The Abductor
The Bank With the Bamboo Door

Two Novels by
Dolores Hitchens

Introduction by Curtis Evans

Stark House Press • Eureka California

THE ABDUCTOR / THE BANK WITH THE BAMBOO DOOR

Published by Stark House Press
1315 H Street
Eureka, CA 95501, USA
griffinskye3@sbcglobal.net
www.starkhousepress.com

THE ABDUCTOR
Originally published by Simon and Schuster, Inc., New York, and
copyright © 1961, 1962 by Dolores Hitchens. Condensed version appeared
in Cosmopolitan, July 1961, as "Abductor! Abductor! Abductor!" Reprinted
in paperback by Popular Library, New York, 1963.

THE BANK WITH THE BAMBOO DOOR
Originally published by Simon and Schuster, Inc., New York, and
copyright © 1965 by Dolores Hitchens. Reprinted in paperback by Lancer
Books, New York, 1966.

"Dolores Was Her Middle Name" copyright © 2021 by Curtis Evans

ISBN-13: 978-1-951473-27-3

Book design by Mark Shepard, shepgraphics.com
Cover painting by JT Lindross
Proofreading by Bill Kelly

First Stark House Press Edition: March 2021

THE ABDUCTOR

It begins with a name whispered to a teacher in the schoolyard… "Marion….*Marion*." Someone is lurking in the bushes, but they run off before Miss Moynton can confront them. There is indeed a Marion in her class, so she tells the principal about the event. She even goes the parent's house to ask if someone was supposed to pick up Marion from school. But Marion's mother has other concerns, and doesn't take the question seriously. However, another nearby family, the Trents, have a daughter named Marilyn, and they have every reason to fear this schoolyard stalker. They have been living in fear of a man who blames the husband for his wife's death, and keeps threatening them on the phone. When the new substitute teacher, Marion Kennick, is kidnapped with one her students, it looks like the stalker has finally decided to strike.

THE BANK WITH THE BAMBOO DOOR

Marlie Renick lives in a town full of secrets. Her own secret is tormenting her. She is pregnant by a man who is not her husband. Then there is Dr. Ferrie, who carries the secret of temptation. He is being blackmailed for his affair with a young woman he refers to as "the barracuda." His wife holds another, much darker secret, one that changes her entire life. And Jim Griffin, the young man who appears so innocently in Karen Evans's gardening store, is anything but what he seems. Their lives, and many others, all intersect when a conniving lothario leads them to a bricked-up cellar wall that hides the greatest secret of them all.

"Tense and exciting"
Francis Iles, *The Guardian*

"Mrs. Hitchens combines strong
cumulative suspense with neat and bitter
sketches of the families involved in a
forceful blend of irony and excitement."
Anthony Boucher,
New York Times Book Review

"The suspense builds and builds....
Dolores Hitchens at her best."
Marguerite Oliver, *Springfield*
(Missouri) *Leader and Press*

Dolores Was Her Middle Name

By Curtis Evans

Sixty-five years ago in the pages of the *New York Times Book Review*, Anthony Boucher, mid-century dean of crime fiction reviewers in the United States, gave to American crime writer Dolores Hitchens what in his male eyes must have seemed distinctly high praise. In his review of Hitchens' latest novel, *Sleep with Strangers* (1955), Boucher pronounced that the author was that *rara avis* among the ostensibly gentler sex: a woman author with the capacity to create credible leading men in her novels. "To a male reviewer," opined Boucher, "it seems that distaff mystery novelists rarely create a wholly convincing male protagonist; even Lord Peter Wimsey and Inspector Roderick Alleyn are men-as-hoped-for-by-women rather than men-recognizable-to-men." Boucher allowed that "[u]ndoubtedly female reviewers have a parallel just complaint" about male authors attempting to fashion women protagonists; yet today the bitter tang of a certain measure of sexism clings to his review, compounded by his vaguely patronizing use of the word "distaff," a term which, The Word Detective has noted, "became weirdly popular in mass media in the mid-20th century, but began to fade in the late 1960s when the practice of labeling half the human race with a word drawn from medieval manual labor began to strike a lot of folks as obnoxious." (See the February 12, 2008 entry "distaff" at The Word Detective website.)

Thirty years later noted crime writer and critic Bill Pronzini praised a later Hitchens novel with the same male protagonist, *Sleep with Slander* (1960), as "the best hard-boiled private-eye novel written by a woman"—a remark which might, like Boucher's, raise some eyebrows today, had not Pronzini judiciously added: "and one of the best written by anybody." Today Dolores Hitchens is being recognized for what she was (and remains today): a noteworthy writer of mid-century crime fiction, who peopled her novels not with colorful outsized storybook sleuths like Lord Peter Wimsey, Roderick Alleyn, Hercule Poirot, Nero Wolfe, Ellery Queen and (on the distaff side, as it were) Miss Jane Marple and Dame Beatrice Adela Lestrange Bradley, but with credible people, male and female—just as did many additional fine women crime writers from Hitchens' day, many of whom now are being recovered and reprinted by Stark House and other publishers.

The fact that these writers were women should not be considered remarkable, here in the year 2021. After the Second World War clever daughters of Eve were doing every bit as much to reshape the murderous landscape of mystery fiction as stalwart sons of Adam were. Women who once might have written traditional detective stories about gentlemanly amateur sleuths and their accomplished lady loves or anal retentive Belgians and inquisitive maiden aunts were now crafting psychologically probing and socially relevant tales of murder and mayhem in which realistic settings and credible characterization were deemed essential features. Dolores Hitchens is a case in point: Like her contemporaries Margaret Millar and Charlotte Armstrong, Hitchens began her crime writing career in the waning years of the Golden Age of detective fiction composing relatively traditional detective novels. (There was even a cat mystery, the beginning of a seventeen-year series.) All of these books she published under a trio of sexually ambiguous or implicitly masculine pseudonyms: D. B. Olsen (*The Clue in the Clay*, 1938, *Death Cuts a Silhouette*, 1939, *The Cat Saw Murder*, 1939, *The Ticking Heart*, 1940), Noel Burke (*The Shivering Bough*, 1942) and Dolan Birkley (*The Blue Geranium*, 1944). Yet by the 1950s, Hitchens had shifted almost entirely into writing realistic crime novels, published under the explicitly feminine appellation of Dolores Hitchens—Dolores being one of her given names and Hitchens being the surname of her second and then current husband. Dolores, it seems, had finally come into her own as an author.

While Dolores Hitchens' impressive productivity had decelerated by the 1960s (she published "merely" ten novels in that decade, compared with fifteen in the 1940s and eighteen in the 1950s), the Sixties was nonetheless a decade which saw some fine work from her hand, aside from the much-praised *Sleep with Slander*. Two of these works are included in this twofer volume, the third in Stark House's Dolores Hitchens series. These are *The Abductor* (1962) and *The Bank with the Bamboo Door* (1965). Before I look at this pair of fine crime novels, however, I want to scrutinize more closely the tangled family life of the author, which I believe had great bearing on her work as a crime writer.

The woman who is known to mystery fans as Dolores Hitchens came into the world, rather grandiosely, as Julia Clara Catherine Maria Dolores Robbins in San Antonio, Texas on Christmas Day, 1907. Julia Robbins, as she was then known, was the only child of William Henry Robbins and Myrtle Statham, who had been joined together in wedded matrimony six years earlier in Caldwell, Texas, when Myrtle, who had left school after the eighth grade, was only nineteen years old. William Robbins, a descendant of the "Old Three Hundred" families who in the 1820s settled the Austin colony in the Mexican state of Coahuila y Tejas and a veteran of the Spanish-American War who had been demobilized in Manila the previous year, was a horse trader by profession. Although a 1910 city directory indicates that William and Myrtle were still residing together as man and wife at 121 Rivas Street, the U. S. 1910 census in April recorded Myrtle and her daughter Julia (aka Dolores) living not with William but rather Myrtle's father, John George Underwood Statham, a carpenter originally from the state of Georgia, who as a young boy had migrated with his family to Texas shortly before the outbreak of the Civil War. Although at the time Myrtle apparently was still married to William, it appears that he had left his wife and daughter, never to return. A few years later, Myrtle, following the peripatetic paths of her own strayed spouse and her restless kinfolk and having divorced William, set out with Dolores, as I shall henceforward call her, for greener pastures—in this case in the Golden State of California, that brightly beckoning oasis, which all too often proved merely a mirage for so many souls seeking to repair their broken dreams.

In 1920 Myrtle and Dolores were living in Kern County in southern California in the small oil town of McKittrick, located some forty miles from the city of Bakersfield and 1500 miles away from San Antonio. Laid out in 1900 and incorporated in 1911, McKittrick by the time of the Great War boasted a population of around 500, a general store, a post office, a newspaper, a railroad branch line from Bakersfield, some tar pits, a grave carelessly marked "Chinaman" which has since become a tourist attraction, and a hotel, originally run by native Italian businessman Almando Bandettini. (Today McKittrick's hotel is known for its "Penny Bar," dubbed such on account of the thousands of Lincoln pennies which its owners have affixed to the bar's surfaces.) Myrtle, who was employed in McKittrick as a restaurant cook, presumably worked at this hotel. She had married and divorced a second time and now carried the surname of Norton, as did Dolores.

Quite possibly Myrtle's elusive second ex-husband was Rex Norton, an oil field worker who in 1920 likewise resided in McKittrick. A slender, brown-haired, brown-eyed man of medium height, Rex Norton had been born Roy Bentley in Paterson, New Jersey in 1887, the eldest of three sons of native Yorkshireman John Henry Bentley, secretary and treasurer of Paterson's Victory Silk Company, and his wife Louise Saxon. Around 1909 the affluent Bentleys had built a fine country house on seven acres on Goffle Road three and a half miles from Paterson, convenient by trolley and train, with a large living room, dining room, kitchen and laundry on the first floor and a den, four bedrooms and two bathrooms on the second floor, as well as a three-room caretaker's house, barn, garage, workshop, chicken house, ice house, swimming pool and orchard. All this material earthly bounty, however, did not prevent restless Roy from leaving home and landing in McKittrick sometime in the 1910s, where under his new cognomen Rex Norton he surely crossed paths with divorcee Myrtle Robbins, now well into her thirties with an adolescent daughter on the cusp of her teenage years. Upon America's entry into the Great War in 1917, the thirty-year-old drifter, who had been employed as a vaquero (cattle driver) at the Rancho San Emidio some thirty miles from McKittrick, was drafted into service as a wagoner with an engineering company. Three years later, while Myrtle was living alone with Dolores, Norton, who had been demobilized in 1919, was residing with other single men at a McKittrick boarding house and working as a boiler cleaner with a local oil company. He later removed to Inglewood, California, married a retired nurse six years his elder and found employment successively as a car painter and a night watchman with the May Company department store chain in Los Angeles. He passed away in 1975 while living in Loma Linda.

Having rapidly run through both a father whom she likely did not remember as a child and rarely ever heard from later in life and a stepfather whom she may not have wanted to remember (see below), Dolores saw her mother marry again in 1922, when she was fourteen, this time to a Bakersfield oil company worker named Oscar Carl Birk, whose surname she took. Birk seems to have shared something of Rex Norton's passion for name change, as he went by Arthur rather than Oscar. The new couple moved with Dolores to Long Beach, California, where Dolores as Julia Birk attended classes, like contemporary crime writers Bernice Carey and Floyd Mahannah, at Long Beach Polytechnic High School, from which she graduated in 1926. Myrtle seems finally to have made a good match of it with her third husband, but in 1933 Arthur after eleven years of marriage passed away at Long Beach at the age of forty-seven. Myrtle never remarried.

In 1931 twenty-three-year-old Dolores, who had qualified as a schoolteacher two years earlier and had since taught third grade, herself had wed Beverley Stephen Olsen, a radio operator in the merchant marine. After her marriage to Olsen, she attended college at the University of California at Los Angeles, obtaining a degree, gave birth to a daughter in 1936 and started writing, publishing her first novel, a mystery, in 1938. Divorcing Olsen three years later (he later died from a heart attack in a Pullman car in the state of Queretaro, Mexico), she soon afterward married railroad detective Hubert "Bert" Hitchens, with whom she had a son in 1944. Her marriage with Hitchens, with whom she would co-author five mysteries, lasted for over two decades, although the union ended in divorce before her death at the age of sixty-five on August 1, 1973, mere days after the publication of her forty-eighth and final novel. Myrtle Stratham Robbins Norton Birk survived her daughter by four years, appropriately passing away at the age of ninety-four in Reno, Nevada, once the divorce capital of the United States.

This outline of the life of Dolores Hitchens has been provided with the intention of suggesting one reason why the author came to write so convincingly in her work not just of crime but of shattered relationships and shameful secrets. Perhaps Dolores' own attraction to pen names—false identities, as it were—was an extension of her and her mother's experiences with her second husband, assuming the man was indeed the mysterious Rex Norton, aka Roy Bentley. In *The Bank with the Bamboo Door*, published forty-five years after Myrtle's ill-fated marriage to Mr. Norton (back when Dolores was eleven or twelve years old), the character Marlie Renick has crossed over from the wrong side of the tracks to marry the local bigwig banker and now lives in a fancy house with two swimming pools. Yet she has not acclimated to such regal surroundings, so different from those of her own adolescence. At one point, she recalls a particularly painful memory, the mere thought of which floods "her face with heat":

When she'd been about ten her mother had been married briefly to a man named Walt. Walt had been big and gross, worked hard, drank hard, cleaned his fingernails with a pocket knife; and he'd been careless. He hadn't thought much about the feelings of a ten-year-old and when he felt like running through the house after a bath, he hadn't done it covered up. Oh, sometimes there'd been a towel around his neck....

Obviously Rex Norton in his former life as Roy Bentley came from a vastly more elevated social sphere and was more appealingly formed than the earthy fictive Walt, yet this creepy passage from Dolores' novel seems to me to carry the force of unpleasant personal retrospection on her part, thereby suggesting one strong reason why Myrtle's second marriage proved so short-lived. (Rex also seems to bear a certain resemblance to the character of Witt Kennick in *The Abductor*, the handsome, charming alcoholic waiter of good background who repeatedly spurns better opportunities in life and whose "thorn must be his family.")

In 1965 Anthony Boucher adjudged of *The Bank with the Bamboo Door* (which he described as "a novel of all the complicated scandals of a small town [in California] and the effect upon them of a complicated professional attempt at bank robbery"): "It's a little as if a Lionel White Big-Caper plot had wandered into the midst of *Peyton Place*." Here Boucher's conceit is apt. In the novel we are confronted with a mixture of suspense—will the planned heist of the local bank come off and just how will it be carried out—and small-town melodrama, what with adultery, an unplanned pregnancy, abortion, drug addiction and life extinguishing cancer; yet the author manages to make these seemingly disparate plot elements hang together. There is even a murder problem as well, including a nice spot of alibi busting, but ultimately the solution to the mystery hinges on criminal quirks of character. Throughout the novel the myriad dilemmas faced by married women like the real-life Myrtle Birk and Dolores Hitchens—not to mention unmarried women who imagine themselves in love—are paramount. The author also manages to find time to limn experiences of Americans of Chinese and Jewish derivation, the former through the major character of second-generation Chinese-American college student Lisa Kim, co-owner of a pet and plant shop adjacent to the eponymous bank.

The Abductor, published three years earlier in 1962, explores a subject which once was deemed too unsavory for "escapist" mystery fiction: child endangerment and abuse. Increasingly in the years following World War Two, threats to children (along with threats from adolescents, or juvenile delinquents as they had become known) featured as a theme in crime fiction, films and teleplays. Some additional notable examples besides *The Abductor*, from both the United States and United Kingdom, are Charlotte Armstrong's novel *Mischief* (1950), adapted as the 1952 film *Don't Bother to Knock*; the 1951 American remake, under the same title, of the classic German child predator film *M*; Philip Macdonald's 1952 short story "Fingers of Fear," adapted as a 1961 episode of the television anthology series *Thriller*; *Psycho* author Robert Bloch's novel *The Kidnapper* (1954); Meyer Levin's novel *Compulsion* (1956), based on the notorious Leopold-Loeb murder case and adapted as a film under the same title in 1959; J. J. Marric's police procedural novel *Gideon's Staff* (1959), in which child murder constitutes one of the multiple plot strands; Hammer Film's crime drama *Never Take Sweets from a*

Stranger (1960); Dolores Hitchens' own novels *The Watcher* (1959), *Sleep with Slander* (1960) and *Footsteps in the Night* (1961)—the former of which was adapted as another episode of *Thriller*—and Margaret Millar's *The Fiend* (1964).

The Abductor opens at an elementary school in a California coastal town with one of the teachers, while supervising children at recess, espying a strange man calling out from some bushes, in a "low, urgent and secretive" tone, the words "Marion…Marion…*Marion!*" The man scrambles away when the teacher approaches, leaving the latter to take the matter to the principal, who promptly downplays it. Is there really a threat to one of the children or was the teacher overcautious? Was the name the teacher heard even Marion? Could it have been, for example, Marilyn? Thus begins a nail-biting tale of doubt, danger and dysfunction, which across the pond in England, Francis Iles, who pioneered the suspense tale with his novels *Malice Aforethought* (1931) and *Before the Fact* (1932), pronounced "tense and exciting" and back in the U. S. Anthony Boucher, ever attuned in crime fiction to nuances of character as well as plot, deemed "a forceful blend of irony and excitement."

Considering the author's own family history, perhaps the most intriguing and moving plot thread in *The Abductor* concerns the relationship between young Marion Charles and her single mother, Betty, who at the age of thirty-seven has hooked a "good catch" in her fiancée Tommy, though the fly in the ointment is that Tommy wants Marion sent far away to boarding school. Betty does not want to do this, but with time ticking away from her she is loath to alienate her boyfriend: "She hadn't met a man of Tommy's caliber since Ben died. There wasn't any use fooling herself either; she wasn't apt to meet another. … she could see how her hair was fading and how the shape of her face was almost imperceptibly not young anymore. Thirty-seven was a tough age for a woman. Forty was staring at you right around the corner." Tellingly Dolores dedicated the novel "with love" to "my mother, Myrtle Birk."

Crime fiction connoisseurs are fortunate that Dolores Hitchens, the former Julia Birk, was able to distil, in the last and most important of her authorial guises, her life experience into so many bottles of powerful brew—and that the stuff is being offered for sale once again. Be forewarned, however: these Hitchens crime concoctions are criminally addictive.

Curtis Evans received a PhD in American history in 1998. He is the author of *Masters of the "Humdrum" Mystery: Cecil John Charles Street, Freeman Wills Crofts, Alfred Walter Stewart and British Detective Fiction, 1920-1961* (2012) and most recently the editor of the Edgar nominated *Murder in the Closet: Essays on Queer Clues in Crime Fiction Before Stonewall* (2017) and, with Douglas G. Greene, the Richard Webb and Hugh Wheeler short crime fiction collection, *The Cases of Lieutenant Timothy Trant* (2019). He blogs on vintage crime fiction at The Passing Tramp.

The Abductor

By Dolores Hitchens

For My Mother,
Myrtle Birk,
With Love

CHAPTER I

It was not quite three o'clock, and yet on the playground Miss Moynton shivered, pulling her blue sweater closer across her shoulders, touched by a sudden breath as of twilight closing in. She glanced at her watch and shook her head. There was a faint smell of fog in the air, though she couldn't see any. The only thing was, high in the sky toward the west, she could see a haze between her and the sun, and she decided that the feeling of twilight came from that. A foggy night on its way, she thought. She was relatively new to Southern California and its weather still sometimes perplexed her.

Miss Moynton was an attractive young woman with curly black hair, a fair Irish complexion, good legs and a look of steady good humor. She was in her second year of teaching. She liked fourth grade. She liked Mitchell School.

The playground was a large paved area, dotted with play equipment. To the north and east in an L-shaped angle lay the school buildings, gray stucco and red tile. To the south was the street, Shelley Road, behind a steel-wire barrier. To the west, shadowed now by trees farther along, was a row of tall shrubs bordering an alleyway which led to the cafeteria entrance. The paved passage was used for the delivery of cafeteria supplies and sometimes as a shortcut to the kindergarten. As she turned now, looking across the playground, pulling the sweater closer, Miss Moynton thought for an instant that there was movement among the shrubs. Some branches shook, not quite the way a stray breeze would shake them. A patch of darkness seemed concentrated behind the greenery.

Perhaps because of that touch of fog next to the sun, or the uneasy sense of a premature twilight, Miss Moynton started to stroll in that direction. She kept her eyes on the certain spot, midway down the alley, where the branches had twitched. There was in her mind nothing more ominous than that a kindergartner had lingered without permission to watch the older children play, or possibly that one of her own fourth-graders might be attempting a prank. A lingering kindergartner would be shooed along home in short order. Her own pupil would be lectured and sent back to join the others.

She passed a group at tether ball and one of her girls, a little blonde with pigtails, and braces on her teeth, caught at Miss Moynton's hand for a moment, and they exchanged a smile.

A jumping boy called to her, "It's almost three o'clock, Miss Moynton."

He was sporting a wrist watch, a birthday gift. "We ought to line up."

"In a minute, Jerry."

The shrubbery was much closer now and the shadow was still in it. Much too big, she realized, to be a kindergartner. A parent, Miss Moynton decided suddenly. Some pupil's father, come to take his child home. She would ask him to wait in front of the building.

It was then that she heard the voice. The tone was low, urgent and secretive, a man's voice. The words—for some reason she took them in with a stirring of alarm—were simply, "Marion ... Marion ... *Marion!*"

She stopped and peered ahead, uncertain. She could make out indistinctly, she thought, dark clothing and the shadowed pallor of a face. The figure was motionless. She called sharply, "Who is there, please?"

The shrubbery shook violently and there were running steps.

For a moment her feeling was one of blank astonishment. The man had been *in* the shrubbery, not behind it. And what a queer place, she told herself, for him to wait! The lanky evergreens, overdue for a pruning, held clotted dust and cobwebs and prickly dead needles.

The running steps were dying in the distance. Miss Moynton suddenly woke up. She hurried toward the street. As she rounded the end of the line of shrubbery there was a flick of motion past the corner of the school. The street was empty.

To her left was a gate in the steel-wire fence; she stepped through. She was still not certain exactly what she should do. Then she heard the sound of a car's motor, the rattle of exhaust, tires on concrete. These too died away.

Silence seemed to wash at her from the shaded tree-lined street, a hollow emptiness in which she listened and looked for clues. Behind her the noises made by the children, the shouts and cries, and the clatter of equipment seemed thin and far away. There was a strange sensation of aloneness. The mood lasted for little more than a moment, and yet it was something she knew she would remember. The harsh dismissal bell sounded at the other side of the yard and there was a simultaneous yelp of escape from her charges. At once they left the games and began to form raggedy, giggling lines, waiting for her to come and tell them that they could go home.

She turned back, walking slowly toward them, thinking of what had just happened, trying to get the nut or core of reality out of it. A man had stood hidden and had called a name and when she had asked who it was, he had run. That was the simplest and clearest way of putting it.

She looked down the line to the head of glossy red curls, the brown eyes impishly alight. "Marion Charles."

"Yes, ma'am?"

"Will you please wait after class for a minute?"

Marion looked hurt and her neighbors gave her sly grins. It seemed obvious that she was in some mysterious trouble, had done something she shouldn't, something known only to Miss Moynton.

The next remarks to the class were familiar routine whose reminder was always necessary. "Those of you who must go back to the room for wraps or books or lunchboxes will stay in line, and go quietly. No running or talking. Others are excused now."

About two-thirds of the group deserted ranks with a burst of joy. The ones remaining formed a single line and waited for Miss Moynton's signal. Marion Charles was at the end of the line. She had a pensive glance for the teacher, as if Miss Moynton had done her a gross injustice. At the door of the room Miss Moynton let all go in except the redhead. "Marion, was someone supposed to call for you at school today?"

Marion's attitude seemed surprised and yet cautious, as if wary of incrimination of some sort. "No, ma'am, I don't think so."

Miss Moynton started to say, "Your father, perhaps?" and then remembered that Marion was a half-orphan, had only a mother.

"How about a relative? An uncle?"

Marion shook her head.

"A friend of your mother's? A man friend?"

Marion looked blank and Miss Moynton prodded, "If your mother wanted you to come home early, would she have sent someone like that? Or a neighbor? A man neighbor?"

"No, ma'am."

"Has *anyone* ever come to take you home?"

"No, Miss Moynton."

Now at a loss, Miss Moynton hesitated. The next step was one she hated to take; but it was necessary. She braced herself. "Has anyone been ... been annoying you, either on the way to school, or going home? Anyone like ... uh ... a man in a car, a strange man, for instance?"

Marion cocked her red head to one side, regarding Miss Moynton almost pityingly. Was she covering a hesitation, even a fib, Miss Moynton wondered? Marion said, "But don't you remember, we saw that movie in the auditorium, the safety movie, and it said that if a strange man ever stopped near us and said anything, or opened the car door and told us to get in, we were supposed to write down the license number and then run? Or try to remember the license number, like saying it out loud? And go straight home? Or go back to school if that was closer? Or even, if we had to, to a house nearby?"

"Yes, Marion, I remember the movie."

"Well, that's what I'd do. Only it never happened."

There was an independent stubbornness about Marion, as if Miss Moynton had accused her of something she wouldn't think of doing.

This was a kind of point of no return, Miss Moynton thought. She was aware of the repercussions if she went on with the thing. Could she just drop it here?

After a brief examination of conscience, she decided she could not. She took Marion in tow to the school office, asked Marion her home phone number, and rang it. Nothing happened. She looked at the now serious child standing beside her. "Isn't your mother at home?"

"Maybe she went to the store."

"Is she always there when you get there?"

"Mostly."

Across the office, the principal's private door was closed. No doubt he was having a conference of some sort. The two office girls were busy with attendance records, and a rebellious-looking boy was waiting, sitting on a bench outside the railing. Miss Moynton turned back to Marion. "Out on the playground—just before the bell rang—did you hear someone call you?"

"I heard you tell me to stay after school," Marion answered, her patience indicating how uncalled-for it all was.

"No. Before that. Did you hear anyone call you by name?"

"That Betty Beekman yelled 'dammit' when she fell off the bars," Marion offered, as if this should suffice.

Miss Moynton spoke to one of the clerks. "How long before I can see Mr. Dobbs?"

The girl glanced at the clock. "It shouldn't be too long."

"Marion, will your mother worry if you are a little bit late?"

Marion shook her head. "How can she worry if she isn't even at home?"

"Sit down on the bench there and wait, please."

In a few minutes the president of the P.T.A. came out and passed Miss Moynton with a pleasant greeting. With a final word to Marion to stay put, she went into Mr. Dobbs's office and shut the door. She poured out her story without sitting down.

Mr. Dobbs was in his fifties, a rather plump man with a reddish complexion, thin light-colored hair, and a manner of acting relaxed and thoughtful in the face of alarm or emergencies. As Miss Moynton spoke, emphasizing the mystery and menace of the man in the shrubbery, Mr. Dobbs picked up a pencil and doodled with it on the edge of his blotter. He nodded a couple of times. His gaze at her was mild as milk.

"I don't know what to do next!" she finished.

"Are you sure," he asked finally, "that this was actually a man? By that, I mean a fully grown person? Could this have been, say, a teen-ager? In other words, not trying to minimize anything—but could you have interrupted some kind of joke, or a gag?"

She tried to sort through her memories of the brief encounter, and found that even this short passage of time had blurred them somewhat. "I didn't place the voice as that of an old person," she decided.

"A young one, then?"

"I—I'm just not sure."

"But it was the voice of a man?"

"Yes. Well, a male voice."

He nodded as though she had corroborated some point he was considering. "And are you sure—are you positive of the name?"

"Marion? Why, yes, I—" She looked uneasily across the desk at him. Mr. Dobbs seemed intent for the moment on his doodling. "Of course there is Marilyn Trent. I hadn't thought of her."

"Might the name that he called actually, then, have been Marilyn?"

Fading ... fading ... The moment by the hedge seemed to grow dimmer as she tried to concentrate. No effort could renew it. "It may have been. I can't seem to pin things down the way I'd like to. It all happened so quickly. The only thing I'm sure of now is that when I asked who was there, he ran."

Mr. Dobbs sat there as if thinking, and the office was very quiet.

"Of course our first obligation is to the children," he reminded her. "Their safety comes above all other things. But then we have a second obligation. You as a teacher and I as principal have a responsibility toward the school."

She waited, dry-mouthed, her heart beating, knowing what he was going to say. She didn't know whether to feel relieved or apprehensive.

"This could be handled in several different ways. Of course you can see that. As one extreme, we could—uh—notify the police." He laid down the pencil carefully and glanced up at her. "They would interview Marion's mother, and perhaps Mrs. Trent as well. If they couldn't identify the man, they'd no doubt keep a patrol car in the vicinity for a while. Even perhaps circling the school now and then. An officer might be sent to ask questions of the people across the street, trying to locate someone who saw the man get into the car and drive away."

"I—I didn't actually see him drive away."

"No, you didn't. The police would be presuming that the person who ran had also started the car. But as I said, this line of action would be at one extreme of the possibilities. It would cause a good deal of comment and even excitement."

She felt behind her for the straight chair that faced the desk, sank into it.

"Parents would become worried about their children. With complete justification. It might seem to them that the school was not safe. A good deal of what we have accomplished, of what our school stands for, could be destroyed. Do you understand what I mean?"

"Yes, I understand perfectly, Mr. Dobbs."

"Incidents of much less importance than this running man of yours have done a good deal of damage," he went on in his soft, calm way of talking. "When I was younger, I taught in the East. The school had a large basement. When the weather was bad, the younger children were allowed to eat their lunches down there. One child went home and told her mother that a man had been hiding behind the furnace, and the story went all over town, and before people were through with it, the tale had the janitor—a perfectly respectable man—doing something quite ugly down there where the children could see him. Do you have any idea what the truth was?"

She tried to smile a little, shaking her head.

"An old overcoat had been hung up behind the furnace, on a nail, by a boy who came early every day in the winter to stoke the furnace."

She waited in silence, not quite knowing how to reply. If she had been one of the older teachers, she might have clucked her tongue. It was a story that needed some such response. Instead she sat quietly, aware all at once of the mixture of odors in the office, the papery smells of ledgers and record books, Mr. Dobbs's pipe tobacco and shoe leather, even the wet effluvium of the ferns outside under the windows.

"Naturally," he went on, his tone hardening, "neither you nor I are going off half-cocked. We don't want to start gossip, or raise apprehension. I don't think we need to call the police. You might telephone Marion's mother later, when she is home, and tell her that while you were outside you thought you heard someone calling Marion from a distance—it was a distance from the child, wasn't it?—and that you wondered if she had sent someone for her daughter. Just say that Marion didn't hear it and you wondered if some plan or other had gone wrong."

"I'll make it very casual," Miss Moynton promised.

"Yes. Do that. Meanwhile I will talk to the other teachers, one at a time, and find out if any of them have had a similar experience." He picked up the pencil again. "And of course—really I don't have to mention this, I know—but you will keep your eyes and ears open on the playground."

"Surely." She got to her feet. "Shall I do anything about Marilyn? Call her home?"

He tapped the pencil several times on the rim of the desk. "Suppose we wait until tomorrow. Let's see— Tomorrow is P.T.A. meeting and you're giving a class demonstration, aren't you? Let's wait until after the meeting, and decide then."

She went to the door. "I'm so glad I talked to you. I feel much better about it now."

He nodded and rose perfunctorily as she went out.

When the door had closed behind Miss Moynton, Mr. Dobbs sat without moving for almost five minutes. All of the mildness and suaveness went out of his manner. His broad face seemed to harden, and deep in his eyes was anger. He put various office paraphernalia away finally, got up from the desk and took his hat from the hanger. In the outer office the clerks were tidying, putting covers on the typewriters and stacking records. Mr. Dobbs spoke to the rebellious boy, dismissing him with a warning. He bade the clerks good evening.

He made a careful circumnavigation of the school grounds. He walked all of the way slowly, looking around. The blocks to the north had been built up with apartments, and there was some traffic there, but the rest of the neighborhood was very quiet. It was a very nice district and the school was one of the best in the city.

Mr. Dobbs noted the increasing haze between him and the sun, the promise of a chilly, dripping night to come. He made a mental jotting to tell the gardener to let up on watering the ferns. They looked sopping. He saw where a curbing had cracked; some child could trip and fall there. The City Street Service would have to be notified.

One lingering stray dog appeared.

But of any lurking figure, any skulking man, he saw nothing whatever. And this was a cause for satisfaction—and relief.

CHAPTER 2

Marilyn Trent went in through the kitchen door of her home. She put her lunchbox on the tiled sink. The house seemed very quiet. She stood listening for a moment. Outside the yard was full of trees and their shadows moved on the windowpanes. "Mama?" she called.

Her mother's voice sounded far away from the other end of the house. "Back here, dear, the bedroom. I'm lying down."

Marilyn crossed the hall to her bathroom, washed her hands and face, removing the playground grime. She dried herself.

"Marilyn?"

"Yes, Mama?"

"Did you come right home from school?"

"Yes, Mama."

"Did anyone speak to you on the way?"

"No, Mama."

"Did you notice anyone watching you?"

"No, Mama."

Marilyn's responses were automatic. She hung up the towel.

"Were there any cars on the street?"

"I don't remember. Can I have a sandwich?"

"May I."

"May I make a sandwich and take it outside?"

"Of course, dear. Stay in the yard, though." Even from a distance her mother's voice had warmth in it, the comfort of love. Marilyn went back to the kitchen, took two slices of bread from the breadbox. She got cheese and pickles from the refrigerator, peanut butter from the cupboard. When the sandwich was made, it was a work of art. She cut it neatly into quarters, then took down a glass and poured it full of milk.

She was a careful, sensible little girl. The blond pigtails and the braces on her teeth somehow made her seem sober and reserved beyond her years. Carrying the plate with the sandwich and balancing the glass of milk, she went out to sit under the trees.

There were some ants scurrying, looking for food, and she gave them crumbs of bread and cheese. She played ticktacktoe with herself, using a twig and a tiny patch of sand. She climbed the lowest branch of the Chinese elm to inspect the old bird's-nest, left from spring. Miss Moynton had told the class that she had read somewhere that sparrows in California bred the year around. Marilyn had kept optimistic watch ever since, but nothing had happened.

She was under the bedroom windows, studying a snail asleep beneath a leaf, when her father came in. She was intent on the snail, not exactly listening to what was said in the room.

"Carol?"

"Hello, darling."

"Is Marilyn home?"

"Yes, she's home. Shall I get up? Do you want some coffee?"

"I'll heat it up. I have to go back right away. I'll be late tonight. Money Mart is showing the new line and I have to be there. Uh—did anything happen today?"

"No, not a thing."

Listening with half an ear, Marilyn knew that in the bedroom her mother and father were sharing one of their looks, her mother's eyes all lit up and full of happiness, her father's warm with love.

"No telephone calls?"

"No, not one."

"Anyone walk by the house and look it over more than casually?"

"Not while I was watching."

"Any new neighbors?"

"No."

Turning the snail over gently with the twig to wake him up, Marilyn frowned. She sensed that in the bedroom the exchanged look of love had gone away. Her father must be standing over by the hall door and her mother, on the bed, must have propped herself on an elbow. And they were just looking at each other in an ordinary way.

And something more. The way her father was asking questions, and the way her mother was answering, reminded her of the exchange that always took place as soon as she got in from school. Her father was asking the same kind of questions, and her mother was answering just as she did, that everything was fine. Puzzled, Marilyn dropped the twig and lifted her head.

"For the first time—today—I began to feel safe," her mother said. "I haven't lain down back here in the bedroom, stretched out, for God knows how long. I always rested on the couch in the living room with the drapes pulled wide so I could see the street. It's wonderful to get over that—that terrible dread—"

"You mustn't neglect your rest."

"I know. And yet how could I relax, really let go, with that—"

Her father made some kind of cautioning sound, and then there were footsteps, and then above her head Marilyn heard the window close almost silently. She was all alone with the stillness and the trees.

The snail had curled himself back under the leaf. The bird's-nest drifted down a few feathers and a strand of twine. The crumbs and the ants were gone. Marilyn was aware of a funny sense of loneliness, of being, as it were, in a suddenly unfamiliar place. She stood up quickly, a strange thud interrupting her heartbeat, and hurried to the back door. She waited there for a moment. She heard her father come into the kitchen and move around, and some of the strangeness went away. She opened the door to go in, and he was beside the sink counter, plugging in the electric percolator.

He turned and grinned and grabbed her to give her a hug. She caught at his big shoulders and squealed. It always delighted and half shocked Marilyn, her father's strength and bigness, perhaps because Mother was small and not well. Mother had to stay quiet and to rest a lot.

"What have you done today? Been expelled from school yet? Made the teacher cry?"

He swung her around, rumpling her hair, and between laughter she corrected him, "Miss Moynton wouldn't!"

"Oh, she's that kind, huh? Tough as nails?"

"No, but she's—" As he let her go, Marilyn ended in a heap, then got up quickly and straightened her dress.

Her father, watching, thought to himself what a neat little old maid of a child she was, prim for her years and utterly lovable, and the primness and the trust in her eyes when she locked up at him filled him at once with a bursting pride and with a dread that it couldn't last. Somehow, in spite of his wanting to be the buffer that took all the blame, it could end—all of them could end—in a burst of murderous violence at any moment.

"Daddy," she said.

"Yes, kiddo."

"Are there awfully bad people everywhere?"

His face changed. He was alert, with a touch of dismay in his manner. "Hey," he tried to say lightly, "what kind of a question is this?"

"I just want to know, Daddy."

"Well, I guess—" He broke off. "No, not many. Not really many. Just once in a while something goes wrong, something happens. A mistake. And people get sick inside. Sick in the head." He quit talking and just stood there looking through the windows at the shadows in the yard. For a moment it seemed very quiet in the kitchen, a listening kind of quiet, and Marilyn waited anxiously for her father to go on. But then what he finally said was, "You know, there's a foggy kind of look outside. A foggy feeling in the air. I want you to stay inside. Don't go out again."

"You'll be gone late tonight," she said, "because Money Mart is having a show."

He shook his head and grinned at her. "Money Mart is a big store, honey. A discount house. They're showing our new line of appliances tonight."

"Are you going to sell lots of refrigerators?"

"Maybe not. But a lot of people will come in to look, and then maybe they'll remember afterward."

"Will you drive carefully, if it's foggy?"

"Very, very carefully," he promised. "I wouldn't want anything to happen to keep me from getting home to you two." He grabbed her and lifted, sitting her on the edge of the tiled sink while he fixed a cup of coffee. "No, I wouldn't want anything to happen like that," he repeated, stirring sugar into the cup.

"The tile's cold," she told him. "It's cold on my bottom."

"Down we go, then."

Her mother came in from the hall and went to Marilyn and planted a kiss on top of the crossed pigtails. Carol Trent was slim, slightly built. She wore her blond hair pulled back simply into a bun, and this plain way of wearing it brought out the clean, delicate lines of her face. She was not a woman who would have looked right in fussy curls. Her skin was pale. She had on a blue linen duster and woolly slippers. "What's being plotted here, you two?"

"It's going to be a foggy night," Bruce Trent said, as if this summed it up.

She was behind Marilyn, her hands on Marilyn's shoulders. Above the daughter's head they exchanged a look, not knowing that she saw it, studied it. "How late will this thing last?"

"Just for us, they're staying open until ten-thirty. If the fog keeps people away they may close earlier."

"Not wishing you any bad luck—"

"I know. So do I."

When he had finished the coffee he kissed both of them and went out through the front door to the car. Marilyn watched him from the front windows, waiting until he had turned the corner. Her mother had come into the front room behind her; she was tuning in the radio for the newscast. "It gets lonesome right away when Daddy goes," Marilyn told her.

"It sure does, kiddo."

Her mother was kneeling in front of the radio cabinet, with her ear turned to listen; her face was intent, closed. It was as if a shadow had passed over her, changing her. The voice of the newscaster mumbled in the depths of the loudspeaker, too low for Marilyn to hear.

This, like the questions when she came in from school, was familiar to Marilyn and yet newly strange, something that seemed just now to have taken on meaning. "Are you worried about something on the radio, Mama?"

"No, darling. Not worried a bit."

"You look worried."

Her mother lifted her head and smiled at her across the room, and the smile was fine. There was nothing scared about it. Marilyn turned back to the window, sat hugging her knees and looking at the street. The fog had drifted lower. Some gray rags and tags of it were among the topmost branches of the big trees. It looked as if a spectral beggar had passed through the sky and left some of his tatters behind.

Miss Moynton and Marion Charles went up the stairs to the second-floor flat. Marion hung back as if apprehensive, so Miss Moynton pressed the buzzer. The door was opened at once by a woman in the process of just shedding a coat. She had red curly hair like Marion's, the same eyes, a hint of Marion's cheerful mischief though in her it was clouded by time and perhaps by rough treatment from the world. Sizing her up in that first moment, Miss Moynton felt that here was a woman who kept up a front in the face of difficulties. "Mrs. Charles? I'm Miss Moynton, Marion's teacher. I wonder if I might talk to you for a minute?" She saw that Mrs. Charles looked worriedly at her child, and added, "It isn't anything Marion has done."

"Come in, of course." Mrs. Charles moved back, inviting her, and there was a whiff-of-whiskey odor. Mrs. Charles had been drinking. Inside the neglected-looking flat, Miss Moynton wondered if Mrs. Charles had just come in from a tour of the bars. "Sit down anywhere. And excuse me for a minute. I'm going to hang up my coat. Marion, get those papers out of the chair for Miss Moynton."

Miss Moynton sat down. Marion hung around uneasily for a few moments and then went out into what must be the kitchen. Miss Moynton heard a refrigerator door open and shut, the clank of glassware. Then Marion came to the door again and asked politely if Miss Moynton would like a drink of milk. Miss Moynton thanked her and said no.

When Mrs. Charles returned she looked refreshed and braced up, as though she might have dashed some cold water on her face and renewed powder and lipstick, and combed her hair. She sat down near Miss Moynton. "Marion pointed you out to me once, in the market."

"I was trying to remember if we'd met at the P.T.A. meeting."

"I never go. Never have time." Mrs. Charles crossed her legs, one foot dangling. She wore a red blouse and a tight white skirt. "What's happened?"

"I was just wondering—" Miss Moynton was beginning to regret the impulse which had brought her here in person, instead of phoning. She saw now that in coming here she might have destroyed any chance of making the inquiry seem casual. "I'm curious about whether you asked someone to come for Marion at school today?"

"Come for her?" Mrs. Charles looked back blankly at the teacher. "Who?"

"I don't know who. On the playground, almost at dismissal time, someone called to Marion from a distance."

"Maybe it was one of the other kids."

"No, it wasn't."

"Well, it wasn't me," Mrs. Charles protested.

"I know that. This was a man. He called Marion's name."

The blankness didn't change to alarm, nor even, so far as Miss Moynton could see, to curiosity. "Well—then what—? I mean, you walked her home just to ask about this?"

Miss Moynton chose her next words carefully. "I was afraid that some plan of yours might have gone wrong. I tried to phone you and when no one answered, I was afraid that you had sent someone for her, someone you were depending on to care for her till you got home. A friend or a relative—something like that, you see." It was said as calmly and as vaguely as she could manage, and she thought with a flash of self-congratulation that it had been put across exactly as Mr. Dobbs had wanted.

Mrs. Charles reached for the purse she had dropped on the coffee table. She took out a pack of cigarettes and a lighter. "Do you smoke?"

"No, thanks."

"I guess teachers aren't allowed to."

"Not at school, that's all."

Mrs. Charles frowned over the job of lighting the cigarette. When she blew out the first breathful of smoke, she gave Miss Moynton a sudden tight smile. "What did this man look like?"

Miss Moynton found no ready words. How could she reply without admitting that the man had been hiding in the shrubbery?

Mrs. Charles seemed now to be staring at her fixedly through the cigarette smoke. "You said he called from a distance? Didn't you get a good look at him?"

"No. Not very. There was some—some shrubbery between us."

"And he didn't come closer?" When Miss Moynton shook her head, Mrs. Charles seemed to shrug it off with a motion of her shoulders. "I don't know who it could have been. Didn't Marion know him?"

"She said she didn't see or hear him."

Mrs. Charles put her head back against the seat cushions and blew smoke lazily at the ceiling. Miss Moynton wondered if it might be the tactful time to go. Then Mrs. Charles lifted her head sharply. "Marion, come in here!" When Marion came, defensive behind a big glass of milk, her mother demanded, "Has Uncle Eddie been around lately?"

"How should I know?"

"Has he phoned, any time I wasn't here?"

"No."

Turning to the teacher, Mrs. Charles said, "I just happened to think of him. My old uncle. He's senile, he gets funny moods and wanders away from the home they put him in. He might have taken a notion to see Marion. He's perfectly harmless, just old and kind of dimwitted."

Miss Moynton was aware of a stirring of hope. This could be the answer!

Mrs. Charles went on smoking and thinking about it. "The only thing—he's so timid. I'd be surprised if he'd hang around a schoolground. You know what they say about old men like that."

Timid. Miss Moynton was remembering the tearing rush with which the man had left the shrubbery. Relief welled up in her.

"What do they say about old men like that, Mother?"

"Go drink your milk in the kitchen!"

Miss Moynton was rising from the chair. She couldn't help smiling. Of course the timid, befuddled old man had been frightened to have a teacher discover him. "You know, I have a strong hunch that the man must have been your uncle. He was reluctant to come closer."

Mrs. Charles also rose, tugging the tight skirt down. There was a shade more curiosity in her manner now, as though Miss Moynton's obvious relief was puzzling. "It could have been Uncle Eddie, all right."

"Goodbye, Miss Moynton."

"Goodbye, Marion, till tomorrow."

At the door, Mrs. Charles said, "If he comes around again, let me know. He's really not supposed to be running loose. For his own sake."

"I'll let you know."

At the bottom of the stairs, looking at the street, Miss Moynton noted that the fog hung lower. It didn't matter. She felt much better about the way the day had turned out.

CHAPTER 3

Marion Kennick was a substitute teacher in the city school system, specializing in fourth- and fifth-grade studies. She was a very beautiful woman, a slender brunette with dark eyes and black curling hair which she wore loose, shoulder length, and fine pale skin. She was in some way not quite the ordinary teacher in appearance, and there was in addition something reserved and withdrawn in her manner. Some of her fellow teachers, drawn by her beauty, had tried to make friends and more than one had expressed curiosity about her, but she kept to herself, and in her particular job, moving about among the many schools, she had an opportunity for privacy. She was soft spoken and solitary.

When classes ended on that particular day she wrote a summary of work progress for the regular teacher and left it in the desk. She took a last look around. The classroom was orderly. She had been in this fifth grade for four days, which was about par for the job. She went to the closet for her coat, stood buttoning it before the windows to the street. She thought that there seemed a foggy look outside. She saw Mr. Dobbs go by, something intent and watchful in his face. She moved a hand in a gesture of recognition, but he didn't glance in through the windows. Taking her handbag from the closet shelf, she went out and closed the door. End of duty, for the time being.

She drove a small foreign car. It was parked in the space reserved for teachers, beyond the playground. As she backed from the stall she saw Mr. Dobbs going back along the other sidewalk. He had apparently made a tour of the grounds; and she wondered about it, briefly.

She turned south at the main boulevard, heading toward the beach. On Ocean Avenue she swung east. Fog was driving in off the Pacific in vertical sheets as tall as a house. The traffic signals wore halos of streaked light and tires hummed on the wet street. When the highway dipped toward the shore area, the fog thickened suddenly and Marion switched on the windshield wipers and kept a foot poised for the brakes.

The apartment house was a block from the beach, a stucco building in two wings with a paved court down the middle, not new but with an air of cheerful respectability, the cheerfulness dimmed now by the low-hanging fog. Going upstairs to the balcony, Marion shivered. She fished her key from her purse, opened her door and went in. She stood still for a moment as if listening.

The place had a closed, empty, almost unused feeling.

Dropping purse and coat on the couch, she switched on the lamps, then went out into the kitchen. It was a very tidy, very bare kitchen. She opened the refrigerator. The interior held very little, a carton of eggs and some butter and cream, plus, on the top shelf, a pint bottle of whiskey. She took this out and inspected it. There was a nearly invisible mark on the label; she compared this with the level in the bottle. Then she took a glass from the cupboard, poured a stiff drink, watered it at the faucet, drank it standing in the middle of the floor. She rinsed the glass and left it on the sink.

She went back to the living room and switched on the radio. The room burst with jazz; she modulated the volume. Then she walked on into the bedroom. In the dim, half dark, she stopped between the twin beds. There was a picture on the wall, a seascape full of wild water; her eyes fixed on it but without any real attention. She seemed to muse over some thought, or memory, and if there was any particular expression on her face it was sadness. She seemed in that moment to be a woman utterly removed from the life in which she found herself.

She went into the bathroom finally, clicked on the light, washed her hands at the basin with an air of simply needing something to do. She inspected her make-up in the mirror. She was turning away when she hesitated. She stood for a long moment as if hung on some point of indecision, as if not quite willing to recognize what confronted her in her mind. Then she swung back to the mirror, picked up a comb from a shelf. She began to tug her hair back from her face, then higher, then pinning it into a puff high off her neck. She pulled bangs loose with the comb, fluffed them across her brows. With a sudden grin she reached for a lipstick, then mascara.

When she had finished, her appearance had changed remarkably. She seemed bold and inviting. Her eyes sparkled. The slash of color across her lips seemed to change the shape of her face. There was no longer any reserve, any shyness. She was a woman on the prowl.

She leaned toward the mirror, laughter spilling from her stretched mouth. "Mrs. Kennick! Oh, Mrs. Kennick!" She seemed to be mimicking some propriety within herself. "You're going to hell, Mrs. Kennick. That's what you're doing!"

With a sudden startled motion she glanced at the watch on her wrist. It was just a minute past four-thirty.

She seemed possessed of energy, now. She rushed into the bedroom and threw open the closet. She yanked a red dress off its hanger. She pulled out red pumps. Inside ten minutes it is doubtful if any fellow teacher would have recognized her.

She took a short black fur jacket and turned toward the door. Then she ran back, bent above the twin bed against the far wall, pulled back the coverlet from the pillow. Delicately she leaned down to put her lips against the fresh white slip. "Sleep tight, darling." She left the pillow uncovered. The bright red mark was blood-colored in the gloom.

She went out through the front of the courtyard to the street. The fog had closed in thickly, no longer blowing, cold and wet. "It's like night already," she said half aloud, her tone pleased. There was no one in the street but herself, no lights except the street lights at the corners. It looked gloomy. She walked quickly up to Second Street, where the main highway cut through the Shore. Here the bars and cafés bounced with neon and traffic rolled by with a hiss on the damp pavement. She turned in at a blue door, went directly to the bar. It wasn't a big place, just a bar and a few booths, no jukebox. The bartender turned and glanced at her as she slid upon a stool.

"Hello, Marion."

"Hello, Red."

He began mixing a drink for her.

"It's wet as frog skin out there," she told him.

"Good night for ducks," he agreed.

"It seems a lot later than a quarter of five."

"It sure does." He was a stolid man, paunchy, with a fringe of reddish hair around a bald spot. He put her drink in front of her and Marion took out a five-dollar bill.

She was halfway through the drink when a man took the stool beside her. She slid a sidewise glance at him. She saw that he was looking at her reflection in the bar mirror. He was about forty, she thought. He looked tired. His clothes were good. He could be a businessman, worn with the day's affairs, dropping in to have a drink. She wondered if she had ever seen him before, here or elsewhere, and decided not.

After his drink had arrived and he'd paid for it, taken it down a little, he poked around in his pockets for cigarettes, then sighed, seeming at a loss. "Damned if I have a match," he said. He turned to Marion and she saw him fullface; he was good-looking in a worn henpecked sort of way. Married, of course. "Do you?"

"Do I what?"

"Have a match?"

"I think so." She opened her handbag. It was either the cheapest and boldest short cut, or else the truth. She handed him the pack of matches.

"I had a bet with myself." He lit the cigarette, the flame glowing against his profile. Marion decided that when he'd been young the women had really chased him. "I had a bet you'd take out one of those little mother-of-pearl lighters."

"I look like that kind of woman?"

"Sort of." He laid the book of matches between them. He had his elbow on the bar now, so that he faced her. Marion realized that she was being taken over. She smiled to herself. "I don't know, though. Since you handed me those matches I'm revising my ideas."

"Don't revise them too far," Marion said. "I could have a mother-of-pearl lighter at home."

It could be a lead, an invitation; and to her inner amusement she saw him deciding whether to chance it. Then the look faded from his eyes. He's really henpecked, she thought. "No, you don't. You're a kitchen-match kind of girl at heart. Or you light them off the gas burners. Ever singe your hair?"

She brushed at the bangs. The man interested her; the conversation bored her. "These are a fake. I've burned myself bald."

"Oh, now wait a minute," he said, as if she might be going too fast for him.

"What did you want me to say?" she asked flippantly. "That I light my cigarettes with barn-size matches, and put up apple butter for a hobby, and sleep in flannel nighties? And that I just sort of strayed in here by mistake? And never have been in a bar before?"

"You're cutting me down with a blowtorch!"

"I'm getting the preliminaries out of the way." She was watching her own reflection in the bar mirror. What a floozie, she thought. Raggedy bangs and too much lipstick and eyes all gooed with mascara, and a neck line right out of *Police Gazette*. "Tell me about your wife."

His exhaled breath struck her in a gust. "Oh, my God."

"No, I mean—why not? Get it off your chest."

He leaned closer. He'd had a couple before he stopped in here, she decided. He was getting into the solemn stage. "Do you know what she did? Do you know what she said to me this morning?"

"No. Tell me." She blew cigarette smoke idly at him.

"There was this vacuum, this carpet sweeper ... well, hell, what's one of them? What do they amount to?"

"Nothing. If you haven't any carpets."

"It blew a fuse or something and she left it by the front door for me to take along. Where I work, it's ... well, there's a repair shop in the same block. And so she left it by the front door for three days, and I kept forgetting it, and this morning—" he reached for the drink as if the tension must be relieved "—this morning she tried to hit me with it. She actually ran out on the lawn."

"She chased you and you ran. What a picture."

His sober eyes studied her, searching for the gibe. "I have a decent job. One I'd like to hang onto. I can't afford stuff like that. It gets back, somehow. She ought to know that."

Marion thought wryly, he's going to have me crying in my drink. "Do you know what's wrong?" she asked.

"No."

"Nothing."

He went on looking at her solemnly, the drinks showing in the uncertainty with which he lifted his glass.

"There's nothing at all wrong with either one of you," she explained with dry patience. "You're both healthy and well fed, you've got a nice home, money in the bank, and you each have a job to do. But there's this kink ... I guess it's in almost everybody. You can't stand it."

"No ... it's her, it's all on her side—"

"I'll bet it isn't. You keep picking at each other, ignoring each other, neglecting and needling each other. Just because you can't stand perfection when it's perfect."

"Where in the hell," he cried loudly, "did you get so goddam philosophical?"

"I'm just handing out advice because I feel like doing it. Look. Why not relax? Why not go home one day and decide to play the game a little differently? Not to needle, not to fail to hear what she says, not to make her miserable? You know what? You wouldn't know the woman."

"I'll bet," he said sourly, turning away so that he faced the bar.

"You don't know what real trouble is," Marion said. "Wait."

He rubbed a hand over his face. "I've got all I can take. Already."

"It's chicken feed. It's stuff you're making up."

"Oh, to hell with it anyway," he said suddenly. "Look, how about dinner? There's a place a half-dozen blocks from here, charcoal broiled steaks ... lobster ... a new place. Nice bar, too."

"It's pretty early." She looked around the dim, ordinary interior, in her mind the half memory of all the hours she had spent here, making it seem like a sort of home.

"We'll have a couple of drinks in the bar. Then we'll eat at ..." He turned his wrist to look at his watch. He had large, well-shaped hands. The shirt cuff was a little raveled. He'd run out of shirts that day, Marion thought; and she wondered if the wife had cut off the laundry in revenge for neglect of the vacuum cleaner. "... six-thirty. That won't be too early, will it?"

"What time do you have to be home?"

"Maybe I just won't go home ... tonight." He tossed it at her but the solemn eyes measured her reaction.

"Aren't you tired of my advice?"

"Hell, yes. Knock it off, won't you?"

They went out to his car. It was a well-kept year-old car in the upper price bracket, and he drove very carefully, a little too slowly, as though he might have had encounters with the law under similar circumstances. He squeezed her hand and then dropped a palm to her thigh and pressed, not looking over at her but squinting at the fog through the windshield, and she removed the experimental exploring hand without comment, and then he kept it on the wheel.

In the second bar they danced. He wasn't at all bad on his feet. Studying him, Marion decided that at some time when he was younger, perhaps when he'd been just out of school, he'd had himself a ball. He had the looks and the manner for it, something in the way he danced holding a nostalgia for better and fleeter-footed times, a little out of date, the bachelor heart not quite tamed. She wondered what he was like to live with. Not fun, perhaps.

Against her ear he said, "Do you want to know my name?"

"Larry," she said promptly.

He drew away, still keeping step, looked at her in mock surprise. "Now how did you know that?"

"I just did."

"And what's yours?"

"Jill."

They danced and he seemed to be thinking about it. "That didn't sound just right, somehow."

"Larry and Jill. All people who meet this way, all strangers on a foggy night, ought to be Larry and Jill. It fits fine."

"What do you mean ... meet this way?"

"The way we did. At a bar, over a book of matches."

"There's something made up about you," he said, to her astonishment, followed at once by a touch of fright. "You're too ... too ... hell, I can't think of the word I want. But you're not just all of a piece. Your voice doesn't go with the rest of it, and ... other things I can't quite put my finger on."

"Don't lay a finger on *me*," she warned, lightly.

"Now that's all right, that's what you ought to say," he commented. "I can't imagine where I get this feeling that you're dressed up for something...."

"I dressed up for you." She reached up and patted his cheek comfortingly, and then unexpectedly, on the dance floor, he bent and kissed her. They clung, and the music beat around them, hollow and mechanical, and the rattle of glassware and the hum of conversation seemed far away, and then the blue lights began to swim in her tears.

She jerked free and ran to the booth for her jacket and purse, and fled out into the street, with him at her heels. He grabbed her at the curb. "Look, I'm sorry. I apologize. If you'll stay, if you'll have dinner with me, I won't do another thing. I won't get out of line again. I promise."

Standing in the misty dark, half-lit by the neon behind them, she heard the miserable loneliness in his voice; and it frightened her because it was an echo of something inside herself, something she didn't want to bring out and acknowledge now. She let him lead her back into the dining room and listened to his voice, under it a running echo of her own thoughts like a counterpoint.

Much later she was home, switched on the lamps, and then went into the bedroom and stopped by the bed, arrested. A mixture of hope and fear and stale familiarity seemed to squeeze breath from her lungs. There was a long inert mound under the covers of the other bed across the room.

She hurried to the bed, pulled down the sheet, and saw his face. He was asleep.

Suddenly she jumped up and ran back through the front room and listened at the door, afraid that the stranger of the evening might have followed her here. Had he driven her home? She thought he had, but now she couldn't remember. They'd had more drinks instead of dinner. There had been a lot of talk about loneliness, and living with a stranger, and at the time it had made sense, but now Witt was home and the loneliness was over.

CHAPTER 4

She went back into the bedroom and knelt on the floor, pulled back the covers to his waist. By the light reflected in here from the other room—she saw that he was fully dressed. All he had done before falling into bed had been to loosen his tie. She felt for his feet under the covers. He was still wearing his shoes.

She tapped his face lightly with her palm. "Witt. Wake up, Witt. Look at me. Here I am. Marion. Can you hear me?"

There was no motion in the pale, still face. The steady, heavy breathing hesitated for a moment, then resumed. She put her head on his chest and heard the slow, laboring heartbeats; listening to them frightened her and she jerked her head up quickly.

"I'm going to take off your clothes."

Usually when she spoke like this, close to him, loudly, distinctly, he made some response. He mumbled, or moved a little. But this time there was no response at all. He was inert. He breathed, and his heart was beating, but the inner man, the person himself, was far away. There was another thing she noticed, the absence of whiskey odor. That meant he'd been on vodka, and vodka was very bad for him. She wondered where he had been all day and what he might have done.

She stripped back the bedding and took off his shoes and socks, his coat, pulled his pants down over his legs, managed to get the shirt off over his dangling arms. Then she covered him again. She sat on the edge of the bed with his clothes in a huddle at her feet. She held her head in her hands and cried for a while.

Then she flung herself on him, inert and motionless as he was, and pulled the unconscious head up so that he faced her in the dim light. "Witt, listen to me. Why are we doing this? Why are we destroying each other?" She let his head back gently and fastened her lips on his. The taste of what he had drunk, faintly sweet, the flavor of whatever he'd used to wash down the vodka, clung to his mouth. She drew away and wiped her own lips with the back of her hand. And in doing it she tasted her own tears. "Witt, hear me! If just once, just once before you took off into whatever it is … the need or the desire or the compulsion … if you'd come to me first …" She leaned against him, sobbing. "… If you'd just ask my help one time, if I could know that you needed me—"

He stirred then. He lifted one arm violently and flung it outward. At the same time he spoke. He said distinctly, "You bastard. You dirty bastard. Gimme a drink."

She drew away, moving down to the end of the bed. She sat crouched and watchful, but he didn't move again. He sank back into the state of immobile stupor. It seemed to Marion that the smell of the fog crept into the room, along with a chill off the sea, and she brought an extra blanket and put it over him.

She went to the kitchen and heated the coffee and drank two cups. She took the whiskey out of the refrigerator and laid it flat on the oven grill. It might delay him two minutes.

She looked at the clock and was astounded at the time, almost three. Then she understood why she and the man she had called Larry had left the bar. It had been closing time. No doubt he'd asked to come up for a nightcap. She tried to remember how they'd come here, whether he had driven or whether they'd walked eight or ten blocks in the fog— Thank God for fog, she thought, we must have been a sight—and couldn't remember one single detail of the journey.

In about fifteen minutes she began to feel horribly tired and weak, and let down. Her mouth grew dry. Her eyes quivered from all the crying, the light stung them and the lids were swollen.

Roaming the apartment, she began to stumble. Marion took a blanket off her bed and curled up on the living room couch, not undressing, not turning off the lights. She lay without sleeping, fighting off attacks of nausea, until the windows began to lighten with the dawn.

She went in then to look at him in the gray light. He hadn't moved except to pull the outflung arm back over beside him.

When she and Witt Kennick had married nearly five years ago he had looked much as he did now, a man almost too perfectly handsome, whose dark good looks had something poetic and sensual just under the surface. He owned a fine muscular body; he had been good at sports. Until lately there had been a sensitive way of dealing with others, a touch of gallantry that made other people notice him. Everyone he met—and Marion had been among them—knew on meeting him that he must be in some way extraordinary. The perfection of appearance, the look of having emerged from some portrait of a cavalier or a poet, the gracious manner, were striking, superior. Women were still always asking her what Witt did, their eyes on him across the room, sure that she was going to tell them of some amazing and romantic occupation;

she always knew that they wanted him to be a spy or a diplomat or some super-brain involved with unfathomable calculations, because that had been what she had expected. What everyone expected. And so usually she tried to avoid coming out baldly with the name of his job.

When he worked, Witt Kennick was a waiter.

He was a good waiter. She knew that. The sensitivity, the natural deference for others, gave him a huge advantage; he could have gone straight up to the very top if he had wanted, to head waiter, to manager, to owning his own place; there would always be men to back someone like Witt. Even here in the obscurity of the beach, working part time with not-too-good a reputation, he had been approached by someone from one of the big Las Vegas showplaces. He had turned it down.

The thorn must be his family. He had never said so. But Marion knew that his father owned a great cattle ranch, or rather two of them, in Colorado and Nevada, and ran unnumbered head over ranges that stretched from horizon to horizon and beyond. He was a gruff old man who had lived outdoors all his life, had worn out and buried two wives, and who wrote to Witt once a year at Christmas and always sent him a check for five hundred dollars. Witt's sister, who still lived at home, or rather at home when she wasn't in the saddle with the old man, also occasionally dropped him a line. Nothing in the letters—Marion had found and read them—betrayed any break among the three. But Marion sensed the father's feeling, one of unbelief and disgust, that his son had come to Los Angeles to go to college and had flunked out and had become a waiter. She always pictured the old man as far out on the rolling range, craggy-faced, sitting on a horse, wind blowing his bandanna neckerchief, bitterly watching the distance for the strayed one who never came home.

She knelt now by the bed and slapped him gently, rolling his head between her palms. "Witt, wake up. Listen to me. Open your eyes, Witt." Usually he managed to look at her, but now the inertness didn't change and she was suddenly afraid. She slapped harder, and his pale face reddened, but still he didn't open his eyes. She rubbed his wrists. She brought a wet cloth from the bathroom and bathed his face. Then, more frightened than ever, she went to the living room to phone for a doctor. She was lifting the receiver when Witt spoke her name.

She hurried back into the bedroom. He was trying to sit up. He squinted at her, rubbing his eyes. "Hello, Marion. Hey, you're all dressed up. That red whore's dress. Where've you been?"

She had forgotten that she still wore the tight, red, low-cut dress. She knelt by the bed. Her head felt giddy, her mouth puckering with the stale taste of last night's drinks. "Nowhere. I've been here with you. Oh, Witt,

I've been scared. You wouldn't wake up."

When he tried to sit up, when he winced with effort, he changed; a gentleness, a touch of innocence and youth seemed to leave him. He looked to Marion's frightened eyes at that moment as he might at fifty or sixty. *Oh, Witt, Witt ...*

"I hate to bother you," he said formally, "but the fact is I'm going to have to have a drink. Just one. And quick. Don't tell me I'm able to get along without it or that you don't know where any is hidden. I'll need aspirin and cold drinks later but right now ... please ... a little something with alcohol in it."

"All right." She went into the kitchen and took the bottle from the oven and poured some from it into a glass, diluting it a little at the faucet.

He drank down about half of it. "Take the glass, Marion. God, take it quick." She grabbed the glass and he doubled in a sick convulsion, gasping and choking, and then got out of bed and staggered to the bathroom. Marion began to straighten the bed.

"Witt, do you know what I think?" She waited, listening to his misery. "I think we ought to take a vacation. A trip. I can put in for a leave of absence. We can go ... oh, somewhere different. I'd like to see where you grew up, your father's place. It would be a change for us. It might help things."

Witt's voice sounded weak and far away. "Someday I'll tell you about the old man, Marion. Until I do, just don't talk about going to see them."

Them. Marion noted the word. She had mentioned his father, but when Witt answered, he had included the sister.

"All right, Witt."

He came back in, wet and shaky, and she put him into the fresh bed, and helped him hold the glass for a second try. By sipping and waiting, and by deep breathing, he managed to hold it.

"Yesterday," she said, "when you knew you were going to tie one on, I wish ... I wish you'd have let me know. Not warning, not like that. But just asking me to ... to be with you."

He let her take the glass. He lay back on the pillow, staring at the wall beside the bed. "If I had, would you have come?"

"Oh, yes, Witt." She stroked his hand. "But you didn't."

"Maybe I tried. Maybe I wanted to."

"I know. And perhaps next time ..." She leaned her head on his bare shoulder, feeling the warmth of his flesh; but in spite of this she was aware mostly of an aching loneliness, a loneliness like that in the voice of the man she had met last night, when she had stood on the curb in the fog and he had begged her to go back and have dinner with him. And then suddenly, like a picture clearing, she remembered something of the trip back here; not all of it, but she could remember sitting in the car while he drove, barely creeping, her head out of the window in the whirling mist, and telling him, "Now you're getting over too close to the curb." Marion thought, we're both living on borrowed time after that.

Carol Trent awoke at first light. She turned her head quickly and saw Bruce asleep in the next bed. He lay face down, with one hand tucked up under the pillow. Without making any noise she got out from under the covers and went over to the window and put a finger between the slats of the Venetian blind. The street still held thinning patches of fog, but not as thick as it had been last night when she had looked out just before going to bed.

She took robe and slippers from the closet, carried them into the bathroom to put them on. She slipped into Marilyn's room for a moment. Marilyn lay curled up, nothing showing except the crossed pigtails on the top of her head. Carol laid her cheek against them for an instant, felt the warm breath stirring from below. Then she went to the kitchen to start the coffee.

She never used to get up early like this. For years and years she had been a sleepyhead. Even when Marilyn had been a baby, Bruce had always fed her breakfast. It was just during the past months, while some inner wellspring of courage and strength had gradually failed, that she slept poorly and woke at the crack of day, and had the doctors commanding her to rest.

She measured coffee into the percolator, noting almost absently how her hands shook a little more than usual. And odd too, considering that she had told Bruce yesterday how for the first time she'd begun to feel safer. It must have been the foggy night, she told herself, and the feeling of silent isolation and knowing that Bruce had to be gone until late. I'll be fine after I have some coffee.

When the coffee was done she took a cup into the nook. The little room had windows that looked out into the leafy yard. Very peaceful, she thought, looking out and sipping the coffee. Closed in and quiet and secure.

It must be, she thought gratefully, that they were safe at last.

Perhaps Bruce didn't believe it yet. But he would. On the wall just beyond the inner door, the telephone rang.

She half rose, pushing herself from the table. But then, there was the rule, the important rule that they'd agreed on. When Bruce was home he answered the phone. She started to sit down again.

She looked at the wall clock, perplexed. It was a little past six-thirty.

There was an extension in their bedroom, muffled as usual for the night, stuck into the closet and buried under an old coat. He might hear it if he were ready to wake up, sleeping lightly. Carol left the table and went through the kitchen and listened in the hall. She couldn't hear Bruce stirring nor could she hear the ringing of the extension phone. It had been muffled too well. She went back to the kitchen, took another unbelieving look at the clock, thought of her mother, ill in the East. She lifted the receiver. "Hello?"

She waited. Two seconds … three … four … ticked by and she knew with sudden fright that she had made a mistake. A shiver like a touch of ice ran across her skin. The receiver shook in her grip. But she forced her tone lower, quieter, and she said, "Who's calling please?"

Just silence.

The way it always began.

She put the knuckles of her right hand between her teeth and bit down hard. In that instant the room around her changed from something homelike and familiar into a part of a stranger's house, a harsh and hostile place to be fled from. The light was gloomy, the view of the leafy yard seemed dim and sinister.

And then a voice spoke. A man's toneless voice said, "Wrong number." There was the snap of the connection closing, then the empty ringing of the dial tone. He had hung up.

She put the receiver on the hook. She looked around, trying to reorient herself. It was still the place they called home, the friendly house with the walled yard where they had felt so safe. Her thoughts were in confusion. In the moments while she had waited with the phone in her hand, something seemed to have broken, some thread of continuity was gone. This was new and it might be nightmare. She couldn't decide.

The doctor had advised her to stop smoking, and she had stopped; but now she needed a cigarette. She went to the cupboard where Bruce kept a carton, took out a pack and opened it. She went back to sit before the cooling cup of coffee. She smoked the cigarette there, looking out at the yard now brightening with morning, the sun coming to burn away the last of the fog, some birds chirping.

Bruce came into the kitchen. He had on robe and slippers. He didn't look as if he had just gotten out of bed, he looked tense and alert. "Did I hear you talking to somebody?"

"The phone rang."

"I thought it did. I heard it while I was half-asleep and then it seemed I heard you talking. Who was it?"

She looked at him, trying not to show the terror inside her. "I don't know. He didn't give a name. At first he didn't say anything, and then he just said, 'Wrong number,' and hung up."

Bruce came to the table. "You wouldn't recognize *his* voice."

"No. I'm sorry, dear. I know I shouldn't have answered."

"Now we don't know."

"It might just be a—a wrong number. There might be dozens of reasons why someone wouldn't bother to say, 'I'm sorry,' or give a name or …" Her voice ran down into a husky whisper. She turned miserably from Bruce.

He took down a cup and poured himself some coffee. "More for you, Carol?"

"No, thanks."

He stood by the sink, frowning. "We know that he's insane, Carol. That we've had proof of. In his world you don't need reasons. He wouldn't feel any need to cover up with politeness. He lumps you with me. And Marilyn with the two of us."

When Bruce spoke Marilyn's name, Carol put her head on the table, cupping her face with her hands.

"Are you all right, Carol?"

"Yes," she said, muffled. "I'm all right. Or I will be in a minute. It's just the thought of going back to that kind of living. Hiding. And being afraid for Marilyn all the time."

"If it was Fecamo," Bruce said, "he's done us a favor. We haven't been on guard. We haven't really been watching over Marilyn as we should. Why shouldn't he try to get at her first? She's the most vulnerable, the innocent one. We've never even explained the danger to her."

"Should we now?"

"I don't know."

The yard was brightening in the sun, the trees glittering with the moisture left by the fog, the birds singing. The room seemed darker by contrast. It seemed to Carol and Bruce Trent that they shared a dark, cold shadow and that the silence echoed the name of the man they feared.

CHAPTER 5

They sat at the table, cups of cold coffee between them, and talked, trying to plan, to foresee. "We could go to the police again."

"What in the hell have the police done for us in the past?" Bruce said bitterly. "You know the answer. Those cops in Louisiana … they didn't even believe the guy existed. They thought I'd cracked up. You couldn't confirm anything, you'd never even heard Fecamo on the phone—incidentally that's when I made up my mind you never would if I could help it. But the cops practically laughed me out of their office. Go take a tranquilizer pill, they suggested. See a doctor. I must be working too hard."

For an instant a memory, like a shade of doubt, clouded Carol's eyes. She must have remembered the pressure Bruce had put on her, his hope that she would back him up with the police, and her inability to do it. "Do you suppose they contacted anyone in St. Louis?"

"I doubt it. It didn't seem important enough. I guess they get nuts like me ... like the nut they thought I was ... all the time. People who hear Russian radio signals through their teeth or who feel they're being electrified through the walls, or who have neighbors giving them the business with the evil eye—"

"But Fecamo is real!"

"How could I prove it? She didn't use his name. She never told me where they'd met or married, there was no way I could even trace a marriage license. Maybe she *never did* marry him. Maybe he imagines that along with the rest of it."

There was a space of silence and then she said half-curiously, "What do you suppose he's like?"

"Looks like? God, I've pictured him a dozen ways. Huge, with hamlike hands and a hairy chest. Or short and skinny, a weasel. No chin. Glasses. He could be anything. Anybody. He's been a voice and a lot of dirty words, that's all."

"I never used to want to believe in him," Carol said.

"You still don't." Bruce put his head in his hands, elbows propped on the table. "And that's dangerous. It's the most dangerous thing you could do—not to believe."

"I know it," she admitted, fright welling again into her eyes.

The sunlight had begun to dapple the windows with moving shadows. A gate slammed in some neighbor's yard. A dog barked and a child squealed.

"I want you and Marilyn to go away," Bruce said, lifting his face from his hands, some inner decision arrived at. "Clear out. Make sure you're not followed. Buy a ticket back to New Orleans and go from there to your mother's place. I'm not going to give up this job. I'm just getting into the good money. I'll keep the house, I'll try to make it look as if we're here, all of us are here, as long as possible. Then in a month or so I'll move into a boardinghouse."

"No, Bruce!"

"Isn't it the sensible thing to do? We've got to protect Marilyn. We couldn't send her all that way alone, even if I'd let you stay, even if you wanted to."

"I'm not going," Carol said. "Neither is Marilyn. Whatever happens to us is going to happen to us together. And anyway, what possible guarantee do you have that he'd stay here and concentrate on you? Wouldn't it be much more likely that he'd follow us? And how could you protect us—three thousand miles away?"

His face tightened with anger, with fear that must be for her and Marilyn. "Don't play right into his hands, Carol. Don't be a fool!"

She looked at him in silence, then touched his hand with hers. "Marilyn's just getting oriented in school, just making friends and beginning to know the neighborhood."

"That's not as important ... as her life."

"Perhaps he wants us to separate. Aren't we a little safer, together? I know I feel safer with you, Bruce."

"You're feeling confident now ..." Bruce controlled his temper, pushed it into the background, while he tried patiently to explain how he saw things. "You're over your bad fright of a little while ago, and you're trying to discount that phone call."

"I'm not over my fright. I'll never be over it." Carol rose and took the cups to the sink, dumped the cold coffee. She turned to face Bruce. "My first instinct was just what yours is. Run. I was ready to pack and to run when I hung up that telephone. But not now."

"You'll wait until he makes another move," Bruce answered, his tone cold and harsh. "It may be his last. It may be the only one he'll have to make. A crazy man can be pretty thorough."

"If he separates us, he's beginning to succeed." She crossed the room and put her arms around her husband's shoulders, forced his head against her breast, stroked his hair. "If he even starts us quarreling— as we are now—he has put in a wedge that can help him at the end. If he makes us stop loving each other for even a moment, he has begun to win."

After a moment Bruce reached up, took her hand in his. "Yes, you're right. I've been out of line, cockeyed. I just wanted you two to be safe and away from danger."

"Don't ask us to go away from you."

"No, I won't. Not again."

"I'm going to wake Marilyn now and start her getting ready for school. Do you want to start the bacon?"

"All right."

Carol went into Marilyn's room. Marilyn was sitting on the side of her bed, already half-dressed. She was pulling on her socks carefully, lining up the heels, in the precise little-old-maid way she had of doing things. "Hello, Mama. Are we going away?"

"No, dear. Not today." Carol opened the closet, trying to keep her hands and voice steady. "What'll it be today? The blue dress and the blue sweater?"

"Is something bad going to happen to us?"

Carol came back to the bed carrying the dress. She stood there for a moment in indecision. Then she sat down beside the little girl. "I want you to listen carefully. I'm going to explain something very important. You know that in the—the world, there are bad people, don't you?" When Marilyn nodded, Carol went on. "Sometimes these people believe ugly things that aren't true."

"Something about Daddy?"

"Perhaps. We have to watch for these bad people, darling—and so if any ... if any ..."

"We saw a movie in the auditorium," Marilyn said matter-of-factly. "It told us what to do if a bad person came up to us, or wanted us to get in a car, or tried to give us candy or money. We can go back to school, if it's close, or run home, or even go to a neighbor's house. If there is a car, we must try to remember the license number."

Carol said a silent prayer of thanks that her job had been made this much easier by the school.

"Did it explain what to do if someone tried to ... to touch you? To grab you?"

"Holler," Marilyn said. "First try to get away and run, and then fight, and yell. Cry for help, I think they said." Her practical attitude seemed more that of a forewarned adult outlining procedure to a nervous child, rather than the reverse. "I don't believe anybody could catch me, Mama. I run awfully good. Well, I mean. And ever since we saw that movie I've been watching."

Looking into the small, serious face, Carol knew that her child had taken the pictured warning seriously and had thought it over afterward. She had had the good sense to apply the lesson to herself. And Carol would have bet that not a tenth of the children had done likewise. In sudden pride she put an arm around Marilyn and hugged her close, and felt the warmth of the wiry figure—the little form, no match for an adult madman—and then there was a fresh rise of panic and the sickening need to run. The thing Bruce had wanted flared in her mind—let her and Marilyn slip away, leave him to fight whatever might come—and then was followed by a flood of shame. Her husband and her child were ready, stout-hearted, prepared for the face of danger. And only she was frail.

"You're shaking, Mama."

"Listen to me. Don't go off the school grounds for any reason whatever.

No matter who comes for you, no matter what story they tell—"

"As if you were in an accident, Mama?"

"Yes." Well, perhaps it hadn't been too bad, their letting Marilyn read the newspapers and watch an occasional adult program on TV. Perhaps it had prepared her for a wholly adult danger. Carol chucked her under the chin. "Breakfast is cooking. Wash your face and come along."

The meal was almost a silent one. Then when Marilyn had put on her sweater and collected her book and her pocket money for lunch and snack, she went over suddenly to Bruce and hugged him with unexpected fervor. "Goodbye for now, Daddy."

He kissed the soft pink ear under the pigtails. "Goodbye, kiddo."

To Carol, waiting at the door, the parting had the terrible sound of finality. She turned the doorknob, bracing herself, forcing away the trembling, filling her thoughts with the day to come.... She must sit on guard by the front window, watching for someone who walked or drove past too many times, or who looked too searchingly at the house, or who pretended an unusually lingering interest in the rental across the street. Her job.

They walked to school in the early sunshine, and nothing could have seemed pleasanter. The fog was gone. Everything looked bright.

At the schoolground gate beside the shrubbery, Carol turned Marilyn's face between her hands and gave her a peck on the end of her nose.

"There's Miss Moynton, Mama. She sees us."

Carol waved to Miss Moynton and for a moment ... for just a moment ... she was tempted to cross the playground and speak to the teacher. A word of caution, a half warning, just something to put her a little bit on guard. But then Carol thought, we're not sure enough yet. It might be what he said it was, a wrong number.

She turned away.

The phone rang at a quarter of eight. For a while Marion Kennick lay fighting off the need to awake, to answer. Let the thing ring itself out. Let them get tired and quit. Let us sleep. Let us sleep if possible forever.

She rolled over, covering her head with the pillow, but the phone went on ringing in the other room.

In the end she got up, staggering, dry-mouthed, and went into the living room where the blinds were still drawn, where it was almost dark, and took the phone off its cradle. "Hello."

"Mrs. Kennick? I'm awfully sorry to be calling you this late—"

"Quite all right," Marion murmured. She'd heard the excuse before.

"—but there has been a slip-up. We thought that Miss Chiroske would be back this morning, but she won't be. She's had a sort of relapse. You know how mean the flu can be this time of year—"

"Any time of year," Marion said. "Yes, I know." She covered a yawn. They were going to ask her to go back for another day to the Knolls. And feeling the way she did, she should say that she too was coming down with something. With old age, with a lack of desire to go on living, with a broken mainspring somewhere inside that no doctor on earth could fix. "I don't believe ..." she began.

"You've been out there four days and the children must be getting used to you," the substitute-supervisor pleaded. "I hate to send another teacher just for today."

"Why not?"

"What?"

"I'll go," Marion said, not even knowing why she suddenly agreed. "I'll have to dress and get ready. I may be a little late."

"I'll call Mr. Dobbs. He can keep the class until you get there."

"All right."

"Thank you so much, Mrs. Kennick."

She went back into the darkened bedroom. Witt lay with his face turned to the farther wall, unmoving. She walked over and stood close, wondering if she should wake him, try to talk to him before leaving. He seemed to be breathing raggedly, almost struggling over it in his uneasy sleep, and she was smitten with compassion, knowing how he was going to feel when he did wake. He was going to need her and she wasn't going to be there.

No, she wouldn't be here to bring the ice water and aspirin, and then the black coffee, and then bromides ... and after all of these and perhaps several more, with Witt still agonizingly shaky and sick, the whiskey. The remedy was always the same, in the end, though God knew he tried everything else first. Say this for Witt, he made it the last resort.

Her eyes filled with tears. She turned quickly, went into the bathroom. Her head felt heavy from the drinking of last night, her limbs were leaden. She got in under the shower, almost cried out at the force of cold water against her naked flesh. Then she tried to dry briskly, to rub some life into herself. After putting on her brassiere and slip, she went barefooted into the kitchen and drank cold tomato juice, made coffee and drank a cup of it, then half sick and not really wanting food at all, she forced down a slice of buttered toast.

She finished dressing in the dark and silent bedroom, listening uneasily for Witt's occasional moans.

At the end she knelt by his bed and touched his hand.

"Witt ... if you need me today, come for me." The words seemed a mockery. He would need her all right, and she wouldn't be here.

As if defending herself from the unspoken accusation, she added, "One of us has to work, Witt. One of us has to make a living."

Witt gave no answer except to let out a long shuddering sigh.

For some reason Marion thought at that moment of Witt's people, and as usual she pictured the old man up and out in the early Colorado sun, the high mountain breeze stirring the cowman's neckerchief, perhaps on his horse right now riding out across the limitless ranges. And the weather-bitten iron-jawed girl riding behind him, as impassive as an Indian.

And then Marion thought, it might not be like that at all. It's just something I've made up for myself. His father at this very moment might be thinking of Witt, grieving for his only son who had gone away and wouldn't come home. He might at this moment be rising from his bed, unwilling to face the empty day. And Witt's sister—I've never even seen her picture. She could be a very nice, sympathetic person. I ought to clear away these old ideas.

She laid her face against Witt's bare hand. "If you need me," she whispered, "come and get me. I don't care when it is. I love you so much. Just come, Witt."

How many times had she said this, how many times had she begged that instead of starting or continuing a drunk, Witt would ask for her help? A hundred? A thousand?

Too many to remember ...

She collected her coat and purse, the car keys, went to the door and closed it softly behind her. It was then for the first time that she realized that last night's fog was almost gone.

Betty Charles woke with a start, knowing in that dazed moment that she had overslept, that the alarm had gone off and run down, that no matter how she felt she must get up and hurry Marion off to school.

She pushed back the bedclothes and sat up, stared at the clock. She needed glasses so badly now, it was hard to make out the time. She rubbed her eyes and looked again, squinting; it was twenty-two minutes past eight.

"Oh, my God!" With a wail she pulled herself out of bed, reached for the cotton duster across a chair. "Marion! Marion! Get up right now! It's awfully late!"

Marion's cot was in an alcove in the dinette. Betty poked the sleeping form as she ran past to the kitchen. There were dishes piled in the sink, a crumple of paper napkins, cigarette butts, burnt toast. She pushed the mess aside to fill a pan with water for cereal. "Marion, get up and start dressing for school! You'll be late!"

"What time is it?" Marion said drowsily from the other room.

"Never mind. It's late. Now get a move on."

"Maybe it's already too late to go," Marion suggested in a sleepy voice. She had been up until midnight, watching a late movie on TV. Betty knew, resisting a pang of self-reproach, how tired the kid must be. "Can't I just stay home?"

"No, you can't. I won't be here. I'm going out."

"I'll go with you."

Into Betty's mind came the picture, along with a bitter taste: Marion following her into the bar, to sit and listen while Tommy planned a future without her. *The kid has got to go. Face it, Betty.*

There's no place for another man's kid in my life with you.

CHAPTER 6

When Marion had been hustled off, still sleepily protesting, Betty Charles sat down for a cup of black coffee and a cigarette.

And to think. To decide.

Today was a day of decision.

A day of destiny—hers and Marion's.

She looked around the room, her glance flickering over Marion's dropped pajamas, her books, her little record player and her beat-up stack of records. A look of grief slowly settled in the mother's eyes.

For a time after she had met Tommy, had started to run around with him, and he had started to show that he was interested in her, she had had great hopes that he would take to the kid. The kid had been without a father for five long years. It would be nice to have a man around, not just for herself, but for Marion too, a second dad.

Marion hadn't talked about missing her dad when he had died. Well, he'd been in the Navy, gone a lot, perhaps Marion hadn't felt the loss as if he'd been home all the time.

The money—that was the problem. At first the insurance and the dependents' allotment had seemed almost like a fortune. Betty had bought a new car and a lot of new clothes for Marion and herself, and they had made a tour to Yellowstone and back, and she'd even bought old Uncle Ed a new suit, though he was already senile and befuddled and hardly knew what was happening. Then the years went by and now they were living on the ragged edge.

What Tommy said was true, though. Marion's survivor's insurance check every month—while it didn't go far here, would keep her in a nice school. He even knew the school; it was back of Pasadena in the foothills.

"We'll put the kid in the school, Betty. She'll get good eats, they'll keep her clothes nice, they'll teach her her lessons. She can come to see us at Christmas … well, between Christmas and New Year's … and maybe a week in the summer."

"They have school in the summer?"

Looking down into his shot-glass: "They keep the kids there if you want them to. Run a summer camp for them. Swimming and everything."

She had asked how he happened to know so much about the school and Tommy had said that he knew the man and woman who ran it. He had done the foundation work on a house they had built for themselves on the school grounds.

As soon as Marion was settled in the school, Tommy and Betty could go to Denver, where he had a chance to go into business with his father. Tommy's father was a cement contractor, like Tommy himself, and making plenty of money, expanding his business now, and Betty could have a nice house and a new car and even glasses—Tommy didn't know that she needed them—and when they decided to throw a party it could be a doozy.

That was the kind of life Tommy pictured for the two of them, and when he talked about the parties Betty could almost taste the drinks.

"I've got to do it, baby," she said to the stack of records. "It's the best thing for the both of us. You'll be in a nice school. You'll learn to be a lady. And I'll be fine, too. I'll be—" Betty's face crumpled. She put her head down on her arm and shook with anguish.

Mad at herself too, at the same time. I'm a funny kind of mother, she thought, wanting to keep a nice kid like Marion in this sloppy old flat when she could go to an exclusive school. Maybe with rich people's kids, even. What wouldn't I have given for a chance like that when I was a kid? She turned her head, seeing her dim reflection in the side of the coffee cup, eyes enormous and faded, hair disappearing into the chalky distance, mouth the shape of a goldfish's. That's me, she told herself. Funny old me. A screw loose. I don't even look right.

When she could control the tears, she went to the sink and tackled the dishes. But Betty was a putterer. With the dishes half finished, she decided to make the beds. She made Marion's cot and stripped her own bed, and then went to straighten the bathroom. She was in there when the phone rang.

"Hello?"

"Betty. Me. How're you doing?"

"Oh, Tommy, I'm just putzing around, trying to get the joint neat.

What're you doing?"

"I'm going to work. I'll be off at four. What say, meet me at Dixie's?"

"Dixie's at four?" she said uncertainly, knowing that this was deadline. This was the time when she would open her mouth and tell Tommy that she would marry him and go to Denver, and that they would put Marion in the school. "Why ... uh ..."

"Order me a Tom Collins and keep it cold."

"Sure I will."

"I love you, babe."

"I love you too, Tommy. I love you an awful lot."

"Give me a kiss."

She kissed him through the phone, but her mouth was shaking. It didn't sound too much like a kiss after all.

"We're going to have a ball together, wait and see. Wait till we get to Denver. We'll warm that town up."

"Sure we will."

"You'll like Dad and Mom."

"I know I will, Tommy." She had a sudden feeling of having been admitted to Tommy's family, a belongingness. with everything that had gone before, the years of Navy life and the five years alone with Marion, wiped away. "Oh, Tommy, I'm so lucky I found you. I'm so lucky we fell in love."

"Me, too, babe. See you at four. Don't work too hard."

"I'll be there with the Tom Collins."

When she had hung up, she stood looking at the phone as if it might produce something further, an answer and a reassurance for the funny emptiness inside perhaps, or a playback of what she and Tommy had just said to each other, only with more reality in it. Then she went back to the bathroom and set about picking up scattered towels.

She *was* lucky. Tommy was a catch, a real catch. He was almost forty for one thing, and most men that age who hadn't ever married before had settled firmly into bachelorhood. He was neat-looking. He was getting gray and it made him look dignified. When he was dressed up you would take him for a professional man, she thought proudly; you could imagine he was a doctor or a lawyer. And he wasn't a sloppy drinker, and he had nice manners, and he made good money. He would make even better money after they were married and settled in Denver, and he was in business with his dad.

She hadn't met a man of Tommy's caliber since Ben had died. There wasn't any use fooling herself either; she wasn't apt to meet another. Even needing glasses the way she did, she could see how her hair was fading and how the shape of her face was almost imperceptibly not young any more. Thirty-seven was a tough age for a woman. Forty was staring at you right around the corner.

There was an alternative to marrying Tommy, but it was pretty weak and she didn't give it much consideration anymore. It was what she should have done right after Ben died, before the insurance money was gone—had her eyes examined and gotten glasses and then enrolled for a brush-up course in typing and tried to get an office job. It would have been easier at thirty-two than now, of course. Office managers looked at you as if you were dead, if you had to admit being over thirty-five.

So it was just better to forget it.

Better to be thankful for what she had now, the chance to marry Tommy. Better for Betty.

She whispered the phrase to herself as she wiped off the bathroom mirror ... *better for Betty* ... and slowly a smile started, reflected in the mirror, and in her thoughts she began to compose the note that she would leave for Marion.

Marion Kennick heard the stir in the roomful of children behind her, and turned to find Mr. Dobbs in the doorway. She laid the chalk in the wooden channel, brushed her hands lightly. Mr. Dobbs nodded to her. A feeling of hope, mixed with dread, set her heart thumping; she was sure that he was bringing some message regarding Witt.

As she walked toward the door it occurred to her that Witt must have called the school, asking for her. He wanted her to come home. He wasn't going to drink today; he was going to fight it out with her help. A sense of happiness and relief swept through her, so strong that it brought tears to her eyes. Witt wanted her. He was ready at last to give up, to beg for the help he needed.

Mr. Dobbs was smiling faintly. Something about his manner seemed mildly apologetic, as if he might be going to ask a favor, the first hint that her wild hope had no basis in fact. He said quietly, "Mrs. Kennick, would you mind taking last-period playground—relieving Miss Moynton? She is to give a remedial reading demonstration for the P.T.A. meeting."

"I don't mind at all," Marion answered, wondering if he could see her sudden, sickening disappointment.

Perhaps he did grasp something of her mood at that. He lingered at the door, giving her a quick little glance out of the corner of his eye. "If there is any ... uh ... incident which is out of the ordinary, anything at all, will you report it at once to me?"

Puzzled, she said, "Certainly, Mr. Dobbs."

"Ordinarily we don't ask the substitute teachers to do playground duty, but I want someone out there from fourth or fifth grades. And keep a close eye on Miss Moynton's group, will you?"

"Is there some situation I ought to know about?" she asked, thinking that some members of Miss Moynton's class might have had a fight—an odd idea, considering that in this nice neighborhood most of the children were well-behaved.

"Uh … no," he decided. He stepped back into the hall. He hesitated for a moment and she knew that he was thinking over something else he might say. But then with another faint smile he walked away.

And Witt hadn't called. He hadn't asked for her help, didn't want it.

By now he had managed his own aspirin and ice water, tomato juice, perhaps a bromide, and if he hadn't started on the whiskey he was staring at the bottle.

With a feeling of numb defeat she went back to the board, took up the chalk and began to write. The chalk made scratchy noises and behind her the children rustled their papers and squeaked their pencils and almost inaudibly whispered about the principal's visit. She didn't turn to correct them. She wanted time to blink away the tears and compose her face, to look again as a teacher should look.

When she did turn from the board she glanced at the wall clock. It was twenty minutes of two. She had an hour and a half of duty, yet, before she could go home to Witt.

If he was there.

Carol Trent had rushed through the house that morning, giving it a surface orderliness, before taking up her post in the living room. The hours had dragged by. No one had walked past except an elderly man with a white poodle; he lived down the block and was perfectly familiar. No one had stopped at the vacant place across the street. There had been very few cars, none that repeated its trip down the block. At a quarter of two, feeling exhausted, caved-in, Carol went to the kitchen and made a fresh pot of coffee.

She took a cup to the rear door and stood there looking out through the pane at the back yard, sipping the coffee. She thought that there was already a touch of haze to the air, the way there had been yesterday. It was going to be foggy again and she dreaded it; the fog made the night so still, so closed in, clammy, the house isolated.

The phone rang. She didn't start; she was so numb with tiredness that a clap of thunder wouldn't have done it. But something sang in her nerves, a rasp of fear, a trickle of terror, and the coffee slopped from the cup into the saucer.

It would be Bruce, calling home to check.

She put the cup on the tiled sink and lifted the receiver, put it to her ear and said, "Hello," and in the moment of silence afterward, the tick-tock of waiting, she knew that it wasn't Bruce.

Without preamble the man's voice spoke in her ear. "How did you feel about them, Mrs. Trent? About your husband and my wife? Did it ever bother you, knowing they went on those trips and must have slept together? Didn't you wonder what it was like, the two of them in bed, didn't you ever picture them enjoying each other?"

She rocked dizzily, clinging to the wall. There had been no warning, no preparation. It was raw shock.

"Didn't you care that he had quit loving you? We were like dirt to them. She couldn't stand for me to touch her. He must have felt the same about you. Couldn't you see it? Couldn't you feel him cringing away from you when you tried to love him?"

"You're wrong," she managed to get out. "You're all wrong. There wasn't anything—"

"Mrs. Trent, shouldn't you have been a little jealous?" The tone was higher and fury quivered in it; and still it wasn't the voice she had expected. There was so much strength in it, such bedrock savagery, and she lost instantly the image of Fecamo she had vaguely entertained, a chattering ferret of a man, a vicious little man with darting eyes and an uncertain enmity. There was nothing uncertain about this man on the other end of the wire.

"Please listen to me," she said. "You have made a terrible mistake. My husband and your—your wife meant nothing to each other. They were friends. They worked together. The trips they made were business trips. Up until the time of the accident your wife hadn't been in my husband's car more than—"

"Lies," said the voice, harshly affronted. "You're lying, Mrs. Trent. I'm surprised that you would lie for him."

"Anyway," she said desperately, hopefully, "it's all over now."

"*His* part is over. Her part ended when she died in his car. Now my part begins."

A wild inspiration burst in her mind, a way to protect Bruce. "Come here, Mr. Fecamo. Come to see me. We can talk about it. I'm sure we can straighten things out."

For a moment he was silent, the wire humming, and then he said grimly, "I see that you are a very clever woman."

"No—no, I don't mean to be. There are things that puzzle me. I can't understand why she didn't use your name, for one thing. Why didn't she call herself Mrs. Fecamo? And why didn't she ever tell anyone ... anyone at all ... that she was married?"

There was another space of silence, longer now; and she began to hope, faintly, that she might draw him into an argument, that he might even come here where she could see him and talk to him and somehow convince him that there was no real reason to hate Bruce. And then the voice, deeper and more hateful, said draggingly, "You are a fool."

The line went dead.

She stood there, sweating, blank-faced, waiting for more, not believing that he had hung up on her, and yet knowing in the depths of her frightened mind that she had said something irretrievable, something immutably offensive, unforgivable. She had put the fat in the fire.

She hung up the phone, fumbling for the hook.

She tried to think what she should do next. Her heart thudded so hard inside her that she felt as if some internal mechanism were running away, out of control; and the backwash of hope and fear had left her weak. She should call Bruce at once, she thought, and have him come home. Then she corrected this idea. For some reason she couldn't analyze she felt that Fecamo was in the immediate neighborhood. If Bruce came home now Fecamo would kill him.

She stumbled to the table and sat down, staring fixedly at the windows where the afternoon light lay mottled by the trees outside.

She thought of Marilyn. She must go at once and take Marilyn out of class and bring her home.

But wait. Perhaps Fecamo didn't know as yet which child was theirs. Marilyn had the protection of a cloud of classmates. If she rushed to school now and brought Marilyn out, wouldn't all possible anonymity be lost? Lost forever?

She held her head, trying to find safety for Bruce, for Marilyn. She felt buffeted by shock waves in tune with her lurching heart, hammer blows that left her gasping. She thought, perhaps the best thing to do is just to wait here alone as long as possible. Perhaps he will come, after all, and I can talk to him.

She felt utterly isolated by silence, by the emptiness of the house. She tried not to feel afraid for herself. He had made no real threat at all. But there was murder in the air.

CHAPTER 7

At two fifteen some of the early arrivals drifted toward the auditorium for the P.T.A. meeting. Mr. Dobbs heard the soft chatter as the women congregated in the passage. He looked at his wall clock, shuffled some attendance reports together and dropped them into the desk drawer. He brushed back a stray lock of the thinning light-colored hair. His calm and thoughtful demeanor seemed to mask an inner tension. He rose from the desk and went into the outer office.

"If anyone asks for me, I'll be back in about ten minutes."

"Yes, Mr. Dobbs."

He went out into the hall, turned right so as to avoid the collected women. He crossed the inner paved courtyard, strode down a second passage and reached the street. He paused at the entrance and glanced around sharply. The only person in view was a Japanese gardener across the street, mowing a lawn. Mr. Dobbs sniffed the air and looked at the sky. There was already that foggy smell, that hint of haze, gathering itself inland from off the Pacific. He had a lodge meeting tonight and getting home would be hell.

He walked down past the playground. First and second grades were out now, twenty minutes of games, and the children were shrill and fluttery and the three teachers stood scattered at even intervals like sentinels at a riot. Mr. Dobbs nodded to the nearest, a gray-haired woman nearing retirement who had been at the Knolls school longer than he had and didn't ever let him forget it. He went down to the end of the block and turned south. He looked carefully in all directions. At the end of the next block a black sedan stood parked but it seemed empty. It wasn't quite the car to fit the neighborhood but Mr. Dobbs knew, with a wry touch of humor, that he could not in wisdom start running to the adjacent houses asking to know who was inside, who belonged to a car that was a little too old and a little too dusty to look quite right in the Knolls. He even smiled a little at the idea.

Ahead of him to his right was the long steel fence of the playground, ending at the row of shrubbery and the gate, beyond it the cafeteria service entry and then the school itself. As he walked he kept a close eye on the row of dark evergreens but nothing could have seemed more innocuous. As he came closer, sizing them up, he decided that they could stand pruning. They looked untidy. The cobwebs and the clustered dirt should be washed away, too, with a good brisk hosing. He was surprised that the gardeners hadn't attended to it.

"Have them trimmed tomorrow," he promised under his breath. "Cut down, lower than shoulder height. Anyone trying to hide in there will find his head sticking out." He gave a last glance at the busy playground and then crossed the cafeteria entry and went down along the south wall of the school. Here were more ladies, coiffed and hatted and gloved, debarking from cars, smiling at each other, turning to greet him, and Mr. Dobbs shook a few ladylike hands and then drifted on to the P.T.A. meeting.

The auditorium was warm and cheerful and its impersonal odor was pleasingly overlaid with a mixture of perfumes. Mr. Dobbs sank into a seat near the rear and looked around with a feeling of pride; the Knolls had the best school in the city and the attendance records of its P.T.A. were a source of satisfaction.

The principal was expected to attend whenever possible, called on now and then for an opinion, as a benevolent expert on children. Mr. Dobbs listened with half an ear to the routine of the meeting, some proposed changes in the bylaws, a complaint about some failure of the publicity committee, a scheme to use a treasury surplus to buy a portable organ for the primary division. All very usual.

He saw Miss Moynton come in discreetly, followed by a half dozen pupils, and sit down near the front, waiting to be called to give the demonstration in remedial reading.

She looked so calm and sensible and assured that Mr. Dobbs found any uneasiness of his own drifting away. She had told him that morning, first thing, about her interview with Mrs. Charles and how the lurking man must simply have been the old uncle, escaped from his nursing home.

And so that's what had happened, of course, and there was no longer any need to worry.

And he could forget about the dark, dusty sedan.

Marion Kennick led her own group and Miss Moynton's down the hall and out upon the playground. It was twenty minutes of three.

Another teacher was already out there, far at the other end of the block, organizing a baseball game. Marion allotted a diamond to her boys, another to Miss Moynton's. She led all the girls over nearer the fence to the volleyball court. When she had the game going, she stepped back, braced herself against the firm steel links near the gate, tried to relax. When the play period was over, she would hurry; she wouldn't spend more than a moment on the lesson summary for the regular teacher. She would rush home to Witt.

The sky was growing overcast and there was a misty smell in the air. She thought about going back for a sweater, but there was a rule and to Mr. Dobbs it must remain inflexible. No groups were to be left unsupervised for any length of time whatsoever.

After some minutes of play, the volleyball group began to huddle and chatter. Marion saw that she had put too many girls on the court and that they were bored waiting for a turn to serve. She went to the court and removed half the players arbitrarily, took them over to the tether ball poles. It was while she was walking back to her post near the gate that she thought she heard her name called.

The sensation was almost dreamlike. She didn't pause; the voice had seemed soft and far away, and in the next moment she wondered with a touch of banter at herself if she could possibly be haunted.

But again she caught the echo of her name, almost a whisper, and she said inwardly, "Well, it's happened. I want so badly for Witt to need me, I'm imagining he's here, calling my name. What do you do in a case like this? I must need a psychiatrist." She turned at the fence and put her back against the steel links; she shut her eyes, shutting out all the wriggling and jumping, and listened to that strange voice as soft and cajoling as a summer wind.

"Marion ..."

Strange that it could seem so real. It wasn't Witt's voice, of course. It was a voice conjured up by her yearning and hoping, it was a wraith, it was a whisper made up of the years she and Witt had had together before the drinking crystallized into a hideousness that couldn't be controlled. It was a dream out of those early times when they had been sure that their love was forever and that nothing that could ever happen—not old age nor poverty nor even death—could change it.

So let me dream a little, she thought, that this is Witt.

The image of his face floated before her, lifelike, the lips twisted in the beginning of a smile, Witt's own unmistakable smile, half mocking and yet loving, the eyes looking into her own with a trusting warmth. Something began to hurt inside her, a terrible squeezing and drawing together in the middle of her breast, cutting off breath, a pain almost like a knife thrust, and in sudden fright and anguish Marion's eyes flew open.

For an instant the playground swam and tilted, and the children were just patches of color distorted by her tears. Then she blinked, forcing the tears away, shook her head. One patch of color had separated from the rest. One of Miss Moynton's pupils, one of her little girls, was walking to the hedge.

Marion glanced to see what might explain the girl's action, perhaps a ball rolling away, but there was nothing.

She straightened and stepped away from the fence, curious to see what the child was after.

The girl wasn't looking at the ground. She seemed to be staring into the hedge itself. For an instant Marion thought of a bird, a bird somehow tangled and trapped in the cobwebby branches, fluttering there, attracting the attention of the child. She waited, expecting the girl to put out a hand, to take from the hedge whatever she had seen in it.

Instead the child stopped some two feet short of the playground boundary, the edge of the asphalt paving, and then Marion saw her lips move. She was talking there alone. It was an incomprehensible bit of action entirely.

She has had a quarrel with the others, Marion thought, trying to explain the inexplicable. She's telling them off, there to herself. The child went on talking to herself, and Marion thought uneasily that it might be best if she went over there.

She started, her shoe leather scraping the paving, and the child threw a glance over her shoulder. Marion caught a puzzling expression of mischief. And in the next instant, looking past the child, she saw there was a person in the hedge. Someone stood there like a shadow, and again to Marion there was the feeling of unreality, of moving in a dream.

But this must be real. It held the continuity of the day, of being here at Mitchell School, of being on the playground in Miss Moynton's place. It was just an odd, an almost unbelievably peculiar, happening.

She tried to think of an explanation. It couldn't be a parent. Not for a moment did Marion make that mistake. A faint memory out of the past returned to orient her, to buzz with a shiver of alarm. When Marion had been small she had been frightened by another child older than she, who had hidden in a closet behind a curtain and jumped out at her. And this was like that, somehow.

She walked faster.

She was almost directly in front of the spot in the hedge when he stepped out to face her. And then the thing he said, without warning, without even much expression, just the bald words, scarcely made sense. "Don't scream," he said. "I have a gun." He had a hand inside his coat at belt level and he allowed the coat to fall open just a little and she saw the gun-butt and his fingers almost touching it.

She had the sensation of having taken root. There was as yet not so much alarm as an inability to believe. She looked at the child, who was staring in fascination at the gun in the man's belt.

Marion said awkwardly, trying to fight off the unreality, "What do you want?"

"I want Marion," he answered. He stood there facing them, quiet for a moment. She saw that he was studying some problem, some predicament. "I want to take her off the grounds quietly. No fuss. No screaming. It's just occurred to me, the way to do that, the way to make it look good, is to take you with us."

"What do you want with her?" Marion put a hand on the child's shoulder, drew her back a little, and he frowned.

"That really isn't any of your business. Don't try to grab her and run for it. One of you will be killed. I promise you that."

She found his flat, steady stare repellant. He was a little taller than she, heavy around the middle. Somewhere in his forties, she thought in that moment of frightened inspection. And she saw that what was in him wasn't anger, exactly; at least, not white-heat rage; it was as if he had come a long, long way, burning all the while with a desire to do what he was doing, and now finally was being allowed to complete his act. "You mustn't take the child," she insisted. "She isn't allowed to leave the playground. She's still in school, really."

"When the bell rings her mother will be here for her," he said matter-of-factly. "So we leave now. Go through the gate there and down the street to the black sedan. Get into the car on the driver's side and slide across. Let Marion sit in the middle."

She shook her head, trying to find words to defy him and knowing suddenly, as surely as if she had been told, that she and the child were facing a madman.

She threw a glance backward, wondering if the other teacher were looking at the odd tableau. But someone in the ball game at the far end was making a home run and everyone there was jumping and yelling.

"Just get going and do as I say and neither of you will be hurt."

"Please don't take her. Take me, just me," Marion said.

There was nothing humorous in the smile he shed on her. "That wouldn't be quite the same, would it?" He put his hand inside his coat again and looped his fingers on the gun stuck in his belt. "It only takes a second to draw this thing and fire it. I'm a good shot. I'm not nervous. And believe me, sister, I have nothing to lose. Nothing at all."

True or not, he believed it. This was a man who wouldn't hesitate an instant if either of them balked him, who wouldn't be swayed by any thought of what would happen to him afterward. Nor would he be influenced by compassion or a distaste for taking a human life. He was, in some way she could sense without knowing how she sensed it, completely beyond such human scruples. He literally didn't give a damn what happened—to himself or to either of them. If she stood stubbornly where she was, she would die. If the child took fright and ran, she would die. It was all quite simple.

She took the little girl's hand in her own. The child didn't seem frightened; her attitude had been one of mischief and fascination, fading now into puzzled quiet.

"Just be careful," he warned behind them as they turned to the gate.

The street looked as she had never seen it before, it or any other, the houses closed as if shutting out the scene before them, indifferent; and on the whole block flowers were blooming, and a sprinkler showering a lawn, and a cat on a front porch licking its paws—all with a malicious apathy, leaving Marion and the child and the man behind them completely alone.

She looked desperately for any stroller, even a child, who might notice and remember. There was no one.

She began to plan. When we get to the car, when I have to open the door on the driver's side and slide over, I'll open the other door quickly and snatch the child with me and jump through. We can keep the car between him and us, and dodge, and there will be a back gate open somewhere

A heavy pulse began to beat behind her eyes, filling her head with a sensation like a drumbeat. Her limbs were leaden, and there was a curious inertia like the aftermath of sickness. For a moment she thought that she would fall. Then he said something in his harsh, complaining voice and she swallowed the dry taste of fear and looked at the car. The car was their last chance.

Behind them on the playground a piping voice was shrilling, "Mrs. Kennick! Mrs. Kennick! Where're you going?" So she knew that one of the children had spotted them.

Let them think to look at the license plates, she whispered to herself. They were at the curb now, facing the car. To their left was a yellow house. It had low, scalloped eaves and a scrolled gate and a small sign at the foot of the steps that said, No Peddlers or Agents.

"Get in without any fuss and you'll be fine," the man said. He opened the door on the driver's side and Marion looked in, gathering herself for the effort to escape, crowding down terror, and then on the opposite side of the car, where the other handle should have been, there was just the bare threaded knob of metal. The inside door handle had been removed.

For the first time panic touched her and she half turned. He had the gun out, sheltered now by the opened door. It wasn't pointed at Marion. It was pointed at the child's head. "No fuss," he repeated.

She looked through the closed pane at the yellow house. Inside its windows were frilled curtains, crisscrossed, and on the window sill African violets turned pinkish faces to the sun.

No sign of a human tenant. It was like a doll's house, fussily decorated, left until the next playtime. Marion crawled across the seat. The car had an old, closed-in smell. The upholstery was worn, the rubber floormats scuffed down to the fabric backing. Above the windshield there was a large mottled stain where a storm had blown in around the glass.

The little girl sat quietly between them, her hands folded in her lap. Was she afraid? Didn't she understand what was happening? Marion was puzzled by the attitude of silent waiting.

He turned the key in the switch, stepped on the accelerator.

"May I ask her one question?" Marion said.

He looked at her quickly, the flat eyes filling with hatred. "Like what?"

"I would like to ask her what you said to her, what you were saying to her, before I walked over to the hedge."

Again the grim touch of fun, the half smile; and he looked down at the child between them.

The little girl looked directly at Marion. "He asked me if my name was Marion. He said it was very important."

Marion ... She remembered the ghostly sensation, that Witt was somewhere near and was calling her. It had been this man instead. He had been whispering the name.

The child's lifted gaze took on a narrowed intensity, as if she were imparting some secret. "He asked me if my name was Marion Trent."

The name meant nothing to Marion. She wasn't familiar with Miss Moynton's pupils. "And what did you say?"

For a moment she thought the child seemed frightened. "I said yes."

The man turned from them with a deep, ironic chuckle. The car moved. It made a U-turn and headed directly away from the school.

CHAPTER 8

At the highway intersection of 101, the crazy traffic circle where cars felt their way through the merry-go-round, the old engine coughed and stuttered and Marion had a moment's hope; they would stall here in the center of the melee and the police would be sure to see them. Then the motor caught, the man at the wheel threw her a sharp ironic grin and they were on their way.

The child between them stirred. "I'm thirsty."

"I couldn't care less," he said.

She looked up at him. "Do you know where we're going?"

A good question, Marion thought. Just where is he taking us? And what makes him so sure he can get away with it? An irrational surge of confidence lifted her spirits. If he continued on the highway south along the coast, he must pass through a series of towns and small cities—Huntington Beach, Newport, Corona Del Mar, Laguna—and constantly on the road were the units of the California Highway Patrol. One little signal, a gesture, would bring a police car following them.

Perhaps he was headed for the Mexican border, Tijuana. And there, under the eyes of the Mexican immigration men, would be the best chance of all. If he keeps us prisoner that long.

She watched the road.

After a moment he said, "Yes, I know where we're going."

"Why are you taking us there?" the little girl asked.

"That's something your mother should have explained to you." Under the words was something like an inward shout, a grating burst of laughter, and Marion's skin chilled.

"Do you know my mother?"

"Oh—after a fashion." He gripped the wheel, his face twisting. He was relishing some great joke. "Enough to know what a liar she can be."

"She is not!"

"Did she tell you this morning to look out for some man who might come for you?"

"No."

"Then isn't that a kind of lying? Not to tell the truth?"

Marion was thinking, this whole thing must be based on some grudge; he had stolen the child to revenge himself on an adult. What kind of man would wreak, would relish, that kind of vengeance?

The answer, as before. A madman.

She looked at him, knowing that all texts supplied one answer: you couldn't tell a madman from the sanest by his appearance.

There was a flattened mark across the bridge of his nose, faintly whiter than the rest of his face, as if he had suffered a blow that had almost broken his nose, and an echo of it shaded the angle of his jaw. His eyes seemed no color, just flat and brilliant, their expression mercurial. Other than these he seemed a very ordinary man. He might have been a salesman, a factory hand, a taxi driver, a grocery clerk. In the past, indeed, he may have been all of these. Right now he was a creature with one purpose, and she had begun to surmise, sickly, what it was. Death. He had death in his thoughts.

Below the Navy ammunition and net depot he turned on a little-used track out upon the sea marsh. It was no doubt a road used by occasional fishermen. He drove indifferently, as if having planned it all before. He stopped perhaps a hundred yards from the highway, braked the car, got out. He held the gun in his hand. "Come on."

The child scrambled to follow. Marion moved more slowly, trying to take in all details of the surrounding area, trying to understand what he intended to do. For acres around them it was all level, flat, covered with scrubby salt grass a few inches high. There was fog in the air through which the sun shone mistily, but everything was clear. She could see the surf far out beyond the rim of the marsh, and behind them the cars on the highway were still almost within shouting distance. She could even see the faces of the people inside, turned to look at them, or at the sea, as the cars sped past. Marion was rigid and yet shivering. Whatever he meant to do to them here, it was to be right out in the open.

Perhaps a police car would come by; perhaps the police would decide to investigate. Then it occurred to Marion, they must seem a very ordinary group, a man and a woman and a little girl, stepping out perhaps to stretch their legs or to relax in the sea air after the rigors of a trip.

"Get in the back seat and kneel down on the floor. Face the seat. Put your hands behind your back, together."

For a moment Marion didn't understand, until he motioned with the gun.

She got into the rear seat and knelt on the floor.

The man looked at the little girl. "Now I'm going to be busy for a minute. I'll be in the car with her. If you want to you can try to run. Know what I'll do?"

"You'll chase me and shoot me," said the child, a strange practical let's-face-it note in her voice that made it sound quite grown up.

"You're so right."

From under the front seat he took a wide roll of adhesive tape and a large old-fashioned and somewhat rusty pair of scissors.

He crawled into the rear seat, bent above Marion. "Hold still and this won't hurt you. You got a nasal obstruction? Any trouble breathing through your nose?"

"No," said Marion, not understanding, and then could have bitten her tongue.

He cut off several inches of the tape. "Shut your lips together." He plastered the tape across her mouth. He waited a moment looking at her. There was a rising moment of panic; Marion forced it down. "Okay. Hands together, comfortable but close. I won't cut off the circulation if you co-operate. Just hold still and don't try any tricks. Keep your wrists steady."

He wrapped her wrists with a double collar of the cold, sticky tape and then stepped out of the car. "Now you," he said to the little girl.

There was something infinitely pathetic about the child's obedience as she knelt beside Marion; into Marion's eyes came a rush of stinging tears.

I'm helpless now, she thought frantically. What if he tries to kill the child? What could I do? I'm trussed like a chicken. I might try to run but what would that get me? But the fright, the pounding of her heart and the almost irresistible desire to struggle, brought moisture into her nose and throat and for a moment she felt as if she were drowning, strangling.

"The floor hurts my knees," the little girl said.

"Well, it won't be too long," he answered. Was he going to kill them? His tone told Marion nothing.

When he had covered both their mouths and bound their hands behind them with the unyielding gluey tape, he took an old blanket from the car trunk and covered them with it. "Keep your heads down. No raising up to peek," he warned. Marion lay with her head on the seat. Under the tent of the blanket she could make out the child's eyes staring into her own.

The blanket smelled of hay and manure; Marion thought that it had been used around a stable.

The motor started, the gears ground. With a lurch that almost dragged them from the seat to the floor, the car began to back.

They were backing toward the highway. Gradually, through the muffling blanket and the noises of the old car, she could sense the hum of passing traffic. If I could struggle up out of the blanket, she thought, get up on the seat, let people see me. The idea burned through her with a compelling insistence. She lifted her head. It seemed that in another moment, defying him, she could be in the open and letting the people in the passing cars see her. No one could mistake the meaning of a woman gagged with tape.

Then she froze.

"He would shoot us," she told herself. He would see her in the first moment she lifted herself, he would see her in the rear-view mirror and without stopping the car and without any warning or reproach he would turn the gun on both of them.

Of course he would be caught, then. The police would hunt him down even if he got away at first. He would be put away, a mad animal in an institution, or perhaps even executed.

But I'd be dead. I would never see Witt again.

He drove for a long time. The terror and the desire to defy him died away and all Marion could think of was the agony in her scraped knees and a burning cramp that extended all the way from the muscles in her calves through her thighs to her spine. Changing positions, lifting herself higher on the rough seat, only increased the discomfort. All the while the little girl lay with her face a few inches from Marion's, eyes wide and unreadable.

Exhaustedly, with a petty irritation that didn't fit the scene, Marion wondered why the girl hadn't denied her identity. Surely, with a madman like this one after them, her parents should have known enough to put the child on guard. This thing hadn't occurred out of the blue. She remembered her impression on first meeting, that he had been planning and working and anticipating this for a long time. For years, perhaps. Whatever had been done to him—real or imaginary—had been done long before or had accumulated for a long period of time. Enough time so that his mind had rotted with it.

And so why had the child admitted who she was?

There was that look of mischief, veiled almost at once, when she had heard Marion's approach. Did that have anything to do with it? Was the child chronically disobedient, rebellious, so that she had disregarded her parents' warning deliberately?

And why hadn't the police been on guard?

Thoughts whirled through Marion's mind like the ghostly dance of a flock of feathers—questions without answers, facts without explanations, cruelty without cause. And it all came to the same end, she and the child were prisoners and their future had the shadow of murder over it.

The car stopped with a harsh growl of brakes.

There was the sound of the car door opening, slamming shut. The smothering blanket was yanked away and the car seemed to fill instantly with the cold sea wind. There was sun dazzle in Marion's eyes, misted by the foggy sky; she looked out through the window. They seemed to be on the incline above a cliff, with a ridge to landward above them. On the ridge were old gray spiney trees, a forest of them, the twisted and withered remains of a fig orchard. The field around the car had been marked thinly with tire tracks, not new ones, that had crushed faint trails through an old stubble.

They seemed far off the highway, far, too, from any house. The street in the distance, running down the hill to the barricade above the bluff, was paved, but the paving had dead grass tufted in its cracked surface.

It was awkward getting out of the car with her hands fixed behind her but Marion forced herself to maintain her balance. She dreaded any help, any touch from the man. She swayed, leaned for an instant against the car. Her legs were numb. She blinked away tears of pain.

"Downhill," he ordered. The gun was out again. The wind ruffled his hair, the flat light of the misted sun seemed reflected in his eyes.

She turned. Down at the edge of the bluff was what seemed to be a long, low wall of concrete with arches and entries into it. It was like nothing she had seen before. As they walked, she studied it. It was not in the right place nor was it constructed to be a sea wall. To Marion as she came closer, there seemed something unfinished about it.

"If you're wondering what this place is—it's the start of what was going to be a big hotel. Nice and fancy. Going to give La Jolla and Coronado a run for their money. Something happened. It won't be finished till a lawsuit's settled, the title cleared."

She wondered how he had found it.

As if answering the thought, he added, "I've been looking for something like it for a long time."

The dry, mocking tone chilled her. Yes, he had been looking ... for a place to do murder.

They came to the brink of the cliff. The earth was scattered with broken concrete, with the bent ends of reinforcing rods. They picked their way through the rubble, into an arch. There was an iron railing, and then Marion saw that down through the great concrete bulwark that lay against the face of the bluff, a stairway led. Sand had been blown down into it and some of the treads were half covered.

"From what I figure," he said, standing close, peering past them, "this was going to be a place for dressing rooms and showers, a way station to the beach. Storage rooms, too, maybe. The hotel itself was going to be on the bluff and all the way back to the fig trees. There used to be pegs out, strings and wires marking the foundation lines."

She looked down into the enclosed concrete stairway ... *Don't, please don't let him take us down there....*

"Down you go," he said. "I'll tell you when to stop."

At the first level, corridors led in either direction, the cement floors and walls vanishing into darkness. She stopped there, chilled, waiting for him to tell them which way to turn. The child was very close to her now, obviously much afraid; she felt the warmth of the little girl's breath, the silky touch of her hair, against her arm.

"Two more floors to go." He touched her other arm with the gun and its coldness seemed to burn her flesh.

It was dim when they stopped. There was a strong, closed-in smell of sea salt and kelp. The child was right against her, pressing her, and she felt the wetness of tears.

He backed from them into the shadows, holding the gun. "Come on." *He's going to kill us now....*

She willed herself fiercely not to think of the horror to come, but of Witt. She tried to fix her thoughts on him. But it was like trying to fasten upon a shadow, and the man ahead of them was the sole, monstrous reality, pulling them forward by the power of his gun. She felt sand crunch underfoot; the air was cold; there were frightened noises from the child; but all of these seemed far away.

"In here." He threw open a metal-sheathed door.

They went in. She had expected darkness, but it was not dark, only dim. At the far end of the narrow room, high in the wall, was an open slit perhaps six inches deep. Through it she could see the sky, milky with foggy light.

"I'm going to leave you in here," he was saying. "You'll be fine. You can't get out, so don't bother to try. Nobody could hear you even if you could yell your heads off. Sit still and behave and I'll bring some food and water. If you have to go to the bathroom, there's the sand heap down there at the other end." The child had stumbled on into the long corridorlike room and he now turned to Marion. There was something new in his expression, directed toward her, a loosening, a grisly approachableness. "You're real pretty. A real pretty woman. Maybe when I get back we'll ... do things."

Bound and gagged, still she looked him coldly in the eye, refusing to let him see how he frightened and sickened her.

CHAPTER 9

Betty Charles bent closer to the bathroom mirror. She gripped the lipstick, tried to draw a taut curve across her lips. The light was poor, she told herself. Her mirrored face seemed to swim in a mist. This old flat, such a miserable place—without a single modern convenience. Take the bathroom globe, high in the center of the ceiling. For gosh sakes, for make-up you needed a light right beside you.

Since Tommy had been talking about the home in Denver, Betty had been buying an occasional homemaking magazine; and she remembered a recent issue—it had shown a bathroom with its own special powder alcove. The big mirror had been rimmed with fluorescent tubes. A fluffy pink rug, wall to wall, towel racks full of flowery colors ...

She frowned, tidied the lipstick with a paper tissue.

She went into the bedroom and picked up her purse from the bed. She glanced at her watch. It was time for Marion to be bouncing in. At first she had intended to leave a note, to get away before Marion came. The easy way. And then she had hated herself for the cowardice. It was time to face the kid and to tell her the truth, explain that though Tommy would be her new daddy she wasn't to live with him and would go instead to a lovely school.

Betty went on into the living room and stood impatiently, listening for Marion's coming. The place seemed awfully quiet. Betty went to the little radio and switched it on. When Marion came it would be better to have music, something cheerful; she switched the dial from channel to channel until she found some rock-and-roll.

She shook up a flattened pillow on the couch, dumped an ash tray in the kitchen sink. Another glance at the watch. Marion was late. Now, wouldn't the kid pick today to fool around on the way home!

The talk would have to be brief. Maybe it would be for the best, too.

Just be businesslike and firm. Casual. Just say, "Honey, I guess you know Tommy and I are going to be married and he'll be your new daddy." And then after a minute or so of surprise, Marion would say, "Is he coming here to live with us?" A perfect opening for what would come next.

Betty, in the middle of the living room, clutching the purse, her gaze on the door where Marion would appear at any minute, tried to phrase what she needed to say. Tried to find the words. There was something the matter, though; the words didn't want to come and her tongue seemed stuck there in the roof of her mouth, wooden with paralysis. Perhaps the little talk had better wait.

Perhaps this afternoon, sitting at the bar. Tommy would change his mind. Perhaps he would say he didn't mind another man's kid in his house after all. It was just a whim and he'd gotten over it. Or perhaps he'd say the school was full. Or he'd been thinking about how lonesome she and Marion would be for each other. Or even, that he'd heard about a better school right there in Denver.

She tried to rouse a glow over these ideas, but no warmth came. The things she had thought of weren't like Tommy at all. He wasn't a man who changed his mind about things. That was the effect of the years of bachelorhood, Betty thought dismally. She went over to the couch and sat down on an edge of the cushion. Her eyes felt tired.

She wondered why Marion had to be so late, on this particular day. She didn't want to talk about Tommy; she had dismissed that idea. But now she felt a curious need to see her child, to stroke the curly red hair and look into the mischievous eyes.

A sudden ache settled in her as she thought about the years ahead, not able to force the image from her mind, of Marion living with strangers and growing up among them, her whole life far removed from her mother's. Why, Betty thought, swallowing a lump of fear, it will almost be as if I didn't have a child at all!

She stood up quickly, a hand at the throat of her blouse. The room dimmed; she dashed the tears from her eyes quickly. A fine thing I'll look, sitting in Dixie's bar, red-eyed!

She went to the door, opened it, looked down the stairs to the open entry to the street. It was getting foggy out there. The smell of the fog, its chilly touch, stole up the stairs to her. She took a final glance at the flat. It would be better to go now, not to leave a note. Marion was used to coming home and not finding her at home.

She went down to the sidewalk. The street looked quiet, dismal with the fog. Betty buttoned her suit jacket, straightened the sleeves. Dixie's bar was five blocks away. She just had time to walk it.

When she went in, Dixie himself was behind the bar. He said, "Hello, Betty. How's tricks?"

"Fine. Oh, hell, no, I'm beat. It's these damned needle heels. I've turned my ankles fifty times on the way here."

"Dames." He put a paper napkin on the bar before her. "Dames and their goofy shoes." He was a short man with black hair and a leathery, whiskey-bitten face. "What'll you have?"

She looked at the watch. It was four o'clock. "A couple of Tom Collins." She put the purse on the bar, glanced around to see if there was anyone she knew. A couple down the bar, both well liquored, stared at her blankly over their drinks. She opened the purse and took out cigarettes. Actually, she thought suddenly, what she needed was an aspirin. An aspirin and about ten minutes to lie down in a dark spot where she could rest her tired eyes.

Tommy came in. He sat down beside her and took her hand in his, squeezed it hard. He kissed her on the familiar spot just under her ear, and whispered, "Miss me, baby?"

"You know it."

She blinked at him, leaning close. The gray gleamed in his hair and his face had a calm, almost judicial intelligence and the hand on the edge of the bar was slim and well-shaped. He was a very nice-looking man and he was hers. He wanted her to marry him. She tried to stir up the familiar pride and excitement over Tommy, but all of her feelings seemed dulled. I'm really pooped, she thought; I walked too fast and my feet hurt. And it's so tiring trying to see things when I need glasses so bad.

"Come on. Let's pick some music."

They went over to the juke box and discussed the records. She couldn't read the titles without bending down close, so she just agreed with what Tommy said. Tommy put in a couple of quarters and they went back to the bar. The drinks were there now, tall and frosty. Betty picked hers up with a hope that it would make her feel better.

There must be some way to throw off this blue dismalness. Tommy would notice, if she didn't perk up. He might get the idea it had something to do with him. She downed almost half of the drink quickly, and Tommy said, "That's not just lemonade, baby."

She felt a hot tide sting her face, partly the effect of the alcohol and partly from Tommy's mild criticism. There was this quirk about him, he hated for liquor to be treated any way but indifferently. You weren't supposed really to need it, nor take it for a pickup, or for any necessary reason. Liquor was something you almost ignored; an excuse to sit at a friendly bar, something to hold in your hand at a party. "I was thirsty," she told him.

"So ... try water then, baby."

"Guess I'd better."

She felt miserable, tight inside, her face still burning. Some men came in then whom Tommy knew, business acquaintances, and he turned from her to talk to them. She quickly drank the rest of the Collins. Tommy muttered an excuse and followed the men back to a booth, standing outside and leaning in at them to finish what he wanted to say. Betty nodded to Dixie and held up two surreptitious fingers. Without any change of expression Dixie made a double Collins and slid it in front of her, and by the time Tommy got back the drink looked exactly like the first, halfway down in the glass, and Betty was smoking a cigarette.

"Where do you want to eat tonight?"

"Oh, I don't know."

"How about some fried chicken?"

It was kind of boring when she felt so let down like this; actually she and Tommy didn't have a lot to talk about except wasn't it marvelous to be in love, and where should we eat, and how things would be once we got to Denver. To herself Betty admitted, right now she would have liked to talk about Marion. There was something on her mind, a faint uneasiness like a shadow; she wished the kid had come home and been settled safely at her homework, before she had had to take off.

"I said, how about some fried chicken?"

"Oh, it's okay, Tommy."

He looked at her for a moment. "Don't you feel good?"

"I'm all right, I'm fine."

Again he hesitated, then he said, "Finish the drink. It might pick you up."

She promptly downed the rest of the Collins and nodded to Dixie. "The same, Dixie."

"Same like that one?"

"Just like it."

Tommy glanced from Betty to Dixie, and frowned a little.

Betty inspected the fresh drink. Something she hadn't noticed before caught her attention; the drink looked greasy around the edges of the ice cubes, and she thought, it's the gin.

"Something on your mind?" Tommy asked.

"Oh, no, nothing."

"I'm not boring you?"

For an instant there was a flutter of alarm; and the dazzle and hope of the last few weeks awoke in her thoughts. Tommy was a wonderful man, a dream of a catch; there wasn't a chance she'd meet anyone like him again very soon, if ever, and she had to be nice to him. She turned to smile, but her face was stiff, dreary, and no smile came. Instead she lifted the glass and when she set it down again she found herself saying, "I've got to go home for a minute."

"Something you forgot, baby?" He seemed concerned, worried.

"Yes, something I forgot. As soon as I finish my drink I've got to go."

"Take it with you. I'll drive you. We can come right back."

They waved a temporary goodbye to Dixie and went out into the foggy light. Tommy backed the car from the slot beside the building and Betty got in. She finished the drink. In the next moment, it seemed, she was looking down the block toward her own doorway and there was a police car parked there, not against the curb the way they made ordinary people park but a couple of feet out, showing that the damned cop was above the law, and then there was the cop himself on the porch, turning away from her entry.

"Hurry, hurry! Oh, my God!" she screamed. The glass dropped from her fingers and ice cubes tinkled on the floor, and Tommy said something disapproving under his breath. She tried to grab the wheel and he slapped at her backhanded.

She got out of the car while it was still rolling and pitched off balance almost into the scanty lawn, then recovered. The cop was standing at the foot of the steps, looking at her. "Are you Mrs. Charles?"

"Yes. Yes. What is it?"

"Could you come with me to the school, please?"

A great black wave seemed to roll up out of the earth and seize her senses. The next thing she knew, the cop had her by the arm, and his face was looking right into hers.

"I didn't mean to frighten you, ma'am."

"That's all right. It's Marion, isn't it? What's happened to her?" Inside herself was a terrible flaming ache, and under the ache was a hideous soul-splitting knowledge, a thing like a sword cutting her brain in two, the fact that she had meant to send her child away and not hardly ever see her again, and live like a queen with a man who wouldn't give Marion houseroom. "Tell me! Tell me!"

"I don't know, ma'am," said the cop, still gingerly supporting her by one arm. "All I know is, I got a call to come and pick you up and take you to Mitchell School."

He turned her carefully toward the police car and suddenly Tommy was there, blocking the way. "What's it all about, Betty?"

"It's Marion."

"Do you want me to come, too?"

"No." He was close enough so that she could see the uneasy alarm, a touch of embarrassment as if he wasn't sure what was expected of him. "I don't need you with me, Tommy. I'll be fine."

"Well ... let me know—"

"Sure, I'll let you know."

He stepped aside to let her pass.

There were three men in the principal's office. She looked around at once for some sign of Marion, but there was nothing. The plump man behind the desk she knew, Mr. Dobbs, the school principal. The others, both lean and gray-headed, sharp-eyed, dressed in plain clothes, gave off an unmistakable odor of cop. "Sit down please, Mrs. Charles," said Dobbs, rising to move a chair; and the tone of his voice was so calm, so unruffled, that a great draft of courage seemed to lift her spirits.

It must not be so bad then, after all. Wouldn't they have taken her at once to Marion? Betty sat down and the quivering weakness died away. A woman came in, Miss Moynton, and stood back of her beside the door.

"Mrs. Charles, we have something here that needs explaining," Mr. Dobbs began carefully. "It seems that your daughter Marion and one of our teachers, a substitute teacher, left the grounds just before the final bell. They went away together with a man who drove a dark sedan. An older model car. We have a fairly good description of the man, but before we went any further in this we were wondering if you might be able to supply the answer." He smiled slightly, and waited.

It didn't make sense to Betty. She had to reorient all of her ideas. She had thought that Marion must have been injured on the playground or by traffic in the street, but this question of Mr. Dobbs's seemed incomprehensible. "What answer?"

"The—identity of the man who apparently came for your child and Mrs. Kennick."

She stammered, "I've never heard of Mrs. Kennick."

He sighed and picked up a stray sheet of paper, opened a drawer and put the paper away. "Mrs. Kennick is a substitute teacher employed by the school district. She has had Miss Chiroske's class for the last five days."

"I don't understand what you're talking about."

He looked at her across the desk and under the calm manner she sensed anger and an affronted meanness. Suddenly she disliked the plump man intensely. He seemed deliberately to be making it hard for her to know what had happened to Marion. "Mrs. Charles, I believe that Miss Moynton came to see you yesterday afternoon."

"Yes ... yes, she did," Betty agreed, trying to adjust to this new tack.

"She told you of a man at the edge of the playground, who had called your daughter by name." The memory of yesterday's interview with Miss Moynton seemed fuzzy and confused, and had nothing to do with this. "I ... I guess so."

"And you told her that it must have been an elderly relative of yours. An old uncle. Senile."

"Well, I just said something about Uncle Eddie because Miss Moynton acted so worried," Betty blurted.

Slack showed in his cheeks as if his jaw had dropped. "You don't really believe that this person who hid in the shrubbery and called your daughter was this old man?"

She frowned at him dazedly. "Nobody said anything about hiding in the shrubbery."

Over her head, Mr. Dobbs and Miss Moynton exchanged a bitter glance.

"Are you telling me," Betty got out, her heart lurching, "that my child has been kidnaped by one of your teachers? Off the school grounds? In broad daylight?"

Miss Moynton made an angry ejaculation. Mr. Dobbs stiffened in the chair. "There is one small fact that is pertinent," he said, looking at her as if measuring the gin in those three Collins. "Your child's name is Marion. The prowler, or lurker, of yesterday, called out this name. We may presume that he did the same today."

She tried not to hiccup. "And what's the p ... pertinent fact?"

"Mrs. Kennick's name is also Marion," said Mr. Dobbs.

CHAPTER 10

Bruce Trent parked his car in the driveway. He looked up and down the street, foggy now and dimming with twilight. He went through the rear yard to the kitchen door. Carol was in there, no lights on. She rushed into his arms. She had been hiding here, terrified, in the dark. A sense of anger and outrage rushed through him, a hot hatred against Fecamo, a man he had never seen.

"Where's Marilyn?"

"In her room. Reading," Carol said, muffled against his clothes. "You can't see her light from the street."

"We're going to turn on the lights," Bruce said firmly. "And we're going to call the police. Whether we manage to impress them or not. Just exactly what did he say to you on the phone?"

"No real threats." She drew away, shivered, touched the light switch. The room came alive, its familiar livableness, but Carol was haggard, eyes hunted. "He was angry when I wouldn't believe, when I wouldn't be jealous, about … about you and his wife. And then he said that though her part was over, and your part was over, his had just begun."

Bruce glanced toward the hall. "What have you told Marilyn?"

"Nothing. I didn't even go after her. I had a horrible feeling that he was near, somewhere in the neighborhood, perhaps even watching the house, and that the longer she couldn't be identified the safer she might be." Carol looked up at her husband hopefully. "Her picture was never in the paper."

"And they got her name wrong," Bruce added absently.

"No one spoke to her, no one came near her, on the way home."

He shook his head. "You took a chance there."

"I—I just didn't know what to do."

"It turned out all right. Don't torment yourself over it." He went swiftly to the hall, Carol following. He found Marilyn on her bed with a book propped against the pillows. When she saw Bruce she scrambled up, not forgetting to tidy her skirts, and held out her arms. "Daddy, you're home!"

"Don't make it sound as if you haven't seen me for a week!" He lifted her, hugged her, and with noses an inch apart they grinned into each other's eyes. "What on earth did you have for lunch? Lead pipe sandwiches? You weigh a ton!"

"I don't! I'm skinny really!"

He pretended to heft her. "Getting fat, as sure as shootin'. Well, come on. We've got talking to do." He walked back to the living room, carrying her piggyback, set her down on the edge of the carpet, went to the front windows and closed the draperies, then turned on all the lamps. "Now," he said, "sit down. And listen carefully."

Carol suddenly sank down on the couch, shutting her eyes. She looked sick and exhausted. Marilyn looked at her mother, then turned back to Bruce.

"We can't put it off any longer," he said, looking straight into his daughter's eyes. "It's something we hoped you would never have to know. But now, because of the danger and trouble, we have to tell you."

She sat down on a chair, tucking her feet into a straight line, her posture prim and grown-up. "Is it about the bad man?"

"Hey!" he cried in surprise.

Carol's eyes flew open as if in fright.

"There must be a bad man after us," Marilyn said in her oddly practical, no-nonsense kind of voice. "You and Mama keep thinking about him."

After a moment of astonished hesitation, Bruce said, "Well … there is. His name—the name he gives—is Fecamo. Paul Fecamo. Neither your mother nor I have ever seen him. He's called us on the telephone." How flat it sounded, Bruce thought; no hint of the cruelty and dirt that Fecamo always conveyed.

"What makes him so bad?" Marilyn asked, getting right to the heart of the matter.

"He is sick, baby—sick in his head. He had a wife, a girl who worked in my office. We all knew her as Susan Spender. Miss Spender. She never spoke of being married to Fecamo—"

"Perhaps he is a man who wanted to marry her," Marilyn offered, with a touch of adult insight.

"It's quite possible," Bruce agreed. "Anyway … if you can remember that far back—you were pretty small—"

"I remember Miss Spender. She came to the house once."

"That was the day of the accident."

"And she got killed. There were things in the paper."

"The other driver tried to blame me. There was a trial. I was cleared of all charges, but that didn't bring Miss Spender back. And it doesn't seem to matter to Fecamo."

"Can't you do something about it?" Marilyn moved to a hassock close to Bruce's chair. It was, he thought with a touch of half-despairing humor, as if Marilyn were a little old lady bent on comforting him.

"We're going to have to." He pulled her against his knee, stroked her hair. "We must call the police. They'll come and talk to us. That's why you had to know, so you wouldn't be confused when they came."

"You thought I'd be scared. I'm not afraid of Mr. Fecamo, Daddy. If he's sick he should be shut up until he gets well."

Bruce put his hands on her shoulders. "No, Marilyn, don't say that you're not afraid of him. That would be a bad mistake. He's dangerous." He looked across the little girl's head to Carol. "Let's call the police."

The officer arrived in a little less than an hour. He introduced himself, showing them his badge and his I.D. in its leather wallet. His name was Renwick. He wore plain clothes, a neat gray suit that minimized his bulk. He sat down and listened to Bruce Trent's story.

After that he spent some minutes thinking about it. Under the light of the lamp at his side, Bruce could see the mark of a scar, cutting down from the hairline to the temple, to the cheekbone below. It gave Renwick's features an off-center look, strangely almost comic. "This Fecamo ever ask for money?" he said suddenly.

The question surprised Bruce. "No, never."

"Think he might be leading up to it?"

"No, I never had that impression. What about the call today, Carol? Any hint of a shakedown?"

"It wasn't that way at all," Carol said in a husky, strained tone. "There was no hint of anything except a kind of—of meanness. Wanting me to be angry and jealous, and then the promise of something ugly to come. He isn't after money. He *has* money."

"Why do you say that?" the detective inquired, staring over at her.

"I don't know." She shook her head. "He has enough to follow through with whatever plans he's made. He doesn't need anything from us."

"But he wants something. There's a motive somewhere," the detective pointed out.

"He's a maniac," Carol said. "I never realized it, perhaps never admitted it to myself, until today. I guess I wanted it to be that Bruce exaggerated. But having talked to Fecamo, having listened to him, I know."

"It's an impression," Renwick said.

"It's the truth," she insisted.

"You don't give me a lot to go on," he said, frowning. "You haven't any idea of his whereabouts. You've never met him, can't give a description. I can check the usual sources of course, California Motor Vehicle Department and so forth, see if he has a driver's license or a car registered to him. We can inquire locally of motels and hotels, places a newcomer might be expected to stay. But you see, if he's what you believe he is, he might not be using his right name."

Bruce looked across at Renwick, wondering what he could offer to help in the search.

"And then, if we found him, he might deny that he had called or had molested you people in any way. We could get a voice identification, perhaps. How good it would be in court, it's hard to say."

"Court?"

"You'll have to sign a complaint against him," the detective said. "And you'd have to be pretty sure it was the right man." His face crinkled suddenly in a look of perplexity, and all along the scar the skin tightened in little ridges. "If you had some idea that the police would serve a purpose, would frighten him for you, threaten him and make him leave you alone—I'm afraid that's not our job. We catch the criminal—after the fact of the crime."

"Isn't what he's doing against the law?" Bruce asked. Under the calm control he forced upon himself, a hot rage boiled, a desire to strike. "Aren't there ordinances against filth and threats on the telephone?"

"Yes. If we can catch him and if you can prove it."

From Marilyn's room came the sound of her record-player.

Renwick lowered his voice so that it wouldn't carry beyond Bruce and Carol. "Unless you're with the police or with the telephone company, you'd have no idea of the extent of this stuff. It goes on all the time. Some people just get frantic. In my own neighborhood for instance, among women my wife knows, women who are widowed or single and have their phones listed in the book under their own names—three of them have had to change listings, use initials—"

"This isn't like that," Bruce said. "I know what you're talking about. Casual drunks or perverts, picking a woman's name at random. This man has followed us across the country. He's got a grudge."

"Get an unlisted phone," Renwick advised flatly.

"I can't. I'm a salesman. My phone has to be available to dealers all over L. A. County. An unlisted phone would cost me orders. It's a simple matter of making a living."

Renwick nodded as if the subject was closed. "That's that, then. I'll do what I can, try to locate Fecamo." Renwick rose from his chair, picked up his hat off a table. "If you get any more phone calls, let me know."

Bruce rose, too. "The thing that worries us both is the safety of our little girl. She's the most vulnerable of the three of us."

Renwick paused, frowning, by the door. "That's a pretty big step even for a maniac, Mr. Trent ... hurting a child. I think he'd hesitate a long time before switching from telephone calls to that."

"I hope you're right," Carol told him.

He nodded at her, a little stiffly. He seemed uncomfortable, perhaps sensing their hostility. "I'll be in touch."

When he had gone the room seemed very quiet. Bruce lit a cigarette and walked around. Carol sat hunched forward, elbows on knees, palms supporting her chin. In Marilyn's room the record came to an end and then Marilyn came back into the room.

"Is the policeman gone?"

"Yes, he's gone. Bruce, you were disappointed, weren't you?"

He didn't look at her. "It wasn't unexpected. It was better than Louisiana. At least Renwick didn't think we were imagining it all. He just pointed out the difficulties. They weren't of his making."

"I hadn't thought of charging Fecamo with a crime, having to appear against him," Carol admitted. Marilyn had come to sit beside her; Carol reached for her hand and held it tightly in her own. "I guess I'd been hoping for just what Renwick said they couldn't do. I thought the police could frighten him, tell him to leave us alone. And that then he'd go away."

"I know," Bruce replied. "I feel the same way. It's natural, not wanting to have anything to do with anything hateful or abnormal. Only, we're going to have to brace ourselves. If they find Fecamo we must identify his voice, and stick with it."

Carol was staring into thin air, perhaps visualizing a courtroom scene with Bruce and herself pitted against Fecamo.

"Don't worry, Mama," said Marilyn, looking anxiously at her mother.

Carol seemed to jerk herself back from anguished introspection. "I'm going to fix something to eat. Look how late it is and we haven't even had dinner." She stood up, pulling Marilyn up beside her, and turned toward the door to the kitchen hallway.

Bruce came quickly and put his hands on her shoulders. "You look terribly tired, darling. Isn't there something Marilyn and I can fix? Frozen dinners, maybe?"

Suddenly she began to shake. She leaned against Bruce, huddling her face against his chest, pulling Marilyn in so that they made a threesome, close there together in the silent room.

Bruce put his arms around her, and at the same time he thought bitterly, suppose Fecamo could see us now? Wouldn't this make him happy? Three terrified people.

"Bruce ... I wish it could be the way it was before. I wish I hadn't heard his voice. Even more than what he said ... It was his voice I recognized, as you recognize some old nightmare out of childhood. His voice was the echo of evil ... of all the evil on earth...."

Bruce knew what she meant. Though she had shared his reaction to Fecamo, it had been secondhand. She had moved when he had thought it best, uprooting herself and Marilyn, she had kept watch through the days for any danger, she had grown sickly with the strain ... and yet, under it all, there had been a core of half hope that Fecamo didn't exist. There had been a secret will to disbelieve. Now that was gone. The evil in Fecamo's voice ... he knew what that meant, too ... had destroyed her inner self-confidence.

"I wish you hadn't heard him," Bruce agreed, hugging her close. He felt Marilyn's warm hand snuggled up under his coat to hug his waist, and he dropped an arm to squeeze her in closer. Maybe this has its good side, too, Bruce thought; maybe we appreciate each other more, maybe we're too scared to take each other for granted. Don't let us ever lose this, once it's over, he prayed inwardly. *If* it's ever over ...

"Why don't you go lie down? We'll see what we can scare up, and when it's hot we'll call you."

She had forced herself to quit shaking. She lifted her head and tried to smile. "No, darling. I'm fine. It was just a—a female vapor or something." She pushed his arms away gently, tugged a pigtail and brushed Marilyn's head with a kiss. Then she went on into the kitchen.

She was brisk and busy. She took things from the refrigerator and the cupboards. She handed down dishes to Marilyn. She poured cream into a pitcher. Her hands shook, but she paused until they steadied and none of the cream was spilled. She lit the oven.

Marilyn opened the drawer that held the silver. She took out knives and forks and was reaching for spoons when the phone rang. Carol was holding a steel saucepan; it fell with a clatter.

Bruce went over to the phone. It was one of his dealers, of course, with a late, last-minute order, something that needed to be brought from the warehouse first thing in the morning, something for an impatient customer who wouldn't wait. He put up a hand toward the phone.

Carol had retrieved the saucepan, set it on the stove. She ran to Bruce. "Don't. Wait! Let me get to the bedroom and listen on the extension!"

"It's just an order," he said, looking down at her, frowning a little. Marilyn had gone to the table with the silverware. She began to place the silver with a soft, precise touch. She glanced over her shoulder at him and he saw the solemn expression, the anxiety. "All right. Go on in the bedroom. When I yell, pick up the receiver."

She ran out, and a moment later he heard her open the bedroom door.

Marilyn had finished putting out the silver. She stood under the light, listening and watching. Bruce nodded to her, trying to grin. "Here's where I sell a refrigerator, baby." He turned toward the hall, and with a sense of ridiculous melodrama, of being involved in something silly like playacting, he yelled, "Now!"

As he lifted the receiver he glanced at Marilyn and winked. He was thinking of how the man on the other end of the line, some staid dealer, would take these shenanigans if he could see them.

"Mr. Trent?"

Every nerve in his body stung with shock. It was Fecamo.

"Speaking," was Bruce's numb response.

"Do you believe in the old adage," Fecamo said conversationally, "of a life for a life?"

All of Bruce's heat and hatred burst out. "Why in the hell can't you leave us alone?"

"No, no. Don't get sore. Answer my question. Weren't you expecting something like it? After all, you know she's missing by now."

The quiet and mocking tone was new, though Fecamo's voice was hatefully familiar. It struck Bruce that Fecamo was highly satisfied over something, and then the sense of the words came, and Bruce said, "Who's missing?"

"That won't get you anywhere, Mr. Trent. You and I know who is missing. I hope that the police don't, as yet. Your chances of seeing your daughter again are much better if you stay clear of them."

In spite of himself Bruce whirled to make sure that Marilyn still stood there watching. He started to blurt out the truth, and then something warned him, stopped him. Fecamo wanted him to believe that he had Marilyn. Before he denied it, he had better find out why.

CHAPTER 11

"I haven't harmed her in any way," Fecamo said still in that hugging-himself, satisfied tone—and then added dryly, "as yet."

"Where is she?"

"Oh, I couldn't tell that! Surely you don't expect it. You're not a stupid person and neither am I. You, Mr. Trent, are a man of experience, of ... discrimination. You and I both know how these things should be handled."

Fecamo was enjoying himself. The fantastic vanity, the triumph, the relish, rang in his voice. Bruce wondered in that moment where Fecamo was, out there in the foggy night. For some reason he sounded far away, an illusion perhaps compounded by the unreality of what he was saying. Then in the next moment Bruce remembered Renwick's suggestion. "You want money! You're asking for ransom!"

There was a muffled noise, made by Carol into the phone, and for an instant Fecamo hesitated as if wondering about it. "No, I'm not asking for ransom." Now he sounded displeased. "Not in the ordinary sense. That would be pretty crude, wouldn't it? Trading my wife's existence for a chunk of money? Your money? I'm seeking an intangible ... something far more imperishable than cash. Not vengeance, though you might peg it at that level. In a way I intend doing you a favor, Mr. Trent. I want you to *feel* ... I mean to widen your horizon. Experienced as you are, there are things you haven't ... tasted, yet."

"Fecamo, listen to me. Wherever you are, you aren't too far from a police station. Go there and turn yourself in and ask for help."

The silence was stark, offended.

"There must be moments for you—even as far off balance as you are—" Bruce said, "when you know how badly you need professional help. When you see your sickness for what it is."

Fecamo made a guttural, explosive, protesting sound into the phone.

"I didn't kill your wife and in your half-sane interludes you must know it. The truth all came out at the trial. Susan Spender and I barely knew each other. We'd been on a business trip, one day. If anyone killed her, if anyone could be blamed, it was the driver of the other car."

Fecamo's voice trembled. "You took my wife ... you took Susan ... in adultery—"

"Fecamo. I did not."

"The accident was a minor part of the disaster," Fecamo said, almost shouting. "She had already discarded me, removed me from her life. Our marriage was over. Death just put a period to it."

"So, feel sorry for yourself!" Bruce controlled the desire to shout in response. "But why hound us? Why make our lives a hell? Why in God's name can't you just leave us alone?"

Fecamo's voice stumbled and hesitated. "Leave you ... alone?"

"That's what I said. Why don't you get off the phone now and never call me again?"

"Now?"

"Now."

The silence hummed in the wire.

"You want me to hang up and not to call again," Fecamo mused, as if over a puzzle. "It's not what I had expected you to say. Frankly, I had expected you to plead with me and to make promises. This way, it sounds as if you don't care much what happens to your little girl. It sounds as if your own comfort means more to you than her safety. That's a funny attitude, Mr. Trent."

The desire to tell Fecamo that if he thought he had Marilyn he was really crazy almost overcame Bruce; but again there was the sense of caution, of warning. For some reason, Fecamo wanted him to think that Marilyn was in danger, had actually been kidnaped. She was gone, and only Fecamo was supposed to know where she was.

Was it a trick? Did Fecamo intend to use this pretended kidnaping to draw him out alone somewhere?

Was Fecamo so far off reality that he actually believed he *had* stolen Marilyn?

He didn't *sound* that crazy, Bruce thought, but how am I to know? I'm no expert.

Then another idea occurred to him. As absolutely mad as this was, wasn't there a kind of safety in it? Could it be true that as long as Fecamo nursed his particular delusion, he wouldn't act?

And how long, Bruce wondered, can I trust the delusion to stay with him?

I need more information.

He forced his tone to be humble, conciliatory. "How is my daughter?" he asked. "Is she frightened?"

"That's better," Fecamo said. "And yes, she is frightened. Very much so."

"How did you manage to get hold of her?" Bruce wondered. "We thought she was visiting a neighbor child. Safe inside another house."

"You know better than that," Fecamo burst out, angry again. "You know by now that I got her from the school."

"Oh, is that how you got her?" Bruce corrected himself, but the tone must not have been right.

For Fecamo said at once, "What's the matter with you? What kind of cold fish are you? You sound as if we were talking about a side of bacon. I've got your *kid*. Your own flesh and blood, the one you've raised. She's red-headed, kind of cute. She's got on a green skirt and a white blouse and sweater. She gave me some sass there at first when I was making sure who she was. I guess she sasses you sometimes, too, huh? And you might miss it when she's gone."

Bruce was at a loss, not knowing what to say. Fecamo sounded so *sure*. The nightmare that couldn't be real seemed to be taking on reality. He rubbed a hand across his mouth, frowning at the phone, hesitating.

Then Carol's voice interrupted.

"Please, Mr. Fecamo! Please! Don't hurt my little girl! We'll do anything. We'll meet you anywhere, go to any lengths to make up to you for what happened to your wife. Just don't ... don't injure our child!" Carol's voice was ragged with strain, with urgency.

And Fecamo was pleased by it. Immensely pleased. His tone took on a rich unctuousness. "Mrs. Trent? At least you seem to see into the heart of the situation. Of course I can't promise anything—"

"No, no—don't say that! You wouldn't hurt a child, you wouldn't punish a little girl, for our mistakes!"

"You admit you made them?" The way Fecamo said this almost made Bruce retch. "You've finally come to the conclusion—"

"Yes. You were right, Mr. Fecamo. Everything you said was the truth. But please don't hurt ... don't hurt ..."

"Marion," Fecamo supplied eagerly.

"Please don't hurt Marion!"

"Well ... You almost move me, Mrs. Trent. I could almost forgive, right now—I could almost promise to release her."

"You will!"

"Uh ... no. I'm going to have to do some thinking."

"You aren't a cruel man," she insisted, with such desperation that Bruce was astonished.

What in the hell were they talking about, anyway?

"I'm glad that you see that, and no—I'm not cruel at heart."

"And you won't just leave us to wonder?"

"Oh, no, I'll call back presently. After I've done my thinking," Fecamo promised.

Bruce thought, Fecamo wants time to enjoy this. Carol has played right into his hands. He feels like God now. He has the power of life and death, of happiness and joy or of disaster. He can make us or break us utterly. And he's completely crazy, because Marilyn is standing in the dining nook listening to every word I say!

"Goodbye for the moment, Mrs. Trent. Goodbye, Mr. Trent."

"Call soon again!" Carol cried, her voice breaking.

Fecamo gave a soft little laugh and the line went dead.

When Carol walked into the kitchen a minute later, Bruce was still standing beside the phone. He looked at her in bewilderment.

"Don't you understand? Didn't you get what he was saying? He has *someone!*"

"What?"

"Bruce, he isn't suffering a delusion! He's got a child—somebody's child! He's too convinced, too sure of himself. And that description he gave—" She swung suddenly to look at Marilyn. "At school today ... what happened?"

Marilyn stood mute, looking from Carol to Bruce.

Carol walked to the dining nook, sat down, pulled Marilyn close to her. "Was anyone in your room ... taken away? Did a man come and talk to the teacher? Did she let a child go?"

"When?"

"At any time."

Marilyn frowned. "Nothing happened, really, except Miss Moynton took some of us to the auditorium. She demonstrated about remedial reading. None of us needed it but it was to show all the ladies what she could do if she had to."

"When was this?"

"When school was almost out. You know. The P.T.A. meeting." The touch of reserve was to remind Carol that she hadn't gone, though all sorts of notices and reminders had been brought home.

Carol sat silent. The tiredness, the haggardness, seemed to have fined down to a fierce concentration. "And where was the rest of the class?"

"On the playground, I guess. That's where we all go, every day. Games in last period."

"And before this, during the day—no one came for a pupil?"

"No, Mama."

Again Carol was silent. Then Bruce said softly, "The name. Marion. It's what the newspapers called Marilyn during that time ... remember?"

Carol looked fixedly at her child. "Is there someone named Marion in your class?"

"Marion Charles."

"Does she have red hair?"

"Yes. It's awfully pretty."

"What was she wearing today?"

Marilyn hesitated. "I think she wore her green skirt. She wears it a lot. It has pockets on each side."

"And a blouse?"

"Kind of cream-colored, with ruffles in front. And a sweater, a white sweater."

Carol and Bruce exchanged a long look.

Carol stood up. "I've got to call the school."

"Wait a minute," Bruce said. "Let's think about this, let's be sure we're doing the right thing. Perhaps we ought to get hold of Renwick first, ask his advice. Perhaps before we do anything—anything at all—we ought to get Marilyn away."

"What do you mean?" Carol moved toward him, and Bruce didn't meet her eyes. She slowed, stopped, still staring at him. "No, I know what you mean. Fecamo has the wrong child. Somehow he made a mistake. And that gives Marilyn some temporary safety. As long as he continues in his mistake, she can be safe."

Bruce spoke harshly, as if past some roughness in his throat. "It's not just Marilyn's safety, Carol. What happens when Fecamo finds out he's made a bad blunder? What do you think he'll do?"

Carol licked her lips.

"He'll almost certainly kill the other child. At once. She's nothing to him, a nuisance, rubbish. He'll kill her and then with that savagery added to his present mood, he'll come for Marilyn."

"Oh, God!"

"If there was something we could promise Fecamo ... if he was doing it for money, the way Renwick seems to think ... then that other child might have a chance. But you know what we're dealing with. You know what he wants. You heard him on the phone."

"Yes, I heard him."

She stood there as if lost, halfway between the phone on the wall and the seat of the dining nook. The blond hair, pulled back severely into the bun on her neck, left her face without any softness. She looked old in that moment.

"It may be that the best course we can follow," Bruce said slowly, "is to let Fecamo go on thinking he has our child."

"You mean ... dicker with him on that basis?"

"Yes."

"And suppose we fail?" she whispered. "Suppose our dickering goes wrong? Can you bear to think of our guilt, if that other child is killed?"

"Can you bear to think of it," Bruce said harshly, "if we tell Fecamo the truth and he kills her anyway?"

Carol shivered, putting her hands up crosswise, holding her arms against her breast. "They're looking for her right now. Her parents are frantic and the school people are at a loss. We have to let *them* know."

"Can we trust them, Carol? Can we trust their promise—providing they give it—to do it our way? Or won't these people rush to the newspapers ... 'Tell this madman he has the wrong child, tell him to let our child go.'"

"We have to leave it up to them." Her lips barely moved; she was hunched over, looking up at him in the attitude of an old woman. "It's their choice, Bruce. Not ours."

He drew a deep, ragged breath. "Yes, I guess it is."

She turned back to Marilyn, hugging her child in her arms.

"Does the bad man have Marion, Mama?"

"Perhaps."

"How would he make her go away with him?"

Carol shuddered. There had been a madman at the school, waiting to waylay Marilyn. The narrow margin by which he had missed her child clogged her throat with terror.

She cried out to Bruce, who had lifted the receiver: "Wait. You're right! Let's talk to Fecamo again before we tell them."

Bruce leaned against the wall, the phone in his hand. Then slowly he put it into its hook.

Witt Kennick stirred in the dark bedroom.

A bell was ringing somewhere. The sound was like a gnat, buzzing tormentingly in his ears, forcing him to roll over, to try to sit up. Holding his head, lurching off balance, he tried to place the sound. It wasn't the phone.

He got his feet on the floor, pulled himself erect, felt his way to the light switch.

The bright light was a bath of shock to his senses; he covered his eyes and sucked in a gasp of agony.

The doorbell, then.

He cursed disjointedly as he staggered into the living room. The outer court was lighted and he could see the windows outlined by the glow and two vague figures out there waiting. He went to the door and yanked it open. "What the hell do you want?"

"Mr. Kennick?"

He peered at them. They were ominous, hulking, with the foggy well of the lighted court beyond them. "Sure, I'm Kennick."

"We're police officers."

His heart seemed to thud like a hammer, two or three terrific pulsing contractions, and then almost to stop. He couldn't catch his breath. It was a moment he had often contemplated. Somehow he had got behind the wheel of Marion's car and had run down a pedestrian. Or collided with another car. And now the cops had come for him. "Officer, I don't remember any accident at all," he said thickly, pleadingly. "Are you positive you've got the right guy?"

"May we come in, Mr. Kennick?"

"Just give me a break, for God's sake!"

"We just want to talk to you for a couple of minutes."

It was a lie, of course. Clammy and shaking, he moved back into the room. The first cop to come in switched on the lights. Again Witt had the aching, agonized stab of pain through his temples.

"Where were you today, Mr. Kennick, at about three o'clock?"

So that's when it had happened…. "Oh, hell, officer, I was home."

Was I?

"Where is your wife?"

"She's … uh …" He looked around, squinting against the glare that seemed to burst and blaze behind his eyes. "I guess she stepped out for a minute."

"Did she come home here after school was out?"

Witt glanced at the cop. A big bastard. Face looked cold and mean. Must protect Marion. "Of course."

"She came home just as usual?"

"Why shouldn't she?" He covered a hiccup with the back of his hand. "You'll find out, my wife's the only one drives our car and she's a very good driver. You can't pin anything on her. And as for me, I don't drive. Haven't driven for—for a year, anyway. Don't even have a license. I let it expire." He faced them with defiance.

"Please sit down, Mr. Kennick. This is something we've got to get straight."

CHAPTER 12

When he finally understood that this had nothing to do with an automobile accident, that it had to do in some mysterious way with Marion's behavior and whereabouts, Kennick felt some of the fog lift and something like cold sobriety settle in its place.

He was sweating inside the pajamas, his nerves quivering, but he forced himself to listen.

"Have you seen your wife since three o'clock, Mr. Kennick? Or in other words, have you seen her at all since she left for her job this morning?"

"I—I guess not."

"She hasn't phoned you?"

"No."

"Haven't you been worried about her? It's almost …" The cop looked at his watch. "… eight o'clock now."

"I was asleep."

"Has she disappeared like this before?"

His anxious ear caught the word. "What do you mean, 'disappeared'?"

"Your wife left the school grounds just before school let out today. She was accompanied by a man, and by one of the pupils. So far there has been no trace of any of them." The cop paused as if expecting him to say something. He glanced at the watch again.

"Who?" Witt said finally. "What man?"

The cop said, "Had you and your wife had any trouble lately?"

"You mean, was I expecting her to walk out on me?" Witt frowned painfully against the light. "I guess it wouldn't have surprised me." He caught the significant stare exchanged by the two cops. "You haven't told me who the man is. Or who the kid is. If Marion was going to leave me, she wouldn't do it this way, anyway. She'd tell me first. And I can't see an elopement with a kid involved." He stopped and let his own words straggle back through his mind. "Hell, it sounds almost like a kidnaping. It doesn't sound like a … like what you're talking about."

One of the cops nodded as if with satisfaction. "Has your wife ever mentioned a pupil named Marion Charles?"

In spite of a growing sense of fear, of a loss of orientation in this thing, Witt tried to remember. Marion had never talked much about her job, or the people she met at the various schools. He'd had the impression more than once, she had compartmented her life, and the kids and the work and daylight were in one part of it, and he and the dark were in another. He rubbed his face. There was the beginning of a beard. He smelled stale. "Not that I can remember, no."

"Any special man friend?"

Witt's mouth tightened. He shook his head.

"Maybe your wife met someone lately?"

"I wouldn't know." Witt was thinking, I've got to get a bath, dress, get out of here and find out what's happened to Marion.

"Does your wife ever go out alone? Uh … say when you're under the weather, or something?"

"You mean, when I'm drunk? Yes, I guess she does. I can't expect her to stay here."

"You have kind of a drinking problem, don't you, Mr. Kennick?"

"Looked it up, didn't you?"

"Well, you do have a record of drunk arrests," the cop said smugly.

"So … yes, I have a drinking problem."

"What about your financial set-up? You make the living? Or does she?"

"Who in hell gave you the authority to ask me questions like that?" Witt flared. "That's our own damned personal business."

"Ordinarily, it might be," the cop agreed. "But now, you see, your wife is involved in a crime. A child has been taken without the permission of the school or the parent. And we have to look for a motive."

Witt squinted at them, his head roaring, angry and incredulous. "Are you on the level? Are you telling me my wife helped steal a kid? Why, you must be nuts. Marion's the last person on earth who would do a thing like that."

"Well, why do you think she did this, then?"

"It wasn't the way you think it was," Witt insisted. "If she walked off the school grounds with the kid and a man, she went for another reason than to share in the loot."

"Such as?"

"Maybe he forced Marion to go along."

The cops exchanged a doubtful glance, and Witt stood up. "Will you guys excuse me now? I've got to dress and go out."

"Why don't you stay?" the older one asked, kind of soothingly. "We were hoping you'd be here to answer any telephone calls. In case your wife wanted to get in touch with you."

Obviously they suspected a conspiracy.

"Why don't *you* stay?" Witt asked. "Answer the damned phone yourselves? You would anyway." He went into the bedroom and began to rummage for clean underwear in the dresser.

I need a drink, bad. Where in hell is the bottle?

He found the bottle—or at least one of them—when he opened the shower stall to bathe. He mixed a quick whiskey-and-water in the bathroom glass. It brought out a torrent of sweat, an inner convulsion, and then for a moment he thought it wasn't going to stay down. Finally he got in under the stinging spray.

They were trying to pin something on Marion. Something she would never have done. He was going to have to go out and get the straight of it. The guy must be someone Marion knew. He hadn't told that to the cops, exactly, though it was what they were thinking. If the guy was someone Marion knew, and knew he was okay, it would explain her leaving the school grounds and taking a kid with her.

Say this. Say the kid's parents are divorced, the kid'd been given to the mother. Only now the father wants her.

Witt stood under the cold spray and sucked air into his lungs and tried to sort his whirling thoughts. Must be a reason.

He dried and stood before the bathroom mirror to shave.

Had to hurry.

It suddenly occurred to him, remembering the foggy courtyard with the cops bulking before it—it was night. What had the cop said? Almost eight? It was dark and Marion hadn't come home.

For a moment he felt a touch of fear for her.

Must take another drink.

When he had dressed he went back into the living room. The cops were still there. They had taken on a look of permanence, a hateful familiarity. Witt crossed the room and stood by the door. "I'm going out to do a little investigating. I'm going to find out ... find out for you guys ... because you can't ... just where Marion is."

"Watch yourself, fella," said the younger cop. "You're kind of two sheets to the wind."

"I love that phrase," Witt told him. "It has the freshness of all outdoors in it. It revives me!" He went out and shut the door on the cop's disgusted face.

Going down the steps to the inner court, he drew in a deep breath of the dank foggy air and had to stop to cough, clinging to the railing, the damp metal cold to his palms. He felt suddenly sick and dizzy.

Should have brought the bottle.

Well, he could stop in the first bar for a pickup.

The pickup warmed and settled him. The paunchy bartender was back in the shadows, his back turned to Witt, polishing glassware. Witt said, "Hey, Red."

Red turned and came closer. There seemed something cautious in his manner.

"Did Marion come in here last night? Don't tell me she didn't come out. I know better. She had on that red dress, those red shoes."

"Yeah—yeah, she came in here for a little while."

"Anybody try to pick her up?"

Red turned around to put the dried glass carefully on its pyramid. "Guess I didn't notice."

"She's disappeared," Witt said harshly. "Some stranger came and got her off the school grounds today."

Red picked another glass out of the water. "That so?"

"What kind of guy was she with last night?"

Red just shook his head.

"Look, I'm just asking for a very small favor, I want to know who she met last night. Who was with her. Who made a play."

"Mr. Kennick, there's no use getting excited. I don't know who the guy was. He'd never been in here before. I kind of thought he was buying a drink because he was mad at his wife, somehow." As Witt started to speak, Red held up a hand. "No, I'm not giving you a line and I'm not covering up. Not nothing. I guess I shouldn't even be sticking my neck out telling you this much."

Witt said doggedly, "But she did meet somebody here last night? Met him and took off with him?"

Red hesitated and then said, "Yeah."

Witt downed the rest of the pickup and pushed the shot glass over, indicating that Red should refill it. "Do your ethics forbid you to give a description of this character?"

"Now, there's no use getting sarcastic. If I told you ... medium height, forty or so, quiet, frayed cuffs on the shirt ... would it mean anything? You going to find the guy on what I can tell you? You going to pick him out of the whole—" Red waved an arm to include the whole town, the whole county as far as Pasadena or San Pedro.

"No. I see your point there."

"That's all I got to say, Mr. Kennick."

"Witt to you."

"That's all I got to say, Witt."

Witt hunched over the bar. "They went on, didn't they? Where?"

"I don't know."

"Goddammit, look, I'm after a son of a bitch that kidnaped my wife. Can't you get that through your frigging thick skull?"

Red paused with the towel in his hands, looking highly offended. "You haven't any cause to use that kind of language in here."

"What in hell are you?" Witt demanded thickly. "A man or a fairy? You've heard ... My God, you're a damned bartender—"

Red said with dignity, "Sometimes I have to listen the other way, if you get what I mean. I'm a family man, Mr. Kennick. I try to live like a respectable person. Don't call me dirty names. Just because I'm in the bar business—"

"Oh, hell, I'm sorry."

"If you'll pardon me saying it, you're one of the pleasantest people I know, when you're sober. A real gentleman, Mr. Kennick. Everyone, everybody here in the Shore, knows that. But when you're drunk you're not like yourself."

"When I'm drunk, I'd better stay home."

"Yes, that's it."

A couple wandered in, laughing together, the girl's lipstick smeared and her eyes glistening, her escort smug. They walked to a back booth and Red went back to get their order. Witt shrank down further inside his coat. He began to shiver inwardly, a quivering that seemed to run up and down the inner surface of his skin like an electric shock. He felt as if he were being shucked loose from himself, that outwardly remained the shell, the chilled skin, and that inside was himself, separated and small, alone. He thought dizzily of the apartment and cursed the usurping cops.

Red came back and glanced his way and then seemed to take in his misery. "Why don't you go home, Witt? Your wife's going to come home. Don't worry about her."

"She went out in that damned red dress and those shoes," Witt whispered stiffly, his eyes watering.

"Yes, I know the get-up," Red agreed. "She don't look like herself in it, that's for sure. But you can't find her running around in the fog. You'll get yourself killed. Run over. Why don't you go home and wait for her?"

Witt shook his head. "Where did she go from here? Where was he taking her?"

Red shook his head. "I don't know, Witt."

Witt got off the stool. "Guess I'll try to find out."

Curtain.

Blessed and merciful, soothing, comforting, mother-warm, womblike, consoling, shutter-quiet, tender, beckoning, *blackout.*

He came out of it sitting at another bar, a brighter bar and more crowded than Red's, where a jukebox was playing and a girl customer was standing in a cleared space singing and wiggling her hips to the music. Witt had a drink in front of him, a shot of whiskey and a beer chaser, a boiler-maker, a drink he never drank, and he was talking to the man beside him. The man was about sixty, bareheaded, wearing a dark overcoat. He had a lot of broken veins in his nose, and the nose seemed puffy and enlarged compared to the rest of his face; and right at that moment, as if a film had begun to run through a projector and a sound track to start, Witt heard what he himself was saying.

"... And you know what my father gave me for my seventh birthday? Believe it or not?" He waited and the man with the puffed red nose stared into the mirror back of the bar. "A horse. A *horse*. Not a pony, not a Shetland with a cart, none of that crap. This was a cow horse, a working range horse, big, dun colored, looked almost like a mule. Hell, maybe it was a half or a quarter mule, as far as I know."

"Mules don't have offspring," said the man without expression.

"Oh, I don't know," Witt argued. "I'll bet sometime during the course of history, during the generations of millions upon millions of mules, there's been one that had offspring. Who can say? Can you tell me, can you positively guarantee, that never, never, never, has a mule had a baby?" He leaned close, argumentatively, clenching his teeth, willing the man to be obstinate and defy him and say no, no mule had ever produced a foal of its own. But the man went on staring into the mirror, nothing on his face but a kind of indifference both for Witt and for the dancing, skirt-shaking, shrieking girl in the other side of the room.

Witt began cumbersomely, "My old man gave me the horse and he put me to work with it."

"That shouldn't have killed you."

Witt could scarcely believe his ears. "Well, no, not exactly. But I was just seven. Would you put your seven-year-old kid to work punching cows and riding fence, would you work him early mornings and after school and all summer like a regular hand?"

"Some kids would eat that up," the man said.

"Well, I didn't. I wanted to go to school and when I got home I wanted to read or draw, or just sit and think. But then, think of this. I *had* a sister—"

His sister's image seemed to burst upon him and he was mute in study of it, the small wiry body with its tuned-down kind of gracefulness, its economy of movement, its dry small step and the face closed and unfearing; and then more, the spirit you sensed within, the spirit that had no need to search, to stumble, that had no time for trial-and-error, for grossness of judgment, the spirit formed like an arrow for its mark.

"I *have* a sister," Witt corrected, "and when I wouldn't stay with my father and be the man he wanted to make of me, he turned to her. He put my sister on a horse and for all I know she's still on one. And do you know what she wanted to be, what she was made to be? A nun."

For some reason the man nodded as if this had been expected.

"She wanted to be a nun and my father made a cowpoke out of her and she remained with him and did what he wanted out of obedience."

A scene swept through Witt's memory. There was a big mirror by the front entry at home, something his mother had put there, a round glass framed in dark wood above a small table, and Witt's sister stopped there every morning before she went out to tie on a scarf and put on a broad-brimmed hat, and once Witt had been watching, idly, and the slim girl in old jeans and faded shirt had lifted the black veiling, leaning close to the mirror, and for a moment she had tucked it tight around her face, hiding everything but eyes and nose and mouth, and a harsh starved look had come into her eyes. Witt had shuddered.

"I'm afraid that if I ever go home to see my old man I'll kill the son of a bitch," he said to the almost silent man beside him.

"Don't do it. It's not worth it," the other answered, as if Witt had been serious and had really intended what he said.

Witt drank some of the whiskey and chased it with the beer, and at once felt sick.

"I came out to find my wife but I'm going to have to go back home," he said.

The jukebox quit on a wailing shriek and the girl quit dancing and looked flushed and foolish.

"Well, that's the way it goes. Thanks for the drinks," said the puffed-nose man, and that was the first that Witt had known that he'd been treating anybody.

CHAPTER 13

For a while after the man had left them, Marion Kennick and the child stood motionless. The dim light, the silence, the strange sea smell and the subterranean cold gave a sense of isolation that seemed gradually to settle and increase, like the incoming of the tide. Finally for lack of anything else to do Marion went to the rusted door and leaned a shoulder on it. It was immovable.

The little girl watched as if Marion were something in a nightmare.

Marion thought, our wrists are bound tight but our fingers are free. He forgot that. She went to the child and knelt down at her side, glancing at the hands taped behind her back, holding her face sidewise so the edge of tape was presented, mumbling an indistinguishable command for the child to pull at it. But the little girl seemed more afraid than ever. Perhaps Marion's appearance scared her; no doubt she had never seen anyone so bound and gagged before. Perhaps she thought that if she took off Marion's tape the man would come back and punish her; or it might be that she didn't know what Marion wanted and the incomprehensible act gave further fright. At any rate, she shrank away.

Marion stumbled to her feet again, awkward because of her bound arms, and this time she tried to reach the child's wrists with her own fingers. And again the little girl fled, this time faster.

She's afraid of me, Marion thought. To her I'm a part of the bad dream, the wickedness come true, the mischief that turned into a monster. For a moment Marion felt a surge of irritation. If the little girl hadn't gone to the hedge, hadn't talked to this ... whatever he was, madman first of course ... if she had called a teacher instead— But all of this was fruitless. I've got to get this tape off. When he comes back to kill us, I want at least to get in a few scratches before dying.

She returned to the door, the one break in the concrete walls except for the high slitlike window she couldn't reach. Where the door had been set in, there was a lintel perhaps six inches deep with the outer corners pitted and unfinished, sharp. She laid her cheek against the rough edge, trying to work it under the end of the tape, and after a while she felt the tape yield, dragging away from the skin, leaving the skin afire, gathering and wrinkling into a mass as she pushed it along. She felt something else, too, slippery and warm, and drew back and saw the blood glistening along the rim of concrete.

She tore her lips on the stony rim and had to stop for a few moments, blinking back tears of pain. Then she went at it again. And every moment that she stood there, rubbing and scraping at the tape, she was taut for some sound on the other side of the door, some indication that the madman had returned.

Finally the tape was a stained, gummy mass clinging to the lintel, and she turned to face the little girl. "Come here." she said. "I won't hurt you. I'm Mrs. Kennick."

The child looked more frightened than ever.

"My face hurts. I guess I scraped it," Marion said conversationally, knowing how the bleeding skin must scare the little girl. "But it will be all right. Did you ever scrape your knee? The main thing is that we must try to do something to help ourselves and we can't with our hands bound."

Her voice sounded silly and inconsequential, the bleatings of an idiot in the face of calamity, but perhaps for the best, Marion thought. Perhaps only an idiot could keep calm in a situation like this. It might even reassure the child, who still stood motionless; she made Marion think of a rabbit under a hunter's gun, frozen with fear.

"When I knelt down beside you a minute or so ago, I wanted you to use your fingers to try to pull off the tape on my mouth. I guess you didn't understand. Anyway, it's off now. And now, could you try to free my hands?" Marion took a couple of steps, waiting for a reaction.

The child backed from her.

"Well, I can free your hands first, if you'd like."

She could see that it took a distinct effort of will, an act of bravery, for the little redhead to stay put; but she did it. She let Marion circle around her. Marion's crossed hands were palms out, almost numb; she had to twist her wrists cruelly to get any leverage, and then it seemed to take forever before she could find the cut end of tape on the child's arms and pry a bit of it up with her nails. In spite of the cold, sweat came out on her body and then the strain of effort, the tension, the knowledge that it might all be useless, *he* might be on the very steps outside, made her head start to ache. But the tape was coming ... *It was coming....*

Something hit the wall of the dungeon with a roar; the earth seemed to shake; and then against the gray light of the slitlike window a silvery shadow darted.

The child screamed, a soundless and muffled convulsion that twisted her from Marion's grip, sent her spinning about. She threw herself at Marion and tried to burrow into her body, crying through the tape.

High tide ...

"It was just a wave." Marion bent over the shaking child, trying to shelter and comfort her even though her arms were fixed behind her. "It was just a very high wave. Don't be scared."

Wasn't it strange, though, that they would start to build a hotel, a huge place such as this was obviously meant to be, a rival to lavish resorts all over the world, on the rim, the very reach, of such destruction? To be battered by the waves? Somebody must be crazy....

The child cried and clung to her as much as bodily contact can be clinging, and Marion's frantic thoughts went on.

Tag ends of confused long-ago reading fled through her memory, all about parts of the coast being eroded, some beaches built up and some almost completely washed away because of new breakwaters and weirs and other things, something that the Army or Coast Guard was supposed to be much concerned about. Well, she thought—while the child burrowed at her and cried behind the tape—how much more likely that the construction here had been abandoned because of an erosion of the beach than because the thing the man had said, some difficulty with title ...

Did it make any difference?

She said, "Look, honey, it was just a wave. It didn't wash us away or anything."

Any minute now *he* would return through that door, *he* would see them here with the child's wrist wrappings half picked off and her own mouth free of tape.

"I'm going to say a prayer," she said suddenly. She dropped to her knees. The redhead looked down at her as if puzzled, the brown eyes very stark above the band of white tape.

She prayed, then. She couldn't have said later what it was, some gabble of terror, some cry to the things beyond human understanding. At its end she rested her head against the wall, and then the little girl came close and said, "You can finish picking the tape."

In the end, they were both free. They huddled close to the inner wall, facing each other; Marion felt stunned with exhaustion. But now they had hands and voices again; they could communicate, and so she roused herself to say, "Your name is Marion, too?"

"Yes, ma'am. Marion Charles."

In the depths of her tired mind, Marion nodded to herself over the memory that Witt had called her. And for a moment her thoughts filled with his image, achingly distinct and yet remote, and then the strange hope came that he would find them and rescue them. But she plunged at once back into cold reality. There was no way that he could find them here.

"This man who took us in his car—had you seen him before?"

The child looked up at her frankly. "No."

"Hadn't your parents told you to look out for him?"

"No."

"Why did you go and talk to him?"

"Doggoned if I know," the redhead said regretfully, the tone adult and touched with wry disgust. "I just did, that's all."

There was a puzzle here that Marion couldn't comprehend. "You just had to know what he was doing."

"I guess so."

At least the little girl seemed to have lost her temporary fear of Marion, though she glanced frequently at Marion's bruised, scraped face. Suddenly Marion remembered something. "Wait a minute. He didn't say Marion *Charles*. That wasn't the name."

"No, he said was I Marion Trent? and it kind of seemed fun to tease. You see, there isn't any Marion Trent."

"There isn't a Marion Trent," Marion echoed, trying to get it straight.

"There's a Marilyn Trent, though."

"In your room?"

"Sure."

"Why didn't you tell him that?"

"He was acting so stupid," the child said scornfully.

"He was really after another child all the time," Marion said, comprehending at last. "He doesn't really want you at all."

"He doesn't want you either," the redhead said practically. Her big eyes seemed to darken in the gloom. "Maybe he'll kill us when he finds out."

A wave hit the outer wall, and though Marion knew that the bastion, built as it was, couldn't actually shake under them, still it seemed to. The silver spray flew by the high window in the darkening light, and then there was a new sound, a sort of deep gurgle.

The child touched her hand. "What was that?"

"I don't know."

Marion had been looking around during the last few moments, thinking—it was going to be dark soon. In this dungeon it would be completely black. The advantage gained by picking themselves free would be lost by the lack of sight. We have to do something, she thought. But what? She forced herself to her feet and went to the door again. It was like part of the wall itself, like stone. She went to the far end of the place and stared up at the window. Even if she could jump and reach it, it was far too narrow for even the child to squeeze through.

A wave came again, not as much of a hammer blow as the others; perhaps the tide had reached its crest; but again there was the strange, deep watery gurgle. Now it seemed directly underfoot. Marion took a few steps and came to the pile of sand. It was under that.

She stooped and plunged a hand into the heap. It was mildly damp, no more; there was no weight of fresh moisture in it. Kneeling, she scooped off the top of the pile and then listened again. There was nothing, now. The little girl came and knelt beside her, pressing her flank to Marion's. Her voice was small and scared. "What are you doing?"

"There's something down here."

"The noise?"

"Whatever makes the noise."

She felt the little girl shiver. "Maybe we'd better leave it alone."

"No, I want to see." Marion went on scooping the sand and throwing it off over the cement floor. The light from the narrow slit went past, over her head; the rest of the dungeon was brighter than where they were. The sand looked almost black.

The little girl put her hands around Marion's arm, hampering her, but Marion didn't push her off. She knew how frightened the child must be in the face of all this strangeness. "See?" she told the child, trying to sound matter-of-fact. "The floor ends here. That's where the heap of sand came in. It came from outside, the hole in the floor. Look, it must be—" She scraped and dug feverishly, while the little girl crawled awkwardly, trying to touch her all the time. "It must be about four feet square. An open place in the cement floor four feet square. Now, isn't that something?"

"Yes, ma'am."

"Where do you suppose it goes?"

"I don't know."

"Won't you help dig?"

After a moment the child let go of Marion's arm and began to toss sand, too, but working in a scared, half-willing way.

Another big wave hit the long outer wall, and the ground seemed to shudder, and Marion caught the child's arm and they crouched, listening.

From far below came the gurgle, muffled, but now added to it was a bowel-like sucking noise that made Marion draw back. It was as if something dangerous waited down there, a muck of quicksand, a trap.

"Suppose the water rushes in?" the child breathed.

"I'll tell you what I think it is," Marion reassured her. "When they built this place—when they started to build what was going to be a big hotel, they must have provided for sewage and drainage, and things like that. Somewhere down there is a big outlet, perhaps an end of pipe. Maybe we could get out through it."

The little redhead looked down into the shallow pit they had scooped, and swallowed hard. "Maybe it'll be too tight. Maybe we'll get stuck," she whispered.

"We're going to try, anyway." Because the child looked so small and scared, Marion caught her in her arms for a moment, hugged her close. She felt the sob that was quickly choked back. The redhead had a lot of spunk for a little one. "And now we'll dig like mad, and soon see what it is."

They tossed damp sand furiously for some minutes, until both were winded. Marion's finger tips were beginning to grow raw. She stopped, caught one of the little girl's hands, examined it. "It's time for you to stop. I'll do the digging."

"We need something like a shovel," the child said.

"Yes. Too bad he didn't leave us one."

"Maybe we could use our shoes."

Marion nodded. She took off one of her pumps; it wasn't a needle heel like her evening slippers; one of them would have worked fine for a pick; but by applying it with a chopping motion she loosened quite a bit of sand in the bottom of the hole. Lifting it then by hand didn't tear the fingers like digging did. "Should have thought of this before."

The little girl squatted at the rim of the hole and looked down at her. "Maybe if we put it all back ... maybe if when he came we'd ask nicely, please let us go—"

In the dark down there, Marion made a bitter face where the child couldn't see her. She chopped sand and threw it away, and tried to measure the depth of the hole. Getting down toward something, anyway; the sand was getting wetter.

She chopped again, and there was a hollow metallic echo.

"I've found something. No, don't jump down here with me. There isn't room."

"Don't leave me alone!" came the cry.

"I won't. Or if I do, for a minute, I'll be right back."

The pipe was huge. For a few moments Marion thought that it must make a floor for the entire opening, and her heart sank for there would be no way through the iron. Then she found the lip, and scratched the sand away and put her eyes down. She had never seen anything that black. She stuck in an arm. There was a space of about a foot at the top which the sand hadn't filled. Below that the sand was packed solid.

"I have to dig some more."

The child on the cement above had begun to cry, soundlessly so as not to annoy the teacher, hiding her face in her arms. Obviously it terrified her to think of her only friend and protector getting down into that strange dark space.

A wave came, and now the gurgle and the sucking sounds were so loud that they seemed to boom up out of the dark, almost alive, animal-like, and the little girl gave a cry and scrambled back from the edge.

Marion bent with her face at the end of the pipe, hoping for some breath from the outdoors, some inrush of air or hint of spray. But there was only the drawn-out lapping and bubbling, as if the tide dwindled out through some complicated maze.

There was not room enough to chop at the packed sand in the pipe; she had to pry it out by handfuls, one at a time. It was wetter, firmer; her fingers were soon bleeding. She thought, despairing, suppose at the end there is a blockage, something we can't get past. Suppose finally after all we simply have to come out and wait for *him* to come and kill us.

The long room was growing darker. The hole was very cold and whatever it was that sucked and bubbled had taken on the features of a monster. The thought of death didn't have the terror that it had had before, and Marion thought, I'm too tired to care what happens now.

CHAPTER 14

Betty switched on the lights and hurried across the room, almost stumbling, her eyes full of tears, her heart thumping. For a moment she'd seen a sweater of Marion's thrown across a chair arm, and there had been the wild hope, soon gone—Marion hadn't worn that sweater today.

The detective stopped just inside the door and before going further, he looked the room over.

"Just take a chair, any chair, Mr.... uh ... I'll find that album in a jiffy. It's right here, somewhere." There were built-in shelves beside the windows in the alcove, alongside Marion's cot. She stooped there; the album of snapshots must be down here, mixed in with the magazines. Some of the magazines slid off under the touch of her trembling hands. When had she seen the album last? Where had she put it? Oh, my God ...

There was a tap at the door, behind the detective's back; he turned around and looked, and then Tommy came in. Tommy looked cool and calm. He nodded to the officer and then glanced at Betty. "Having trouble?"

"They want a picture. I've got one somewhere."

"Hasn't Marion come home yet?"

Her head snapped up. He was dim through the tears, through the nearsightedness, but she caught the careful poise, the lack of urgency. "How can she come home? One of the teachers kidnaped her!"

"What?"

"Off the school grounds!"

"Oh, look, Betty, it isn't possible."

"I'll say it's possible." She was almost yelling at him. He wouldn't like it, either. "The woman damned well took Marion off in a man's car and no one's seen hide nor hair of her since. Nor the teacher. Nor the car." Betty took up some of the magazines and threw them out into the middle of the floor. Then she crouched and pounded on the floor with her fists.

"Betty ... Betty—"

"You shut up!"

He sat down and coolly began lighting a cigarette. The cop sat down too, but with an air of wariness, as if he might have to move again suddenly. Betty straightened up and wiped her eyes with the backs of her hands. Oh, God, if I could only *see!*

"It's got to be here somewhere."

She found the album under the foot of the cot, where Marion must have put it. She got to her feet, snagging one of her nylons. She took the album over to the detective and spread it open on his knees. "Here she is. This was taken last summer. You can see, it's a good plain picture … she has on an outfit a lot like—" She broke away and staggered to the couch. "I can't talk anymore, I can't." She bent over, knowing the eyes of the two men were on her, Tommy's wry and contained, the cop's indifferent, his emotions all worn away years ago through a million scenes just like this one; she wadded her skirt against her face and wept into it.

The cop looked over at Tommy. "You a … uh … friend of the family?"

"Mrs. Charles and I are going to be married."

"Oh, I see. You know the little girl pretty well, then."

"Ummmm … well, pretty well."

Through the tearing grief, Betty was aware of such rage that it seemed to shake inside her skull like the thud of a machine. You dirty, dirty liar, she said into the wadded skirt; you never had time for Marion. No time for a word, a thought; no, not even a minute. You don't know her any more than you know the man in the moon….

"Is she the sort of kid who might go off with strangers? Out of curiosity, maybe? Or easy to take in?"

"Oh, I wouldn't say so," said Tommy, as if he knew all about it.

"You think she'd spot a phony?"

"Oh, sure." Tommy tapped the ash off his cigarette into a tray. "You mean this is on the level? One of the schoolteachers really did snatch her?"

"We're not just sure yet what part the teacher played in it," the detective said cautiously. "She went along, yes. Maybe not willingly."

"What kind of a teacher was she?" Tommy demanded.

"A substitute."

"I never heard anything like that before," Tommy marveled.

Betty's teeth ground together until her jaws ached. She couldn't endure to look at the two men, the indifferent cop with his mild uncaring curiosity and Tommy, full of bull.

She heard the rustle of paper as the cop took out the pictures of Marion. She said soundlessly, I want them back when you're through. They're all I have of her. She's gone. I haven't got a little girl anymore. She was a bother, an encumbrance; I couldn't take her with me to the bars so she had to stay home alone while I drank with Tommy. She had to be shut out of even my plans for tomorrow.

No tomorrow for my little girl …

No bother to anybody now.

She heard the cop get to his feet. "Mrs. Charles ..."

"Yes," she mumbled into her skirt.

"We'll call you the moment we have any news of her."

"Thank you. Thank you so much."

"Try to get some rest, and try not to worry." The cop actually seemed to mean it, but Betty wouldn't lift her face, wouldn't let him see her tears.

With a couple of passing remarks to Tommy, he went on out and shut the door, and then she heard his steps going down.

"Betty."

Her face felt hot, scalded against the skirt, and her eyes—always tender from strain anyway—stung with pain. "Please just leave me alone now," she said.

"Betty, look, he's right, there's nothing to do now but wait, and to try to wait as calmly as possible, with as little wear and tear on yourself as you can. Like lying down. Why don't you go in and stretch out on the bed in the dark and I'll run out for some whiskey and come back and fix you a hot toddy? You've got to unwind. It'll relax you."

"Please just go," she said stubbornly.

She heard him get to his feet; he must be standing there looking at her. "It's not a good time for you to be by yourself. You mustn't try to go it alone. You've got to remember, you've got me now."

The rage had all died away in the last few moments. She felt sick and lost, and the thought of Marion was like a knife, a hot cautery gnawing inside, twisting, twisting....

"Betty, aren't you listening?"

"Go away."

"I'm trying my damnedest to be patient. I can't help but feel, all this business is some kind of tempest in a teapot, a fuss over nothing. Marion's a smart kid, she'll look after herself. I'll bet she's on her way home now. Maybe the woman was drunk, maybe it was some crazy impulse, but Marion will straighten her out."

He waited, as if she might agree with him. He came closer.

"When Marion comes home again, things will be just the same," he said, as if pointing out something significant she might have overlooked. "Of course you'll want to cuddle and pet her for a while. Get her some new clothes. Spend a little time home with her. I know that. But the point is, Betty, don't go overboard. Don't act as if the kid must be ... uh ... lost, or something."

She heard the scratch of a match; he was lighting another cigarette.

"Keep your head and wait for what the cops turn up. Simple. Easy. And don't treat *me* like this."

"Get out, Tommy."

"What?"

"Just get out."

"My God, Betty, you must know how I feel—how this makes me feel—you all cut up and hysterical. You can't mean—"

"Yes. Yes. Just go."

He didn't start walking, just stood there, and the room grew very quiet. Betty was tired. She was sick. She didn't want to tell Tommy these ugly things, but he was going to make her. Some little dream still lay in the back of her mind, the last tag ends of what she had hoped, the new life in Denver and the money and the lovely home and the parties, and Tommy's people.

She thought, I guess I never really believed in it anyway. It was just something I imagined.

It was a way to keep from facing what I have to do, to go to work and make a living for Marion and me, not try to scrimp by on my little survivor's allowance.

Tommy said, "Let's not just forget everything we had planned. Let's not throw it away. This is just a temporary upset. A mistake. Of course, I'm worried about Marion." He paused as if wondering whether he had sounded worried enough. "I'll be honest with you, though, I'm not a bit scared of how it will turn out."

As he talked on, Betty found herself experiencing a revelation. A light seemed to dawn inside, and all of her motives and intentions seemed suddenly laid bare. She drew in a harsh, sobbing breath.

It was like having her eyes jerked out and stuck in backwards, so that they looked inside. It was like being peeled.

She saw now that she had never really intended to abandon Marion at all. Underneath, down in some buried layer of her brain, she had planned to go along with Tommy for a short time, to let Marion board here in California for perhaps six months, then to switch her to a school in Denver, then to have her at home more and more frequently, then to move her in finally right under Tommy's nose.

He'd have blown his top, of course; she could imagine what he'd say.

At the same time, mixed with the shame over her duplicity was a kind of soft relief; she hadn't actually meant to leave her little girl. She wasn't such a frightful mother. She began to cry again into the skirt.

"Well, there's nothing for me but to go now, Betty."

I'm a cheat. I meant to lie to Tommy, to fool him. And I'm so damned glad....

"Goodbye, Betty." He was over beside the door now.

He waited a moment or two longer, and then went out.

After Tommy had been gone for a while and she had quit crying, Betty rose and went into the bathroom and threw cold water on her face from the faucet, and patted the coolness into her tired, aching eyes. She dried herself with a towel and leaned over to peer in the mirror with her habitual air of worry. I look awful, she thought, shocked. Red and shiny and bleared. No, the blear was because she couldn't see well.

She thought wistfully, a lot of women start to wear glasses along about my age. It's nothing unusual.

Some of those glasses, the slanty-eyed kind with cute rims, aren't bad at all.

She started to smile into the mirror, the way she had of cheering herself, and then her face crumpled.

Marion, come home.

Bruce Trent had begged Carol to take Marilyn and go to a hotel, but Carol wouldn't go. She put Marilyn to bed at nine. Then she moved soft-footed through the house, looking at everything as if for booby traps. The exhaustion, the trembling, any trace of weakness, seemed to have gone away. She made Bruce think of some catlike animal sniffing the wind. At bay, Bruce thought; this is what it means. The last line, where danger shall not pass. Finally she went into the kitchen and started a fresh pot of coffee.

Bruce wanted to ask what she was thinking and then decided the question would be silly. She was thinking, as he was, when would Fecamo call again and what would he want? And what could they offer him? What could they promise, what cleverness might suffice, to save the life of that other child, the one he thought was Marilyn?

Where was Fecamo now?

Bruce sat on the couch, hunched over, listening to Carol moving around in the kitchen. She had the lights on; she seemed to have lost the desire to cower in the dark. Had Fecamo gone back to the hiding place, wherever that was, to do some ugly thing?

Bruce shut his thoughts on this. It was unendurable.

When the phone rang, it was with a sense of release that he got up and hurried to the bedroom. He lifted the receiver. Carol was already on the wire from the kitchen.

She was saying, "Yes, Mr. Fecamo, we're both here. Waiting."

"Your husband, too?"

At the sound of Fecamo's hated voice Bruce felt such rage that a red dazzle seemed to close in, shutting out sight; he had trouble getting himself oriented again. "I'm here, Fecamo," he managed.

"Not quite yourself?" said Fecamo smugly.

"Hoping you've come to *your*self," Bruce answered.

The brief silence was offended. "But you're still reasonable, now, still admitting your guilt and your part in the ruin of my marriage?"

Carol answered; Bruce couldn't get it out. "Yes, Mr. Fecamo. We agreed to all of that."

"Let him say it," Fecamo snapped.

"I admit ... everything," Bruce said.

"You committed adultery with Susan?"

"Yes."

"How many times?"

Bruce thought for a moment he couldn't go on with this, couldn't force himself to the lie. "A ... a good many times."

"So many that you can't exactly recall the number?"

"Yes."

"The first time ... did she want to, was she perfectly willing, or did you have to force her?"

What did Fecamo want, what did he expect?

It came to Bruce then, Fecamo wanted a victim, he wanted someone to blame *now*, he wasn't interested in blaming even partially the dead woman. "I forced her," Bruce said woodenly. "She didn't want to. I made her."

"In other words, you raped her."

The words were like an increasingly bad taste, almost vomitous. "Yes."

"Where did it happen?"

"In the ..." Bruce found his mind a blank, rebellious, sickened. "... the car."

"In the car," Fecamo repeated, as if rolling the words over his tongue. "I see. Was she dressed? Or did you force her to take off her clothes?"

"I don't remember."

"You'd better," Fecamo told him. "You'd better put your mind to it, Mr. Trent. It's pretty important. It's a kind of test, you know. Your memory isn't as bad as all that. You know what you did."

Bruce forced himself to say it. "I took off her clothes."

"Now, where were you parked? This couldn't have been by daylight, in the open—you must have taken her somewhere first, and then, still inside the car, done these things to her. Where had you taken her, Mr. Trent?"

This is more than I can take, Bruce thought. There's something so loathsome here no one could be expected to go on. He held the receiver over the cradle; he was going to hang up. Then something Fecamo had said returned to him. *She's red-headed, kind of cute.... She gave me some sass there at first.... I guess she sasses you sometimes, too, and you might miss it when she's gone....*

Someone was going to miss the redhead, in the very same way he would have missed Marilyn, unless he handled this frightful madman in just the right way.

He put the receiver back against his ear. "Fecamo?"

"Waiting, Mr. Trent," said Fecamo, smugly gleeful.

"We drove to a large park, out of town, a closed picnic area. No one else was around."

"What did she think you were going to do? Wasn't she suspicious?"

"No. Well, perhaps a little." Bruce forced his mind to the fiction, trying to recreate the imaginary scene. "I teased her and called her chicken. She was a spunky kind of girl. She came along."

"I see. And this was the first time?"

"Yes."

"And what about afterward?"

"I guess she got to like me a little, in spite of my rough treatment. I never had any trouble after that first time."

A long breath came over the wire, a sigh, as if Fecamo had at last forced into the open what he had known to himself.

"When can I see ... Marion?" Bruce asked.

There was a hesitation as if Fecamo hated to tear himself from a reverie of satisfaction. Then he said sharply, "You'll see her soon, Trent. I'm going to take you to her."

"I'm ready any time."

"No, not right away. After midnight, perhaps, I want a chance to think again."

Bruce almost said, You horrible freak, you want a chance to digest and enjoy this little victory; but he controlled his feelings enough to say, "I hope she isn't too far from home."

"Oh, she's quite a way from home. But ... you'll see, Trent, you'll see."

The line went dead.

CHAPTER 15

Betty sat up with a jerk, on the bed in the darkened bedroom. Her eyes stung with pain and her throat was hot and scratchy and for an instant all she knew was that she felt terrible, almost like a hangover. She saw dazedly that a light burned in the other room. She'd been lying here with her clothes on. She brushed back her hair and stared around at the ill-defined room. Something had wakened her. What?

The phone?

The moment she thought of the phone it all came back—Marion, the detective, the fright, the nightmare. Crawling to the edge of the bed, she whimpered.

She hurried into the front room and stood there looking at the phone, waiting for it to ring again; but nothing happened.

It hadn't been the phone. They hadn't found Marion. They weren't trying to reach her. She ran over to the clock on the mantel and stuck her face close and saw the time, almost eleven thirty; and a terrible bolt of fear shot through her, knowing that Marion had been gone all this time, over eight hours now, and no word of her.

Then the doorbell rang and Betty knew that this was what had wakened her. She rushed to the entry and threw open the door, expecting the detective to be out there on the landing, and instead there was another man, someone she didn't know. She was too dazed to be afraid, to think that this might be the man who had Marion, or anything to do with him. She said, "Who're you?"

"May I come in?"

He had a nice voice and his tone was gentle.

She moved back, admitting him. He brought in the smell of the outdoors, the night, a faint aroma of tobacco and damp wool, and something else. Liquor. He'd been drinking. A faint, half hope that he might be bringing some word from the police died in Betty; they wouldn't send someone like this.

He turned in the middle of the room, taking it all in, her along with the furniture, and now that he was out in the center of the lighted space she got a better impression of him. Even through her stinging, nearsighted eyes she could see how good-looking he was. He was terrific! And again she revised her ideas; he must be someone important after all. Some high-up.

"You're Mrs. Charles?"

"Yes."

"You have a daughter named Marion?"

"Yes."

He nodded as if this checked against some information he already had. "May I sit down?"

"Go ahead."

She watched him take a chair, sat down facing him, more puzzled now. He wore good clothes, a nice dark suit and a light coat over it. Maybe he was a doctor. Or a lawyer. Maybe he'd heard about Marion somehow and had come to offer his services. Did doctors … did lawyers … ever do that? Betty didn't know. She began to feel uneasy.

"My name is Witt Kennick."

"How do you do?"

He waited as if patiently, smiling a little at her—she saw that it was a miserable kind of smile, forced, as if he must feel inside just about the way she did. "Doesn't the name mean anything to you?"

"Should it mean something?"

"My wife is Marion Kennick. She's a teacher. She disappeared today along with your little girl."

It hit Betty with a shock. To her, ever since this afternoon in Mr. Dobbs's office, the teacher had remained a faceless villainess. She hadn't even considered that the woman might be married—might be anything as *normal* as married.

Come to think of it, Mr. Dobbs hadn't told her very much.

Maybe the police hadn't let him.

Betty gripped the arms of her chair. "What did you come here for?"

He looked down at his hat, turning it in his hands. "I need some information."

"Do you think I don't need information?" Betty started to get shrill. "Your wife kidnaps my child and keeps her all these hours, God knows where—"

"No, Mrs. Charles. That's not possible. You mustn't think it."

The tears began to spill from Betty's eyes, she felt as if she were crying fire. "That's what happened. The detectives said so."

"They didn't say so to me," he answered quietly.

They were sparing his feelings, Betty thought; he's a fool not to know it. "I don't care. It's true. True." She choked up and couldn't say any more.

"You'd have to know my wife," he went on, still very quiet of tone, "to know how impossible it would be for her to hurt a child in any way, or even to be a part of any crime concerning a child. We don't have any children of our own … for one reason or another …" He brushed over it as if, underneath, there was something he couldn't endure to examine just now. "… and I guess Marion transfers some of her … unspent … mother love on her pupils."

"She … she took Marion away … in an old car.…"

'She *went* away with your child and a man," he corrected. "Either she was forced to go, as your little girl was, or else she went voluntarily with an idea of protecting her. You've got to believe this, Mrs. Charles. We can't stop here and argue over it because if we're going to get at the truth we have to agree on this, and then go on."

Betty felt a curious reluctance to give up the image of the unknown, vicious woman who had taken Marion. And then she saw that what she had hated to face was the thought of Marion in the hands of a bad man. A bad man would be worse for a little girl than any number of bad women.

"I know my wife, and what I say about her is the truth," he insisted.

"M—maybe I ought to be glad she went along," Betty stammered.

"Perhaps you should."

Betty squinted, trying to see him clearly through her tears. "Have you been married long?"

"Several years."

"Was she a teacher when she married you?"

"She was finishing college in Los Angeles."

"What do you do, Mr. Kennick?"

She thought his mouth twisted a little, something not quite a smile. "I'm a waiter."

"Oh, I see."

"Temporarily unemployed."

"Well, like me ..." She smiled back at him, though her mouth shook.

"Now, about this man who took them away," he said, suddenly businesslike. "The police said you told them you had no idea who he could be."

"I don't."

"But you see—I called this principal, Mr. Dobbs, just before I came here, and he said the man had called your little girl by name. He said something in passing, kind of brushed over it—the man had been there yesterday too and one of the other teachers had heard and seen him."

Betty thought about Miss Moynton's visit of the day before; there was nothing to it yet but a blank mystery. "I can't understand it."

"He *knows* your little girl. You must know *him*."

"I don't though."

He waited, watching her, and Betty tried to think hard and came up with exactly nothing.

"Really, there just isn't anybody at all like that."

"Do you have a man friend?"

"Sure. But it wasn't Tommy. He isn't a bit like that, and besides he was with me about the time ... well, no, later...." She shook her head. "It just wasn't Tommy."

"He likes your little girl?"

"Look," Betty told him. "You asked me to believe your wife wasn't to blame in this and I'm telling you Tommy isn't either."

"All right. Now ... how about ex-boy friends?"

She shook her head. "Mr. Kennick, you're way off base. You're flying blind."

"I sure am."

He sat turning the hat, his head bent; Betty thought he seemed terribly tired, perhaps almost at the end of his rope. "Could I fix you a drink?"

"Thanks, but I had some earlier, a little too much I guess, and now I'm kind of sobered up and I want to stay that way."

She sensed what he didn't put into words: he wanted to be sober so that he could find his wife.

"I went off on a wild hair of my own," he said, "and then when I simmered down I went back and talked to the cops, listened to them this time, and I saw that this couldn't have anything to do with Marion, really. Not the way it had happened. It was all tied up with your little girl. And he *has* to be somebody you know."

"If he thought Marion was the one he wanted, he just damned well made a mistake," Betty said, trying not to cry again.

"A mistake? But then ... the name. Is there someone else in the class with her name?"

"No, I'm sure not. Marion would have mentioned it."

"What about appearance? Could he have mistaken her for ..." He sat frowning, his face tight, and then shook his head. "No, that won't account for his using the name. Mr. Dobbs said that one of the other pupils noticed your daughter heading for the shrubs where he must have hidden. He must have called her, called her by name."

"He made a mistake," Betty insisted. "That's what happened."

"Marion. My wife's name, too, of course. She heard it too."

The room grew quiet.

"Maybe it was your wife he wanted, after all."

"He tried to entice a child the day before, remember, when my wife wasn't on the playground."

"That's so. Still, it's got to be a mistake. He got the wrong one. The more I think about it the surer I am." Betty turned her face, trying to squeeze back the tears.

"Let's figure that way, then. He wanted someone else. Perhaps the child of some wealthy family. I noticed some big homes south of the school."

"Yes, there are some nice places. Doctors and business executives, and like that, I guess. I don't know how these apartments got into the district. They've been here a long time, they're pretty old, so maybe they were built here before the zoning got strict, or something."

"But if someone down there, who? Who?" Again there was a long, silent space of thinking. Finally Betty offered, "There's a *Marilyn* in her room."

"Marilyn ..." He seemed to be letting the name echo in his mind.

"Maybe she could be the one."

"A chance in a million. Marilyn who?"

"Trent. Let's see, Marion said something once— She said that Marilyn's mother came for her and they walked home down Lime Avenue." Betty nodded at him. "I'm sure. Lime Avenue. And it wouldn't be too far."

"What does the child look like?"

"I don't know."

"I wonder if—by some impossible miracle—"

"Why don't you go see them? I'll ... I'll go with you. It's better than sitting here, getting the jitters. I'll find the address in the phone book. Shouldn't be too many Trents living on Lime." She got up and went to the phone, knelt on the floor, dragged the heavy book from the lower part of the stand, spread it on the floor. A couple of tears fell on the open pages. "Here it is. Bruce Trent. Thirty-four twelve Lime Avenue."

He had risen. "I'd hate to take you out and then have it all fall through. Let me go and see them alone." He moved over to the door. "They must be in bed by now, and if there's just me it can be short and sweet, no hard feelings."

"I won't cry! I won't say a word. I'll wait on the sidewalk."

"You might miss a call from the police, being gone. They might need you in a hurry."

She hadn't thought of this. On the way to the closet for her coat, she paused, undecided; the urge to get out, to help with something, no matter how remote its hope, was almost more than she could stand.

"I'll call you," he promised, "however it turns out."

She swallowed a bitter taste. "Well ... All right, then."

He opened the door. "If this is any comfort, Mrs. Charles—as long as my wife is with your little girl she'll do everything in her power to keep her safe. Even at the cost of her own life, if that's necessary."

Betty didn't know how to answer; there was still the doubt, the fixed idea of that afternoon that Marion had been kidnaped by a teacher. But then, he seemed so sure. She nodded at him.

When he had gone she sat down close to the telephone. Somehow she expected it to ring any minute. Perhaps the police had found Marion by now, perhaps they'd want her to phone before coming home to relieve the anxiety. Or maybe Tommy had found out something, though she couldn't think how.

She waited, and time passed, and a dull cold wretchedness settled in her, as tough as stone.

Witt Kennick was surprised to see, as he approached the house, that lights burned in it. Several rooms seemed to be lit up. The neighborhood, otherwise, was dark.

He went up the walk to the front door and found the button on the wall, rang the bell. He could hear the bell ringing, away off in the house somewhere, and then he caught quick footsteps, and then there was silence. It seemed a funny kind of silence to Witt; it seemed arrested, watchful. I'm imagining things, he told himself; they were getting ready for bed and I interrupted that. Somebody's scrambling around inside for robe and slippers.

He waited. The foggy dark was cold, the street was still. The liquor had almost entirely died out by now and he felt horrible.

The door opened without warning, no approaching steps, nothing.

A man looked out at Witt. He was completely dressed. Behind him in the room Witt glimpsed a woman, a blonde in a blouse and skirt. She stood in the middle of the floor facing him and something in her attitude had instant impact. Hatred, Witt thought, trying to grasp it. She hates me.

The man just went on looking at Witt, no expression on his face, saying nothing, and something here was out of focus, too. Distorted. They acted as if he had come to ... *what?*

Witt spoke, half-apologetic, puzzled. "Mr. Trent? My name is Kennick, Witt Kennick. I wonder if I might talk to you for a couple of minutes? I'm sorry about the hour...."

The minute Witt spoke something changed in the room. It was something like a magician's trick, Witt thought. The man still stood at the door, looking out, the woman was still behind him; only now somehow they were different people. It was as if someone had changed the picture in a frame, while he watched, using the same background, the same figures. "Mr. Kennick? I don't know you."

"I live in the Shore. My wife teaches at the school here. I mean, she was a substitute, she was there temporarily."

"This concerns the school?"

"Yes, in a way."

Trent still had some kind of guard up, there was a certain caution, but he said civilly enough, "Come in, then. This is my wife, Mr. Kennick." The woman nodded stiffly at Witt. The hatred was washed out.

"I'm pleased to meet you."

Platitudes. How could he begin what he had to say?

"Will you sit down?" she asked, motioning to a chair.

It was a nice room, an entirely different place from Betty Charles's flat. "This may only take a minute," Witt said. "Do you by any chance have a little girl named Marilyn?"

A sharp hesitation, and then Trent said, "Why, yes, we do."

"Is she in the same room with another child named Marion Charles?" Witt had turned a little; he happened to be looking at the woman when he asked this, and he saw something like a shadow pass over her; she seemed to gray, to lose color, to recede, and then to recover as if with an act of will, and suddenly Witt saw all the signs of strain, of the grip she had on herself, and he *knew*.

He knew without another word among the three of them that he had stumbled, by some impossible miracle, on the truth.

He turned to Trent. Trent wouldn't meet his eyes.

There was more here than fear. There was knowledge. Witt fought down the sudden illogical conviction that they knew everything that had happened. "My wife was kidnaped today, along with Marion Charles. A man forced them to leave the playground just before school was out. There's been no word, no trace of them since."

"Your wife?" The whisper was as sharp as a scratch of paper in the silence, a thin sound filled with fright.

"Didn't you know that?" Witt looked at them with rage, with disgust. "Didn't you know that he took a teacher, along with the little girl?"

CHAPTER 16

The dungeon had gradually grown dark and was completely black now, and terribly cold.

To Marion, shivering and exhausted, it seemed that she had been digging in the pipe forever.

At first she had merely scratched the sand loose and tossed it out the end of the pipe, but soon the heap there became a problem, threatening to shut her in. She saw that she must use the last of the dim light to make a systematic removal.

She had an inspiration. She took off her slip and tore it open along a seam, making a large irregular square of silk. She scraped the pile of sand into it and then using the material as a sling, threw the sand as far as she could off across the cement floor. Then with the end of the pipe cleared, she spread the silk there and pushed out what she scraped into it, and then threw it away, over and over, while the long room slowly turned dark.

The child came down into the pit and crouched at the lip of the pipe, and reached in occasionally to touch Marion's stockinged feet. The first time she did this Marion was seized with fright; she thought, in her dazed exhaustion, that the man had returned and was grabbing for her. In another instant she realized that the child was afraid, was trying to reassure herself that the teacher was within reach and that she wasn't alone.

Then every once in a while the child would whisper, "What are you doing?" And Marion always said briefly, "Digging." In the hollow pipe their whispers had an eerie echo.

Marion had one piece of luck. In the packed sand she found a chunk of clam shell, perfect for scooping, and thus saving her hands.

The tide had long since gone. There were no more gurgles.

"Can I come in there with you?" the little girl whispered.

Marion rested her hand against the face of the hard-packed sand, put her forehead against it, and considered. Was there room for two in here? Could she let the child take over briefly, dared she rest a little, and so last longer? After a moment of tired thought she rejected the idea. There was no way of knowing what lay ahead, even what might wait within the next foot of unexplored space. For all she knew, the pipe, though it seemed sturdy enough, might be in danger of collapse. "You'd better not," she said. "You can rake sand out of the end of the pipe, though, and pile it on the cloth, and let me know when the cloth won't hold any more. That will help."

"All right," came the disappointed whisper.

Marion tried to estimate how much she had cleared; she thought that she must be under the wall by now, perhaps even a little past it.

She started digging again, trying to ignore the cold, the damp, and her own quaking tiredness. Almost at once something happened which was ominous.

The pipe began to descend.

She encountered a rough collar of metal, some kind of joint, projecting into the pipe perhaps an inch. Beyond this seal, or hoop, the surface sloped away. She chipped hurriedly now, afraid to believe, hoping to find some other similar joint where the pipe would rise again. Sand was packed solid now, there was no free space at the top.

She cleared a couple of feet through the middle, felt ahead in the dark. It went down.

She crawled back to the level section and crouched there, trying to reassure herself. This unreasoning fright was silly. She had much more to fear from the madman who might even now be returning. There was nothing in the pipe, no threat, no danger, that could even approach the evil he represented.

But the fear, the shivering, wouldn't go away. "Did you stop?" came the whisper.

"Just … just for a minute."

"I could help dig."

"No. Stay outside."

"Aren't you almost at the end?"

In her exhaustion, light-headed, Marion almost laughed. "How would I know?"

"I'm scared to stay out here alone."

"Don't come in."

She forced herself to go back, to cross the collar of metal where two sections were sealed, to dig further, to pile the sand behind her and then to push it on within reach of the child, all in the dark, sightless, and with the feeling that she was now excavating a pit into which she was about to fall headlong.

"I can't panic now."

"What did you say?"

"Nothing. I was just talking to myself."

But I can't panic, she repeated to herself. The pipe doesn't slope *much*. It's just that if it keeps on going down … She foresaw how it would end in that case, a sand-filled hole ending at nothing; and this vision might be the bitter truth. The place had been abandoned. The pipe might have been run out of the foundations so far, supposed to connect up with some drain or other from the hotel built on the bluff above, and then left.

Well, I won't give up yet, she thought. I'll see where the thing ends.

It seemed then that she worked steadily for a long time, though progress became slower and slower. She became more or less accustomed to working on the slope, to the feeling that she was headed for the middle of the earth.

She grew careless about pushing the sand on out to the opening. The pipe began to fill up behind her, heaps of sand leaving little room at the top, and she was too tired to worry about it. She had a dogged determination to get to the end of this, whatever the end was, and either crawl free or fail. But at least to have done. To rest.

The thought of just getting out upon the cement floor and lying there to sleep was almost irresistible.

She paused in the work of digging. She was crouched, eyes shut, the piece of clam shell hanging like a hundred-pound weight from her numb hand, when she became aware of something going on behind her. A sound, movement. She listened, trying to place it, and for a moment she thought that the child had crawled into the pipe and was trying to whistle, was making some kind of hissing sound between her teeth, and yet it wasn't like that, it was more of a rustle and it went on longer than the space of a breath. In fact, it didn't stop at all. It went on and on, sibilant in the dark.

She tried to gather her flagging senses.

Surely I've heard something like it before, she told herself. It's a sliding kind of sound. Something is sliding in or over or through.... That's what makes the whispering noise, the rustle. Something is sliding into the pipe.

Behind me.

Between me and the open end.

She turned to the dark behind her, no less dense than the dark in front, and stretched herself across a heap of sand and spread her fingers. Instantly something touched them, a dry soft contact, and she jerked back her hand.

She sat still again, her heart thudding, and listened, and the dry whisper went on and on.

The pipe was filling up.

There was a crack, a hole, there at the seam. The dry sand from the beach above was trickling through.

She brushed at her face, and the sand on her palms stuck to the sweaty skin. She was sweating, here in this icy hole.

She was sweating because she was going to die.

No.

From somewhere, from some deeps of being, from resources beyond herself, came the strength to fight. She found herself clawing away the heap behind her, sliding across it and then she was in an enveloping curtain, a blizzard, all invisible in the dark. She was breathing sand, it was in her eyes, her nose, her mouth, it was sifting through her hair and her clothes.

Her hands fought for a way through and now there was a perversity as if the stuff had come alive. It yielded and yet there was always more of it.

She was screaming. The noise was shocking in the narrow black space.

She fell forward, stretched out, her hands buried, the almost noiseless whisper of death going on and on. She couldn't breathe. She was choking, dying.

And yet the screaming went on. It didn't stop. It was a mirage in her mind. A long echo out of the time when she could still draw air into her lungs. Music to die to.

Echo, have an end, she thought. How many times can you bounce back and forth in this little pipe? A hundred? Five hundred? I won't be here to listen.

But the screams took on words. Not her words. The screams said, "Come out! Come out! *Come out!*"

Now that's funny, she thought drowsily, that I can be outside and yelling in at myself.

I'm splitting up. Two parts. Schizophrenia.

Something touched her face, not the way the falling sand touched it. A scream said, "Come out!" right in her ears, shrill, terrified, goose-pimpled, lost, and Marion lifted her head and tried to see. Nothing but the dark, of course. The touch came again, then a tug at her hair.

"Ouch," Marion said. "Wait, I'm coming."

The little girl dug like a squirrel, hands flying, and Marion inched over the barrier and then on out to where the air was.

She got out upon the floor of the dungeon and lay flat, face down, while the child patted her and bent close occasionally, so close that Marion felt the warm breath on her cheek, and said, "Are you all right? Can you talk?"

When she could, Marion answered, "I'm fine."

"What was down there? What scared you?"

The fear of nameless horrors haunted the child's voice, so Marion forced herself to rouse, to explain. "There was a seam in the pipe and when I went on digging, when I got further along, my weight or my moving around must have opened it and let the dry sand in. The pipe was filling up and I was scared I couldn't get out."

"Oh, is that all?"

"That's all."

The desire to just lie there on the cold floor and go to sleep, her face cradled on her arm, her exhausted body relaxed, was so strong that it was almost irresistible. It was like a drug. Like Nirvana. Heaven. But there wasn't time. As soon as she could move she had to be up and doing, planning, making some sort of fight for her life and the little girl's.

The pipe was a lost cause. The knowledge brought weak, stinging tears into her eyes.

By now it was filling with the tons of dry sand above tidemark, in unlimited voracity.

Where did it go? Down, she answered, her mind hammering the words into bitter clarity; just down to nowhere.

Their only hope was here, inside the dungeon. Somehow.

In the warmth, the brightness of the Trent living room, Bruce had been talking for several minutes to the dark, quiet, intensely angry man sitting across from him.

"This is the part you've got to understand. Our only link to Fecamo is through the telephone—when he chooses to use it. There is no way we can trace or discover him. He could come to the door and we wouldn't know him. In fact, we both thought in those first few moments that you were Fecamo. It wasn't until you spoke that we knew you weren't. Handicapped as we are, with no way to lay hands on him, we can only wait. And we thought that if we were to do this other child any good—we didn't know anything about your wife—we had to keep our mouths shut."

"It didn't occur to you that keeping still served another purpose?" Witt asked, leaning forward a little on the chair, dividing the bitter glance between Bruce and Carol.

"I'd be a liar if I said no," Bruce agreed wearily. "So I won't say it."

"I can't help thinking that what you're really trying to do is to wash your hands of Fecamo's mistake. To get out from under. To refuse any responsibility. You've explained, almost a little too carefully, it began a long time ago, in another city, where a reporter got your child's name wrong and printed it in the paper where it was copied that way by other papers. You seem to want the blame to lie there, on that unknown reporter. But it won't stay put, Mr. Trent. Fecamo wanted your kid."

"I've tried to give you the picture, the whole picture," Bruce said, his own anger singing along his nerves.

"What you should have done in those first minutes of talk was to tell this crazy man the truth."

"We thought of that," Carol said, her voice almost breaking, "but then, he might have turned on the little girl. What would she have been to him then? A nuisance, trash, something to be got rid of."

"If I happened to be in the power of a maniac," Witt said harshly, "I'd a damned sight rather seem a nuisance than the thing he's been itching to get his hands on for a couple of years."

"Perhaps we have made a mistake, then," Bruce admitted. "At least it has worked out to this point—he says he's going to take me to see the little girl."

"And my wife?"

"He's said nothing about a woman."

"Maybe he let Marion go," Witt said slowly. "Maybe she's out in the dark now, trying to get home. Trying to hitchhike." He sat a moment hunched in the coat, his gaze on the floor, as if deep in thought. "I don't believe it, though. I think he's got her. My wife's a beautiful girl. Maybe he has plans for her, too."

The room seemed to stifle in the moment of silence.

Carol said, "It's too horrible to endure. It's too hideous. I keep thinking it can't even be true."

"Shut your eyes, Mrs. Trent. Maybe the nightmare will go away. Or maybe I'll go away and take it with me, out of the door and out of your lives and you can stay here safe, with your child safe in her room, while I hunt for my wife and that other child and the madman who has them."

"I don't mean that," Carol said, "and you're cruel to pretend that I do. Do you think that I'm so insensible that I can congratulate myself on my child's safety, while this other child takes her place with Fecamo?" She got up and walked back and forth across the rug for a couple of minutes, almost staggering, and Witt felt a stir of compassion. "You're blind, too, Mr. Kennick, if you can't see that we shouldn't be quarreling, trying to fix blame, accusing each other. We have to work with what we have. Right now we have one thing in our favor. Fecamo wants to take Bruce to see the child. Why couldn't you go with him?"

Witt glanced sharply at Bruce Trent.

Bruce said, "I thought of it. No doubt Fecamo will demand that I come alone. It will mean some careful work to slip you in."

"My wife's car must still be parked in the school lot," Witt said. "I know where she keeps an extra key under the floor mat. I could follow you and Fecamo in her car."

"Before we do any of this we're going to call that detective, that Mr. Renwick," Carol said, standing straight in the center of the floor.

Witt lifted his head, staring incredulously. "Call the cops? They'll botch it! Suppose we find Fecamo, locate Marion and the little girl, and then the cops swoop in with sirens—what do you think will happen then?"

"They'd have more sense than that!"

"How do you know they would? And since you've played it solo this long, keeping it all to yourself," Witt said angrily, "what's the point of dragging the cops in now?"

Two spots of stubborn color burned in her cheeks. "You talked about responsibility, that we'd tried to shove it all on some reporter. And I'm talking about responsibility now—the duty we have to share it with the police. If we fail, they can continue. We've shared a job with them. It's what we have to do."

"But the plan you just talked about, Fecamo taking your husband to see the child— What suddenly happened to all that?"

"It will still work," she insisted. "They'll let Bruce go on with it. They'll have to."

"You're thinking about the danger to your husband," Witt said. "You want the cops there to protect him. But if that's worrying you, look, here's a new idea. A fresh switch on all of it. Since you don't know Fecamo by sight maybe he doesn't know either of you, and maybe I could—"

She jerked up a hand sharply.

The telephone was ringing.

CHAPTER 17

Only the loudness of Fecamo's voice on the wire betrayed any excitement; his words were evenly spaced and had a biting explicitness. "Mr. Trent? You're there? Waiting, ready, eager?"

"I'm here," Bruce said, his tone shallow with the effort to control his anger. He shared the kitchen receiver with Witt, who had crowded so close that Bruce became aware of the whiskey odor and started to move away impatiently, then realized how anxious the other man must be, and realized too his own insensitivity in not thinking of it.

"Now let's hear from Mrs. Trent, too," Fecamo said.

"Speaking on the extension," Carol said evenly.

"Well. Everything's just as it was? You haven't done anything foolish like calling in the cops?"

"No, nothing like that," Bruce said.

"I've been doing a little thinking," Fecamo said, "and I can't help wondering how you satisfied the people at school."

Under the brisk remark was something cunning, some kind of trap; Bruce stiffened, held the phone away a little, looked at Witt. Witt mouthed two words, "My wife."

Bruce said into the phone, "They said that Mari ... Marion had been taken away by one of the teachers." He had stumbled in saying the name, wondered if Fecamo might have caught it. "No excitement, especially. They just asked if there had been some arrangement between the teacher and us, looking after Marion, and we said yes, there had been. I guess you looked like a teacher to them, Fecamo."

Bruce's hand shook; he was in a cold sweat as he finished outlining this weak lie. Could Fecamo possibly be taken in by it?

"Just when was this?" Fecamo asked with the same careful distinctness.

"I don't remember exactly," Bruce hedged.

"Before my first call?"

Bruce started to say yes and then saw Witt shaking his head.

"No. Afterward. That's how we knew enough to stall them off, to reassure them."

"I have some information for you, Trent. There is a teacher involved. A very pretty teacher. You'll see her later."

"You took a teacher when you took Marion?" Bruce tried to sound surprised, though his throat felt like cotton, his head was thick with the effort to outwit this madman.

"It couldn't be avoided," Fecamo said. "She proved to be quite manageable, though. No trouble. I'm warning you now: She doesn't enter into this business with your kid."

"What do you mean by that?"

Witt's eyes were no more than four inches from Bruce; he saw the tightening between the brows, the shadow of rage.

"I haven't decided yet what I'll do with her. She can identify me of course." The line was silent as Fecamo must have spent a moment in thought, or perhaps in a sly effort to add to Bruce's fear.

Bruce was thinking, after I meet Fecamo tonight, *I'll* be able to identify him, too; does this mean that he intends to murder us all?

"Well—" Fecamo suddenly became sharp. "You're waiting to find out how and when you'll see your little girl. I'm going to explain this just once and then hang up. You'll have a time limit. A very strict time limit, Mr. Trent. You'd better be on your toes."

"Go ahead," Bruce said tightly.

"Before I tell you where to find me, I'm giving a warning. In the time schedule I've allowed for a few things. Very few. You can put on a hat and coat, if you do it fast. You can spend perhaps ten seconds warming up the car before you put it in gear. Then you can drive without exceeding the speed limit, but just barely."

The two men's eyes met over the close-clenched phone and Bruce thought, with a shock: If we had Fecamo here, the two of us, we'd tear him to pieces with our hands. The knowledge of what they were capable of, two supposedly civilized beings, almost made him shiver.

"You won't have time to turn out the lights, Mrs. Trent won't have time to powder her nose providing she's in a mood for it. You'll have to run to the car. Now in case you think this is pretty finicky, in case you think I'm talking through my hat, let me tell you I've timed it all. From your house to here. Ticking off everything by a watch."

"You want me to bring my wife."

"Yes. That's important. If she weren't along I'm sure she'd be getting into mischief."

"I won't bring her, Fecamo."

"You won't see the kid again, then."

"Why bring her into it? Suppose she would promise—"

"No promises. I'm not as gullible as I used to be." Fecamo was actually laughing. "When I hang up I'm going to wait exactly ten minutes. If you aren't here when the second hand sweeps around that last circle on my watch, your kid is as good as dead."

"Where do we meet you?" Bruce asked, feeling an insane desire to tear the phone off the wall.

"Do you understand the purpose of my time limit?"

"I don't know that I do."

"It doesn't give you even fifteen seconds to spend on calling the cops."

"I wouldn't risk—"

"Perhaps not. But you've thought of it."

Bruce knew that Fecamo was baiting him; he kept still.

Fecamo said, "If you call police headquarters you'll get hold of a dumb desk sergeant. You'll have to give him your name and address and state your business and he'll have to fill out a form. Then he won't get the name or the street right and you'll have to correct him. Then when he's gone through this official mumbo jumbo he might consider putting you through to a detective. He'll have to check first and find out who's in and who's stepped out for a beer, and so forth. He'll do this checking very slowly, very deliberately, because detectives have such tender feelings. They can't be hurried. So by now you're yelling over the phone and he snaps back and puts you in your place. And you try to quiet down."

Witt drew in a harsh, sucking breath through his clenched teeth.

"At about the time that the phone begins to ring on a detective's desk I'll be putting my watch back into my pocket and starting my car. And as the detective reaches for the phone, very slowly, very careful not to hurry, I'll be gone."

"You've made your point, Fecamo."

Fecamo said, "Mrs. Trent?"

"Yes," Carol said.

"Do you get the picture?"

"Quite clearly."

"I'm at the corner of Thirty-seventh and Atlantic Avenue, on the southwest corner, in the parking lot behind the drugstore."

He hung up.

Carol came running from the bedroom, two coats dragging from her hands, headed for the back door, her face a mask of shock and fright. Bruce caught her and spun her around. "Hold it. Fecamo doesn't know about Marilyn being here. But we can't forget it. You can't leave her alone. You'll have to stay."

Carol peered at him as if through a quaking light. "He's going to kill them!" She tried to tear free.

"You're going to stay here and call Renwick. We'll stall Fecamo as long as we can, argue with him, delay him—" Bruce shoved her bodily into a chair, yanked the coats away, threw hers across the table. "Come on,

Kennick. He'll expect to see two figures in the car and by the time he knows the difference—" Bruce was hurrying to the back door, shrugging into the coat, feeling for keys in its pocket.

Witt paused for a moment. He touched Carol Trent on the shoulder. Her eyes lifted to meet his. "Call the cops. You were right. It's time now. And be glad your child is home safe. That's a perfectly natural way to feel."

He went on out. The car was sitting in the driveway and Bruce was already in it, had the motor running. Witt jumped into the front seat beside him. "Can you dim the lights on the dash?"

Bruce turned a knob and the interior of the car grew dark; they couldn't see each other's faces. Bruce put the car into reverse and swung around in the seat; the car began to back.

"He's playing a trick on you," Witt said suddenly. "It's not anywhere near ten minutes to Atlantic. What are you here—Thirty-fourth? Then Thirty-seventh isn't more than four or five blocks, counting these little streets like Beech and Tolliver ... Atlantic can't be more than ten or twelve, west of here. It won't take ten minutes—it's going to take about five—"

The car rolled through the fog, the curbs and houses indistinct on either side, and Witt sensed that Bruce Trent threw him a sharp glance, not exactly pleased.

"Whatever he has planned, it's not simply to meet you at the parking lot," Witt added. "So let's keep our heads and look sharp."

Yes, he thought, let's keep our heads. Too bad my own isn't clear. Even with the fear for Marion there's underneath a fine dark craving for a drink, sharp enough to taste. And suddenly he *could* taste the flavor of whiskey. He could taste that last drink he'd had at the bar when his drinking buddy, the perfect stranger, had got up to go and had thanked him for the drinks and had walked away.

He shook himself, blinked; the lights swam in the fog and Bruce Trent drove with a grim air of patience.

He's got a fine noble air of doing somebody a favor, Witt told himself sourly. Going out to rescue somebody else's kid, somebody else's wife. Hell, it's us doing him the favor when you think of it; my wife taken instead of his, the kid a substitute— Then Witt forced the sourness and the cynicism away. Bruce Trent wasn't like that. He was a man worn down fine by a long, long time of suspended dread and his wife Carol had come running, all ready to go out and meet the madman who hated them.

They passed under a street lamp and Witt slipped back his sleeve to look at his watch. Elapsed time about two minutes.

At Atlantic, a big boulevard, they had to wait for a traffic signal.

Bruce said, "We've got plenty of time. I'm not going up the street where he can see us. I'm going to cross Atlantic and take the alley."

"Good idea."

We're playing with lives, though, Witt thought. Suppose we make a mistake, make him sore?

What we do next here, Witt told himself, could mean whether Marion lives or dies, whether I ever see her again. And then the thought of trying to live without Marion had a strange, stark reality as though he had just thought of it for the first time, and he remembered all the times when he had talked to her of separating, of living apart, and he saw that those times had not had any meaning. They'd been words and nothing more. This minute now, this dark-shrouded moment in the car, this stranger named Trent beside him, a fantastic story of persecution by a madman—this was real and Marion's death could be real, as real as the walls of the alley slipping past them, and the life they had lived which seemed to be teetering always on the verge of separation: that was a dream.

He gripped his hands, the nails cutting into his palms; the inside of his mouth felt hot, dry, and stretched, and his eyes burned. He was trying to see through the fog to the parking lot ahead.

"Marion," he whispered to himself, and the taste of her name had a cleanness, a roundness, sweetness, and he felt a strange trembling in his throat.

They were at the parking lot and there was a car waiting.

Bruce stopped, still in the alley, and they waited.

The car parked with its nose to the back of the drugstore, under an overhanging light, dimmed in fog, was a red Cadillac, a convertible, almost new. The fog had condensed all over it and it glowed like a ruby. But if Fecamo was in it he was crouched down out of sight, because the car looked empty.

"Don't go out where the light hits us," Witt said. "I'll get out and go over and see."

Bruce made some kind of objection, something about Fecamo taking fright at a stranger, but Witt was already out, crossing the blacktop to the standing car. As he approached, he saw that the rear door of the pharmacy was open, he could hear the music of a radio and some other kind of racket, as if somebody in there were moving crates around.

He looked into the red Cadillac. The only thing in there was a pair of men's gloves, old ones, gray leather with the shape of hands worn into them, lying on the front seat.

He went back to the other car, almost invisible past the wall of the adjoining building.

"It's empty." He started to open the door, to get in again, and then didn't. "As long as I'm out here I'm going to walk around a little. Maybe he'll be here at the end of ten minutes. Maybe the extra time was a safety point. I want to be off somewhere watching, where he can't see me."

"Don't you foul this up," Bruce warned.

"Who's got reason not to?" Witt said, coldly, almost indifferently. He put his arm on the door, shoved it to latch it, then turned and walked off around to Thirty-seventh. Ahead of him was the intersection of Atlantic, brightly lit but with not much traffic. It was getting late. Most of the show crowds, the uptown theater crowds, had gone. Across the street at a café, a man in a white apron was taking in a sidewalk sign. Behind him, in the café, most of the lights were out and a single waitress was doing something desultorily behind the counter.

Witt drew in a deep breath of the chill, foggy air.

Fecamo was playing with them.

It could go on for a long time. The longer it went on the more desperate the game could become.

Suppose it went on and on. For days. For a week. Suppose it went on so long that all reason told you they were dead, you knew their bodies were decomposing somewhere, and yet you couldn't quit playing because there still might be some slim miraculous chance....

You still went on trying to meet Fecamo on lonely corners. You still listened for his voice on the phone.

Witt stumbled. His heart seemed squeezed flat by a terribly dry fear.

I'd get drunk, he thought. Yes, I would.

He forced the despair away—forced himself to quit thinking about the future. He turned to trying to imagine where Fecamo might have taken them. He's got them salted away somewhere, Witt told himself. As he walked up the block to the corner, he made himself pick at the puzzle, where Fecamo could have hidden Marion and the little girl—some place where there was no chance of escape, where Fecamo could be sure of them no matter how long he left them.

A place so lonely they could die.

He stood by the traffic signal, listening to the gears in the steel column, a growl like the growl of guts; he felt stunned with fright, with tiredness, with hangover, with rage.

The fog seemed drearier. When cars swept past they had a closed-in look, as if occupants had huddled down into their coats, not looking out.

I should have gone and looked for Marion's car on the school parking lot, Witt thought. If Fecamo doesn't show, that's what I'll do. I'll go back to Trent's place but I'll have a car to use.

He turned around and walked back the way he had come. There were big homes to the west of Atlantic here, almost mansions, set in large plots of lawn and shrubbery. He could see the outline of the dark roofs against the foggy sky; and, like the passing cars, there seemed something shut in and safe about them. He had never thought about the shut-inness or safety before, not before Marion was lost; it seemed that his perception had a whole new dimension.

He thought suddenly of his father.

I could offer the bastard a ransom for Marion. Plenty. Dad would do it. Of course there would be some conditions attached.... He began to run in the direction of Trent's car.

Bruce had pulled back further along the alley where it was quite dark. When Bruce saw Witt coming he started to get out of the car, and then recognized Witt and waited. Obviously he had expected Fecamo.

"No sign of him. It's been more than fifteen minutes."

"He's having fun."

"I'm worried, just what kind of fun," Bruce said. "I keep thinking about Carol. Suppose he was outside our place, had no intention of being here; suppose he knows now he has the wrong child and this was a way to get the right one...." Bruce's tone betrayed how afraid he was for the two left unguarded at home. He added, "He just isn't going to be here. I know it."

"Go home and check and come back," Witt said. "I'll wait and see if anything happens."

"I can't even give you a description."

"Yeah, I know."

Bruce Trent got into the car and backed away into the dark pocket of an open space, turned and drove off.

Witt went to stand near the red Cadillac.

When he had been there about two minutes a car turned into the lot from Thirty-seventh. It was an old clunk, battered and shabby and filmed now with moisture from the fog. The front window by the driver's seat was rolled down and a face looked out at Witt as the clunk came to a slow stop.

Bruce Trent hadn't left any description but Witt wasn't put off for a moment.

This was Fecamo.

CHAPTER 18

Witt thought that they were the meanest eyes he had ever seen.

The eyebrows sheltered them like a black thatch and they gleamed, snake-cruel, from the impassive face. There was more to the face than just the eyes, of course; there was the shovel-shaped chin, dark with beard, the pursed venomous mouth, and under the hat brim narrow ears, dead white. Witt thought that the hat was silly-looking, somehow. He was a silly-looking guy altogether until you remembered who he was. Then he was terrifying.

The car slowed with a small groan of the brakes, and a squeak. The face smiled. "Mr. Trent? It's good that you had the patience to wait. I take it that your wife has given up and has gone to notify the police. And that's all right. That's fine. We'll be long gone by the time they get here. This has worked out just as I expected."

Witt realized that Fecamo had had Bruce Trent's car under some kind of distant observation. He had seen Witt get out and walk around, had seen the car leave.

The first shock of Fecamo's appearance had worn off and Witt was remembering that this crazy man had Marion somewhere, and his temper was rising.

"You're ready to come along?" Fecamo said, half opening the car door.

"Sure, I'm ready."

For a moment Fecamo stayed there, half in and half out of the car, staring oddly at Witt, and Witt realized that his voice had puzzled Fecamo. Probably it hadn't sounded much like Bruce Trent, on the phone. "What the hell's the matter?" Witt said roughly.

"Oh, nothing. Nothing." Fecamo got out slowly. He went on looking a little thoughtful, as if still considering the change of voice. He stood facing Witt on the blacktop; the fog seemed to drift in close around them. "Get in the car. I guess what surprised me was, you've been drinking. You never did strike me as a man who needed any extra … bucking up."

Was this really what he was thinking of, Witt wondered? He looked into the car. There was no door handle on the other side, just a threaded stub of metal. This is how he trapped them, Witt thought. He glanced at Fecamo, and Fecamo had his coat open and his fingers were touching the butt of a gun stuck in his belt.

"Get in, Mr. Trent."

The politeness was overdone. It was sly and ironic. "You think I'm drunk?" Witt asked, staring into Fecamo's eyes.

Fecamo shook his head. "It's not important."

"Where have you got them?"

"I'll explain as we go."

Witt got in. The car was old, worn, the upholstery battered. He turned and looked into the back seat. There was a blanket back there, nothing else that he could see.

Fecamo got in and shut the door. He put the car into gear and pulled off down the dark alley. "In case you have any idea of doing something foolish, I'd better explain about your little girl. She's quite helpless, she's in a place where there is no possibility of escape. If I don't supply her with food and water she'll die. If you succeed in injuring or killing me, my friend, you'll sign her death warrant."

"What about the teacher?"

Driving, peering through the fog, Fecamo answered, "As I said before, the teacher doesn't enter into our negotiations at all. She's something quite separate. Taking her was a mistake, of course. By that I mean it wasn't in the original plan."

"Why didn't you let her go, then?"

Fecamo pursed his lips, perhaps covering a smile. "For one thing she's a very pretty woman. I feel drawn to her. I want to know more about her." He turned out upon Atlantic and headed south toward the beach. "My wife ... Susan ... remember? She was attractive but she was nowhere near as good-looking as this young woman. And since Susan was taken away from me in such a ruthless manner, I feel deserving of a reward."

"This girl had nothing to do with your marriage breaking up," Witt said, trying to control his nervousness and his inner rage. "Why take it out on her?"

"I should take it out on you alone? Is that what you mean?"

Witt had to keep reminding himself that as far as Fecamo knew, he was Bruce Trent. He had to remember to speak and act as Bruce Trent would have, if he had been here. "Why not?"

"From the beginning ... from the first call I made this afternoon ... your attitude has puzzled me. For that reason I'm not going to treat you quite the way I had planned, the way I treated the others." The car turned suddenly into a side street. Here was an old section where oil derricks still filled the vacant lots, where only a dim riding light on a walking beam lit the dark here and there. Fecamo parked at the curb abruptly and got out. He held the gun on Witt. "Turn around and kneel down and put your hands behind you."

Witt slid off the seat and turned slowly to his knees, trying to watch Fecamo.

"No, no," Fecamo said, "put your face down on the seat. Turn your head the other way. Now I'm putting the gun here, about six inches from your head, while I work on your hands. If you try to jump me one of us will get killed. I'll have the advantage because I don't care much who—" His tone had taken on a grisly amiableness as if he were indifferently explaining some point to someone who might be slow to understand. "I'm going to leave your mouth free so you can talk. That's the difference." The next moment Witt found his hands jerked together and held tightly; he had expected a rope or cord and it took a moment for him to understand that Fecamo had used adhesive tape. "I want some answers. I want to know what the mystery is."

"What mystery?"

"You can get up now. The mystery is ... what kind of cold fish are you? It's plain that you aren't worried about your kid. Even here, even in the car, you were asking questions about the teacher."

"Oh. Was I?" Witt tried to sound offhand but he was thinking that he had failed to play his part. He got up awkwardly, inched into the seat, leaning back against his bound hands. The tape gave a little and he began to work on it. He had to keep his mind off Marion, to play the part of a man whose child is gone. "I'm kind of confused. The waiting, I guess."

"You don't even sound like yourself," Fecamo complained. He slid into the driver's seat, put the old car into gear. The street ahead was dark and empty. He drove south through the oil fields, then turned on Highway 101 toward San Diego. He drove in silence and seemed deep in thought, and Witt began to be afraid that Fecamo suspected the truth.

In spite of all of Fecamo's careful planning he hadn't touched Bruce Trent at all. He didn't have Trent's child, and now instead of Trent himself he had a stranger, someone who meant nothing to him.

Fecamo said suddenly, "Tell me some more about yourself and Susan. Tell me how she acted on dates. What you did. Where you went."

The information Witt had on this subject was sparse. Trent had said that Fecamo thought he had been responsible for his wife's death. The girl's name had been Susan and she and Trent had been on a business trip. Fecamo had insisted that there had been more to it.

Witt didn't know what to say, and Fecamo waited, not looking at him, and then Witt decided that it must be a test.

"When we went out we kept to ourselves," he improvised. "Little cafés where nobody knew us. Out-of-town shows."

"Didn't your wife suspect at all?"

"No—" Witt tried to think of Mrs. Trent's name; he had heard her husband call her by it; but the name wouldn't come. "No, she never did suspect us," he finished.

"Carol," Fecamo supplied, as if knowing all about Witt's dilemma.

Witt felt sweat come out on his face. "Carol never suspected."

"Does she look at all like Susan?"

What should he say now? "I—I can't say that I ever noticed any resemblance between them."

"None at all?"

"Why in the hell do you want to keep torturing yourself with this thing?" Witt burst out. "Why not let it go? Your wife is dead."

"You make that sound very casual, Trent."

"Nothing you can do, no revenge you can take, will bring her back," Witt said.

"Well, as a matter of fact," Fecamo said, almost musingly, looking out at the road and the foggy night, "I guess I really wouldn't want Susan back if she *were* alive. And that's good. That's for the best. I feel better about it. More relaxed. I guess that's why I made you tell me about the first time you had sexual intercourse with her. It took away some of my longing for her. It changed my memories of her, somehow."

Witt was astonished at this, and aware too of a bolt of fear. He saw that there was a great area of information, or misinformation, about which he knew nothing. Bruce Trent hadn't reported any such conversation. "Not that it changed my ideas about *you*," Fecamo went on. "I still see what you are. I want to pay *you* back."

Witt thought, I've got to get him off this subject because I don't know enough about it to sound convincing. He cast around, and then said, "What about your marriage to Susan? How long did you live together, and where did you get married, and so on?"

Fecamo threw him a sharp look. "She must have told you."

"No." He remembered a remark made by Bruce Trent at home, he'd never heard of a husband until after Susan's death in the accident. "Not a word."

"You've always said that, of course," Fecamo said slowly. "It could be true. Looks like, though, in some of those intimate moments you might have asked her about previous experiences and she'd have told you she had been married. I don't think Susan would have let you figure she was just loose."

"It never came up at all," Witt said brusquely. "Where *did* you marry her?"

Fecamo waited a moment. They came to a big intersection on the highway, to the right was the beach drowned now in fog, to the left on two corners facing each other were a couple of large filling stations. The neon made a huge glare in the fog. Fecamo waited for the light, then crossed. Witt's hands were going to sleep; he had twisted the tape and it was ropelike, cutting into the flesh. Fecamo said, "We were married in Fresno, California, in August of 1953."

"Almost ten years ago."

"We lived together for three months."

"That was short."

"Don't be flippant, Mr. Trent. You'll find flippancies all paid for with interest, in the end. Susan and I didn't get along, but it wasn't my fault. She was a cold, frigid girl. I tried to teach her. I was loving. I was patient. I made her quit her job and stay home. I bought her beautiful lounging clothes, silk robes and nighties and everything like that."

Witt thought, What in hell made the girl marry him in the first place?

Fecamo had an uncanny way of answering the unspoken. "Susan told me before she left that she had married me on the rebound. She'd been in love with some other man. You see, she'd been going to State College in Fresno and this man was a student, like her. I knew him, too. He was learning newspaper work, though they say you don't really learn it by going to college but by working for a paper."

"She went back to him?"

"Oh, no. He already had another girl. Susan left Fresno and I had a lot of trouble following her. When I caught up with her she was working in Detroit."

"She came back to you?"

"She got sick," Fecamo said bitterly, "and so she needed me. I paid her hospital bills and when she was better I rented an apartment and furnished it. I bought her a lot of new clothes. I tried again to teach her about being married."

Witt thought, the girl must have lived in hell; he felt a sudden sense of pity for her, regret for the mistake she had made in marrying Fecamo.

"I was a relentless lover," Fecamo said with a sly touch of pride. "If she would have co-operated we'd really have had something." He slowed; they were coming to Huntington Beach; even through the closed window on his right Witt could hear the breakers.

They passed through the town at a decorous rate.

"Now, Mr. Trent," Fecamo said, "getting back to our little mystery, why aren't you anxious about your child?"

"I am," Witt insisted. "I'm terribly worried."

"You haven't asked how she reacted when I took her off the playground."

"How did she react?"

"She's full of sass," Fecamo said, giving him another quick glance.

"Didn't she try to fight?"

"I showed them the gun right away," Fecamo explained. "I told them that I would kill them if they ran. I guess they believed me. That teacher looked like a smart girl. Smart as well as beautiful. I think she got the idea right away that I meant to do just what I said."

"Look," Witt said, facing him. "Why take the child at all? It's me you've hated—"

"Oh, I figured this out a long time ago. Say you'd known me years ago and wanted to get even with me in some way—though of course you didn't. I'm just saying this—well, doing what you did, taking Susan away and then causing her death, that's exactly what would have punished me the worst."

"And now, taking me to see my little girl—"

"I want you to understand the kind of place she's in," Fecamo said.

"You don't intend to let her go, do you?"

"I guess I don't," Fecamo answered, his teeth gleaming.

"And there's something about this place, this thing you've hidden her in—"

"Yes."

"So that afterward, when you let me live for a little while, I'll know that she'll be dying of neglect."

"Yes."

"And what about the teacher?"

Fecamo turned to stare and Witt saw that he was frowning. "That's what I mean, Mr. Trent. The mystery. Why aren't you begging for your little girl's life, why aren't you making promises and offering money, and things like that? You've just taken my word, the kid has to die, and now you're asking about the woman." He looked at the road, turned the wheel a trifle, faced Witt again. "It's almost as if it's the *teacher* you're really interested in."

"I am interested in the teacher," Witt said boldly.

Fecamo drove, and thought it over; he wore an expression as if he had come on some amazing surprise. Finally he said, "You mean that this girl, this pretty young teacher, is one of your ..." He chewed his lip. "Like Susan was?"

"Yes."

Fecamo shook his head. The old car rattled and bucked, and through the fog to the right Witt thought he caught a far-off sheen of surf. They must be close to the ocean here. "It doesn't seem possible," Fecamo objected.

"Well, you kept talking about the mystery and I thought I'd better explain," Witt said. "Don't you understand? When the school principal called, right away I knew it wasn't just my kid who was missing. It was someone more important than that, though I couldn't say so to Carol."

"I see. I see."

Witt wondered how the weak, spur-of-the-moment lie could have fooled Fecamo, but apparently it had.

After a while Fecamo said in the greasily amiable way he used, "You know, it's a good thing you told me this. I was just about ready not to take you there, after all."

Witt thought, I knew it. Some hunch told me.

"I was just about convinced you were some kind of ringer," Fecamo said. "I didn't hardly see how you could *be* Bruce Trent."

"But it all fits now, doesn't it?"

"Oh, sure," Fecamo agreed. "It fits right in with all that I knew about you and Susan. And it gives me some great ideas for tonight. Yes, great ideas." He began to laugh.

CHAPTER 19

The car turned from the highway into a rutted track; the tires swerved and bounced and the old chassis complained. The fog lay thick and feathery under the headlights, throwing a reflection back into their eyes. Witt sensed that they were approaching the sea. He suddenly glimpsed bare black trees on the flank of a rise, beyond these a sloping field. Fecamo pulled off upon the bare ground and set the brakes.

He reached across Witt and opened the glove compartment and took out a big flashlight. He tested the light, flicking it on and off, then left it on and switched off the car's lights.

Witt's arms were asleep, his whole body stiffened from the awkward position.

"We have a short way to walk," Fecamo said, getting out, keeping the big light centered on Witt.

Witt climbed out. The fog filled his lungs and settled on his face; it felt wet and sticky. The thought that Marion must be somewhere near, perhaps bound hand and foot, terribly frightened, in a dark place, filled Witt's mind. He had to think of something to do to save all of them. If there was any kind of cliff, any drop down near the beach—

Fecamo twitched the light off him, shone it down the sloping field, and Witt could see some sort of building. It looked like a ruin. There were archways, dimmed by the fog, opening it seemed upon nothing. "What's that?"

"People in Dana Point say it's going to be a big hotel—someday. It seems they ran into trouble, or ran out of money. This way, now."

Motioning with the light, Fecamo urged Witt to walk ahead. Witt glanced back. Fecamo carried the light in his left hand, and below, gleaming dully, was the gun in the other.

They came to the archways and Witt realized that something lay beyond, a kind of great bulwark built against the face of the bluff. There were openings in which the fog swam, black holes that led down. Sand was thick underfoot, a few spiky weeds grew in the crevices. It had been quite a while, Witt thought, since any work had been done here. A vast beginning, and then nothing. And Marion and the little girl were down in there somewhere.

He glanced back at Fecamo. "It's really isolated."

"Oh, now, Mr. Trent, we don't have to keep up the chitchat," Fecamo said. "I'd expected much better from you. I thought you'd run forward and yell, try to warn them to be ready, try to scream some kind of encouragement and instructions." He shot the light into the throat of one of the nearby openings and Witt saw the shape of stairs, almost buried in sand, and the thick darkness down below. "But then, perhaps you have some idea of doing something yourself, of keeping them out of it. Let me tell you, Mr. Trent, all the moves were marked out long ago. And being surprised isn't written into it for me. Go ahead and yell."

He wants a show, Witt thought.

"You know," Witt said, "you're not going to get a damned bit of fun out of me. I'm too pooped. I've been on the merry-go-round too long. All burned out. I love my wife and I'll do what I can—well, you know that— but the fireworks are fizzled out. I'm a wet spark."

"It's an odd time to be thinking of your wife."

Witt jerked himself together. "It was just a slip."

Fecamo flicked the light here and there over the yawning arches. "Still the mystery, Mr. Trent. Still something that warns me: You aren't what you ought to be. A premonition I don't understand. But it's as if from the beginning you've known something I haven't."

If I keep on making blunders, Witt thought, I'm going to ruin this. He's going to figure out that I'm not Bruce Trent. A look at my wallet would do it. Then he's going to shoot me and head for town again. And bring the *real* Trent next time.

"Just when I'm feeling better about you," Fecamo went on, "you make some strange remark. You slip out of character."

Witt kept still. He knew how close he was to being shot.

"I would have thought by now you might have begged a little," Fecamo hinted.

Witt had to say something. "I'm begging all right." He thought that behind the light Fecamo smiled. "Please let me see my little girl."

"And your … ah … mistress?"

"I want to be sure she's alive, too, of course," Witt said, trying to sound pleading, "but somehow at a time like this it's the little kid…. I can see what kind of spot they're in, a kind of mausoleum. Helpless. Please let them go and take out your feelings on me."

"Well, that's better." Fecamo sounded more mollified.

"If I could kneel down here, beg from my knees, I would," Witt added. "But with my hands bound like this, I might just fall down and not be able to get up very well."

Fecamo waited as if weighing Witt's words and manner, and then said, "Let's go down now."

Witt went to the edge of the steps. He saw with a sudden start of fear that the thing was much bigger and much deeper than he had supposed. The steps went on and on. Fecamo's light made a tunnel but even so at the end there was darkness, the dim shape of more steps.

He knew suddenly how Marion and the child must have felt here, even by daylight, being forced down into this catacomb.

"Don't be afraid," Fecamo said mockingly. "It's all quite solid. Under the drifted sand there's solid cement. I don't believe even dynamite could move it."

Witt thought of Marion's frailness, her slim hands and slight body. No, there'd be nothing she could do, nothing the child could do, in the midst of a monolith like this.

They went down to the first landing.

"Oh, this is just the beginning," Fecamo told him.

"And when we get to the end?"

"You'll see how little hope there really is."

Witt sensed that it was hard for Fecamo to keep his gloating, his satisfaction, under control.

"Please let them go," Witt said.

"I want you to see them first."

The further down they went the more the damp smell of the sea intruded. "You didn't put them in a place that floods at high tide?"

"Oh, no, nothing as crude as that."

Now they were facing a sheet of steel set into the cement wall. The metal had been painted with red lead but was flaked with rust now. Across the middle was an old hasp on a steel bar and this was locked into place with a brand-new padlock. Fecamo put the light under his left arm. Still holding the gun, he managed to extract a key and open the lock. "Push the door in."

Witt pushed the door as far as it would go. It stubbed on some obstruction and stopped, almost against the wall inside.

The light in Fecamo's hand struck the opposite wall and reflected the length of the chamber, a long narrow room.

"Wait a minute," Fecamo said, his tone full of alarm.

Witt looked but couldn't see any sign of Marion or the child. There was a lot of sand on the floor at one end of the room. High in the wall was a narrow slit, or window, that only a cat could have gotten through. "Where are they?" He turned to Fecamo, anger beating through him, a rocking nauseous jolt. "What kind of trick is this?"

Fecamo just stood there. His astonishment seemed genuine.

For a long moment there was no sound at all except the faint wash of surf outside, far away.

"They've ... they've gotten out," Fecamo said then, his tone disbelieving. He began to walk across to the end of the room where all the heaped sand lay, concentrating the light there. Witt followed a few steps behind.

There was an open pit, about four feet square, and as Witt approached he saw that a couple of feet below the surface there lay exposed the end of a huge pipe.

Fecamo's breathing filled the silence, a hot ragged pulse, and Witt suddenly saw how furious he was. He was literally alight with fury. The hand holding the light trembled. "How could they do it? How did they manage?"

"They've escaped through the pipe," Witt said in sudden exultation.

Then, as they stood there with the light concentrated on the pit, the huge stub of pipe, Witt heard a sound. The hairs rose on his neck and he wanted to cry out, "No, no! Keep still!" For the sound came from the pipe, a faint scratch like that of a mouse.

"Did you hear it?" Fecamo shouted, and began to look around as if for a way to get down into the pit.

It was a time to do something, no matter what. He had to act now, to distract Fecamo now. Bound or not, and dragging from hangover and exhaustion or not, and Fecamo's gun or not, he had to—

Something strange was happening.

From the direction of the door, from *behind* the door, something was running, headed like a shot for Fecamo's back.

Marion ...

Barefooted. Her clothes rags, her face torn and swollen, her outstretched hands bearing terrible wounds. A witch with hair flying. A ghost risen from the dead. Witt's throat convulsed with the need to scream, to warn her back, away, before Fecamo turned with the gun.

She hit the middle of Fecamo's back headlong and the rush carried them on into the pit. The light bounced and dazzled and then jolted to a stop pointed at the ceiling and by the reflection Witt saw what was happening in the pit. He'd heard something hit the pipe with a hollow echo—Fecamo's head, he hoped—but now he saw Fecamo beginning to stir groggily and Marion sliding down the heap toward the mouth of the pipe.

Where was the gun?

Without waiting to find out, Witt jumped. He landed on his knees, a sharp jolt that shook through him viciously. He pulled automatically at the binding tape. And then Marion's fingers were busy, there behind him. She was pulling the tape away; his hands were almost free.

Fecamo was rising like a tiger, eyes glittering.

In that moment she pulled the tape completely free.

Fecamo reached for him.

They rolled, and Fecamo's fingers found his throat, and sand choked his breath away. Lying there under Fecamo, under the tiger, he suddenly knew what Fecamo had held inside himself all this long time, in a way no one else could know it, and even half-conscious and trying for a last quick breath, Witt marveled.

The sound of the shot knocked through the narrow place like a hammer blow. For a moment there was no difference, the throttling fingers didn't loosen; and then they slowly relaxed, unwilling, and Fecamo began to slide away like a sack of salt.

Marion crouched there in the strange glow from the ceiling, this Marion he would scarcely have recognized, this wounded-faced woman with the hollow exhausted eyes, the ragged hair, and all they did was look at each other. The dead body of the madman slumped all the way down and then there was a short, shrill cry and a little girl came scuttling up out of the pipe. She grabbed Marion around the shoulders and cried, "Did I do it right? Did I scratch at the right time?"

"You did fine," Marion said, still staring.

After a while she whispered, "Witt?" as if she didn't believe it.

He crawled over and laid his head in her lap and for a while there was silence, the three of them clinging like that with Marion in the middle as if she represented some rock of strength and sanity, a refuge.

He had Fecamo's keys. They climbed up to the top of the steps and then walked over to the car. Witt kept an arm around Marion and the little girl clung to her hand on the other side.

When they got into the car, the child was the only one who spoke. "Won't my mama be surprised? She's worried, I'll bet."

When they came to a town Witt went into a service station telephone booth and rang Bruce Trent at home. It was quicker than trying to find out which detective was in charge of the affair. He told Trent what had happened.

"Wait where you are," Bruce Trent commanded.

"The hell I am. I'm going home in Fecamo's heap," Witt said. "We're taking the kid with us, her folks can come get us there. The cops know the address."

It seemed forever, a forever of silence and foggy night, and the kid going to sleep in Marion's arms and his own head nodding with tiredness and a wish to sleep, and the old car clunking along; and then at last they were home.

When they got inside the apartment the child fell on the couch and went to sleep again at once. Witt took Marion into his arms.

It was such a crazy thing to say, right then; he couldn't imagine where the crazy words came from. They were born out of this night of revelation.

"Marion ... life's so damned short. I want to send for my sister. I want to get her away from Dad. Do you mind if she lived with us for a little while?"

"I don't mind," Marion said, her voice loving and compassionate.

Bruce Trent turned at last from the telephone, from the echo of Renwick's dry civil voice, and looked at Carol.

"Well, it's over."

She was on the edge of the bed. "Isn't it strange that in the end it wasn't you at all that he ... he punished?"

Bruce was looking past her at nothing. The lines in his face were gray-shadowed. He waited as if examining what she had said and what he must say in answer. "I'm not sure about that," Bruce said slowly. "I'm not sure that I'll ever be able to forget that it was another child he took instead of Marilyn, nor that another man stood in my place at the end."

She moved anxiously, edging toward him. "Do you mean that we should have done it all differently?"

"When I look back," he said, his tone bitter and wondering, "I can't see a single step that I might have changed, then. Each act and each decision seemed right at the time. It seemed the only way to protect you and Marilyn. And yet in the end, somehow, it added up to what Witt Kennick said. We gave away our responsibility. Somewhere. We passed it on to others and they acted out our parts for us."

"Name me one thing," she cried, becoming agitated. "Name one thing we might have changed."

"We could have warned the school," he said flatly.

She bent against her skirt and began to cry, almost soundlessly, and her shoulders looked thin and defenseless and the way her hair had let down, the knot loosening, was somehow vulnerable and childlike.

"Don't cry, darling." Bruce went over and sat beside her and lifted her so that she rested against him. She felt frail, disjointed, a doll-woman without strength. "It's all over and done with. We'll do what we can with the memories. Fecamo—I can almost pity him—is finally done with the hate and the craving. And we must try to live in peace. Even if we don't quite deserve it."

There was a touch of gray dawn through the window blind, like the intrusion of a ghost.

He held her and after a while she stopped crying, and Bruce dried her eyes and got her to go to bed.

Betty Charles had fallen to sleep on the couch in the living room. She awoke when the doorbell clamored.

For a while she thought she must be dreaming, for there was Marion in the arms of the detective who had come earlier, and when Betty started to scream he told her sharply that Marion was okay and was simply asleep. He took Marion into the bedroom and laid her on the unmade bed and covered her gently. Then he took Betty back to the living room and told her a long involved story about some man with a strange name, and the schoolteacher, and what Betty got out of it at the end, firmly, no mistake—the cop saw to it—was that the teacher had saved her child's life. The teacher and the teacher's husband.

"Why, he was here!"

"Yes. He said that."

"I want to look at her again!"

"Mrs. Charles, let the kid rest. She needs rest and sleep. The doctor looked her over and she's fine, just got some sand in her hair and she'll be hungry when she wakes up, but she wasn't hurt."

Betty got herself under control. She tried not to cry. She blinked at the cop, wondering what he might look like if she had glasses and could see him good.

"There'll be an inquest on Fecamo," the cop said, "but we'll keep the little girl out of it. She may have to give a statement, how she and Mrs. Kennick were taken from the schoolground and how she lied about who she was, saying she was the other little girl, and all of that, but it can be taken down and read into the record later."

"Oh, thank you," Betty cried, seeing he was meaning to do them a favor.

"You've got a fine plucky little girl there, Mrs. Charles. I think that teacher, that Mrs. Kennick, kind of hated to see her go!" He laughed and Betty laughed a little too, trying to see the humor of someone else getting attached to her child, but he was so fogged up now, her eyes were stinging, she couldn't really see the expression on his face.

Betty sat up the rest of the night and smoked and drank coffee, and Marion slept.

They were eating breakfast about ten-thirty when Tommy came and rang the doorbell. Betty spoke to him through the crack.

She didn't even open the door.

THE END

The Bank With
the Bamboo Door

By Dolores Hitchens

To Vera

It's a pretty little town, Jimmy boy. A picture-book kind of place, your ma would say. Not crowded and smoggy the way it's got down around L.A. Nice wide streets, clean streets. Big old trees. Lots of flowers and big garden plots. Some new houses and plenty of old ones. This town got started around 1880.

There's maybe twenty-five thousand in the town and even more than that outlying. Commuters. You know, the government put in some big space and missile outfits along the coast and that brought a lot of employment. Money, too. New money.

The rich people live out along Old Mill River Road. There never was a mill that I knew of, nor more than a creek after a good rain. But the money is real enough and the people along Old Mill River Road have got it.

So they've always had a good bank. The government must have money in it too, now, and the remains of all that payroll. It's a nice little bank and I've had an eye on it for a long time. Just watching. Not that I think you've got to do anything about it unless you want to. It's just there.

Now the thing about this particular bank, the reason I've kept an eye on it, is: it's got a bamboo door.

And that bamboo door is what I have to tell you about....

WEDNESDAY

One

When you looked out of the breakfast-room windows of the Renick house, you saw the big trees of Old Mill River Road like a tall green wall, and between you and them the sloping lawn and the beds of rare pink iris and the white-rimmed marble pool like a little mirror reflecting the sky. A quiet formal dreamlike view, it had the qualities due to every Cinderella who gazed from her castle.

Marlie Renick put her forehead against the pane and gazed out, with the white marble pool's rim distorted by her tears and her heart thudding. She was afraid. Here in this silent room at six o'clock in the morning, alone, dressed in a white chiffon nightie and negligee that still looked nice though it was part of her trousseau, alternately she burned with chill and shivered with heat, consumed by terror. Everyone else in the house was asleep.

She tried to tell herself that none of this was real; she tried to will herself back to the beginning and then awake. It's a nightmare. Tod Bonnay was a nightmare and the gambling clubs at Tahoe were a nightmare and the scene in Dr. Ferrie's office was just part of the whole, a dream; and now this thing that has me scared to death is just something I'm imagining. I'm just sick in some strange way.

In the window, in the glistening pane, she seemed to see her mother's face, worn and tired, sometimes a little cynical and world-weary; and she thought that she could hear her mother's voice, the warning voice, saying: "Don't marry Warren Renick, Marlie. Listen to me. People like us don't know anything about people like him. We really don't, at all."

How silly.

And now, how true....

I married Warren anyway.

"I don't think you'll be happy with him, Marlie," her mother's voice said from the image in the window. "Everything will be so different. You will have to learn so much, and be so careful. And then this ... this thing about having children. Don't you understand the safety in having a family? Don't you know why girls who marry rich men—oh, look at any of them in the papers—right away start having kids? One after another. One, two, three—"

Shut your ears.

Don't let her take away the warm, wonderful happiness!

"—and if you aren't wise you'd think, for heaven's sake, what a love match. But it's because of this, Marlie. The money. If she has to divorce him after a few years ... usually it's him with his eye on someone younger and prettier ... if there's a divorce and she goes before the judge, the judge will say, 'Well, it's plain that this woman married this man for his money. She wants to be supported now for the rest of her life, but she didn't even give him a family.' So she gets nothing. But now look on the other hand, she has three or four kids, a pretty young mother, and what does the same old judge say? Why, she gets the works. Anything she asks for. And that's what the babies were all about in the first place. Insurance. Plain old insurance. And you won't have any."

Mother, don't make it worse than the things boys like Buddy Harkens whisper to you in the halls at school!

I won't let you spoil it, Mother!

And I didn't let you spoil it. And now I'm here alone....

The pane was icy against Marlie's palms, and the air of the room was chilled, and the view of the wide lawns and the iris just beginning to bloom and the marble pool, all of it seemed as cold as death; but inside of her, her heart lurched and battered away with a great hot beat.

I'm so scared, Mother.

I deserve it, too.

But living here with Warren isn't the way I thought it would be. And it's not the way you told me it would be. It's a lot more complicated than that. Neither you nor I, nor anybody who hadn't lived on Old Mill River Road, would have guessed about the Old Hens. In fact, if you tried to tell the rest of the people in this town about the Old Hens, I don't think they'd believe you.

You just couldn't know about the Old Hens unless you lived right here among them.

Because here the Old Hens hold the power of being in or being out, of being wanted or unwanted, welcomed or disdained, living or crucified.

You know, Mother, you told me once, when you'd sort of been thinking about life in general and things like that, that when a woman got older she got kind of invisible. Lots of people just didn't seem to see or notice older women. On the street and in the stores and on buses and in restaurants ... just everywhere ... it was as if people could see right through you. And sometimes you felt amused by it. You wanted to test them by doing something ridiculous. Like wearing your shoes on your head.

But the Old Hens would never have to wear *their* shoes on *their* heads because here on Old Mill River Road—

Marlie turned suddenly, hearing a stir behind her, but it was only Suzabell covering a yawn, looking at her from the swinging door.

"Mrs. Renick? You up so early?"

"Yes. I couldn't sleep. I felt restless."

Could Suzabell see the stuck lashes, the smeary cheeks, the redness?

"Would you care for a cup of coffee?"

"No, thank you. Not yet."

"It's real pretty out there, those trees and all, isn't it?"

A chance to turn to the window again, to conceal the marks of fright, the signs of tears. "Yes, it's very pretty. Mr. Renick's father planned it all. He planned it so that you see different things from each part of the house. He brought the pool from Italy or somewhere."

They had this in common, Suzabell and she—both were strangers and discoverers in this house. Sometimes it seemed Suzabell fitted in easier than she did. After all, Suzabell had been in a few great big houses before, lived in them and knew what it was like.

"What do you suppose Mr. Renick would like for breakfast this morning? French toast, maybe?"

"I think he'd like that."

"He never says, so I don't know if I've pleased him or not."

"Don't worry. He's easy to please."

A funny pause, then. *Easy to please*. He married me, didn't he? Wouldn't you say that makes him pretty easy to please?

It was her own reflection she saw now, tawny hair all wild, the skin too white, the eyes with their funny tilt.

Buddy Harkens: If you weren't so good-lookin', people would call you cockeyed.

"I like a man doesn't complain," Suzabell was saying, "but I want to know his favorites, too."

"Don't worry."

The door swung in with a slight *whush*. Marlie stole a glance back but Suzabell was gone.

The quiet came back, the fear crowding again, but Marlie made a determined effort to think now, instead of panic. To whom could she turn? To her mother? No. Not yet.

It was then that she thought of Karen Evans. Funny. She hadn't seen Karen for almost two years, at least.

Moving out to Old Mill River Road sort of cut you off from people. You lost old friends, you lost ones that you really liked because in your mind you were always rehearsing, you were introducing them to the Old Hens and you were seeing in your mind how the Old Hens would react.

But funnier too, Marlie decided: Karen would probably have been all right as far as the Old Hens were concerned. She came from nice people and she knew how to behave. The only thing about Karen, she wouldn't have given a damn what the Old Hens thought of her, and perhaps they'd have sensed this.

It has to be Karen. I'll look her up today.

All that she'd heard recently, Marlie remembered, was that Karen was working with Lisa Kim in that little pet shop next to the bank. The two girls had expanded the place and put in a kind of nursery sideline, potted plants and mulch and stuff like that.

That's all I know about Karen, Marlie thought, looking out at the peaceful view that might have been painted on a postcard. I haven't spoken to Karen for ages, and yet we were such good friends in school. I wonder what she thinks of me. If she ever bothers to think of me.

Marlie shivered. She rubbed her arms below the soft fabric of the puffed sleeves. She had better go back upstairs. Warren would wake and he might want her.

All of the warm secret pleasure, the loving and giving, had gone out of that idea, too.

She looked around at the breakfast room, studying it. Why, a dozen people could eat in here, she thought. Why do we need all of this? What's the big sideboard for, with knickknacks that Suzabell dusts all the time?

And the big polished brass light that hung from a chain above the table ... Marlie thought it must have been made somewhere ... Italy, like the pool, perhaps ... but surely not just to hang here where two people ate just once a day.

A lovely home, said an echo in her mind.

A lovely home ...

A lovely home. She went back up the stairs and down the hall to the bedroom where the windows looked out upon another pool, and ranunculuses and ferns and willows and a wrought-iron bench with a sundial.

Warren wasn't in the big bed. The door to the dressing room was open, the lights on in there, and she could hear the shower.

The rug was thick, like fur, and the bed was huge. She got in under the covers. The electric blanket was still on. Marlie curled into a ball and waited, wide-eyed.

We have five beds in this house, not counting Suzabell's downstairs. Who's supposed to sleep in all these beds?

Who's supposed to be using all those other bathrooms?

Who sits in the satin lounges, who looks into the mirrors? Who needs all those fluffy pink-and-white towels, changed every week?

Who walks through the rooms I never see from one month to the next? Ghosts? The ghosts of Warren's mother and father, his uncles and aunts, the people who had come to Old Mill Road in the beginning, who'd been its first rich?

A lovely home.

A lovely haunted home....

Well, we could use all those bedrooms, we could give slumber parties, she told herself, almost with a desire to giggle in spite of the fear and anguish that wouldn't go away. She could even imagine Warren, big and prematurely gray, wholesome as a boy somehow, engaging in a pillow fight.

"Well," he said from the dressing-room door, "I see you have a smile for your husband. What'd you run away for?"

"I couldn't sleep." She felt a stab of guilt because she hadn't really been smiling for Warren. She hadn't even seen him standing there. "So I went downstairs to look at one of the views."

"The breakfast room." He said it matter-of-factly, unsurprised.

"How did you know?"

"Oh, it's the morning view. Dad planned it for morning, just past daybreak. He was an early riser all his life. Didn't you notice, the pool's like a mirror under the early sky and there's usually a trace of mist from the water. It's thoroughly romantic and Dad was a romantic." Warren had one of the big pink-and-white towels and he was rubbing his neck and chest. Now he turned and threw the towel at the hamper behind him. He wore a terry-cloth pareu, tied at the waist. The skin of his chest and arms and legs looked ruddy and healthy. Warren really didn't seem almost fifty. He never did run around naked, either, Marlie reminded herself. It was something very decent about Warren, a way he had of showing respect for her and for himself. It was also what the Old Hens would think was proper, but this wouldn't be Warren's motive.

A memory came, flooding her face with heat. When she'd been about ten her mother had been married briefly to a man named Walt. Walt had been big and gross, worked hard, drank hard, cleaned his fingernails with a pocket knife; and he'd been careless. He hadn't thought much about the feelings of a ten-year-old and when he felt like running through the house after a bath, he hadn't done it covered up. Oh, sometimes there'd been a towel around his neck.

Warren wouldn't dream of acting like that.

He was over by the big chest of drawers now, getting out his underthings.

Marlie shrank deeper under the covers. How can he look at me and not know, she thought desperately. He's decent and good, and I'm ...

I'm so sick inside.

It isn't real. It's some kind of terrible dream. When things are at the very worst, I'll wake up.

But I've been waiting so long now and I haven't waked up. And nothing else has happened, either.

Today I'll go see Karen Evans....

Warren turned with his things in his hands. "You know, kitten, you might not like my saying it ... I'm not criticizing ... but it seems to me that you're looking kind of fine-drawn. A little thin in the face. What my mother used to call peaked. You know I'm not the fuddy-duddy type, but ... well, why don't you drop in and see Doc Ferrie?"

In that stunned moment Marlie thought that she would faint.

"You seem paler, too," Warren said, puckering his eyes a bit the way he did when he stared hard at someone. "I don't want you fading away. I can't have you looking puny and sick. What will people say? I had such a beautiful bride at my wedding, they'll think I'm not treating you right." He smiled to let her know that he was joking.

She forced herself to rally, though now Warren seemed shut behind a quivering wall of light and all the bits of bright color in the room, the gold and crimson and deep blue, seemed to be bits of broken puzzles scattered here. She raised herself on an elbow, propping her head on her palm. The sense of unreality shut her in. Warren was still there looking at her but she couldn't meet his eyes.

"I'm all right. I'm just fine," she managed. "Why should I look sick?"

"I don't know. I just thought you did, a little." He seemed to be apologizing, afraid of having hurt her.

She felt cold and drained. Suddenly she wanted to tell Warren the truth, just blurt it out, just force it on the silence, baldly, without leading up to it. The naked nasty fact of what had happened to her and what she had inside her. It was too much to endure, keeping still and knowing what she had done and what she was. It was too much, all alone.

I can tell Warren and then I can quit thinking about it, and he'll have to plan what must be done. I can stop worrying and he'll have to figure out a way to get rid of me. Gracefully. And to keep the Old Hens from knowing. That's the main thing, to get rid of me without any scandal, without affecting anything at the bank.

If we keep it all away from the Old Hens and the bank ...

Nerving herself, she opened her mouth to tell Warren about Tod Bonnay and what had happened at Tahoe, and then she saw that Warren wasn't in the room. He must be in the dressing room putting on his clothes.

I'll tell him when he comes back...

She turned over, turned face down against the pillow. There was a hint of lavender sachet and the pillowcase felt smooth against her cheek. She shut her eyes.

All at once she knew. With a new, wrenching anguish she knew how Warren was going to look when she told him. She knew what expression would come into his eyes, and the sick way he was going to swallow. He was going to feel worse than she did now. A million times worse.

And he hadn't done anything.

Well, you could say, he'd married a tramp.

A tramp.

A lovely home, with a tramp.

A lovely haunted home, haunted by a tramp.

Five beds in the lovely haunted home, but she had to go to bed at Tahoe.

I can't tell him. I can't tell him until I've tried in every way I can to solve it.

Today I'll go see Karen Evans at that funny little store she and Lisa Kim are running beside the bank.

Lisa Kim had been a senior in high school when she and Karen were sophomores. And Lisa's father had died that year. She couldn't remember just when Karen and Lisa had become good friends.

Hadn't Warren said something once, that the building where the bank was now, and Lisa's store, and even the whole block beyond had all been Chinese once? A sort of Chinatown? A long, long time ago?

Two

Karen got to the store about eight-thirty. The street still had the early look. The pavement had been washed, and the bank next door was shuttered, the flat-cream venetian blinds hanging against the glass. Karen's gaze dwelt for a moment on the bank door, and in the back of her mind, as usual, was the fleeting thought of the money and what she should do about it.

Do nothing.

Well, nothing today at any rate. Just for today, I don't have to do a thing.

She opened the shop door. The little bell tinkled. Lisa was already there, in the rear where the clutter centered around the desk and the file cabinet, pounding the typewriter. Karen paused by the door and drew in a breath. There was the funny animal smell, the bird smells, still, but now much sweetened and improved since they'd added the line of potted plants and garden mulch. Down in the dragon's den were sacks and sacks of peat moss and leaf mold and redwood chips, and she imagined that their odors came up through the old floor, like incense.

"Hi," she said to Lisa's back, taking off her jacket.

"Hi," said Lisa, not turning around. Lisa's hands looked slim and pale against the black typewriter. She tapped out a couple of lines, drew out the letter, then looked at Karen who came to hang up her jacket. "Mrs. Carpenter called."

"Oh, no."

"He won't eat. She thinks he has a hair ball. A big one. Maybe he was born with it. Inherited it from his mother through the placental membrane. Mostly she thinks that we deliberately sold her a diseased Siamese."

"I like that," Karen said. "Diseased Siamese. Why don't you try writing for Disney?"

"He's already done Siamese. He won't do them again."

"You're good, though."

Mockingly, Lisa said, "Honorable ancestors were not scholars. All of honorable ancestors were merchants."

"Tradition dies hard in you Orientals," Karen agreed. Lisa giggled. Karen went to inspect the guinea pigs. There was a mother guinea pig with a trio of babies, now a little more than a week old. Karen took out a brown ball of fur, bright-eyed, nose twitching with curiosity, and cuddled him inside her palms. "I like this one. I'm going to keep him. He's too cute to sell."

Lisa nodded and started another letter.

Karen rubbed the brown fur against her cheek. "That's the trouble with running a pet store. I hate to sell any of them. I always wonder what kind of homes they get when we send them out of here."

Lisa's fingers raced across the keys. "You should be running an adoption agency."

"We are, in a way."

Karen put the baby back with the others and started to check and clean cages. There were families of white rats, very friendly, and tiny mice with pink eyes. There were parakeets and finches and a whole rack of canaries. The goldfish gaped at her through the glass. Two striped yellow tom kittens slept, ignoring the noise she made.

Filling the kittens' water jar, Karen thought, I'm going to have to do something about the money pretty soon. It's no good pretending that the money's all right, there in the bank. That's not a solution. The situation's ugly and it won't get less ugly. I should try to decide. I should come to a conclusion and act on it.

Like giving in, and giving up the money.

Or like moving entirely away from here, taking the money with me.

She slopped some of the water and exclaimed with bitter impatience over her clumsiness. Lisa had stopped typing and was looking at her. Her thoughts must have been following Karen's, for she said, "Anything more from Tod Bonnay?"

"No."

"You aren't rid of him that easy."

"I know it."

My father hated Tod almost more than he eventually hated Tod's mother, Karen thought. His name for Tod was "educated bum." He called Tod other things that I prefer not to remember. During that disastrous marriage, my father's relations with his stepson deteriorated even faster than with his wife.

Lisa's tone was quiet. "How much justice is here on Tod's side?"

Karen wanted to ask: *What is justice?* But instead she said, "I don't know. None, perhaps. Or perhaps a little."

"That's what worries you? Being completely fair to him?"

"No." What's worrying me is that I loved my father very much and even though he is dead I want to go on pleasing him. I wanted to please him by punishing Tod, by denying Tod any share of what he is so sure is his.

"Why don't you tell Tod Bonnay to go to hell?"

"Maybe I will." One of the kittens opened his mouth in a yawn and Karen saw the frosty pink tongue and the sharp little white teeth.

"What he gets out of you—if he gets anything—he'll throw away. He'll be seen in the ski resorts and in Las Vegas, and he'll rent a yacht the better to skin dive off Baja California—briefly. No matter how much you give him, it will be briefly."

For a moment, bent there by the kittens' cage, Karen listened not to Lisa's words but to the tone of her voice; it seemed there was a surprising bitterness there. And a surprising knowledge of Tod. "Yes, Lisa, I know that."

"So shall I shut my big mouth?"

"What would you have done if it had been your father? I mean, wouldn't there have been some set of rules, some long-ago tradition? Some way that your people always handled such things? And you'd have been guided by that?"

Lisa looked at her thoughtfully. "You know, I kid around. I do the inscrutable Oriental bit. Confucius say, and all that. But no, I wouldn't have had any long-ago set of rules. And no tradition. My father never encouraged me to live in the way of our Chinese ancestors. I was never to forget that I was an American. And, most of all, in a thing like this, what remains when a man dies ... I don't believe there's much difference between people. Between *any* kind of people. Ages ago in China there must have been stepsons who coveted what Mama had almost got. And who tried to do something about it."

"He's started a lot of gossip."

"And do you really care?" Lisa seemed surprised.

"I think he's telling things that aren't true," Karen said, flushing a little. Lisa's eyes met hers; Lisa's eyes looked blue-black, full of liquid lights, above the sheet of paper in her hands. "And I can't seem to figure out how to fight back, except to give him part of the money, maybe the biggest part of it, to show I'm *not* a thief."

Lisa shook her head. "No, no! It would be like paying off a blackmailer. In fact, that's exactly what it would be."

Karen scratched a kitten ear through the cage and got another pink yawn in answer. "Well ... I don't have to do anything today."

"No."

"Only ... I feel more and more as if I'm being pushed closer to something. To an edge. To the brink of something. To a place where I'll have to ... to surrender."

Lisa typed a few words. "He's very clever," she said softly.

The doorbell jingled as someone came in at the front of the store. For a moment, looking up at him against the brightness from the show windows, Karen made out only a tall, unfamiliar, well-set-up male form. She rose from the cage of kittens, and went forward. He was watching her, smiling a little. He wore a gray suit, dark shirt, and a plain black tie, and Karen noticed his clothing because there was something more formal about him than about their usual customer. Many people came in hastily in their gardening clothes, having run out of something in the middle of planting or trimming or fertilizing. Scarcely anyone ever came here all dressed up, except perhaps the older women from Old Mill River Road, who brought along a handyman to carry stuff for them, and who performed the entire transaction of purchase and removal in white kid gloves. This man had a dark hat in his hand. His hair was black, close-cropped. He had a tanned, enigmatic, high-cheekboned face. His eyes were quite blue.

"Yes, sir. May I help you?"

He looked around the shop, taking his time about it, studying their layout of gardening truck and the little collection of pets. Karen got the impression—ridiculous, fleeting—that he had been sent to inventory their stock.

"You carry soil conditioners? In bulk?"

He had been looking at the gardening display, the African violets and the flats of begonia seedlings and the philodendron's mass of green.

"Yes, sir."

He glanced at Lisa now, and something came into his expression that Karen couldn't understand. He knew Lisa. He recognized her. As he stood there waiting, Karen wondered if he expected Lisa to speak; but Lisa was looking over her shoulder at him, her gaze only mildly pleasant and interested.

"What do you have? And where do you keep them?"

"We have a few sacks up here." Karen started to lead the way to the opposite end of the shop where, in a pyramidal display, were some stacks of processed fertilizer and leaf mold.

"I'd need a lot more than that."

"Well, we have quite a lot stored downstairs."

"Could I see it?"

It meant taking him down into the dragon's den, a place where Karen never felt easy, a place where she disliked to go alone with strangers. But of course Lisa was here. It wasn't as if she were alone in the store, which happened often enough in slack hours.

"This way, please." Karen went to the rear of the shop, paused to click the light switch on the wall above the stairs to the cellar. She felt the heavy masculine tread behind her as she went down.

The cellar light was bright at the foot of the stairs, but because of the length of the cellar, and its shape, with the other end wider and partially hidden, with a lot of old crates and cages and storage barrels and boxes, there was something uncheerful and remote. Karen never came down without renewing a twin resolve to get rid of some of the junk back there and to put in an extension cord and light.

The man had stopped on the lowest step. "Well, what a surprise. It's big down here."

"Yes, isn't it?"

The sacks of fertilizers and soil additives were stacked neatly along the east wall in a solid tier about five feet high. Putting in this large supply had been the reason for a great deal of deliberation and questioning on Karen's and Lisa's part. It had meant extending their finances somewhat. Lisa hadn't been sure at first that the garden supply line was going to succeed. It had been Karen who had pointed out that there was no similar business in the downtown area; and that if both of them were going to keep busy and make enough profit to enable them to stay at least part-time in college, something had to be added.

As it had turned out, the gardening end of the shop was the one which was growing and which showed the principal profit.

But now the customer was looking at the other wall, the west wall, where red brick enclosed a space perhaps six by fourteen feet, taking up that much of the original cellar floor.

She thought that he was going to say something about it. And again she got the odd impression that he had recognized something—in the same way he'd recognized Lisa. He had found something he had expected to see.

He seemed to have forgotten her, forgotten why they had come down here. "It must be an old closet," Karen said into the stillness. "I've often wondered why it should have been bricked up like that."

His gaze turned on her swiftly, something almost like anger in it, as if she had no right to speculation. Then he smiled, covering what had flashed in his eyes a moment before. "Makes you think of ... oh, those old stories by Poe. You know. Cellars and winding passages 'The Cask of—' whatever that cask was full of."

"Wasn't it in 'The Black Cat' that the man walled up his wife?" she offered, answering the smile.

"And the cat got in, too, by mistake?" He had half-turned his back on the brick wall now.

"I have a name for this place. I call it the dragon's den."

He thought it over. "Is this a Chinese dragon?"

"Oh, yes. It would have to be. Mr. Kim built this place. He built the whole block originally. And it was Chinese, for a while." She had the feeling she was telling this man something he already knew. "So much has been changed since then, remodeled— But yes, this has to be a Chinese dragon's den. I haven't seen him but I feel he's back there in the shadowy part."

"He might help out a little by incinerating your old boxes and barrels, wouldn't you think? One good breath should do it."

"I wish he would."

They laughed together, laughed above the trace of an echo in the long, still room; and there was a shared feeling of friendship. She could like him very much, Karen thought, and wondered why she had thought it.

"I guess I ought to look at all the different brands of sacks here," he said, walking over toward the long tier against the wall. "I don't know much about it, really."

"What kind of soil do you have?"

When he looked back at her blankly, she added: "Is it clay? Heavy adobe? Or light, nothing to it, too sandy, not enough humus?"

"Everything looks sick around that house," he said. "The dirt's in clods. Big clods. Like rocks."

"You're out on the north side."

"How did you know?"

"I've lived here all my life. My father had a house on Holloway Drive once. You must be in that neighborhood. We kids used to throw those clods at each other when we had fights. I wonder how we lived through it."

"I'm just off Holloway, on Edwards."

"Well, I think you could try a mixture of redwood chips and vermiculite and humus. About two, one, and five. It will be kind of expensive. But things will grow then."

He leaned against the bright yellow sacks and looked at her as if thinking about her suggestion. He had a scar through one eyebrow, she saw, a white line the heavy brow didn't conceal. She wondered if he had ever fought with clods. Probably. He looked like a man who would have been a tough kid. If, for instance, some mythical monster *should* happen right now to jump out from the shadows back there, he would turn and be ready instantly to do battle. She knew this. And still, he had read Poe somewhere. And had cared enough to remember.

"When will you want it, and how much to start?"

He seemed now to be measuring her slight figure and the height of the cellar stairs. "How will you deliver?"

"Don't worry about it. Miss Kim's uncle is our delivery man. He owns a small truck and he's very good about helping us."

His eyes dropped away from her. "Does he live near here?"

"Not far." She was wondering why he wished to know; the question seemed out of place.

He slapped one of the sacks and shook his head slightly, almost with an air of regret. "Do you mind if I ask someone, a friend of mine, about those proportions you mentioned? Do you mind if I check up before I order?"

"No, not at all."

They went back upstairs. She noticed that he paused by one of the rear windows—it was dusty—and looked out into the alley. There was a back door, too, and she saw him looking at it.

A long time ago, Lisa had said, this rear part had been living quarters for her parents. The store had been very small, half its present size. Her mother had hung washing in the alley, her very young mother, and had trained sweet peas beside the windows.

The customer thanked her and left.

Karen thought, *He came to see the store. He knew Lisa would be here, and he wanted a look at everything.*

Actually, he hadn't been a *real* customer, at all.

Unable to explain why, Karen liked him anyhow.

Three

Lisa said, "What did he want?"

"Nothing really, I guess. He looked at the sacks downstairs. He lives out on Edwards Street and his yard is horrid."

"I'll bet it is. Why didn't you tell him to just plant castor beans like everyone else out there? Or you could have explained that there are nicer parts of town."

"We lived out there for a while. When I was little. Before Dad got into the construction game."

"I know you did. Before I forget, there was a phone call for you while you were down in the cellar. A girl. She said to tell you Marlie had called. I offered to get you but she said she'd call back in about ten minutes."

Karen stood as if dumbfounded.

"What's the matter?" Lisa asked. "Did I say something off key? Marlie. There was a Marlie at school. That horrible Buddy Harkens, that cesspool of a boy, used to corner her in the halls. But wait ... of course ... you and Marlie were friends."

"Yes, we were. Good friends. But I haven't seen her for ... oh, for over a year! She married … Oh, I *know* the name! He's in the bank. Warren … Warren Renick."

Lisa nodded "I remember something about it. He's older isn't he? And she's terribly pretty. There was something catlike, slant-eyed, about her face. Not slant-eyed like me. Something hard to explain. And yet very interesting, that face."

"I wonder what she wants?"

"Well, what she wants is you. I offered to take down a message but she wasn't interested." Lisa scratched a nail across a row of typewriter keys and frowned. "She didn't sound as if she needed a Siamese cat. Nor a parakeet. Nor a load of fertilizer."

"I didn't hear the phone ring," said Karen, thinking back. "That's funny."

"I could hear *you* laughing, though," Lisa pointed out. "Just what did go on down there anyway?"

Dr. Roland Ferrie opened his office door, came in, let the door close on its automatic air-cylinder behind him. The waiting room wasn't large but it was opulent. The walls were covered by a fabric woven of maguey fibers, imported from Mexico, and there were several pseudo-Aztec masks hung between the windows. The carpet was deep, a russet-and-pink plaid that seemed to reflect the sun. Two couches were upholstered in turquoise Naugahyde, and a couple of cream-colored chairs had cream-colored ottomans before them. The desk was in the back of the office, beside the inner door, and his nurse-receptionist was already there and looking confusedly through the drawers for something—for the appointment book perhaps. Dr. Ferrie noted grimly that the phone was off the hook.

She glanced up, angering him as usual by her air of surprise, as if he were a stranger; and he put a cautioning finger to his lips and then pointed to the phone and shook his head.

She quit fumbling through the desk and picked up the receiver and said, "I'm so sorry, Mrs. Quigley, but Doctor seems to be so busy today that we won't be able to fit you in. No, I'm sorry. Not anywhere. How about tomorrow?"

His expression cold now, and full of disgust at her stupidity, he shook his head a second time, and she stuttered, "Look, Mrs. Quigley, let's do it this way. When Doctor comes in I'll find out from him just when he can see you. Yes, of course. I'll call right away. And I won't forget."

Mrs. Quigley, horrible old hen, had a voice that rattled the phone. Dr. Ferrie listened impassively while the nurse grimaced, and twitched under the white uniform, and said *thanks* and *of course* and *no, never*, and finally in relief was able to hang up the receiver.

"Now you can find the appointment book," he said evenly.

"I know—I just *know* I put it in the top drawer."

"When you find it, go through the morning's appointments and cancel."

"All of them?"

He nodded. He felt the pressure pounding behind his eyes; he looked at her with hatred, with loathing, remembering that his wife had hired her and so of course she'd hired someone exactly like herself, a slut and a slattern, incapable of the least efficiency.

She opened a drawer and then glanced up as he passed. "You're early this morning, Doctor."

He turned at the inner door. "What hospital did you graduate from?"

Her eyes were round in her rather fattish face. "Why, Dr. Ferrie, you know that! Mercy Hospital. Mercy Hospital in Tacoma, Washington." When his sour, distant look didn't change, she repeated, "You know that!"

"I just like to be reassured about it once in a while," he said quietly, and went on into the hall. *I don't really believe it, though*, he told himself, getting out his keys. *No nitwit like that ever got past the head of a nursing school.*

His private office was roomy. Its atmosphere was savagely bare and clean and sterile, however, as if the office took something of the mood of the man who worked here. Beyond it, connecting by means of an inner door as well as by way of the hall, was a second room with instrument cases, locked drug cabinets, a sterilizer, and other equipment. At the end of the hall were two closets, one in which linens were kept and another used for storing records. Three examination rooms completed the suite.

Dr. Ferrie took off his lightweight spring suit-coat and hung it in a small closet. He washed his hands and wrists, slowly, with plenty of soapy lather. He inspected his tongue in the mirror above the basin and then spent a bitter moment examining his own face, its blunt features and heavy-lidded brown eyes and brown-turning-to-gray hair above a wide forehead. "You're a goddam sap," he told the mirror.

Then he shrugged into the stiffly laundered white doctor's jacket.

He went to his big desk and stood there staring at nothing, and said calmly aloud, "I feel like hell." His glance swept over to the open door and to the locked drug cabinet in there; but then he shook his head and sat down behind the desk. "Have to think. Have to think today, and think hard."

I'm in a spot.

I'm in a damned spot because I've been a fool.

I'm in a worse spot, a much worse spot, than most people could ever get themselves into, because I'm a doctor and there's so much to lose.

So much to lose....

"That's what I've got to decide," he said under his breath. "How much is there to lose? That I can never have again—anywhere—any other time?"

He looked around and decided that there was the office to lose, to start with. He liked it here, he liked the whole suite. He liked the way the waiting room looked, and the nice straight short hall, and the neat examination rooms; and especially he liked the clean gray linoleum under his desk, and the desk itself, bare and shining. He liked his framed diplomas on the wall.

Well, he could take the diplomas when he went.

The only thing that spoiled his pleasure in this office was the nitwit in the white uniform, the boob with her blunders and inefficient slowness. Take her out—

No, put losing her on the credit side. At times he could scarcely remember her name and then when it came to him—Miss Spilling— he felt like retching, as though she had accidentally put a hand on him.

He'd be everlastingly getting away from Miss Spilling.

Carry it a step further—*I'm just dying to*—and he'd be getting rid of Janie, too. Janie didn't look like Miss Spilling, but they were sisters under the skin. He wondered if Miss Spilling felt fat inside her cotton nightgown, in bed, the way Janie did, and then couldn't endure to wonder any longer because he could *feel* Janie....

Janie, the slob.

Janie, the slut.

He leaned on the desk and put his hands out and laid his face in them. His palms felt cool. The sense of sickness went away.

Then, of course, there were the two barracuda. Getting rid of them, getting them off his back—that was the mainspring, that was the whole motive, the thing that must make the rest of the loss worthwhile. The two barracuda were the reason he must think today, and decide.

The barracuda were going to eat him alive.

Unless he could cut and run. They wouldn't expect that.

His head lifted off his hands with a jerk as the door opened. Miss Spilling's capped head stuck itself in at an angle. "Doctor," she said humbly, "if we aren't to have any patients all morning, what will we be doing?"

Several perfectly shocking and unspeakable replies sprang ready-phrased to his lips, but he repressed them. When her head remained there, though, the cap wavering, he had to grunt, "Please go away. I've got a lot of worrying to do. I think I've got syphilis."

She turned white and her mouth twitched. She shut the door. He knew— *What a bastard I am*—she was out at the desk now, realizing how mean he had been, again, with tears welling in her eyes and her fattish lids blinking and blinking to blink them away.

And also hunting for the paper tissues, lost in the desk like the appointment book.

To hell with her.

And to get back to the summing up, the evaluation.

Credit: To lose the barracuda, Janie, Spilling, and the damned boredom that had led him to be involved with the barracuda in the first place.

Debit: Losing the office, the house almost paid for, the modest store of blue-chip stocks that were all, dammit, in his and Janie's names together. And the career, the business of being a doctor. Not quite the kind of doctor he'd planned to be, but still a very decent living. Maybe only temporarily, but face it, at least temporarily, the career.

He licked his lips and thought about his career, the long years of it, what it had meant and what it had become.

He'd had a hell of a time getting through medical school at all, because he'd been so damned poor, and he had had to take time off, a semester here and there, to work.

Lousy work. The incredibly low-paid work of the thirties, the depression. Janie's father had shown an interest in him, the kid who once had mowed their lawn and chopped wood for their fireplaces; and in the end Janie's father had even, in a magnificent gesture of kindness and confidence, bought him into old Dr. Annison's practice, when Dr. Annison decided he needed a younger man.

And then, when it seemed he was finally set, Pearl Harbor had exploded and he'd been in the Navy; and for eleven wonderfully lucky months he'd had the fun and excitement of Navy wartime experience; and then had come the torpedo. Even today, seeing one of the American Japs, the Nisei, on the streets, Ferrie couldn't help cursing the torpedo.

He had been shipped home in a cast, very fortunate to be alive at all. Janie's father had been a literal rock of a man, never failing him for an instant, full of courage and optimism—why in hell couldn't Janie be, *in one tiny way*, like her decent old dad?—and Dr Annison had turned out to be a very good doctor indeed.

A month out of the cast and he and Janie had been married in the Presbyterian church. He'd had no family, nobody. Janie had had the whole mob from Old Mill River Road.

But now, sitting with his head propped on his fists, Dr. Ferrie was remembering that what he had wanted to do was to become an internist. In medical school he had chosen gastroenterology because he liked it.

And now there were all sorts of new techniques to deal with the stomach, and what chance did he have even to study them? He was tied up hand and foot with the horrible old hens from Old Mill River Road, with their neurotic nothings, mostly imaginary "female trouble." If another one of them came in here simpering under the over-powdered wrinkles and used that expression, so help him, he was going to bust her one in the chops. Or better, he was going to set up a camera to take pictures of them while they were on the table with their legs propped apart; he was going to explain, in some pseudo-medical gobbledegook, that this was a scientific study of the whappiglottis; and he was going to have the pictures enlarged and framed and hung in the bank, at the back where they had that art-exhibit corner, trying to bring culture to this place, and he was going to label the exhibit "Matrons of Our Upper Crust."

That would teach them.

But the very thought of those pictures, the undersides of the old hens, made him want to vomit. He leaned back in the chair.

Anger was so close under the surface now, all the time, like an untriggered bomb; he felt a clinical, wry, detached interest in this emotion in himself, almost as though it were a growth he had discovered in somebody else, like a polyp in the gullet, for instance. The anger was there and it was going to blow up. It had almost blown up at Miss Spilling.

He had to get away, *or do something*, before it did explode.

He could give the female barracuda something in her vein that would put her out of the picture forever. That wouldn't be any trouble for him at all. But it wouldn't remove the male barracuda, either, and the eating alive would go on faster than ever.

He had a pretty good idea who the male barracuda was, though there'd never been anything but the phone calls. But this male barracuda wouldn't let Ferrie get closer than ten feet, much more likely fifty, with anything resembling a hypo needle in his hand.

Whereas the female barracuda was on the steps practically every night....

(You gave it to her first.)

The hell I did. She'd been on what she calls horse for a year or more, by the time I first met her. And before that, marijuana. Marijuana in junior high school.

Seventeen now....

God.

At eight minutes to ten, Miss Spilling opened the door a crack. He could see one eye, and it was reddened, the fattish lid fatter than ever.

"Go away before I say something else."

"Please, Doctor. Mr. Renick is here. You know how he is. He's your friend and he just thinks you're having putting practice in here, or something."

"Why in hell did you tell him I was here at all?"

"I ... I ..."

Take some time out. "Oh, all right. Let him come in here. Shut the hall door and if you let anyone else know I'm sitting here, so help me, I'll cut your throat."

"Yes, Doctor."

Warren Renick came in at once, and Ferrie found himself looking at *him* with a wry, clinical attitude. They were contemporaries, practically. But Warren almost always managed to look as if he'd just spent the weekend on a yacht, working in the sun and spray. His middle was as flat as the top of Ferrie's desk. His big clean hands with their square clean nails had just laid down the hawser.

"Hello, Warren."

"What the hell are you doing?"

"Oh, I've got a thing to think about and I can't do it at home."

This didn't rouse the curiosity it might have in someone else. Warren always accepted remarks at face value; he never looked for secrets. He sat down now in Ferrie's extra chair and said, "I've got a problem at home, too. Marlie."

My God, she told him. Ferrie sat erect fast. This was something he would never have expected.

"She's not looking right. She says she feels okay, but I have a hunch she doesn't. You know, there's an old-fashioned word, my mother used to use it—peaked. Marlie looks peaked to me."

Ferrie leaned back again in his chair. He smiled a little, briefly, to himself, and Warren didn't notice this.

I never thought of it before, but this thing has untold possibilities. Warren's family was on Old Mill River Road even before Janie's. And God only knows how much money he inherited.

I could, with the proper encouragement, become a barracuda myself...

Four

The phone almost always rang before ten o'clock for Janie Ferrie, and this morning was no exception. The colored maid, Grizzie, came out to the little stone-floored porch where the sink was and where the vases were kept. "Mrs. Ferrie? My, oh, my, but those roses are pretty!"

"I should have cut them earlier. While the dew was on." She pulled the long-stemmed pink buds up to loosen the bouquet, fussed a little with the fern and baby's breath. "What is it, Grizzie?"

"Mrs. Winniger on the phone."

"Tell her I'll be right there."

"Yes, ma'am. Sure're pretty," said Grizzie, turning away.

Janie came into the kitchen after a minute, sat down, picked up the phone at the little wall desk, and then said, "Grizzie, please bring me an ash tray." She took a pack of cigarettes from her housecoat pocket. The housecoat was knee-length, full, and it had a pattern of huge pink rosebuds that strangely were almost enlarged dead ringers for the ones she had left in the vase on the porch. It made Janie look enormous.

Mabel Winniger had a deep, scratchy note in her voice that was unmistakable; not unpleasant, once you got used to it, and Janie had known Mabel all her life. "Hello, Mabel. How're tricks?"

"Tricks are fine," said Mabel, deeply and scratchily. "What's new with you?"

Down through the years certain fads of slang had come and gone, and their vestiges could be found in Janie's and Mabel's conversation, like mastodon bones in a swamp.

"Boy, oh boy," said Janie, "have I got some dirt for you!"

"And I have a t.d. for you," grated Mabel huskily.

"Yours first!"

"No. Yours first."

"Oh, come on!"

"Not a word. Not a single cotton-pickin' li'l old word!"

"Is it a good one? A real good one?"

"A real nice t.d."

Briefly, Janie wondered why trademarks were called t.d.'s and not t.m.'s. In a way it didn't match. But this went back to high school.

"It's precious," Mabel amplified in her deep scratchy tone, promising all sorts of pleasant surprises.

"You'll tell me who said it?"

"I promised not."

"Oh ... come *on!*"

"Promised. Anyway, you've got to tell me first."

"Well, this is about ..." Belatedly, Janie glanced about, especially at the open door where Grizzie had vanished after leaving the ash tray and the kitchen lighter. The kitchen lighter was a solid silver lighter that a grateful patient had given Ronnie almost fifteen years ago. It was shabby now but still worked marvelously. "... this is about someone in *Ronnie's profession!*"

It didn't bother Janie a bit, reminding Mabel that she was married to a professional man. After all, Mabel had come to her for advice before getting engaged to Sam Winniger, and she'd told her not to do it. Of course Sam made a terrific lot of money now, and always had, but in the end, what was he? He kept his mouth shut around people like Ronnie, that was for sure.

"A doctor? Another doctor here in town?"

"Yes." Janie couldn't control a giggle. She dropped ashes from the cigarette onto the bosom of the housecoat, brushed at them disgustedly.

"Who?"

"This is *just* between you and I, Mabel."

"Just between you and me," agreed Mabel, getting in a tiny dig of her own to pay back for "Ronnie's profession."

"*Dr. Farmer.*"

"That young doctor? The blond one? With the little wife that—"

Janie broke in. "He changed his name from *Farbenstein.*"

"*What?*" It was a shriek of dismay.

"Farbenstein. F-A-R-B-E-N-S-T-E-I-N."

"You're kidding! You've got to be just kidding!"

"I am not kidding," said Janie with immense satisfaction, "and I know what I'm talking about."

Mabel seemed to spend a few moments thinking it over. "How'd you find out?"

"Tell me who gave you a t.d. for me?"

"Can't."

"Just take my word then. It's Dr. Farbenstein."

"Are they both ...? I mean, is *she* ..."

"They only marry each other. So of course she is."

"I've got her on my Ways and Means. I've got her on the Committee to Improve Housing for Elders. She's even ... oh, my God ..."

"What is it?"

"The Martin Luther Hospital Benefit."

"So what? What's so cat's-pajamas about the Hospital Benefit?"

"Martin Luther, you ninny."

"Well ..." Janie thought all at once that Mabel actually was kind of over-reacting, kind of overdoing it. "Still, so what?"

"Don't so *what* me!"

"She won't damage your old Martin Luther."

"Oh, Janie! It's the idea!"

"What's my t.d.?" Janie demanded flatly.

It seemed to take a while for Mabel to get her thoughts straightened around, after finding out about Dr. Farmer. "Well, someone was saying—

I'm not mentioning names … Oh, doggonit, Janie, I don't feel like talking about it now."

"You promised," said Janie grimly.

"You've made a wreck of my day."

"The t.d."

"Well, *someone* was saying about how kind you were, and they were using as an example how nice you've been to that little Mrs. Renick. When the rest of us held back, because—you know—"

"Because the rest of you were running after Mrs. Dr. Farmer."

"No, no. Now doggonit, don't rub it in! But there was *someone else* there, and they were kind of criticizing that book report you gave a couple of weeks ago … you know, that historical novel by what's-his-name; and this other *person*, your real friend—not me, it wasn't I, don't think it—I was ready to pitch in but this other *person* got in ahead of me—"

"My real friend," said Janie softly.

"Now, look."

"I know you're slow on the uptake," said Janie, deciding to be forgiving. "And the reason I was nice to that wife of Warren's is because, my gosh, someone had better be. You and the rest of the girls seem to have kind of forgotten who Warren Renick *is*."

"We were just using … uh … good judgment."

"You were giving that girl the cold shoulder," said Janie calmly. "Now, Mabel, I've got an idea, something that's sort of been on my mind for a few days. Something I want us to do—just you and me."

"Just you and *I?*" cried Mabel, still stung over Ronald's being a doctor while Sam was merely a financial genius.

"We've got all summer. Club will soon be over until fall."

"So?"

"You just ease Mrs. Farmer out of those committees one by one. Nicely and sweetly. Like saying there's been a temporary hitch about having her name approved."

"She'll catch on."

"I know. Probably. But you ease her out and you get in that young Mrs. Renick, you get Warren's wife in there or, I'm telling you, someday the roof could even fall in on *Sam!*"

"My Sam? Oh, Janie, there's no more chance of Warren hurting Sam than there is of that new Dr. Farmer putting your Ronnie out of business. And anyway I just don't discuss—"

"Money? You aren't interested in *money?*"

She heard Mabel's long, breathy, frustrated sigh in the phone.

"You know who owns that bank," Janie said softly. "You mean to tell me Sam might never need any financial assistance? That he's right up there ... invulnerable?"

"Oh, all right. *All right!*"

"Mostly, I guess, I think that girl got a dirty deal in a way. She can never have any kids married to Warren. And that's what you look forward to, when you're young. I know I did. Even though they ... in the end, they never came."

Humble now, because she had sat beside Janie on some long nights while Janie cried, Mabel said, "Yes, I remember." She hesitated for a moment, and wondered if Janie felt the tug of old memories, old dreams, even as she. "Janie, is it okay if I let Mrs. Farmer stay on the Housing for Elders? We've already had one meeting and she sort of ... she had some really good ideas."

Janie, softened, relenting, said, "Yes, and keep her on the Ways and Means. That's dull as ditchwater and Warren's wife would go to sleep. But you put that girl on the Martin Luther Benefit!"

Mabel sighed again. "Okay."

When the conversation was finished, with an agreement to meet at lunch downtown, Janie sat peacefully smoking at the little desk. She could picture Mabel, in *her* kitchen, finishing up *her* cigarette. Mabel's kitchen was much bigger than this one, ridiculously huge, in fact, with an enormous brick barbecue built in alongside the range, and opening at the end into a lanai where there were a lot of planter boxes and a fountain and game equipment. Sam's ideas.

Then Janie thought about Dr. Farmer. There was actually much less malice in her attitude than she had displayed in talking to Mabel. She had dressed up the bit about Farmer's name to get a bigger rise out of her friend. Thinking about it now, Janie sort of liked Dr. Farmer the better for having changed it; he had showed good sense, and a shrewd, appraisal of the town and who mattered in it.

I ought to make an appointment with Dr. Farmer, Janie thought, *and see if he can find out why I sometimes have those pains down there. All my friends go to Ronnie, but of course I can't.*

Grizzie was using the vacuum at the front of the house, and the faraway buzz was a part of the peacefulness and the comfort here.

I have a lovely home, Janie thought, eyes half-shut, dreamy. *A lovely home and a social life, and a good husband.*

Looking forward into the day—the prospect of lunch with Mabel and then the style show at Harrigan's, and some bridge later at Vivian's house—she was aware of a feeling of gratitude toward Ronnie.

She could have been an old maid ... in fact, she was sort of on her way to being an old maid when Ronnie had asked her. And an old maid, money or no money, in this town was *nobody*. Look at Caroline Huff and those Pekingese, for example. Or Julia Leffingwell and her Worldwide Orphans. Just passing the time. Outside looking in.

She and Ronnie had never had children, but the raw grief over that had subsided into regret.

Not that there hadn't been rough spots. Her heart still thumped a little when she remembered that young widow, almost five years ago now, a black-haired girl with a haughty face who'd gone to Ronnie because of a whiplash injury caused in an auto accident. For months Janie had been terribly frightened. She had even lost weight. She had wanted to talk to Ronnie about the girl, but the fear was too deep, too paralyzing.

Ronnie had drunk a lot during those months—something utterly out of character for him—and one night he had cursed her.

But then miraculously, the widow had suddenly married somebody else and things at home had gradually returned to normal.

Janie started to get up from beside the desk, and brushed the cigarette on the housecoat again, leaving a long smear of ash on top of the earlier smudge. She brushed her bosom hastily, but the ashy smudge didn't go away and after a moment Janie proceeded to ignore it.

Lisa Kim had to study for a test that afternoon. She sealed the last of the statements and stacked the envelopes, put the cover on the typewriter. Behind the file cabinet was a private nook with a big chair, a small table with dictionary, thesaurus, and an ash tray, and a pole lamp. It was understood that when you settled yourself in the tiny nook you were, for all practical purposes, away from the shop and not to be disturbed.

It saved having to go back to the apartment to study, since the campus was in the opposite direction.

Karen was wiping out some goldfish bowls which had collected dust. "Lisa, before you open your book, there's something I want to ask. I meant to ask about it before. Down in the dragon's den, there's a place, a bricked-up part. It looks as if it might have been a closet."

Lisa was at the file cabinet, reaching up to take the two biology texts off the top. For a minute—a few seconds longer than necessary, perhaps—she remained there with her hands on the books.

"Do you know what's behind those bricks?" Karen asked.

"I think it must be a place where the wall needed to be braced," Lisa said, turning around with the texts in her hands.

"You mean, it's ... it's just cement in there?" Karen wondered, trying to figure it out.

"I'm not sure."

Lisa liked to play-act the inscrutable Oriental, but what she was doing now, Karen realized, was trying to be inscrutable without Karen's knowing it. Karen said, "Is it some kind of secret?"

This must have put Lisa on some kind of spot; she seemed to be trying to make up her mind, searching for something to say.

"It's either a secret or it isn't," Karen pointed out.

Lisa smiled, throwing her a quick undecided glance. "A long, long time ago there was a family conference. I remember it. I was very small, but still I remember. My two uncles came, and my grandfather. I remember thinking how terribly old Grandfather was. It must have been about the time we were ready to move out of the rear part of the store and go to live in the apartment, because the partition wall had been destroyed. There was a lot of rubble on the floor. And still ... most of the furniture was still here...."

Karen felt a little uncomfortable. She had intended mildly to tease Lisa, and now something seemed to have opened up, something Lisa didn't remember too well and which, from her tone, bothered her.

"My father and my uncles and my grandfather sat around the dining table. Over there." Lisa pointed to a spot midway between the desk and the rear door. "My mother and I didn't have any place to go where we would have been out of earshot, and so we sat by the wall and kept very still, and I think the idea was, we weren't really supposed to listen. You see, my parents, even though both of them were born here and were very American in all ways, still respected my grandfather very much. And so while he lived they tried to show respect, too, for the old ways. And it's funny—I've just remembered something—but my mother wore a brocade shift and pantaloons, a Chinese woman's garb, the day Grandfather was here. And there were things in her hair. Pins. I'd never seen them before. I never saw them afterwards, either."

Karen was looking, fascinated, at the spot where the table had once stood. In her mind's eye she could imagine Mr. Kim and his brothers, the ancient grandfather, very dark and wrinkled and thin of hair. What had they talked about?

Startlingly, Lisa answered the question as though Karen had spoken it aloud. "I don't know what they talked about. I learned very little Chinese. Just a few respectful greetings and such. But they were all very serious, and they seemed to do a lot of thinking. I remember that later—perhaps a year or so afterward—I had decided that the talk had been about our moving, not living in the rear of the shop anymore, and some work that had been done in the cellar."

One of Lisa's slim brown hands stroked the cover of her biology text.

"There was something more, too. Something I didn't understand then and don't understand now. I always meant to ask my father about it, but he died suddenly and the chance was gone."

The shop seemed very still, as if waiting.

"For some reason, the family had suffered a disgrace. I remember my mother telling me, if the other children teased me, I wasn't to answer, and I was to come home unless it was at school, and then I must go where I could be alone, and ignore them. But no one ever teased me. So I never knew what the disgrace was. I don't think my father and mother felt it as much as Grandfather. You know, to the Chinese, the shortcomings of one reflect on the whole family. But my father and mother had gotten away from many of the old beliefs."

Karen said, "You thought the conference had something to do with that bricked-up place in the cellar? What had the dragon's den looked like before?"

"I don't know. When I was small I was never allowed down there."

Five

Karen lit a cigarette. She wondered for a moment why Marlie Renick hadn't called back yet. Then her thoughts returned again to the puzzle of the dragon's den. "What about your uncle? Couldn't you ask him about what you remember, piece out the rest of it?"

Lisa nodded. "I have thought about it, more than once. But then, perhaps I'm not supposed to know. And if that's the case, Uncle Lee wouldn't tell me. He'd just look at me—you know the way he can look— and I'd feel very young and foolish."

A couple of the canaries decided to sing, trying to outdo each other, and for several minutes the little shop reverberated with trills and crescendos, and sharp single notes that punctured the stillness like the point of a knife.

When the two had quieted a little, Lisa said, "There is something I've wanted to do. Get a little pick of some kind and loosen a couple of those bricks and take them out and use a flashlight just to have a look in there."

"You think it's hollow?"

"I don't know what it is."

"Why did you say it must be a place where the wall had weakened and needed to be braced?"

"It's what I tell myself," Lisa admitted dryly.

"I don't know whether I like that idea of peeking in there," Karen said after a moment. "Something spooky about that idea. Suppose we found something awful?"

"I'm sure there isn't anything really awful," Lisa assured her.

Karen folded the cloth she had used to dust the fish bowls, put it away on a low shelf. She kept listening, expecting the phone to ring. Marlie had said she would call again in ten minutes, but it was long past time now. Lisa had to study for the test. Karen herself had classes from eleven to one. If Marlie wanted to see her—

Lisa broke in on her thoughts. "My father was a good, kind man, Karen. I wish you might have known him, really known him. He wouldn't have kept this shop all those years, and left it to me, with something horrible down there in the dragon's den."

"That makes sense," Karen agreed, wondering why she had brought up the subject of the brick wall in the first place, and sorry because it seemed to have carried disturbing memories for her friend.

She had a sudden vivid picture, though, of herself and Lisa, down in the cellar, removing some bricks, shining a light in and finding ... *what?* And the sensation she felt then was goose-pimpling.

The telephone rang, and it was Marlie Renick. She would be downtown in fifteen minutes and could Karen go somewhere and have a cup of coffee with her?

It was an hour and a half before Karen got back. Lisa wasn't in the study nook, since one couldn't see the front door from it; she was at the desk with one of the books open, studying.

Karen came in quietly. She put her purse away in the lowest drawer of the file cabinet and then just stood there staring at Lisa Kim.

"What's the matter? You look kind of ... sick."

"Lisa, do you know of an ... an ab—" The word stuck and Karen had to give it a second try. She grimaced as if at a bitter taste. "... an abortionist here in town, or anywhere close by, or ..." She just quit talking and went on looking at Lisa.

On her part, Lisa seemed to struggle with something like an unexpected blow, or a sudden revelation, shocking, brutal. The hands holding the textbook began to shake. "Why should I ... Why do you ask me? *Me?*"

"I don't know one," Karen said simply. "I just don't know of one anywhere."

"Why ask me?" Lisa persisted, her tone rising, sharpening. A swift anger, almost rage, flooded her face. She started to rise from the chair. "I said, why are you asking *me?*"

"And I told you, I don't know of one. And a friend of mine needs one. Or she thinks so ..." Karen leaned against the filing cabinet; she shut her eyes and rubbed a hand across them. "Oh, God."

Lisa's face cleared all at once. Slowly she sat down again. "You went to talk to Marlie Renick. You hadn't heard from her for a long time. The call surprised you. You couldn't imagine what Marlie wanted. That's it, isn't it?"

"Yes."

"I don't see the difficulty. Why can't she have Warren Renick's child? Is something seriously the matter with her? But no, she'd have a doctor of her own and it's not impossible ..."

The canaries were quiet; there was only the chirp and flutter of the parakeets at the front of the shop.

"It's not Renick's child, then."

"No, it's not."

"Why can't she just ... lie a little?" Lisa wondered.

In a dry thick tone, Karen said, "Warren Renick is sterile."

"Oh." Lisa's breath went out with a rush. Suddenly she looked almost as sick as Karen. "I liked her. I never knew her, really, except just to say hello to, in high school. But she seemed like a ... a clean sort of girl."

"She doesn't deserve this."

"Well, still, perhaps Renick would agree to some kind of compromise, passing the child off as his own—"

"It's not just her husband," Karen said. "This happened to him when he was eleven or twelve, some complication of an illness he had then, and Marlie's sure that everyone who knew the family at that time—and that means all the old families out along Old Mill River Road—that they know, too."

"What a mess."

"She looks beautiful," Karen went on, as if still not quite believing the interview she'd had with Marlie. "She wears her clothes nicely. There's nothing wrong-side-of-the-tracks about her. She has poise ..."

"Take my advice," Lisa said, her tone grown much quieter. "Stay out of this thing. Keep away from her."

"How can I do that?" Karen asked incredulously.

"I don't know, but do it. This thing can't end well. You know it. A bad ending is inevitable. And don't let it be blamed on you, Karen."

"She's going to do something pretty desperate before long. I *have* to help her!"

"No, you don't."

"There's no one else she can turn to. Just me."

"She has a mother somewhere here in town."

"She can't go to her mother except as a last resort."

Lisa's tone took on an added urgency, almost a note of fear. "Just believe me—believe me this one time, Karen—someday she'll hate you for helping her get rid of her baby."

"It's not what I *want* to do," Karen said. "I tried to reason with her. I brought up every argument I could think of. Mostly I tried to make her see that it will be murder. The murder of someone innocent and helpless." All at once, standing there looking very frightened, Karen began to cry.

Lisa sat silent for a while. Then she said, "Do as I tell you. Don't see her, don't talk to her again."

"Suppose she k-kills herself?" Karen wiped away the spilling tears with the back of her hand. "How will I feel then?"

Lisa sat hunched over, not looking at Karen now. "Don't find an abortionist for her. She'll never forgive you. And you won't forgive yourself."

It seemed to Karen, even upset as she was, that there was something strange and unspoken in the room, a near-visible presence, something from the past, from Lisa's past. Lisa's manner seemed to be telling her something, telling it without words, and the lovely Chinese eyes weren't inscrutable at all. They were full of pain and of some horror from the past.

Karen went back into the study nook and sat down, trying to control her own anxiety, and the tears.

Lisa came to stand at the corner by the file cabinet. "Karen, a million things happen every day that we can't do anything about. Kids are beaten. Animals are abused. Men die without reason or justice. And these things we had better not worry about, or we'll go crazy."

Karen nodded.

"Promise me," Lisa insisted, her tone tough and yet pleading, "that you won't do what Marlie Renick wants you to do."

"I can't promise. I have to think about it."

Lisa kept looking at her, as if to force the promise out of her by the power of that look, but Karen just went on wiping tears away.

"You're going to be late for your eleven o'clock. Can you afford a cut today?"

"I'm going. In a minute, I'll start getting ready."

Lisa turned and went back to the desk and the open biology book. She sat down, but she no longer read. The shop grew very quiet. No customers came in and even the birds were silent.

In the kitchen of the house on Edwards Street, James Griffin worked at the table with pencil and T square on a large piece of tagboard. He was drawing a map of Lisa Kim's shop, both on the street floor and the cellar. He took frequent glances at the scribbled notes and drawings that he had made in the car as soon as he had left the shop.

He made several erasures on the tagboard and then sat frowning.

He was going to have to have another good look at the shop. There were spots here he couldn't fill in. The trip he had made had been too hurried, and he'd tried to take in too much all at once. Most of all—he smiled wryly to himself—the girl had thrown him off. It had been hard not to look at her all of the time he'd been there.

He put down the pencil, took cigarettes and a matchpack from his shirt pocket, and went to the open kitchen door and looked out through the screen at the sunlight, and stood there to have a smoke.

Outside, the yard was a mess. This place had gone through the hands of a succession of tenants, obviously, and just as obviously none of them had been yardkeepers. A couple of starved lantana bushes crowded rankly against the back fence, and moved by a kind of pity, James Griffin went outside and found the old hose and connected it to a faucet and let the water run to give them a drink. The lantana had threatened to spill over into the neighbor's yard and Griffin could see where it had been severely hacked. The rest of the yard was covered with dead grass and weeds.

Tomorrow he'd get someone with a tilling machine to come out and break up the heavy earth. Then he could go back to Lisa Kim's shop.

He was going to have to plan this second trip carefully in order to get as much from it as possible.

It had been a remarkable break, his getting this kind of place and then finding out that the shop now carried garden supplies. The letter from his stepfather hadn't mentioned anything but a pet store. With the kind of yard he had here, it would be logical to pay several visits to the Kim shop. First the soil had to be dug up and prepared—and why not go back and ask the girl about someone to do it? Then a lot of manure and other junk was plainly needed, to be followed at last by the new plantings. They didn't carry much in the way of actual outdoor plants, he had noted, mostly house stuff; but there was no reason the girl who had taken him down in the cellar couldn't give advice.

Maybe he could even ask her out here and have her look at the yard. Would she come?

Lighting a new cigarette, sitting down on the back steps, Griffin imagined himself showing her this horrible yard.

The girl had been the unexpected element, the surprise, the thing that didn't fit and that now he didn't want to fit. She was outside, far beyond the outline of this ... well, call it a crime. He didn't think of what he intended to do as a crime; but then for a long time the edges of right and wrong, of must-do and don't-do, had been pretty fuzzy and intermingly.

You might say, he decided, that he was floating on a river and that the river had begun to meander, cutting old banks and changing the familiar countryside into something new and insubstantial and grotesque.

Was the girl employed at the shop by Lisa Kim? Somehow the shop didn't seem as if it would support paid help.

Perhaps the Chinese girl had found an optimistic partner.

That could be it, he thought. It would explain the little expansion into plants and fertilizers, a search for something more to sell in the limited space, a small addition to the profits. But still—he shook his head—if the two were living off the shop they were far from being in a high income bracket.

He was curious about the girl, the brown-haired girl who smiled more on one side than she did on the other, when she smiled—and had anyone ever told her so?—and he wondered what her motives had been, to go into Lisa Kim's shop. He sensed, without knowing why, that the shop filled a gap and was a means to an end. So what was the girl really after?

Perhaps she was just passing the time, like some girls did, fooling around until she got married. Had she worn an engagement ring? He felt a sudden angry impatience with himself for not having noticed what was on her finger.

Perhaps there had been a wedding band …

This idea caused him to jerk erect and to toss away the cigarette. Was she one of the bored young marrieds who have to have a job, any job, in order to feel alive? The ones who can't stand housework because it isn't a career?

No. Not this girl.

After some thought, he decided that he would have noticed a wedding band automatically, and would have classified her at once as being taken. In spite of his preoccupation with the measurements and contents of the shop, he wouldn't have missed that.

I'll have to find out her name.

I can ask her. Or I can find out from someone else before I go there. I can greet her by name; and surprise her.

He thought then: *Whatever may happen later, I don't want her to be involved in it.*

Wouldn't you think they'd be wary of taking anyone down in that cellar? The Chinese girl must know what had happened there.

And what might happen again …

The female barracuda hadn't even waited for Dr. Ferrie's business day to end. She came tripping in at a quarter past twelve, wearing the geranium-pink sweater and the tight brown skirt. Her thighs looked firm, round, shapely inside the brown corduroy and the sweater was so tight across her breasts they didn't even bounce.

Ferrie was at the receptionist's desk looking for a certain file. He looked up when Betsy came in. "What in the hell are you doing here?"

"Your nurse came into Charlie's. I was there having a bromo. She said she had a headache and then she told Charlie something else. She said she had the rest of the day off and thank God because today you'd been horrible." Betsy the barracuda came close and tried to cup Ferrie's face between her soft young hands. "Are you really horrible today? Are you mean and awful?"

He struck her hands away. The surge of pressure, the pounding, came into the space behind his eyes and for a moment he saw great red waves of light, like the apex of a forest fire, or of Hell. If he could have had Spilling there in that moment he could have killed her.

"She's kind of unprofessional, isn't she, talking out in public like that?" All of Betsy's ideas of the medical and nursing professions were garnered from watching television; but here she was on sound footing. "I don't think it can be according to the rules."

"Why are you here now, in the middle of the day?"

"She's gone, isn't she? You're all alone?" Betsy leaned on the edge of the desk and slyly, carefully, undid the top button of the pink sweater.

There were still so many things to decide …

There was so little time …

"He told you to come here at noon," Ferrie decided. "It's a way of putting more pressure on, of increasing the danger. A way of finding more money in his pockets, you might say. Wouldn't you say, Betsy?" He reached out and grabbed the front of the sweater and pulled it open all the way down, the buttons popping out of the wool with a tiny series of soft little *bumps*. Betsy looked down at the silk slip and her own soft flesh, and giggled. "He put you up to it. Button up your clothes, Miss Barracuda. You look lewd."

Unperturbed, still smiling, the big brown eyes still filled with the light of admiring mischief, Betsy slipped the buttons back into their knitted holes. She had to tug the pink wool across her bosom to make the two edges meet. "You are horrible today. But I still love you. I still think you're adorable. You're cross, and adorable, and antiseptic, and grim, and intelligent. You can shoot me, baby. And then we can go back to the examination rooms. There are three examination rooms but we'll only need one."

"I won't give you drugs in the middle of the day and have you weaving out of here in broad daylight."

"I don't weave. I just feel good inside, all tingly and good."

He slammed the drawers shut and stood there looking at her. She was beautiful. She had skin the color of cream. Her hair was washed with silk and gold, and her mouth had a soft hurt look like a child's. It was too bad, Ferrie thought as usual, and regretfully, that she couldn't belong to him, that she had to belong to a hypodermic needle and the male barracuda, and that Ferrie himself was only given the loan of her at frequent intervals as you might pass another man a pack of cigarettes and let him help himself.

She came closer, an air of caution under the mischief and the pretend-love. "Shoot me, baby."

He thought of the idea that had come to him this morning, to load her veins with something lethal. *Have to have time to think that over.* "Come back after five o'clock."

"Now."

He hit her across the face with the back of his hand, seeing the flare of shock and stunned pain in her eyes, hating her, hating himself, and hating all the days that had led up to this one.

He grabbed her, turned her and walked her stiff-legged to the door and shoved her out into the hall. The light from the stair-well threw her shadow against him, made a nimbus of her hair.

"Don't!"

"Go tell him it didn't work."

"He didn't send me. Please, please! Why do you think I needed the damned bromo a few minutes ago? I'm dying!"

He slammed the door.

… And you know how long I've been in this place, Jimmy, and so you might think I'm not up to date about the bank and the town. That maybe what I think I know isn't true anymore. That things have been changed. Well, let me tell you, I keep my ears open and I've got friends. I've got friends a lot closer to that bank than I am now. And they pass me the news. You'd be surprised at the amount of news that seeps in through these old walls.

That's why I know about the smog and the traffic these days down around L.A., and how this particular town still stays clean and kind of old-fashioned, with the same wide streets and the big trees, not even a freeway through the place yet. That's how I know the rich people still live out along Old Mill River Road. Other places, you know, the rich district gets all built-up and then the young rich move on, and the new spot gets more stylish, and then after a few years—my God, the places I've seen it happen; I must really be an old duffer, Jimmy—anyway, after a few years the old district where the rich used to live gets to be a slum or it gets built up with big apartments. That's the pattern. It happened in the town where I was born, back in Oklahoma, and it happened in L.A., and if you want to see the results just drive out and take a look at what used to be called the Wilshire District.

Believe it or not, your Ma and I once had the idea of living out on Old Mill River Road. You were just two years old and you'd been sick and your Ma wanted to get you out of town. I was in the chips then, I had a couple of good things going for me. I know you don't remember anything about those days but it's the truth, we did look at some property once, a nice piece of land out on Old Mill River Road. I can't recall why we didn't buy it.

The funny thing about that town, the pattern changed downtown. They crowded out the Chinese. I doubt if there's a Chinese store left in that whole block, except for the Kim girl's pet store.

Most of the Chinese I've known, I got acquainted with through gambling. They're great gamblers. Most of them, though, were what you'd call working-stiff types. I never knew one to be in the rackets. Of course there was that one, the Kim family figured he'd disgraced them, but I'll get back to him later. Besides being strong for gambling, I think the Chinese are secretive. A good word; I looked it up and it means what I want: they mind their own business and keep their mouths shut.

The Chaplain here keeps saying a whole race of people don't share a single quality, like all the French are maybe not such good cooks, but this is my opinion and I'll stick by it. The Chinese are a secretive race and a lot of the old-timers among them would rather conduct their business in such a way that no one saw them going and coming. Maybe they brought the idea from China, or maybe it came about because of the way some of the white people treated them. Anyway, they often connected their places of business, and often with a tunnel. You're way, way too young to remember any gossip about the broken tunnels they found in Frisco's Chinatown after the big quake in 1906. There must have been a horrible howl that went up all over the country, because my folks talked about it, and this was in Oklahoma. White slave traps, and other bogeyman yarns. I was too little to know what a white slave was, and I used to crawl into bed at night scared stiff, looking for some Chinaman to come and grab me and carry me off to his little secret tunnel. Cook and eat me, I guess I expected.

The Old Man of the Kim family harked right back to whatever part of China the family came from. Maybe he's the one who had the tunnel built. Later on there was a stairway, too, though I'm not sure how long that lasted.

The bank was at fault, too, of course. They should have investigated those walls. It cost them. There's sixty-nine thousand dollars gone that never was seen again.

Sixty-nine thousand isn't much compared to what's inside the bank vault. But you might just keep in mind, it's possible that the bundle, almost twenty years old now, is still somewhere in the cellar...

THURSDAY

Six

She awake, and the room was bright with morning, and Warren was propped up on an elbow looking at her from the other side of the bed. There was a small space between them as if he had wanted some perspective on her. He looked ruddy and vital as always but there was something uncertain, undecided, and worried in his eyes.

Marlie's throat dried out instantly with fear. She wondered what he had seen, what secrets her sleeping face might have betrayed. She couldn't even manage a smile. Her eyes locked on his and she lay still.

"Hello, darling," he said. His voice was kind, soft, quiet. It made Marlie want to cry. She wanted to weep, and to creep close to him and to whisper the terrible secret.

But she couldn't. She was fixed here like a woman of ice.

"Do you know what I did yesterday?"

She managed to shake her head, her hair sliding on the pillow. Her heart was pounding now, the dreadful thump and bump beating inside her like a clenched fist.

"I went to see Dr. Ferrie."

If he had picked up a sledge hammer from the floor on the other side of the bed, and had hit her right between the eyes with it, she couldn't have felt a greater sense of poleaxed shock. The bed, the pillow, even Warren's face, seemed to expand suddenly in some vacuum in which she lay suspended, slack, dying, immobile. There was nothing beneath her, nothing beside her, nothing above her. She floated, the icy body breathless, brain in a state of paralysis.

"Do you know what he said?" Warren's voice went on, as though the room and the bed and she were all unchanged. "He asked me how much recreation you'd had recently. Did we go out much? And did you have a chance now and then to be with people your own age? He made me see things a little differently, Marlie. He made me understand how selfish

I've been. Of course I told him about your Tahoe jaunt with those youngsters you'd known in high school. Less than a week at the lake … how long ago now? Two months? Almost three?"

Two months and two weeks, Marlie wanted to say. *Two months and two weeks old …*

"And he thought it wasn't enough. He was interested and he wanted to be helpful, but he thought he'd better see you. In a day or so, I guess he's kind of busy now. Just call his nurse and make an appointment."

Warren stopped talking and the room filled with an eerie, vibrating silence.

"I can't have you looking sad and run-down," he added, when Marlie said nothing. "This has to work, kitten. I had one marriage and it didn't work, and when she died I said I'd never marry again, and then I met you. And you mean everything to me. You literally are the world for me, Marlie."

The look he bent on her was so full of love and compassion that Marlie tried to make her terribly dry throat and her cottony mouth perform, and tell him the truth so that he would turn away and take that look off her.

He reached an arm, and took up one of her hands. "If you want to make a trip somewhere, we can do that. Things aren't so busy at the bank that I can't take time off. We could fly to Hawaii, or Mexico City. They're just minor hops now, with the jets."

Her eyes swam with tears, and a tear crept out of a corner of her eye to drop into her hair. Warren saw it and frowned, not in anger, but in worry and concern.

In the desperate moment, Marlie remembered. *Karen.*

Karen would help her, save her.

Karen would save Warren from that terrible look she had pictured on his face, the look of sick disaster and unbelievable loss …

She heard herself whispering, "Could we really go … to Hawaii?"

"You'd like that?" He moved closer, the look of worry fading.

"Oh, yes." She lifted his hand, put it against her cheek. Some of the pounding fright went away, now that she had remembered Karen and their talk yesterday in the café. Things could turn out all right. Karen was her friend. She could trust Karen to help her. Suddenly it seemed quite possible that shortly she and Warren could be in Hawaii, could be lying in the sun on one of those wonderful beaches. She could even imagine the lazy contentment, the warmth, the well-being.

Free by then of course of this inside her …

She couldn't imagine how that would happen. Her mind refused to create an image. It would be some kind of surgery, an operation, metallic instruments stuck inside her, pain perhaps; she turned fearfully from the thought.

Warren began to kiss her gently, and she moved into his arms.

At ten o'clock she was dressing to go downtown, to drop in on Karen at the shop, when Suzabell rapped at the bedroom door and looked in. "Mr. Bonnay is downstairs. You want to see him?"

Marlie already had on her slim blue sheath, the white pumps, and she was at the dresser, leaning toward the mirror to rearrange a few locks of her tawny hair, a brush in one hand and a can of hair spray in the other. She looked over her shoulder at Suzabell's brown face across the room, feeling nothing for a moment but a surge of irritated astonishment. What business had Tod Bonnay coming here? She hated him.

"He apologized for not calling on the phone first," Suzabell said. She kept all expression off her face and something in her manner indicated a dislike for Mr. Bonnay. Marlie couldn't help but wonder why, even as a sense of alarm began to stir. Tod usually made an excellent first impression. People liked him, felt at ease with him. Suzabell usually judged people by their politeness, their charm and social know-how, and Tod Bonnay was loaded with all of them.

"I'll see him on my way out, I guess," Marlie said uncertainly, trying to figure out whether Suzabell thought she should see him or not, and what might be behind Suzabell's antagonism. "Where is he?"

"In the hall."

"That's all right."

An evil glint came into Suzabell's eyes, as if Tod's being left to stand in the hall was exactly what she had expected. "You look nice in blue, Mrs. Renick. Real nice."

"Thank you, Suzabell."

"Will you be back for lunch, do you think?"

Marlie stared at her reflection, trying to think. She had hopes that Karen would have good news for her, that they might go somewhere, a coffee shop as they had yesterday, and make plans to do what was necessary.

Would Karen think that Marlie was rushing her, that she was asking the impossible?

"I ... I guess not. Don't fix anything. If I do come home, I'll get a snack from the refrigerator."

"Fine." Suzabell shut the door.

Marlie finished fixing her hair, picked up her purse and a pair of short white gloves. She left the bedroom and walked to the carpeted landing. From the landing you could see part of the hall below.

Tod Bonnay was down there. He had one hand in his jacket pocket and he was snapping the fingers of his free hand as if in time to some tune running through his head. His hair was a little darker than Marlie's. She could see one side of his head from above, the smooth hair brushed back, the line of the jaw, a cigarette held loosely. All at once a kind of panic seized her, and she wondered if she were able to go down there and face him with composure, with indifference. She hadn't seen him since the time at Tahoe, but the impact of those meetings was roaring down upon her like a tidal wave.

She clung to the balustrade, and then he turned and looked up at her. He quirked one eyebrow, took the cigarette from his mouth and said quietly, "Hi, there."

It was unbelievable, but she had forgotten a little how he looked. She had forgotten the focus of his features, the way that the gray eyes, the quizzical mouth, the slant of temple and cheekbone all led your eye to his deeply indented chin, to the cleft like a knife-cut that made his face a mask both of bedeviled humor and sensuality.

"Hello," she said, starting down the stairs.

He met her at the foot of the stairs. "We need to talk a little bit. Somewhere kind of lonely. Just you and I."

She stammered the words one by one. "I … don't … have … anything … to … say… to … you.…"

"No, but I have something to say to you. To be grim about it, something kind of private. Away from your little brown hen."

"Suzabell?"

"Or whoever. The watchdog."

"I'm on my way. Walk out with me to the garage, to my car."

He swung her around by the arm, so that she faced him; she found his eyes frightening. "Let's don't brush this off. Let's act like a lady of the house and her welcome guest, shall we? Take me out to the lanai, or whatever you've got, and order me a drink.… Yes, I know it's just past ten in the morning, but I've been thinking hard, and I'm tensed-up. So move."

She tried to pull away. "Please just let me walk out to the garage, and you come too—"

"I said, it's not going to be that way." He pulled her closer still, and then quickly slipped a hand behind her head and forced her mouth against his own.

She had forgotten what that was like, too.

She was trembling. She felt behind her for the banister, the stairway. She wanted to run and could not.

"Where do you take casual drop-ins? Not upstairs?"

"No. This way." She forced herself to move, to leave the support of the banister and lead the way to the back of the house. A paved patio was sheltered under a fan of canvas wings. There were white wrought-iron tables and chairs, strange potted plants whose names Marlie didn't know, another pool, this one an opal teardrop under the brilliant colors of the canvas.

She gestured awkwardly. "Take any chair. I'll bring your drink."

He sat down and leaned back, narrowing his eyes at her. "If you try to run out on me, Marlie, you'll be sorry. I hate to tell you how sorry you'll be."

"I'm not going to run out."

She left her purse and gloves on the table beside him and went off to the kitchen. She was terribly afraid now, her limbs wooden, a horrid quaking inside her like the working of a wobbly erratic clock. She opened Warren's liquor cabinet and stared at the bottles.

Where was Suzabell?

Upstairs, perhaps, working on the bedroom and their bathroom.

She took down a glass, got ice from the refrigerator. Out of the foggy confusion in her mind, a remembered fact emerged: Tod Bonnay liked what he called waterballs, Scotch with a dash of plain water over ice. She put in the Scotch, not measuring it, her hands shaking. She put in what looked like the right amount of water, and took the glass and went back to the patio.

He was lighting a fresh cigarette.

When she put the drink in front of him, he jerked a hand toward the opposite chair. He picked up the drink and took two swallows and she saw his eyes widen. "Damn."

"Is it too strong?"

He laughed. "You'd made a hell of a bartender. No, the drink's okay." He set the glass down, took the cigarette off the edge of the ash tray. "You saw Karen Evans yesterday, downtown."

He spoke quietly, without expression, and it took Marlie a moment to catch the change of subject. For some reason then, though he hadn't changed expression, and his eyes weren't even on her, she felt more frightened than ever.

"What were you telling her?" Tod Bonnay asked.

"We just ... We hadn't seen each other for a long time."

"Since when were you and Karen friends?"

"We've always been friends. That is, since grammar school, since about fifth or sixth grade and all through high school."

He was quiet then, and appeared to think this over. Perhaps he doubted it. He took the drink down by about a third, and then said, "So what was all the talking about?"

Marlie didn't answer at once. Some other things were coming back to her. When she and Karen had been in junior high school—about the eighth or ninth grade—Karen's father had been married for a while to Tod's mother. For how long? Marlie couldn't remember. A year? Two? During the time Karen's father had lived with Tod's mother, Karen had never asked her to her home, and that was funny too, now that she thought of it.

Tod Bonnay reached across the table to seize her wrist. "Come on!"

"What?"

"What did you and Karen talk about?"

Her thick tumbled wits would not produce a lie. She tried to evade. "Why do you ask? How do you even know that we ... we talked about anything?"

"A friend of mine, a little bird, happened to see you and Karen, and this friend—my canary friend—thought that the talk seemed extra long and full of meaning."

A sick weight settled in Marlie's body. Something dreadful was about to happen. But then she made a sudden resolve. Nothing—*nothing at all*—was going to force her to tell this man what she had told Karen yesterday. No threat, no abuse, no fright, would get it out of her.

He read the look she gave him and got up from the chair and came around the table toward her. Marlie stood up to meet him. Her legs were rubber and the thumping clockwork inside seemed about to pound her to pieces.

He stood over her, half-smiling, his eyes promising violence. "Tell me. What did you tell Karen about me?"

Again she felt disoriented, off balance. She must have shown her confusion and surprise. "About you? Nothing about you." She tried to step back, to get away from him, but the chair arm pressed her legs from behind.

"Don't lie, Marlie. You're not good at it."

"I'm not lying. Your name wasn't mentioned. Why should it be? I'd even forgotten, until a minute ago, that you knew Karen."

"My mother married her father. You knew that."

"I guess I did, once."

She thought he was about to say something more, and changed his mind. He shrugged, and went back to his chair, and without sitting down again he drained the glass. When he put the glass down he stood without speaking, finishing the cigarette, staring at her. His eyes roved her body and Marlie felt as if she were under some prying ray, all secrets laid bare; she wanted to crouch, to shelter herself from his look.

"I like your dress," he said finally. "You've got a good shape, baby."

She felt a hot flush race into her skin. She swallowed. It seemed to her that she had gained a short sweet tick of time, a little respite from danger, a brief comfort. A trap had been open at her feet but she hadn't fallen in. Not yet.

"I want you to stay away from Karen," he said, crushing out the cigarette. "Leave her alone. No more talks downtown over coffee. No more talks, anywhere, anytime. Do you understand me?"

She shook her head. "No."

"Very simple. Just don't see Karen again."

She wanted to stammer, but I *have* to see her; but his manner warned her. If she persisted in wanting to see Karen he would find a way to stop her. Not a nice way.

"And thanks for the drink, Mrs. Renick." He laughed at her under his breath, turned, and walked back through the house, disappearing from Marlie's stunned sight, leaving her there by the white iron table under the brilliant wing of canvas, nothing left of him but the faint cloud of cigarette smoke and the empty glass.

Marlie sat down. The whole interview seemed unreal now and out of focus, a poorly organized play in which she as an actress had said all of the wrong lines. And yet, being misspoken, it was all the more terrifying. A day would come in which all of the lines, his and hers, would fall right, and on that day she would die.

Why? ... Why did it have to be like this?

Why couldn't *he* die?

Her heart shook with the dark thought.

It came again. Why couldn't *he* die?

Seven

James Griffin walked into the shop just after noon, and found Karen at the desk eating a sandwich and a bag of potato chips, with an open thermos on the pile of books at her elbow. She recognized him and smiled, a smile that was both pleased and shy, and there was a funny regretful moment when Griffin wished that he had really come here just to ask about soil conditioners, or to see her again. But in his mind was the map, unfinished at home; and it was important not to forget what he had missed before.

She started to rise, but he shook his head. "No, sit down. I want to talk for a minute. I'll prop myself on the end of the desk."

"I could offer you half a sandwich. Or some chips."

"You mean, you throw in meals, too?"

"Oh, we try to serve the public as best we can."

"You're going too far."

She picked up the thermos cup. It had milk in it. She sipped from the rim of the cup, looking over it at him.

He said, "You didn't think I'd come back."

"Well … no. I thought you had decided to let your yard go its own way while you went yours. That's the policy out there where you live. I shouldn't criticize. Anything else is expensive and involves a lot of work.

"I have two fairly healthy lantana bushes."

"I'll bet you do. And what else?"

"Well, as a matter of fact—nothing."

"And how far do you want to go to get rid of … nothing?"

"I've been thinking it over." He found himself fascinated by the stack of books on the desk. They were college texts. If Karen Evans was trying to get through college, if Lisa Kim was too, then that could explain their efforts here, their toleration of small profits. "It occurred to me that if I could put in a good easygoing ground cover, I could gussie up the edges, concentrate on the borders, and have something not too awful."

She looked interested and impressed. "Yes, that's true. Once you get away from the idea of having a lawn, temperamental grass or dichondra, you've solved a lot of your problem. But I warn you, even ivy takes longer than usual out there unless the ground's broken up well before you plant."

"I'm going to have the place tilled. That's one reason I came back today, to ask if you knew someone with a machine."

She nodded, taking a bite of potato chip. "Lisa's uncle, the one I mentioned yesterday who has a pickup truck, can do it for you."

"Is he a gardener?" Griffin didn't want the job taken away from him entirely, turned over to someone else; that would mean no more trips here to ask advice, to study the stock, the stuff in the cellar.

"Not anymore. He hurt his back a few years ago, and he can't do anything heavy. But he works a day or two at a time, and he can come out and run a tilling machine over your clay stone yard."

"That's a good description of what I've got. I don't suppose … I guess this is really asking too much service … I don't suppose you'd come and look at my place."

She laughed a little. "It must be awful if you need the advice of somebody like me."

He nodded toward the stack of textbooks. "For all I know, you're a botany major with all sorts of exotic possibilities on tap in the way of greenery."

"No. I'm a speech major. I'm a speech major because I don't know, yet, what I really want to do. And so for now I'm doing debates and plays. After all, everyone has to argue and to dramatize a little, all of their lives."

He found himself laughing at her solemnity, at the direct and offhand way she had laid out her motives. He wondered what her real motives were. They went far below the surface nonchalance, he was sure. "Are you coming to look at my place?"

"Why not? When do you want me?"

"Are you busy this afternoon?"

She shook her head. "No. Lisa will be back by three. I don't have classes today—or rather, I've had them, early."

"I'll come by again at three. Do you mind if I go down and read the brand names, and the table of contents, on those sacks in your cellar?"

"No. I'd go with you but I really should stay here to watch the door." As he started for the rear stairs, she said, "Don't forget to switch on the light, there at the top of the steps."

He looked back at her. She had the smile, the smile that was wider on one side than on the other, that made her look as if she were playing a game or a trick, a very young sort of smile that could go away quickly. "Does the light make the Chinese dragon disappear?"

"It puts him back in the corner where he belongs."

Down in the cellar, he wasted no time or glance on the stacked peat moss and fertilizers along the left wall. He took an envelope and a pencil from his coat pocket and made a careful sketch of the floor area, including the section walled off by the brick. He estimated and wrote in the footage and he was most careful of the area at the rear, where all of the boxes and crates and barrels were stored, some of them seeming to teeter from the mere sound of his footfalls.

He kept an ear tuned for any sound from the stairs.

He didn't expect her to come down, however. When Karen Evans had said that she must stay up there to watch the door, she had looked over at the door, and Griffin remembered that look and tried to analyze it. Someone was coming in, someone was expected. And someone had Karen Evans kind of worried. Perhaps she would have betrayed even more worry, looking at the door, except that he'd been there watching.

Griffin had the feeling that the imagined river on which he floated was pushing a little faster now, the current strengthening, and that as the sandy banks broke and caved into the water, the scene around him changed by the moment. Karen Evans was worried, and this had more interest for him than the job he had to do, and even more than the possible close proximity of sixty-nine thousand bundled-up dollars; and even as he rapped the brick wall with his knuckles and listened for an inner echo, he was also somehow up there with her, wanting to comfort her because someone was coming and she wasn't ready to meet this person. The current was pushing him in a direction he hadn't intended to go, and the caving banks showed him a lost country, a land shrouded by time and memory and pessimism, the long-ago place where it was possible to love someone else and to care what happened to them, and for them to care about you in return.

He needed something more substantial than his knuckles to rouse an echo through the brick wall, if such were possible at all, and there was nothing heavy at hand and no time to look around through the junk at the rear of the cellar. Besides, Karen Evans might hear him and be very curious as to why he wanted to pound the wall down here.

He had found out her name from the florist shop, two doors away, and now remembered that he had intended to surprise and perhaps impress her a little, by addressing her as Miss Evans.

He decided that he could do it when he went back up. He walked over to the stairs, stood still, and listened to the sound of voices from above.

On Tuesdays and Thursdays, Karen had classes from eight until ten. She had hurried to the shop in order to allow Lisa to leave for school, and also with the thought that Marlie would call and that she would urge her to come downtown for another talk. But from ten-twenty until just past noon, when the stranger had reappeared, there had been eight or nine customers shopping briefly, and no phone calls at all.

The stranger had been down in the cellar for just a couple of minutes, and she was finishing the milk in the thermos, when a shadow darkened the door momentarily; someone looked in and then walked on. Sipping from the thermos cup, Karen had the startled impression that she knew who the outlined figure was. With a tightening of dread and apprehension, she put down the thermos cup, and as she had somehow expected, in a short while the figure returned. This time he walked on in, and it was as she had thought: Tod Bonnay had come.

After all the snarling ill-will, the accusations, the jeers, the not-quite-joking threats, it was practically beyond belief that Tod would show up here, simply walk in without warning.

When he got close enough so that he was not just a shadow against the brightness, Karen saw that he looked as usual; he wore a good sport jacket, good slacks, he was clean and smoothly barbered, bareheaded with well-brushed healthy blond hair, tanned, handsome.

When she had been much younger—about twelve, she thought—and her father had first brought Tod to the house, with his mother, and had introduced him to her, she had been instantly aglow and thought him the most handsome thing in the world, a god. How old had Tod been then? Seventeen? Now he was still handsome; his face had matured and held a mocking humor and wit ... sensuality, too. He had always had a way of holding his head back to look at her, jutting forward the big chin with its unnaturally deep cleft. He did this now, not speaking. He seemed to be waiting for her to speak.

"What on earth are *you* doing here?" Karen asked coldly.

He made a brief, abortive attempt to grin at her. "I just came to see you. To say hello. Uninvited. Unwanted. I've had a kind of ... of funny experience. Funny for me, that is. Completely out of my usual line. You could call it a change of heart—except of course no one thinks I've got a heart." He took a pack of cigarettes from his jacket pocket and Karen noticed with surprise that his hands shook. He had trouble then striking the match; he muttered in vexation around the cigarette between his lips. There was sudden sweat on his face. Karen had never known Tod to be at a loss, off balance, or put out in any way. Was this real? When he got the cigarette going, he said, "I'm ... I'm kind of tired of acting the hateful juvenile, Karen. It's not a role I have any appetite for, anymore. I guess you're getting ready to order me out of here. Can't blame you. I guess an apology on my part doesn't ..." He stopped as if he had run out of words, or as if embarrassment had overwhelmed him. The shop was quite still for a moment. "... doesn't mean anything, anyway."

In spite of all that had happened in the past, Karen felt a terrific rush of pity and compassion for him. He seemed like someone proud and highborn and invulnerable, suddenly come upon shocking days.

She rose from the chair. She didn't know what to say to him.

He looked down at the smoke rising from the cigarette in his hand and said, "I feel like a fool. I knew I would. But after I looked in, I couldn't just walk away and say, to hell with it, the way I wanted to. I had to come in and get it said, somehow."

Uncertainly, Karen answered, "I'm glad you came, Tod."

"I'm really sorry, Karen. I'm sorry for ... everything."

"I believe you are."

Her words, or perhaps her quiet tone, seemed to surprise him. "You aren't going to give me my just deserts, and all that?"

"No."

"You hate me, though. You've got to hate me. It's logical."

"I don't hate you. Do you want to sit down, Tod?"

"Well ... Really, you don't have to be decent and forgiving. I'd understand it if you weren't."

She took a birdcage off a stool and brought the stool over beside the desk. Tod sat down, awkward and apparently uneasy.

For a minute they watched each other, as if trying to understand what was supposed to come next, how the hostility and anger might be buried.

"Ever since Dad died," Karen said finally, "I've wished that we could have a talk, just quietly and calmly. Like friends, not like enemies. Of course, as long as Dad lived—"

"I know."

"There were so many things I wanted to ask you. And I couldn't. And then it seemed I had to fight you, because of Dad. I couldn't ask you to come and help me decide about Dad's estate, help me decide what should be done."

"I made sure you couldn't do that," he said bitterly. "Karen, I promise to undo, as much as I can, anything I might have said in anger. Actually I don't think people paid much attention to me. They put my ravings down to ... what prompted them."

She was aware of a stab of mistrust. He had skirted the word that had leapt into her mind. *They put my ravings down to ... greed.*

Greed?

"Part of the way I felt was due to a disappointment you might not believe," he was saying. "I had some crazy idea, for years, even after he and Mother split up, a weird notion that I was *still* going to win your dad's liking. Win his liking and his trust and his approval. I used to imagine myself, picture myself—fantasies, day-dreams—going to him to show him some remarkable thing I'd made, or done. In my imagination, then, the bars were always finally broken down and he came to regard me, or to halfway regard me, as a son. I'd redeemed myself, proven my worth."

Remembering her father's contemptuous scorn of Tod, his unfailing belittling of Tod at eighteen, nineteen, twenty, Karen felt a sense of shame, of deep regret.

"I know he thought I was just wasting time in college, but there were weeks and months when I worked like a dog, hoping to impress him with my good grades. And then he and I would have a ... a kind of collision. An argument. A fight. And the grades would drop like a kite tied to a brick. But still, I kept the ... the dream, or whatever you want to call it. I guess I just *had* to have an old man."

Karen was remembering, Tod's own father had died while he was still a baby. There had been plenty of money in Tod's young life, but no father.

She was also watching the cellar stairs, expecting the stranger to come up, to make himself visible. Was he actually eavesdropping? It seemed that he had to be.

"Your dad was just never impressed by anything I did. Not that I did much. And then when he died and I found out the terms of his will, especially the codicil that mentioned me, I just ... Oh, I don't know how to explain it, Karen. I wanted to hit back. All those years, and all that trying and hoping—I'd been a sap. He had hated me, despised me all along. He wouldn't have been impressed if I'd been the first man on the moon and had flown there by flapping my arms."

It was true. Karen wished that she could deny it, could prove that her father might have relented as far as Tod was concerned, but she knew better.

"Did your mother know how you felt?" Karen asked finally.

"I don't know. The marriage lasted such a short time, and she was so bitter.... I don't think she listened much to me. She had her own problems. I won't go into that."

Karen flushed. Tod's mother had claimed that she had loaned Karen's dad money which was her own, which she had received on the death of her first husband. Karen's father never admitted that this was true. He hadn't called his wife a liar, either. He had said she was mistaken, he had given her what the law said was her share of their community property. Two years later Tod's mother had killed herself in an accident with her new sports car.

The money left to Karen, when her father had died, now sat in the bank, drawing interest. Creating bitterness, too, Karen thought to herself. It was time to have a settlement with Tod, end the conflict.

"I'm glad you came in," Karen told Tod. "I wish we might talk longer now. But I think it might be better sometime tomorrow." He looked up at her quickly, his glance puzzled and a little suspicious; he thought she was trying to get rid of him. "I have classes tomorrow in the middle of the day, but then I'm free."

She reached over and put a hand on one of his, and his face cleared, the look of suspicion vanished.

"How about dinner?" he said.

"All right."

"Where shall I pick you up? Here? Or the apartment?"

"We stay open late on Friday," she said, "but it's Lisa's turn to keep the store. Why don't you come to the apartment around seven?"

When Tod had gone, the stranger came up promptly. He looked at her face, and shook his head. "I know. You think I stayed down there because it was all so fascinating. But after the first minute or two, I just didn't see how I could barge up and interrupt. It was a pretty embarrassing situation, but I could have made it worse."

"I guess so," she admitted coolly.

"Now I'm in bad with you," he said, his tone full of anger at himself.

"No, no, you're not."

"You'll still come out this afternoon to see my unpleasant yard?"

"Yes. After three, after Lisa gets here."

He seemed to cheer up, then. He came to the desk where Karen stood with an air of dismissal. "I wished I could have had a look at this ... your stepbrother, wasn't he? Am I out of order to ask questions? Is it a sensitive area, as the saying goes?"

"Yes, it is."

He nodded. "I'll keep my mouth shut. I'm just a passing stranger, so far."

When he had gone, she thought about those last two words. There was a promise in them, a hope that she and he would become friends, perhaps more than friends. And Karen had to admit to herself, that in spite of not knowing anything about him, she liked him.

And so far, she didn't even know his name.

FRIDAY

Eight

Janie Ferrie came out of Dr. Farmer's office at about eleven-forty on Friday morning. When she had called on Wednesday afternoon, the nurse had said the doctor had a full schedule for the next three weeks, but then Janie had explained who she was, and an opening had been found for her today.

She walked through the building's patio, where tropical plants grew lavishly up through pink crushed coral, and went on out toward the street, her gait uncertain and her face drained and stunned. The lightheartedness, the blithe confidence of that Wednesday afternoon seemed lost in time now, aeons away. The world had changed in a thunderous twitch of time; it had shifted under her and now there was no footing anywhere, no sureness, no escape. Even the sun felt different, shining on her. It touched the skin of her face and arms with a faded warmth, not really wanting to waste itself on her at all because ...

She found herself at the car, suddenly, and it too seemed strange and removed from reality. It was hard to remember that Ronnie had bought it for her less than a year ago, that she had planned all those trips, the jaunts to the coast and to Tahoe and Reno with the girls. She hadn't even gotten around to the trips yet, and now ...

She looked down at herself. She was wearing a straight-cut peach linen suit. It had nice straight lines, and the little jacket concealed some of the weight she carried in her bust; but there was no pride in Janie now, looking at it. What was she, after all? She couldn't decide. She was not what she had been when she had walked into Dr. Farmer's office earlier today. That cheerful fool was gone for good. She still wore the linen suit and the gray patent pumps, and carried the big gray patent bag, and she still tried to stand quite straight because to do so tightened the waistline a little, but this was all part of the chilling unreality that no longer mattered.

Her thoughts, diffuse and stumbling, tried to draw to a focus but the point at which reality began was too terrible to contemplate:

"Mrs. Ferrie, you shouldn't have waited so long." And: "We'll have to take a biopsy at once."

These two phrases ran around in her head, trying to connect themselves either to the past, where all had been secure and understandable, or to poke a way into the present, Janie Ferrie standing by her car, the pretty yellow convertible, taking her keys from her gray handbag.

"Hold still, now. This will only take a moment."

Why didn't I get up and run?

The feeling of brutal indignity, embarrassment, sinking terror, returned now with such impact that Janie Ferrie almost fainted. She felt a strange lightness rise into her head; she staggered against the side of the car. In the next moment tears came. Her throat closed and she thought that she would strangle. She had to get to Ronnie at once, to the office just down the street near the bank; Ronnie would tell her that none of it was true.

Ronnie ...

She was in the car now, no memory of opening the door, of putting the key in the switch. The motor was running. She made an effort to remember what you did next.

Reverse.

She parked again near the bank, across the street from Ronnie's upstairs office. She couldn't make the car behave. Even after several attempts to straighten it against the curb, the rear fender stuck out into the street, and when she got out of the car a policeman started toward her from the corner. He must have recognized her then, because he slowed down and with a casual air turned around.

Janie crossed the street and entered the building. It wasn't new like Dr. Farmer's place and there were no tropical plantings or fountain. It was just a plain tile-floored entry with a directory on the wall by the stairs.

The familiar dim light, the undefinable smells and the stairs with their rubber treads and dark banisters brought back to Janie a feeling that the world could not have entirely crashed and that sane, dignified surroundings could support her. There was almost the sensation, giddy and boisterous, of returning courage. She went up to the carpeted hall. Ronnie's door stood open a little.

Ronnie, Dr. Farmer has given me some ridiculous story that I ...

The words were ready, but the outer office was empty and so was Ronnie's consulting room.

Miss Spilling didn't seem to be around, and this was odd.

From the office Janie caught sounds from the end of the hall. Two voices, she decided, after a moment of listening. Ronnie's and another. A woman.

I'd better go.

The thing that Ronnie had always impressed upon her, that she must never know anything about his patients, that she must never even speculate about them, urged her to leave. It was a training of years.

There must never be the least chance that any bridge-table gossip, any libelous rumors, originated with her. Her protection, and Ronnie's, had been her complete ignorance.

But now, driving her, was this other, this pitiless hunger for reassurance. She *had* to see Ronnie, even if it meant interrupting, or seeing some patient in the examination room. Ronnie would just have to understand.

But Janie, my God, listening to this complete amateur, this beginner ...

Somehow these words didn't seem right, even though they were comforting to imagine. Ronnie never ran down other doctors. There was a kind of code, or something.

Janie was moving ever so quietly down the carpeted hall toward the examination rooms at the back.

Ronnie's voice said something, a low tone, and the woman answered. There was a silent moment or two, and then the woman's voice took off on a trill of giggling mirth, with little squeals, and Janie stopped moving. A funny cold shrinking feeling crept through her. This didn't sound at all like the usual doctor-patient exchange.

She felt trapped there in an incomprehensible ambush, unable to make a noise, afraid to go forward to see whatever there was to see, unwilling to retreat.

Suddenly a woman's hand, a woman's arm as far as the elbow, thrust itself from the open door of the examination room into the hall.

Shoulder high, the arm moved jerkily while from the fingers dangled a white silk garment. The giggling grew high and shrill. Some kind of tussle seemed to go on inside the room.

The garment was a brassiere.

Through gasping laughter, the woman's voice said, "I'm going to toss it out the window. The front window. Where your name's on the glass!"

Ronnie's voice in reply was low, vicious. He was cursing the woman, and the way he spoke was exactly the way he had cursed Janie on that long-ago night when he had been drinking, and upset over the haughty young widow.

There was something here that Janie couldn't understand. The woman's voice seemed so young, for one thing. The giggles and squeals were young. And Ronnie hated her, and was afraid. But still ...

Ronnie must have jerked her back into the examination room, because the weaving arm suddenly vanished. The squeals stopped, too. Now there were murmurs. And Ronnie wasn't angry anymore.

Janie leaned against the wall and closed her eyes. The examination, the things Dr. Farmer had told her, the frightful terror that had driven her here, now seemed as remote as her childhood. As remote, for instance, as that safe happy life which had enveloped her as late as ten o'clock this very morning.

The murmurs continued, and then there were other sounds, and then silence.

Ronnie said, "You'd better get dressed, Miss Barracuda."

Janie stirred, then. She checked herself to make sure that she still carried her handbag, that she hadn't laid anything down anywhere which would give away the fact that she'd been here. Then she walked stiffly back through the hall to the lavish reception room. Across the room were the windows facing the street, with Ronnie's name, there, reversed, in gold leaf.

It occurred to Janie that she was seeing this place for the last time, and that she had better take a good look at it. There were memories here. And so, seeing it in a way for the first, as well as the last time, she examined the strange bright rug and the Mexican wallpaper and the Aztec masks. Ronnie had done this, and it spoke to Janie of a restless urge, a desire to change and to break free—of what? Of his work? Of the town? Of her? And she saw then how completely she had lost him. She had lost him a long time ago.

Janie went downstairs then, to wait in her misparked car and to see who came.

There wasn't anyone left now but Ma.

Funny. She hadn't called her mother "Ma," hadn't even thought of her as "Ma," since she'd been about ten years old. When she had started running around with Karen, she remembered, she had liked Karen's little formality of "mother"—of course Karen's mother had been dead, and formality seemed proper—and somehow Marlie had desired that her own mother be endowed with some formality, too. Formality would seem to make up a little for the indignity of Walt, who had run around without his clothes on.

Marlie looked at the splintery steps, the sagging porch, the screen door with its patches. Ma hadn't had any luxuries in these last years, hadn't wanted any. Warren would have been glad to have helped. Ma would have refused. She still did cleaning part-time, and baby-sitting. The rent was cheap here, she ate little.

Marlie went up to the screen door and rapped. "Ma? Mother?"

"Marlie!"

Hugging Ma close, being hugged by her, it seemed to Marlie that the shape was frighteningly smaller, frailer, than she remembered, and that this small frail person could not help bear the burden she must share; and for a moment Marlie felt thrown back upon her own nonexistent resources.

"You're trembling so!" her mother said, pulling back suddenly to look up into Marlie's face.

"Ma, I have to talk to you. I have to tell you something. And you've got to help me!"

A strange quietness came into her mother's face; and the eyes lost their inquiring sharpness. It was almost as if her mother knew, already, what had happened. "Well, sit down. Here. Let me shake up that old feather cushion. It's worn out, really."

The chair too was small and frail, and creaked when Marlie sat down. Marlie looked around the small shabby room. There was nothing here for her, she thought, no strength, no support. Fear welled up in her.

She managed to stammer, "I'm going to have a baby..."

Her mother seemed to bring her attention to a sharp focus, staring into Marlie's face. "You are? But—"

"It's not his." Tears stung Marlie's eyes. She wanted to huddle down in shame and fright and wretchedness.

The silence drew out. Her mother seemed to be thinking. She seemed a little paler than before, but the faded eyes held no fear. "Legally it will be Warren's child," she said finally.

"That doesn't make any difference."

"What do you want to do, Marlie?"

"I've got to find an abortionist."

"Marlie!"

"I must! I just must."

Marlie put her face into her hands and cried. The silence seemed all around her, shutting her in, and she felt entirely alone until her mother's hands settled on either side of her face, forcing her own hands away.

"Marlie, it's too dangerous. Women die from abortions. A decent doctor won't do them. You'd have to find a quack." Her mother pulled Marlie's face up until Marlie's eyes met her own. "You'd have to find some amateur—the last one I heard of around here was a male nurse, and he did his jobs in a garage out on Sheeley's Road. A dump. And he killed a girl."

"I don't … it's a chance I'll have to take."

"No, Marlie." Her mother pulled her chair over now, and sat close, still clinging to Marlie's hands. "You know—let me tell you—when you walked in today I thought, how beautiful my baby looks? My little girl, and all at once you're a lovely lady, and what I'd expected, that you wouldn't fit in nor be happy married to Warren, it hadn't come true … and I was so glad in that little minute, Marlie, I thought my heart would break. And I won't have it all lost for you, and dirtied, and you maybe crippled or dead. I won't have it. I won't, *won't, won't* have it!"

Her mother sounded so firm, so determined, and looked so fiercely into Marlie's eyes that some of the terrible fear lifted a little. Marlie wiped her tears with the back of her hand.

"What can I do?"

"You're going to have a baby, and it is Warren Renick's child."

"That's lying—"

"And lying is what you're going to have to do. A little lie is much, much better than this other thing you thought of. I'm not so sure now that I think about it, that it won't be far the best for Warren, too—"

"Even if Warren, even if in his kindness, he was willing, there are the Old Hens, they've known him all his life—"

"The Old Hens, the Old Hens," her mother mocked, impatiently. "Do you think any of them are going to fight Warren and that bank of his? Who do you think owns the mortgages on those big houses out along Old Mill River Road? Don't you know that there *are* mortgages? I baby-sit for some of that bunch. They're always anxious to have ready cash. Ready cash makes more ready cash. So they borrow on those big houses. They borrow from your husband."

"But suppose, when I tell him about the baby, Warren wants a divorce. Think of the ugliness. Publicity in the papers. Think of what my name will be then—"

"Your name is Mrs. Warren Renick," her mother said firmly. Then with a touch of caution: "Who else knows about this? Have you gone to anyone?"

"Dr. Ferrie."

"His nurse, too, then. But she's not a bad sort. Did you say anything to him, that it couldn't be Warren's, or anything like that?"

"No."

"Who else, then?"

"I ... without saying anything about the man, I asked Karen Evans to find an abortionist. And she hasn't called or come out."

"And about the man ..."

Marlie stumbled through the story of the trip to Tahoe with old high school friends, of meeting Tod Bonnay at Tahoe, being introduced to him at a cocktail bar, gambling with him in the big casinos. And then the final night, the drinking, the disaster.

"Tod Bonnay," her mother said reflectively. "That snake in the grass. To think my girl would be involved with him."

Marlie was astonished that her mother knew anything about Tod.

"You're not the first one with him, Marlie. Far from it. He's got a bad reputation in this town."

"I didn't mention him to Karen."

Her mother sat quietly again; she seemed to be thinking it all through. Marlie was aware of a sense of relief, of having found help, even though what her mother expected her to do seemed unthinkable.

Finally her mother said, "Tod Bonnay is really the only one you have to worry about. He's the only one who knows the truth of what happened. To anyone else—to Warren, Karen, *anybody*—you can insist that the child must, after all, be your husband's."

Marlie thought, I couldn't do that. "Warren was married before, Ma. You know that. That's when he found out, really and truly found out, that he couldn't ever have any children. So even if I tried to fool—"

"He found out that he couldn't have children *then*," her mother said with a sort of fierceness. "Marlie, believe me, the human body changes all the time. Warren could have been sterile all his life until he met you. He's a big strong healthy man, and his glands or something just naturally got better when he found a pretty young wife."

"Ma ... Mother, I know it's a corny old phrase, but I'd be living a lie."

"How do you know you wouldn't be making Warren awfully happy?"

The idea surprised Marlie, and then she sensed the truth behind it. Warren *would* be happy. The conviction seized her. There would be no need to shock and grieve him, to bring that awful look into his face, the look she had imagined.

"You go home and take care of yourself, Marlie. You don't want to lose this baby. You and Warren are going to be happy, and no doctor on earth is going to say that Warren absolutely *could not* be the father. There's too much chance of a mistake. Lawsuits and such. You tell Warren right away that you're pregnant, and you act excited and surprised, and you let him make love to you. All he wants to."

Marlie blushed at her mother's final suggestion. At the same time she felt elated, and excitement was beginning to build in her.

"There won't be any more, though, after—"

"So his glands have died down again, or whatever. Relax. Be pleased. Make him feel pleased. He will, anyway. I'll bet Warren will be happier than he's ever been before. There's just one fly in the ointment. Tod Bonnay. And maybe there'll be a way to take care of *him*."

Nine

Karen was waiting on a woman who wanted a potted plant for a sick friend, but her eyes and her attention were directed toward the door. Lisa was late, which was unlike her. The street outside had darkened, the neon signs and the traffic lights bloomed against the dusk. In the block of buildings opposite, only Doctor Ferrie's office still showed lights at the windows.

The woman, who had a puzzled, petulant face and stood as if her feet hurt, finally chose a dwarf begonia, and Karen took it to the counter to add fancy paper and ribbon to the pot. As she worked with the ribbon and scissors, she thought about James Griffin and his neglected yard, and the absence of personal history he seemed able to offer, and the feeling she had about him, the liking and interest he stirred in her. They had spent over an hour sitting on his back porch steps, talking first about the horrors of living on Edwards Street, and then generally about the town, its social stratification, the State College out on Weller Boulevard, her goals in going to school, and things they both liked.

One thing they both liked, it seemed, was a yard which made it possible for two people like themselves to get acquainted.

That had been yesterday, but the memory still had the power to warm and somewhat confuse her.

James Griffin had once lived here, long ago when he had been very small. He had not described his family, though Karen got the impression that he had been an only child. There was something about him, to Karen, of the footloose wanderer, not in a derogatory sense; he was a man who just happened not to have settled down, and who had enjoyed moving on to new places. Along the way he seemed to have worked at a variety of jobs and to have acquired an education at an unusual number of educational institutions.

With the plant tied nicely, Karen made change for her customer. Two more people came in. A second woman needed birdseed; and a man, a grandfatherly type, showed interest in the kittens. By the time she had finished with them, Lisa had come bearing a wrapped package.

When the shop was empty of customers, Lisa said, "Come over to the desk and see what I brought, Karen." She was snipping string, looking over her shoulder at Karen. The package gave off clanking sounds.

Karen came to see. "A chisel. Hammer. But we have a hammer."

"It's too little. Look at the size of this. I asked the man at the hardware store for something to remove a few bricks, and this is what he suggested. He said to work carefully or we'd chip the bricks; that is, if we intended to use them again. I didn't know bricks were fragile, did you?"

The chatter seemed to cover other things, Karen thought. Lisa was anxious, almost flustered. At the same time there was an undercurrent of determination, of having made up her mind about something. The dark eyes didn't quite meet her own.

"You're going to take some bricks out of that wall in the dragon's den?"

"*We* are, Karen."

"Lisa, you know I have a date to go to dinner."

"Yes. With Tod Bonnay. Don't go. Stay here with me and we'll see what's down there."

"But I promised him, Lisa. I couldn't back out now. He wouldn't understand at all."

Lisa's hands hovered above the hammer and chisel. "Does it matter? Do you care what Tod Bonnay thinks of you?"

"It's been such an ugly situation, for such a long time," Karen said, hoping to make Lisa understand. "I know he told things that weren't true. He tried to make me out a thief and a liar. But if there is a chance of changing things, I want to do it. He has apologized—"

Lisa gave a snort of scornful anger. Her fingers lingered on the handle of the hammer.

"—and perhaps, as he says, he really has had a change of heart."

"The only thing you can be sure of, where Tod is concerned, is that he is forever money-hungry. If he's coming around acting humble and apologetic—"

Karen interrupted. "You talk about Tod as if you knew him very well. Do you?"

Lisa's eyes dropped off Karen's instantly. "No. Well ... at one time I did know him. Just briefly. I was in my last year at high school." She shook her head as if dismissing some memory. "But knowing him isn't important. Tod Bonnay's reputation is all over town. He's a ... a louse."

Karen didn't know what to say in the face of Lisa's vehemence. She thought for a moment of trying to call Tod now, this late, and postpone their dinner date; but then she remembered his hesitation, the moment of suspicion when he had obviously thought she was getting rid of him. If she were to call now, he wouldn't believe any excuse. He would be angry and offended. And the situation between them would go back to what it had been, hateful, degrading.

"He will be very convincing," Lisa prophesied. "You'd swear that he was turning over a new leaf. But in the end ... Don't let him get control of you. Don't ever let your guard down."

"I promise to be most careful."

"He's your enemy, Karen. And he has some plan in his head."

Karen had been looking forward to the evening, the hope of being on better footing with Tod, but now all the shine was gone, and thinking of sitting opposite Tod at a dinner table, trying to carry on a conversation, held nothing but dread. She would not be able to forget these things Lisa had said, and it would affect her manner, and Tod would notice it.

"Please, Karen, please don't go."

"I just have to."

"Then go with your eyes open."

"Yes, I think my eyes are open now."

Karen busied herself with a few last odds and ends and then hurried from the shop. She and Lisa, for the past six months, had shared an apartment a block and a half away. It was not at all fancy, but it was close to the shop and they could neglect the housework when necessary without too much disorder showing. When Karen's father had divorced his last wife, Tod's mother, he had bought a home for himself and Karen on the outskirts of town. The business he owned had begun to prosper, and so the house he bought had been a very nice one. After his death Karen had sold it; it was too big for her, too filled with memories of her father.

When she reached the apartment she hurried into the shower and then dressed quickly, put on fresh make-up, tidied her hair.

She tried to recapture the feeling of hope and optimism that she'd had earlier, but it was gone. In the midst of her frustration and depression, she thought of Marlie.

Several times in the last two days, she had been on the verge of calling

Marlie, and then at the last minute she had changed her mind. Offering no help at all to the desperate girl was cowardly, inhuman. But what was she to do? In the end, what *could* she do?

Still, Marlie had turned to her for help. And she had done nothing at all. She had not even offered the comfort of another meeting.

Upset now, filled with guilt as well as dejection over what Lisa had said shortly before, Karen sat down beside the phone.

A man's voice answered her call. Warren Renick was home, then. Marlie wouldn't be able to speak freely. But anyway, she could let Marlie know that she hadn't forgotten her. "Could I speak to Marlie, please?"

"Just a minute."

When Marlie came on the phone she sounded breathless, almost gay. "Karen? Oh, how are you? I've been meaning to call and talk to you, but things have been rushing along so. I've been asked to be on the committee for the Martin Luther Hospital Benefit! Isn't that something? Mrs. Winniger asked me. She's chairman!"

This merry, prattling, lighthearted, and enthusiastic Marlie was the last thing Karen would have expected. The happy voice seemed to explode into the phone. Karen could scarcely believe her ears.

"And then ... oh, Karen, other things, too. Really wonderful things! I'm not ready to ... to tell everyone yet. But for you ... a secret. And you mustn't tell." Her voice dropped to a dramatic whisper, and somehow Karen knew that Warren Renick was standing there listening, just as happy as Marlie was. "I'm going to have a baby!"

Karen wanted to cry, "But Marlie, I know that!" but somehow found the wits to stammer instead, "Oh, Marlie, it's so wonderful, and I'm so happy for you."

Marlie must have turned from the phone to address her husband, for Karen heard her say—muffled, indistinct—"Now Warren darling, run out for a minute. We want to have some girl talk." There was a pause. Perhaps he was kissing her. Then Marlie said into the receiver, "Warren was right here. He's so pleased, Karen. He's just ... wonderful. I guess you were surprised when I didn't come back, or telephone, or anything." Her voice dropped to a whisper and Karen thought a touch of fear had come into it. "Someone came and warned me not to see you again."

"Warned you?" Karen echoed incredulously. "But who?"

"I can't tell you. He's somebody you know, though. And he might have some idea of trying to make a good impression on you, or have you like him, because he said I absolutely had to stay away."

It didn't make sense to Karen. Why should anyone—wanting her to like him—demand that Marlie stay away?

Then the light dawned. "Who, Marlie? You have to tell me *who!*"

"I wouldn't dare. Except for that, everything's fine. Don't worry about me, Karen. And thanks for … for listening."

"Please."

"I'd be afraid to."

And there it ended. Marlie refused to say who had warned her to leave Karen alone, but now a name shot through Karen's mind like an arrow.

He looked at Karen across the candlelit table. "You're so quiet. Quiet and thoughtful. Let's have some more of the bubble-water, shall we? And drink a toast to better days—the days to come." He reached across the table to touch her hand. "I want us to be friends, Karen. Real good friends."

She tried to respond. She made every effort to throw off the feeling of apathy and pessimism. She smiled, with her lips alone, and answered the pressure of his hand.

"I've done things, said things, that make me want to kick myself," he said, sounding wryly sincere. "I really did want to hurt you. I thought I hated you. But you know, sometimes hate isn't really hate at all. It's something else. It's the other side of the coin, you might say."

Karen's throat was dry and she was suddenly tired, wrung out. Much of the evening so far had been like this, Tod throwing out hints about his real feelings for her, and she smoothing them aside or pretending to misinterpret his words. Not in her wildest dreams, she realized, could she picture herself falling in love with Tod Bonnay. It was queer, too. When she'd been twelve and thirteen he'd been her secret idol. He was handsome, charming, winning, sophisticatedly dashing; but he was not for her. Not ever. She found herself comparing him to James Griffin.

"We really don't need any more champagne, Tod. Let's order."

He took his hand off hers and picked up the ornate menu. "The seafood cocktail's good here. Let's start with that."

Karen couldn't help seeing the prices on the menu. She wished in that moment that they were going Dutch treat, or that she had taken Lisa's advice and stayed at home. She didn't want Tod buying her a meal. Not a meal as expensive as this one was going to be.

She read the gilt-printed page. "I haven't eaten out in so long," she murmured. "Not in weeks and months. Not for ages. I just never get into a restaurant." And she waited for his answer.

"That's not the way I hear it," he said quickly, and then a curious silence fell, and she knew that he was watching her above the menus between them.

Now I know, she thought.

Marlie in her fear and innocence had given away too much. Someone had seen them at the café; not Tod, she would have noticed him. Someone had seen them in the booth, where Marlie had cried, and dried her eyes, and cried again. That someone had told Tod, had played the spy. But why?

Tod had made a bad blunder and now he was waiting to see if she had caught it. Waiting to see if she had heard from Marlie and was putting parts of a puzzle together, perhaps.

"Oh, I go out for coffee and such," she said, not even looking up, shrugging it off, "but I can't count that with this."

Then she lifted her eyes and smiled at him.

He warmed at once. His eyes sparkled in the candlelight. "This can't be the last time for us, Karen. We'll have to come here again, this same table ... many times."

She wished he would start talking about the money.

She dragged herself upstairs to the apartment door. She was completely worn out, drained, exhausted. Nothing on earth, she told herself, is harder than acting a part—offstage. The pretense tonight had been more demanding than anything she had done in drama class at school.

She put her key into the lock and the door swung in. Lisa must not be at home. A light was always left on, if one of them were out, and the room was dark. Karen snapped on the lights. She dropped her wrap and her small gold bag, and glanced at her watch. It really wasn't much past ten-thirty. The long, wearying deception with Tod had only lasted a little over three hours. Not three hundred....

She looked into Lisa's room to make sure she hadn't actually come in and just forgotten the light in the front room, but Lisa's bed was smooth under its white spread.

For a few moments Karen stood there undecided.

Could Lisa still be at the shop, working down in the dragon's den as she had proposed?

Karen hadn't taken Lisa's purchase of the hammer and chisel seriously, because she thought she recognized in them simply an excuse to cancel the date with Tod. But now she wasn't sure. Could Lisa have been serious in wanting to tackle that brick wall? And should she go to the shop now and check on what was happening?

Her own room, her own bed, seemed too inviting. She thought, I'll wake up later and check on Lisa, and make sure she's come in.

It seemed that she slept for a long time.

"Karen? Karen?"

It was Lisa's voice, and Karen tried to rouse to answer.

From far away, from the world outside the deeps of sleep, she heard Lisa say something. She thought at the time that Lisa said, "It's ten-thirty, Karen. It's just ten-thirty," and she wanted to answer, scolding, "How can it be?"

A little later she did wake, fully wake, and heard splashing sounds from the bathroom. Lisa must be washing out something in there. A light burned in the hall.

When she awoke again it was morning, bright and sunny.

Karen showered and dressed, had a cup of coffee and some juice and a piece of toast. Lisa wasn't up, but this was as usual. The one who kept the shop on Friday nights didn't go in on Saturday morning. Karen left the apartment shortly before nine-thirty.

The woman who had bought the potted plant the evening before was there waiting for her. Not to complain—she wanted a duplicate plant for herself. It seemed that it would fit some garden scheme which Karen didn't quite understand. Karen unlocked the shop, drew the shades up in the front windows, looked in at the pet guinea pig she intended to keep.

The woman wandered around while Karen selected a plant for her. Suddenly she came stumbling from the rear of the store. "There's someone back there. Lying on the floor. A man. Must be sick, or drunk, or something. You'd better call somebody ..."

Unbelieving—it was too incredible—Karen went to see.

She recognized the clothes at once. She went closer.

Tod Bonnay lay on his face and there was something wrong...

The big new hammer lay a few feet away.

SATURDAY

Ten

Karen looked at the clock on the wall beside the breakfast nook. It was a little over an hour since she had walked into the shop with the woman customer at her heels.

Lisa was at the other end of the couch. She looked tired and chilled. Her skin seemed grayish, the black eyes desolate. Her hands lay folded in her lap. She wore a black silk kimono over her nightdress, and she sat as still as stone.

Across from them in the green chair was the detective.

He was a man of about fifty, with a ruddy face and big hands. He wasn't holding a notebook and pencil, the way detectives did on TV and in the movies. His hands lay flat on his knees and he was watching the two girls carefully. Karen thought that neither of them could have winked an eye, nor swallowed, nor moved the toe of a shoe, without his seeing it. His hat was on the floor beside the chair. It wasn't a new hat. He didn't look like a man who worried much about his hat. It dropped where he chose and it looked after itself while he watched people.

Karen tried to search back through the hour that had passed since she had found Tod's body in the shop.

She recalled the noise of a siren; she remembered uniformed men in the shop, and a lot of hurried questions, and people crowding at the door, looking in, their eyes filled with an avidity that shocked her. There wasn't much more, though it seemed she should have remembered making a phone call to police headquarters.

She remembered that an officer had pointed to the hammer and asked if it belonged on the premises, and that she had said yes.

Another uniformed man had escorted her back to the apartment and had waited there until the detective had come. It seemed to Karen that his purpose had been to overhear, or perhaps to prevent, any private conversation between her and Lisa.

The detective had turned his glance to Lisa now, and was saying, "What time did you leave the shop last night, Miss Kim?"

"It must have been"—Lisa seemed to make an effort to rouse herself, to respond—"about ten-fifteen. I got home around ten-thirty. I closed the shop at ten o'clock and drew the front window blinds, and the blind on the door. Then there were a few things to do. I looked at the canaries' water. Things like that."

Karen, remembering that the clock had indicated almost ten-forty when she had come in from her date with Tod, and that Lisa hadn't been here, almost spoke out. Then she checked herself. But she was sure that the detective knew it. He had sensed her surprise, and then the chilling sense of caution that followed.

"I called to Karen when I came in," Lisa went on. "She was in bed. I remarked to her that it was just ten-thirty."

"Why?" he asked flatly.

"Well ... she'd gone on a date. I guess I expected she'd be gone until at least midnight."

"And your date?" the detective said, turning to Karen.

Karen was sure that she had already told him the date had been with Tod Bonnay. She met his eyes, confused. "Yes?"

"Where did you go?"

"We had dinner. At the Mill Wheel. Then we drove out toward the coast. We didn't stop. I guess Tod drove for a half hour, perhaps forty-five minutes. He just ... talked."

He shifted his weight a little and the chair creaked. "You know—excuse me for saying this, Miss Evans—but we detectives get to be a hard-bitten lot. Pretty cynical. We take a lot for granted ... like perhaps, Mr. Bonnay might have made a pass or two."

This man took nothing for granted, Karen knew, and he was a far better actor than any of her fellow students in the drama classes at school. "Mr. Bonnay was my stepbrother," Karen answered. "Even though our parents had been divorced, and both were dead—still, you don't forget that kind of relationship. Of course there weren't any ... what you called passes."

Did he believe her? She couldn't tell.

"Well, then, just forgive an old hard-case, Miss Evans. You'd been Mr. Bonnay's stepsister for a while, and now you had something to talk about."

"The estate my father had left. Part of it, you see—"

"Mr. Bonnay thought might be his."

Karen felt her face stiffen. This man knew a great deal and he was cutting brush now, trying to get at the center of things. Of course the gossip about Tod had gone all over town and the police made it their business to listen. Why had she thought they would not? Because you want to think of the police as noble enforcers of the law, above the traffic in slimy whisperings? Because you dread the advent of Big Brother, and this would seem to be a step in that direction? "Yes. He thought some of the money should be his. Actually, though, we didn't get around to discussing the estate. It was a just a pleasant ... friendly ..."—Karen's voice broke for a moment—"... evening with someone I'd known a long time. And I'm glad now—"

"Yes, of course you are. It's always a good feeling when you bury the hatchet. It might surprise you to know, though, that one of your friends came to the police not too long back, to complain about some of Mr. Bonnay's remarks about you. I had to explain that libel or slander is a civil matter and that it would be necessary to get an attorney and file suit, and round up witnesses, and so forth."

Lisa? Karen turned to stare at the immobile Chinese girl.

"Not Miss Kim, by the way. This is an older lady. Someone who knew your father, and knew you when you were little. She'd been at some party and Mr. Bonnay had been broadcasting some opinions, and she had resented it."

"I see."

Easily, smoothly, the detective switched his line of questioning. "Miss

Kim, will you try to remember exactly what happened when you left the shop last night? Perhaps there was something a little different in your routine, some change that didn't seem important at the time. Now, you turned out the lights? Locked up?"

Lisa nodded stiffly.

"Will you tell me just what you did?"

Lisa licked her lips. "There is a night light.... We leave a low-wattage bulb on, it's near the stairs to the ... the cellar. The main switch is by the front door. I clicked it off, and then closed the door from outside and checked the night latch to make sure it had caught."

"Was anyone passing the shop? Anyone seem to be watching from across the street, for instance?"

"Downtown is deserted by ten," Lisa said. "Actually, we usually close the shop by nine. It was just ... I got to studying, and let the time pass. I don't remember seeing anyone on the street. I may have passed a pedestrian or two coming home. I don't really remember."

"What about that rear door?"

"I didn't go around into the alley and check it, if that's what you mean."

"The rear door wasn't locked, apparently," the detective said, "and it seems Mr. Bonnay must have got in that way."

For the first time Karen's thoughts came face to face with the strange puzzle of Tod's being in the shop at all. When he had left her at the apartment he'd said he was going home. Why should he have gone instead to the shop? What could have taken him there? Why should he have slipped into the dim, closed place with the pets and the plants and the stacked fertilizers ... Karen felt like shaking her head in disbelief. The improbability of Tod's acting in such a way, and under such conditions, was insurmountable. When Tod did something, there was purpose behind it, usually self-seeking; and he did what he needed to do without lost motion.

She found the detective's eyes on her. "Did you unlock and open that rear door yesterday, Miss Evans?"

"Not that I remember."

"You and Miss Kim share the running of the store. Is it possible that one of you opened the rear door and forgot to mention it to the other? And that the other might have forgotten then to lock it?"

"It ... it did happen that way a few times," Karen admitted.

"But you're not sure that it happened that way yesterday?"

"No."

"Now, this business of the blinds being drawn—do you know that there is no other store on the block whose windows are covered at night? And that drawing the blinds defeats the purpose of the night light, since a passing officer couldn't see what was going on inside anyway?"

Lisa spoke up quickly. "My father had blinds installed in the front show windows a long time ago. Once we kept several cages of birds there, where people passing could see them, and early one morning some children came. They were playing with cut palm fronds. They waved the palm leaves back and forth against the windows to see the birds flutter. The birds were terrified, and quite a few of them died. We no longer keep birds in those windows, but still—having the blinds there and drawing them every night is a habit." She seemed to search the detective's face for some sign of disbelief. "And anyway, there's nothing in the shop that's valuable enough to steal. The night light, like the blinds, is just a habit."

He nodded, though he seemed to answer Lisa's look with a sharp glance of his own. Then he turned to Karen, and again the transition was smooth and patient. "You said that the weapon used to kill Mr. Bonnay belonged on the premises?"

"Yes."

"For how long?"

She waited for Lisa to speak up again, to explain about the big heavy hammer, but Lisa was silent. "Just ... recently."

"Remember where you bought it?"

"No."

"We'll need to trace it just to keep the records straight."

Karen was confused, fearful, lost. Under his stare her skin grew cold, her throat dried. Why didn't Lisa say something? Why didn't she explain about the dragon's den, the brick wall that had roused their curiosity?

"I ... I don't know ... which store—"

"I see."

There was something in the air, unexplained, secret. The detective's eyes were neutral, almost inattentive; and behind the mask Karen sensed how his mind toiled. He was looking now at Lisa, still mild, still indifferent. "How old are you, Miss Kim?"

"Twenty-one," Lisa said. Her voice was hoarse. Her hands made nervous motions in the lap of the silk kimono with the dragons embroidered on the sleeves.

"You're too young to remember anything about the bank robbery."

"I don't recall anything about it."

"Uh-huh." He appeared to withdraw into thought, and the apartment grew so quiet that the traffic noises outside seemed loud by contrast. "It was before my time, too. I've only lived here for a little more than ten years. I heard about it, of course, from some of the older men in our department."

He waited as if Lisa might say something more, and the quiet invaded the apartment again, more thick, more meaningful than ever. Karen tried to remember anything about a bank robbery, but nothing came to mind. What possible connection could a long-ago crime such as this have with the murder of Tod Bonnay last night in their shop?

Again her thoughts returned to the sense of shock and unbelief, the feeling of complete nightmare, which had seized her when she had seen Tod's body.

It couldn't be.

But it was.

"Well," the detective was saying, "just to sum up: Miss Evans, you had no disagreement at all with Mr. Bonnay during the hours you spent with him last night?"

"Not at all."

"And he didn't mention any errand that would take him to your store after he'd left you?"

"No."

"And you, Miss Kim, are positive that you left the shop before Mr. Bonnay came there?"

It was a whisper. "Yes."

"And neither of you has the faintest idea what he could have been doing there around eleven?"

Karen thought, *That's when they think he died.* She said, "It still seems impossible that he went to the shop right after dropping me here."

"Yes. Hmmmm." He picked up his hat and looked it over as if to see how it had fared on its own under the chair.

"Lisa, what did he mean, a bank robbery?"

Karen had gone to put on water for coffee, not that she especially wanted a cup right now; it was something to do. Lisa sat in the corner of the couch. She hadn't moved since the detective had gone.

"Lisa!"

"It happened a long time ago, and I was too small to understand."

"That conference, the family conference you told me about, when your grandfather and your uncles came—"

"Perhaps it had something to do with the robbery."

"You told me that the wall, the inner wall that separated the store from the living quarters, had been demolished. That there was a lot of debris on the floor—"

"They searched for something. Missing money, perhaps. I didn't know what was going on at the time. I remember my mother seemed shamed and terribly afraid." Lisa leaned forward and put her forehead into her palms, and sat with her face covered as if to shut out something from the past. "Something had happened in the cellar."

"Something to do with the brick wall down there?"

"There used to be a kind of ... of tunnel."

"Your father built it?"

"No. I don't know, Karen. It was old. Old."

Karen sat down close to Lisa. "Were you ever in it?"

"I was never allowed in the dragon's den, never." Lisa lifted her head, shook back a wing of heavy black hair. "There was a little gate at the top of the stairs to keep me from falling, or from going down. Chinese children are obedient. I understood that I was not to go down the stairs."

"What did your father, or your mother, ever say about the bank robbery?"

"Nothing."

"Lisa, what happened last night?"

Lisa's eyes focused on her swiftly. "What do you mean?"

"About Tod."

"Nothing at all happened about Tod. I didn't see him. I have no idea what he might have been doing in the shop."

Looking into the direct, brilliant black eyes, with the only sound that of the kettle beginning to sing on the stove in the kitchen, Karen felt that she had reached a crossroads. She had a choice and she must choose quickly. She could accept what Lisa was saying, she could pretend to believe it—or she could give up Lisa's friendship forever.

There was no compromise whatever, no middle road.

She wanted to touch Lisa, to say, "But Lisa, I know. You came in long after ten-thirty. Then you washed something out in the bathroom, clothing from the sound of it, and something more substantial than nylons ..."

The suddenly strange black eyes warned her. Karen felt a wrench of sorrow, of loss, and for the first time she sensed the difference between them, the difference she hadn't known was there, the separation of race.

She tried to force a smile. "I'll fix us some coffee."

She knew that Lisa watched closely as she rose and walked toward the kitchen. What was Lisa thinking?

The detective who had just left had not asked Karen if she remembered exactly when Tod had dropped her off. He had appeared satisfied with Lisa's statement that she had come home at ten-thirty and had found Karen already in bed.

But one of the uniformed men at the shop had asked Karen for the exact time of her last sight of Tod, and she remembered telling him that it had been around ten-forty.

Eventually the two conflicting statements would be weighed against each other, and the detective would be back again.

What should she say then?

Eleven

Miss Spilling went up the stairs toward the office door, her throat tight and her knees almost shaking. She had a headache, already, and now she saw that her uniform was missing a button right over the bosom, which made it gape unattractively and was sure to draw some cruel comment. It was all the fault of that dreadful man, Dr. Ferrie, and if it weren't for the kindness of his wife, she, Miss Evelyn Spilling, would walk off this minute and go back to private-duty nursing, as hard and ungrateful as *that* was.

She opened the office door timidly, finding it unnecessary to use her key and knowing that he must already be in there.

He was in there. He was at the windows that faced the street. He turned to look at her as she came in. She ducked her head, cowed and fearful, and he nodded in return. Somehow the nod didn't seem to have the usual snap of anger in it. "'Morning," he said.

"Good morning, Doctor." He turned back to the window and Miss Spilling went toward the desk.

In nursing school their instructors had drilled and drilled into them the great respect they must show to doctors. They must stand when a doctor entered the room. They must never in the least way question or criticize a doctor's orders for the patient. A doctor's word was law. In person he was second practically to God. And now she had ended up with ... with *him*. Wasn't it only fair that if the nurse showed great respect for the doctor, that he in return treated her decently too?

The desk looked queer. She saw that there was a great heap piled on it. For a moment she thought he had yanked out all of the clutter inside and piled it here for her to sort and for him to make remarks about; but then she saw that the heap consisted of folders from the little closet down the hall where records were kept.

She circled the desk warily, opened a drawer and put away her purse, opened a second drawer and took out her white cap, and pinned it to her hair. Then she waited.

"Miss Spilling...."

"Yes, Doctor."

"I want you to do something for me. Something a little unusual. I want you to go downstairs and across the street and find out exactly what happened in that shop next to the bank."

The request made so little sense, was so far from what she had expected of him, that she stood glued there, staring.

He threw her a glance. "Didn't you notice a knot of people over there when you came along the street?"

"I ... I guess so."

"You weren't curious?"

In more carefree days, Miss Spilling knew, she would have trotted over there to see what was brewing; but now from the moment she left home in the morning she was bracing herself for the dreadfulness of Dr. Ferrie. "I was in a hurry, I guess."

"I heard a name shouted," Dr. Ferrie said. "Someone was answering a question from across the street. They took a body out of there, well wrapped. Would you just take a few minutes and go find out?"

"A body?"

"Especially find out whose body," Dr. Ferrie said, but not unkindly. In fact, it now occurred to Miss Spilling that Doctor's attitude was quite changed. He seemed benign and reasonable, even almost polite.

Once this change had made its full impression on Miss Spilling, she rushed for the door.

Unbelievable—*but he was almost human!*

Downstairs, she darted across the street. Seeing the white uniform and the starched hospital cap, the small group of people parted to let her through. Probably they had some idea she had been summoned officially. But the cop in the doorway had no such illusion. "Just a minute, miss."

"Oh, I didn't intend to go on in. Dr. Ferrie sent me over. You see, he ... he ..." She bogged down, wondering why Doctor should have sent her here on an errand of idle curiosity.

"Dr. Farmer's our new medical examiner, ma'am—when we need one, which ain't often—and he's been and gone. You thank Dr. Ferrie, though—"

"Doctor wanted to know who it was you sent off on a stretcher," she got out. "He ... he thought it might be someone he knew."

The cop shrugged. "A feller name of Tod Bonnay."

Even Miss Spilling had heard of Tod Bonnay. "The young society man? The one they write up for skiing and skin diving and things like that?"

A flat, disillusioned expression came into the cop's eyes, as if he and Miss Spilling had heard of Tod on different wave lengths. "Yes. The same."

"And he took sick here?"

The cop sighed. "It's going to be in the papers, so ... He was killed in there, ma'am. His head was beat in. With a hammer."

"Oh, dear."

"Ma'am, I'm afraid that's all I can tell you."

"I know. And thank you so much!"

She went back to the office. She opened the door cautiously, half expecting Doctor to be his latter-day self again. But he was still at the windows and his eye on her seemed still mild, still just gently inquiring.

"Tod Bonnay, the young society man," she gasped, breathless from hurry on the stairs. "He was horribly murdered, his brains dashed out, with a hammer."

Dr. Ferrie didn't look particularly shocked. Of course he had been there at the window and had seen a body taken away and must have known something bad had happened.

"Hmmmm," he said. He seemed to think for a moment or so. "Did they seem to be questioning anyone, have anyone handcuffed in there? A suspect, I guess you'd say?"

Miss Spilling was aware of police procedure from watching television. "They wouldn't do it there.... No, they didn't.... They'd do it at the police station where they have interrogation rooms," she told him.

"Hmmmm," he said again.

She went over to the desk, trying to ignore the mess on its top, because she was sure that when Dr. Ferrie got around to talking about it, things would be very unpleasant. She sat down and pretended to be looking inside the desk for the appointment book. Appointments were quite sketchy these last few days. Doctor was very temperamental about whom he wanted to see.

"Those folders, Miss Spilling ..."

She gulped, knowing the evil hour had come. "Yes, Doctor."

"Will you just go through them quickly, and separate the folders of people who haven't been in for ..." He rubbed his fingers along his chin while he came to a decision. Looking at him across the office, Miss Spilling allowed herself to admit that when Doctor was calm, not snarling and nasty, he was a nice-looking man. "... haven't been in for six months. And get at the rest of the records, too, and separate them all on that basis. Put the inactive stuff in a big box and stick it in the back of the closet. Or better yet, tape it so that it's dustproof and I'll have the janitor store it in the cellar."

"If someone comes in—"

"If they come in, and their file's downstairs, you can get it out before their appointment."

"Yes, Doctor." This was going to take all morning. How could she answer the phone, too? And write down appointments? And make note of cancellations? On Saturdays, the office closed at a quarter of twelve.

"Don't worry about answering the phone," Dr. Ferrie told her, as if her worried frown told him what she was thinking. "I'll do it."

"Very well, Doctor."

Dr. Ferrie nodded to her, really a nice respectful nod as if she were a person who filled a need here, and went into his private room and shut the door. Miss Spilling was aware of a lift of spirit, a feeling of freedom. All she had to do, all morning long, was to sort and classify records. She smiled a little to herself now, picking up a folder.

She felt no curiosity, no morbid interest, in Tod Bonnay's death. She had made a mental note, crossing the street to return to the office, that the pet shop was a peculiar place for Mr. Bonnay to die. But this was as far as her observation extended.

For a long time—or at any rate what seemed like a long time—her mental faculties, her will and her attention and her endurance, had been engaged in a struggle to survive in this job where the doctor made each day increasingly more difficult. It wasn't just the money; she felt a debt toward Doctor's wife, who had hired her, who had accepted the very mediocre recommendations and the lapses in professional engagements and had set the generous salary.

Something else made her feel cheerful, too; something she hadn't as yet analyzed. With a folder in her hands, Miss Spilling stopped to think. Wasn't there something more, something beyond Doctor's merely being pleasant?

Yes, there was.

Recently Doctor had seemed like a man who was fed up, who was getting ready to ditch it all. She hadn't put it into words even to herself, but that's just how Doctor had been.

Now he seemed to be settled in some way, reorganized, tranquil.

He had decided to get the records in order, to bring them up to date, and this spoke of plans for the future. Wherever his mind had been, it had apparently returned. And high time, thought Miss Spilling, humming to herself contentedly as she worked on the folders.

In the private office, in his chair behind the desk Dr. Ferrie sat with his head leaning in his hand, his eyes half-shut. He felt completely at peace in spite of the possibilities that flickered out at the edges of thought like heat lightning along a horizon. He wanted a cigarette but felt too relaxed to bother to light one. It was very quiet in here, very peaceful. He could not hear that silly goose of a woman—he never thought of her as a nurse—out in the reception room or trotting in the hall. He was shut away from the street.

Of course the phone could ring at any moment, and it could be the police saying that Tod Bonnay had left certain papers among his belongings and there seemed to be something that needed explaining in them, in regard to the doctor. And then all of the possibilities he had conjectured would come true.

But just for now he didn't want to worry about it.

He wanted to enjoy the feeling of relaxation, and to consider the other possibility, that he had been handed a new lease on life, an absolute miracle out of nowhere.

Of course certain plans would have to be made to take care of the female barracuda, to keep this possibility from going sour. The plans didn't have to be complicated or elaborate.

The female barracuda was nothing, by herself. He'd always known it. She was a puppet, manipulated by the male. And if Tod Bonnay had had the decency to keep his bookkeeping in his head, the female barracuda could be swept under the rug. Kaput. Forgotten, finished. There would be some pleasurable moments in watching her writhe and beg. She was going to get pretty feverish and disorganized before it was all over, before the doors of some institution closed on her delirium.

Well, what would be explained was that she'd been his patient, he had been trying to help her—the police would understand that and they'd have complete sympathy for his difficult course. He pictured the scene to himself, calling the cops, acting detached and regretful while the naked girl—a good touch, he thought; it gave the right touch of madness—the naked girl groveled and gibbered and tried to spit up her gullet on his clean floor.

For three days, he decided.

For three days she would be given enough to keep her quiet and in control of herself, and then he would start shooting her veins with straight milk sugar.

He had drawn his head back as the moments had passed, and now he found himself regarding his own hands, folded on the desk in front of him, the hands that were going to do these things. A tag-end of memory, an old scattered dream, came back to him; he had once thought that a doctor's hands should *look* merciful, compassionate, as well as clean and capable, an idea born in that first flush of ambition to become a doctor.

I used to have a lot of funny notions, he told himself; and then he found that he couldn't go on studying his hands.

"Mrs. Ferrie, aren't you going to fix them flowers?"

"No. No, I guess not."

"You look kind of washed-out, ma'am. It might make you feel better to go sit in the swing and let me bring you some lemonade."

"Grizzie, I'm all right. Just leave me alone."

"Yes, ma'am."

Janie was sitting in a corner of what was called the family room. If there had ever been any children this place could have been filled with ping-pong tables and a fountain-bar and a home-type jukebox and a place to toast hot dogs. As it was, Janie had made it into a sprawling and informal parlor. This morning she had pulled down the blinds and lain down on a canvas lounge. The pains flickered through her body under the enveloping folds of the muumuu. The pains had started when she had reached home last night and hadn't stopped since.

I'm going to die.

The thought was like the slow, soft pulse of a bell ringing in her head. *I'm going to die.* Me. Janie Linden Ferrie.

I've got this thing and it's filling me up and pretty soon there won't be room for it and for me, and I'll be the one to go. The main thing is not to panic. If I panic I won't get done all the things that must be done. I won't leave everything in order for Ronnie the way I want to.

She remembered suddenly that she was supposed to go back to see Dr. Farmer today.

She decided after a moment's thought that she wouldn't go. It was too late. Dr. Farmer had been kind and he had tried to cover his dismay, but she knew. I've torn it all loose, she thought, with the exertion, with the shock of being so scared, and the thing that had happened in Ronnie's office yesterday. It's worse than when Dr. Farmer examined me just yesterday, and it was bad enough then to make him turn pale.

At the end, if the pain got quite terrible, she would have to tell Ronnie. He was a doctor and there should be ways to make things easier.

It was going to be a shock to him, Janie thought. Well, maybe not such a big shock after all. She hadn't realized it until yesterday but Ronnie hadn't paid much attention to her for a long time. She had thought it must be the pressure of his work, or his age—when men got to be middle-aged they went through a bad time, she'd heard, almost as bad as women's. She knew the truth now.

She knew about Miss Barracuda.

It was funny, the love she felt for Ronnie now. He had disregarded all their marriage vows. He was an adulterer. But she loved him very much. He was the husband, still, who had saved her from being an old maid who fussed around with Pekingese or Worldwide Orphans.

When I'm gone ...

He could have Miss Barracuda unendingly, if he wanted her.

He could fire Miss Spilling.

He could sell this house and move away from Old Mill River Road, and quit having her friends as his patients, and study all the new things to do with people's stomachs, the way he wanted.

She whispered in the stillness, "Maybe I haven't been such a good wife, Ronnie. I guess there was a lot I never did understand."

Now, in gratitude, she had a last lovely gift to offer.

She had her own death.

There were four of them in on it, not counting the Chinaman, and I guess that might have been a couple too many. The Bug figured he had to have some experts. That wall might have wiring in it, from the time the bank had taken over, so he wanted somebody who would know a hot wire if he found one, and that was Tommy Schafer, who learned his electrician's trade the best way, plenty of time to study, five-to-eight in good old San Quentin.

Then The Bug wanted a vault man. The first plan was to go in at night and shoot the time-machine. Or whatever it's called, it controls the thing opening up.

So there were these, and The Bug himself, and my old sidekick, Rappsy—he had the machine guns, having got into an arsenal in Benicia. Count the Chinaman and you could say, five.

They got through the wall, that was nothing. You'd think a bank would take a look the other side of its cellar walls, but I guess everybody trusted everybody.

The Chinaman's job was to get his relatives out, they lived right in the back of the store, and keep them out, all night. They weren't supposed to know anything about this.

But things started to go wrong right away. When they got through the wall and into the basement of the bank, the vault man took a look—I can't remember the joker's name now, for some reason—he took a look and gave his head a shake. It was the wrong kind of box. There was no way he could get at the alarm.

He was a small-time joker anyhow. Rappsy knew it and I can't understand why he didn't tip The Bug.

Well, they waited, hoping the Chinks stayed away long enough, and they didn't get any money until morning, after all the clerks and the manager and the bank president got there. The timer opened the vault after nine o'clock. They hadn't had any sleep. Tommy Schafer especially was plenty nervous. When the Chinaman wandered up from the cellar while Tommy had his gun on the bank president, Tommy sprayed things a little with the machine gun, and he killed the bank president deader than hell. An old duffer name of Renick, as I recall. One of the big shots out on Old Mill River Road.

The whole job was a mess, and it didn't have to be. It could have come off smooth as cream, with them leaving by the pet store doors one at a time and nobody noticing them at all.

As it was, Rappsy and The Bug got as far as Pismo Beach, and hid out two days in a motel before they were picked up.

The money was all found, except for sixty-nine thousand dollars. Tommy Schafer died right there in the bank. Somebody stepped on an alarm when he put a burst through old man Renick...

Twelve

James Griffin walked along the street in the sunshine, passing the bank on the corner and taking a quick look inside. The place was crowded. It seemed that the bank must surely want to buy Lisa Kim's property before too long, for an expansion of the building.

If anyone meant to use that bamboo door, it had better be soon.

He started to turn into Lisa's shop and then noticed that the door, though half-opened, had a hand-lettered sign taped to the glass: CLOSED.

Several men were in there. One was sitting on the end of the desk at the rear of the shop, running through a sheaf of papers. The others weren't far away. There seemed to be a conference going on. No sign of Karen or of Lisa Kim. A big man in shirt sleeves, whom Griffin couldn't see clearly, seemed to be cleaning the floor.

A sudden sense of warning, of danger and trouble, woke in Griffin and he felt himself tighten. He put a hand on the doorknob. Now he had attracted the attention of the men inside and a second warning told him not to show surprise or alarm.

"You," he said to the group, as if he didn't know they were cops, "is Miss Evans here?"

"No. You looking for Karen Evans?"

The man stood up, away from the desk, and the smell of cop was so distinct that Griffin almost grimaced.

"Well, Miss Evans was supposed to find somebody to help with my yard work," Griffin said, trying to sound like an irritated customer. "Do you suppose she just forgot about it?"

"I wouldn't know, mister." The man was only a few feet from Griffin now, staring hard. "When was this? When did you see her?"

Griffin started to ask if something had happened to Karen, and then decided that the cop wouldn't tell him. "I saw her a couple of days ago. Thursday, I think. Yes, that's it."

The cop chewed his cigar, studying Griffin. "And haven't seen her since?"

"Why, no." Griffin tried to sound abrupt. A leaden fear was spreading in him, though. The atmosphere was ominous.

"You're a personal friend of Miss Evans?"

Beyond the plainclothesman Griffin could make out the interior more plainly now. The man who was cleaning the floor back there, using a wet mop and a bucket, was a middle-aged Chinese.

"No. I'm one of her customers."

The cop examined Griffin's face and build suspiciously. "She's doing you this special favor, though."

"I'm going to buy a lot of her soil conditioners, and I need the yard tilled. It's like brick."

The cop nodded as if this much might be believable. "You live here long?"

"No, not long."

"Name?"

"Griffin."

"Got a job?"

Griffin hated himself for not being ready for the damned question. "I'm looking. I've got some good prospects."

The cop was going to ask about the prospects, but the Chinese man interrupted. He had propped the mop against the wall and had come to the door. He touched the detective's sleeve. "I'm the one Mr. Griffin wants to talk to." To Griffin he said, "I'm Lisa Kim's uncle. Karen spoke to me about the job you wanted done."

"Has something happened to Miss Evans?"

"No."

Griffin couldn't conceal his relief. "Oh. Well, good." He offered Kim his hand.

"My name is Kim, too, like Lisa's. I can't come out to your place today, though. Somebody has to stay here and feed the pets and keep an eye on the other stuff while the officers go about their business. The place will be open and people coming and going, maybe some curiosity seekers, and not all of them exactly honest."

Suddenly Griffin wanted to grin. The bland Chinese face held no hint of sarcasm, but Kim was implying that the cops, if not watched, would take whatever pets and plants seized their fancy, not to mention possibly tons of fertilizers.

"What is going on here?" Griffin asked.

Kim looked at the cop, who shrugged and started back toward the desk. Griffin thought that the back of the cop's head had a listening look. Kim said, "A man's body was found in here this morning. Karen and a woman customer found him when she opened the store. He'd been killed with a hammer. His name was Tod Bonnay."

That one, Griffin thought. The one I heard putting on the big act of what a good boy he'd become. Then he remembered a further fact, that the conversation between Karen and her stepbrother had implied that things hadn't always been pleasant between them.

"Is Karen all, right?" Griffin asked quickly. "She's not ..."—he started to say "*a suspect*," and then bit back the words—"... upset, or anything?" He knew it sounded inane.

"Oh, yes, Karen's very upset. She's known this Bonnay for years."

Griffin was remembering the date that Karen had made with Bonnay for last night. What could have happened on that date? How bad a time were the cops giving her?

Kim said, "I haven't had a chance to talk to Karen. Lisa called me this morning. She told me what had happened here, and I figured somebody ought to be in the shop." He glanced back at the detectives, who returned his look stolidly. "I'd better stay here all day."

On an impulse, Griffin said, "Do you think Karen would mind if I went to see her? I know they live not too far from here, in an apartment—"

"I don't know why you shouldn't go. Maybe it would help, for her to talk to you. All she has is Lisa. No family at all. And Lisa's one who'll draw into a shell and stay there when anything bad happens."

"Well, then, what's the apartment address?"

He drove the few blocks and parked again.

Karen answered the door and the sight of her was instantly, though illogically, reassuring to Griffin.

She looked at him for an instant without recognition. She had been expecting a cop, Griffin thought. Then the stunned expression changed and she said, "Oh, hello."

"Do you want to talk to anyone? Me, for instance?"

She opened the door. "Come in."

He glanced around for some sign of Lisa Kim. Karen said, "Sit down. Would you like a cup of coffee?"

"I would, yes."

She fixed two cups and brought them into the living room, on a tray, with cream and sugar. Griffin took his black. He studied her over the rim of the cup. She was paler, all right. Her manner was puzzled and unsure. Griffin asked, "Do you feel like talking about Bonnay?"

She shook her head. "I can't understand it. It's like a bad dream. That's a hackneyed way to put it, but it's exactly the way I feel. As if I'm living a nightmare and have to wake up pretty soon. And there's a … a feeling of being pushed along faster than I want to go." She set her cup on a small table, brushed at her hair where it trailed against her cheek.

"I guess that's a normal way to feel, under the circumstances. Where is Miss Kim?"

"Lisa's lying down."

"Did she know Bonnay?"

He saw at once that the question frightened her.

"I … I don't know."

She knew, all right, Griffin decided; and the answer was yes, Lisa Kim had known Bonnay.

Perhaps Lisa had known Bonnay in a perfectly casual way and there was nothing more to this than a desire on Karen's part to keep Lisa from any suspicion whatever. Or perhaps it went deeper.

"You had a date with him last night. I overheard you making it, remember?"

"We had dinner at the Mill Wheel…. It's a fairly big restaurant, in case you don't—"

"I've been there."

"And afterward we went for a drive in his car." She sat looking at him, not seeing him really, Griffin thought, but thinking about the drive and perhaps something that had happened during it.

"If you want to tell me—how *was* Bonnay during all this?"

"He made such an effort. He tried so hard. He was charming, and he was ingratiating. You never saw him, so you don't know how good-looking he was, and the way he could smile at you, and … oh, a million things. When Tod was my stepbrother, years ago, I had such a crush on him. I'd have given the world for a tenth of the attention he showed me last night. And yet, last night, the harder he tried and the more winning he was, the further away from him I felt. I just seemed … frozen."

"Of course, you know I heard what he said to you that day he came to the shop. He sounded pretty sincere, especially that part about wanting your father to like him."

"Yes. I know how he sounded." She had an elbow on the chair arm, and she leaned her face into her palm with an air of weariness.

"You didn't believe him?"

"About Dad? Yes. I believed that. Tod had a funny way of setting up someone to admire, of kind of … well, contrasting them with his mother. In spite of a surface affection, I don't think Tod liked his mother much. I really believe that he did need and want a father. And he wanted that father to provide for him when the father died. It might have been that just as much as wanting the money for its own sake."

"You're giving him the benefit of a lot of doubts."

"I believed that much."

Griffin waited, but she didn't say what there had been that she hadn't believed. Finally Griffin asked, "Do you feel like talking about what happened this morning?"

"I found him." She shivered, straightening on the chair. "It doesn't seem real. It was horrible, and I remember it, and still I can't feel that it happened."

"Was Bonnay dressed the way he was last night?"

"Yes. He must have gone to the shop some time after he left me off here. But that doesn't seem possible, either. What on earth took him there?"

"Had Miss Kim come in when you got here?"

Well, that question hit home. There was no mistaking the fear in Karen's eyes. To cover the awkward moment while she hesitated, trying to frame an answer, Griffin asked, "Was anything valuable kept in the shop? Anything more than the pets, and the plants, and so on?" and then could have bitten his own tongue; what on earth had possessed him to start *anyone* thinking along that line?

"Nothing."

"You can't think of any reason for him to go to the shop?"

She shook her head.

"Maybe he wanted a look at your books there, to see how well the place was doing, how much money you might be making."

She almost smiled at this. "Anyone, anyone at all, can see that we're not making much in the shop. And Tod would know that." She busied herself for a moment, stacking things on the tray on the table in front of her. She took the empty coffee cups to the kitchen and returned. "That's part of the impossibility of it all—that there was no reason whatever for Tod to go to the shop."

Chalk up two items, Griffin thought. Lisa Kim had known Bonnay. Lisa Kim hadn't been at home when Karen had come in last night.

These weren't just facts, in Griffin's opinion. They were facts that had Karen scared to death.

Lisa kept the shop on alternate Fridays, so there seemed a good chance she had still been at the store when Bonnay had dropped Karen off here. Had Bonnay known that Lisa wasn't at home?

"Did Bonnay want to come here after the drive was over?"

"No. We said good night downstairs."

"Did he press you for another date, soon?"

"He kept insisting we'd see each other often now."

Well, Bonnay might have driven past the shop and seen the lights on, might have seen Lisa Kim in there. Bonnay had been putting on a big production, the switch from bad boy to good boy, and maybe Lisa Kim could have spoiled the act somehow. Maybe Bonnay had had to placate or threaten the Chinese girl before he could feel safe about impressing Karen. And maybe Lisa had played the part of a woman scorned to the hilt, and had killed Bonnay for being faithless.

It was corn. It was soap opera. It was something out of a 1920 silent movie. With a player piano in the background.

It happened somewhere every day.

Once the cops got past their suspicions of Karen, they'd begin to think along just these lines. They wouldn't be bothered a bit by any dislike for corn and soap opera.

Of course the Chinese girl was kind of slim and small to kill a grown, conscious man with a hammer; but then, fury lent anybody a lot of energy.

Right now the cops would be concentrating on Karen.

I don't believe Karen killed Bonnay, but then I'm in love with her and believing in her is easy.

He sat looking at Karen across the room, acknowledging to himself with a feeling of wry surprise that he did love her. It was a complication he hadn't expected. For a long time now he'd thought of himself as a kind of emotional paralytic, lost in a world where there was neither hating nor loving, but only indifference. A world in which he observed only, floating on his imaginary river, removed from what had once seemed to be reality. That was changing. And change, Griffin reminded himself, can be both painful and dangerous.

She blushed a little under the intensity of his look.

Griffin said, "Is there anything I can do, Karen?"

She nodded. "Yes, there is. Would you drive me somewhere?"

"Sure."

"I want to go back to the Mill Wheel. And then ... a drive."

"You want to retrace what you and your stepbrother did last night."

"Yes."

"Timing it," Griffin said.

She moistened her lips. "Yes."

"I think it's a good idea," he told her, "but I wouldn't mention anything about it to the cops."

"Oh?"

"Their minds don't work the way ours do. They'd try to see a lot of funny implications in the fact that you went over your night's drive with a possible witness along."

"I hadn't thought of it that way, at all."

"They will."

She gave him a wondering, slightly puzzled glance.

"I know quite a bit about cops, Karen. Let's say, I know their worst side."

She wanted to ask him about it; he could see that. But she was too afraid of hurting him, perhaps. Griffin added, "I never served any time. People with money enough to hire clever lawyers rarely do."

"Had you done what they ... they thought you'd done?"

"Not exactly. I'm not a model of innocence, either. Karen, if they can, they'll pin Bonnay's murder on you because it will save them a lot of work. You're the obvious one, an ex-relative of sorts, with a quarrel over money between you. You saw Bonnay before he died. What could be more logical than that you fought during the evening, you made an innocent production out of coming home, but you'd also promised Bonnay to meet him at the shop later. After Miss Kim was safely asleep, say."

"It didn't happen that way."

"I'm showing you what you'd better expect."

She nodded. The weariness had come back. "I see. Thank you, Jim."

"Get your coat and let's go."

Thirteen

When they reached the Mill Wheel, the front of the sprawling building had a shuttered appearance. Griffin drove through the parking area to the rear, found a couple of delivery trucks. and figured someone must be around. Karen asked him to wait, and left the car.

He smoked a cigarette and watched the driver at work from a liquor wholesaler's truck. The uniformed man had a small hand-dolly, and from the amount of cased liquor he was wheeling inside, Griffin judged that business was good. The other truck belonged to a linen supply outfit. It was very quiet in the service area; sunny, serene, with a lot of carefully arranged greenery, palms, dwarf evergreens, and what looked like star jasmine. When Karen emerged from the rear of the building and walked toward him, Griffin knew at once that her errand hadn't gotten her anything.

She slid into the seat beside him, brushed a lock of hair back from her cheek. "Nothing. A man who seems to be an assistant manager thought I might try coming back tonight and find the waiter, and perhaps talk to the cashier. But he told me not to expect anything. The waiter wouldn't know the exact time, unless it was just when he was due to go off. And there's no time stamp, or anything, on the meal checks."

"Let's drive, then."

She told him where to go. They left the main highway after a few miles and angled out toward the coast. The orange groves gave way to salt-marsh flats, and Griffin could smell the ocean. Then they turned back toward town.

He parked in front of her apartment. She looked over at him with a wide-eyed, worried expression. "It *had* to be past ten-thirty when I got home. It just had to be!"

He tried not to show undue curiosity. "Why shouldn't it have been?"

Suddenly she had nothing to say. She bit her lip.

"When did your friend Miss Kim get home last night?"

Her eyes dropped away; she rubbed a hand nervously across the clasp of the bag in her lap. Her breath came in a sigh.

"There's the snag, then," Griffin said. "You want to tell me about it? Or perhaps not?" He offered her a cigarette. She shook her head and then Griffin hesitated, asking mute permission to light one for himself. She gave him the ghost of a smile. "Go on. Of course."

He lit the cigarette. "Do you know when Bonnay is supposed to have died?"

"When the detective was at the apartment this morning he said something about eleven o'clock. But that would have been *right after* he let me out. And now, since you said what you did about the police, I can't help wondering. Maybe the detective was testing me, somehow. Trying to catch me."

"Don't believe what the cops tell you. Or that is, not necessarily. Sometimes they let things slip. But most of the time there's a motive for giving you any information. True or not." Even as he spoke to Karen, something else had come into Griffin's mind, a disturbing thought. He had to get home and burn the damned letter before some cop came snooping. It was in a place at home where a cop might not think to look. Or then again, just might.

"I have to believe Lisa. Don't I?" Karen asked, in a tone oddly childlike.

He put a hand on hers, felt the thrill of the warm, firm flesh under his touch; checked his rush of feeling. "Don't trust anyone. Don't accept any-thing as true except what you know by seeing it yourself. And you might even question that a little." He saw the flinch of doubt; he sighed. "Don't even believe me. Don't follow any advice without checking it against your own common sense and self-interest—not even *my* advice."

"I see."

"No, Karen, you don't, see. This is out of your world, beyond it."

"But it's in *your* world."

He knew that his features changed, took on the hooded look of withdrawal. It was nothing he could help. "It's in my world, all right."

She waited as if thinking something through. "Why did you come to the shop in the first place?"

He shrugged.

"I ... I find that I like you a great deal," she said quietly. "Does that make me a fool?"

"I hope not."

"But you won't tell me the truth?"

"No."

She thought that over. "You think I'm better off not knowing?"

"You're a million times better off. And you can believe it."

"The officer who questioned Lisa this morning kept bringing up something that happened a long time ago, when Lisa was small—"

Abruptly he put a hand over her mouth, cutting off what she was going to say. He saw the flare of surprise, of offended hurt, in her eyes. "Don't say any more."

He let his hand drop. Instantly she reached for the door handle.

"Karen, will you call me later? Let me know what's happening? Here's the number ..." He jerked out a pen and stray card and scribbled hastily.

She had the car door open. He thought for an instant that she would refuse the card. And in that heartbeat it seemed that every value he'd lived by, every cynical premise on which his existence was built, shattered and dropped away. What mattered now was Karen. If she shut him out, he was done.

I couldn't take it, he thought with inner astonishment. *She means too damned much to me. I can't endure to lose her.*

A funny thing happened to me on the way to the bank—

I found somebody to love.

His mouth was dry and inwardly he was shaking.

She twisted around on the edge of the seat and reached for the card.

"Thanks," he said.

"I'll call you after a while. Perhaps after I've talked to Lisa."

"Thanks," he repeated, unable to think of anything more to say.

"I'm not going to press her to tell me anything. I just want her to know that I'm still her friend."

"I guess that's best."

"Will you be at home?"

"Yes."

She got out of the car into the sunlight. He watched her walk to the stairs of the apartment. She didn't want him to escort her, he sensed; she wanted no show of courtesy; what had happened between them, unexpressed, not put into words, had shaken her as much as it had him.

She didn't turn at the entry, didn't look back; she simply disappeared, leaving him there in the car feeling unutterably alone.

It was nearly twelve-thirty before the silence made Dr. Ferrie aware that Miss Spilling had gone.

There were no longer any heel-tappings in the hall, the busy and self-conscious rattle of folders as she passed, efficient skirt-swishings, the multitude of silly things she did to let him know that she was there and trying to please. And to drive him nuts.

He had been leafing through a medical journal at the desk. Now he lifted his head, savoring the quiet; and then suddenly he was struck with a feeling of being back *before*—before Miss Barracuda and the compulsive flirting with disaster and the weighing of what he could salvage if he could cut and run—unreasonably, because the cops could still call and say that they'd just run across some documents in Mr. Bonnay's stuff and wouldn't he co-operate by coming in to be interviewed. Mixed with the feeling of having returned to this previous condition was something more, something he recognized and hated and dreaded, a sense of stifling, throttling boredom.

My God, he told himself, I was bored. I was bored to stupefaction.

He sat there in the quiet, searching his suddenly uneasy mind, trying to recapture the knowledge of deliverance which had dazzled him all morning.

He tried to laugh at himself.

What's wrong? He spread his hands on the pages of the magazine without consciously seeing the print, the illustrations. *You can't stand security anymore?*

He tried to revive the emotions of the past few days, the sense of ruin hanging suspended from moment to moment, the choking rage over the phone calls and the blackmailing bastard who'd laughed at him, the futility of taking out his fury on the soft body of the girl—none of it seemed real anymore. He was back in the old world again, Janie's world, the world of Old Mill River Road, of steady money piling up, and the rightness of knowing certain people and of being admitted to their homes, and the everlastingly same faces, and *dammit*, no excitement whatever.

And then he knew the danger he'd really skirted. He knew at last, with an insight into his own self, what the cut-and-run dream had been all about. It had had nothing to do, really, with the two barracudas. It had come into being because of what he was, now, his own present predicament.

The things that Janie's dad had done for him, the hesitant beginnings, the slow building of the years—he had been so bored with the end result that the thought of throwing everything to the winds and escaping had had the impact of some *Arabian Nights* adventure. Costly but beautiful. A new world full of the wonder of all things new.

I'd been on the point of saying Open sesame! he thought with a kind of wrench under the thinking, I was ready to cry Open sesame! to my future, to all the rest of my living years, and then that cursed Bonnay had to get himself murdered. The lousy pimp.

And now for the first time he wondered, almost idly, who else had been caught in Bonnay's claws and who had chosen to be free by killing him.

Somebody he'd pressured harder than he did me. Somebody with more to lose, with something irreplaceable to lose.

In that pet shop, of all places.

Dr. Ferrie got up from the desk, leaving the magazine lying there, and went out into the silent hall and on into the reception room. He glanced about, aware that it looked bizarre and pleasing still, that he found satisfaction in the riot of color on the floor, the Aztec masks; and he knew that this had been the beginning, the first stirrings, of what had led him finally to Miss Barracuda and her soft compliance and her drug need. And would have led him on into the wilderness of a new beginning— except for what had happened to Bonnay.

A few fragments of gossip, whisperings half-overheard under the man-chat at some garden doings, returned to mind. The women, old and young, married or single, had found Bonnay fascinating.

He walked over to the window and stared down at the pet and garden shop across the street. It looked deserted now. He felt no curiosity about Bonnay's murder, beyond the puzzle of its location; and no doubt that would shortly be explained by some release to the newspapers by the police.

He was reaching into his coat pocket for cigarettes when the phone rang. Miss Spilling had switched the incoming calls to his desk, and he heard it now, from there, muffled a little by the intervening walls. He finished getting out the cigarettes, lit one, inhaled and exhaled slowly. He was quite sure who was on the other end of the line.

She would be anxious now, nervous, her hands sweaty on the phone in the public booth at the drugstore.

The booth would be filled with the smell of her perfume and the clerk would be staring at her from the soda fountain.

My beautiful barracuda, he thought, and then something that almost amounted to shame came after, because without the male barracuda she was defenseless, directionless; she had no weapons, nothing but the desperate torment and need.

Down on the sidewalk across the street, from the direction of the bank, came a short stocky man in a blue suit and a brown hat. He proceeded carefully and exactly down the middle of the sidewalk, as if he might be afraid of breaking some ordinance or other, or as if the speed of pedestrians had been regulated by law and he were being clocked by a policeman. He slowed at the Kim girl's shop and glanced at the window, the display of fertilizers and garden tools, and this too with an air of guarded caution. He seemed to wish to attract as little attention as possible, in his tight careful manner, though this escaped Dr. Ferrie's idle regard, because Dr. Ferrie was listening to the phone ring and he was thinking how it had all begun, the day Miss Barracuda had first come, on some silly pretense, and had wanted him to examine her, and had pretended to feel dizzy and faint. And he had sent the Spilling wretch out in a hurry, on some fool's errand, anything, to get her away while he confirmed this new delight. And it had been like being snatched up on a tidal wave, on top of a wave that reached enormously above all other waves, a crest of unbelief and tearing ecstasy and ferocious lust, a lust he wouldn't have believed, not for him; and then it had been like drowning and dying, and he had known then all that Janie had cheated him of down through the years.

Before she had put on a single garment, she was begging for drugs.

Later there had been the man's voice on the phone, and Dr. Ferrie had seen the plot, and he had grasped the cunning of the male barracuda, and the male's shrewd measure of himself as ripe for plucking. For a while it hadn't mattered. She had mattered.

On the sidewalk across the street, the man in the blue suit and the brown hat had swiveled his head so that he could take a casual interest in the Kim girl's window display, even though he was slightly past the shop by now. His pace had neither quickened nor slowed; he was still doing the legal limit and still under the eye of an imaginary policeman. Dr. Ferrie, upstairs and across the street, made no mental note about this other man except that he'd never seen him before. He was new. He was a stranger.

The phone had quit ringing some minutes since.

Dr. Ferrie smoked, and waited.

There was a scratch of sound in the hall, a footstep, and then small knuckles rapped at the door.

The buzzer sounded under the edge of Miss Spilling's desk and in his own private office, a rough little sound like an imprisoned bee in a bottle. Then there was another spell of rapping.

He knew what he would see if he opened the door.

He didn't move. He regarded the street with introspective disinterest. He finished the cigarette.

She was murmuring something now, secret words, whimperings, at the rim of the door. She had checked the parking space behind the building—it was in a direct line from the drugstore, right on her way—and she was almost sure that he was in here. Almost. Not quite. He could have gone to play golf with a crony. That's what Janie would have thought, under the circumstances.

I could let her in and quiz her about what happened to Bonnay, he thought. She probably knows something. Maybe quite a bit. But of course she might not be as co-operative about talking as she might be … say, tomorrow. Tomorrow she'd be very co-operative.

He debated whether he could let her hang fire until Monday and then decided he could not. She'd be shattered, frantic by Monday. She'd talk to anybody.

Tomorrow, Sunday, he'll tell Janie that there were a few things to check at the office, some kind of test to run, anything—she was too ignorant ever to be in the least suspicious—and he could come downtown and leave the car in front, where Miss Barracuda couldn't miss it.

And then he could ask questions, and make her answer them, and then give her what she wanted, beginning the plan he had formulated. It would be a first step toward the end he had planned for her.

The scratchings, the whisperings, had died away. Dr. Ferrie turned to look at the room again.

I'm lucky, he told himself. I'm very lucky to have got out of this thing in this way.

He sighed. He didn't feel lucky.

On the sidewalk across the street, the stranger was coming back. He was passing Lisa Kim's shop again, staring now at the letter hung inside the door. The sign said CLOSED.

Fourteen

Warren usually got home on Saturdays before two o'clock. He spent Saturday mornings at the bank with one of the vice-presidents and the head accountant. He was very conscientious, Marlie sensed, though she had only the vaguest idea of what his work must involve. He had told her once that he *liked* Saturday mornings at the bank. He could check up on a lot of things without the clutter of a lot of employees and customers. Marlie had a mental image of Warren, going through fictitious checks perhaps, doing some kind of detective work on them, though she realized that this probably wasn't a true idea at all.

When Warren came in at two, she was in the kitchen with Suzabell. They were concocting a salad dressing for tonight. A cookbook lay propped open between them and an array of spices was clustered by a bowl. The little gold-colored radio played on the shelf over the counter, and Marlie, in white shorts and dark blue shirt, rope sandals on her feet, had been tapping time to the music. For Marlie, it was a gorgeous day.

"Hello, kitten." Warren bent to nuzzle the back of her neck, before she could put down the spoon. There was a new tenderness, carefulness, about Warren now that was heart-touching.

She turned against the counter, the tawny hair swinging; she touched his lips lovingly with the tip of a finger. "I'm *cooking!*"

Suzabell, always tactful, gave Warren a brief smile of welcome and then found something to do across the big kitchen.

"Cooking, is it? Cooking what?"

"A salad thing. A dressing. It's going to be garlicky and full of sage and mace and stuff."

"Wonderful. Kitten, come upstairs while I change. I want your company."

"Sure." She left the wooden spoon in the big blue bowl, put the cap on the bottle of wine vinegar, and went arm in arm with her big husband to the stairs.

They were a third of the way up, bouncing together, his arm around her, when he said without preamble, "The damnedest, absolutely the damnedest thing happened downtown this morning. Right next to the bank. You know that little shop, the garden and pet things—Lisa Kim's little store—

"They found Tod Bonnay in there, dead as a mackerel. Beaten to death with a hammer. I just … it seemed so unbelievable that I—Hey! What're you doing? Trying to break your neck? Watch your step, baby, you can't afford any head-over-heels tumbles downstairs, not now. You're pretty precious, you know that Marlie … Marlie!"

She was sagging, falling, and then Warren had picked her up and was carrying her, and the stairs and the walls and the ceiling high above swung on a great revolving wheel, and Warren was cursing under his breath, breathy cursing that blamed himself for what had happened, telling his pregnant young wife such a shocking thing. "I'm a damned fool. Marlie, look at me."

She was in bed, Warren was chafing her wrists, the room looked sunny and distinct. "Let me sit up."

"Of course you're not going to sit up. I'm going to call Doc Ferrie. Right now."

"Oh, Warren ..." She struggled for control over her fuzzy senses, the fright, the tearing sense of disaster. "No, no. You mustn't bother Dr. Ferrie—"

"*Bother* him? For Pete's sake, Marlie—"

She was surprised that her thick tongue could form words, that the words even made a kind of sense. "He'd just ... It's nothing. It happens all the time. I ... I had a dizzy spell like it this morning, while you were gone. It's because of changes in your system, something ... nothing. Warren—"

"You're not making me change my mind, baby."

"Warren, just let me lie here for a minute. Then if I don't feel better, if the dizziness doesn't go away, you can call him."

"Look, kitten, this could be *important*—"

"Warren. Please."

He was sitting beside her, he wasn't rushing to the phone. She'd won a moment's respite. She had to know more about Tod Bonnay, had to know at once. But this knowing had to be gone about carefully.

"You're as pale as a sheet."

"As white as a sheet. Pale as a ghost."

"Or whatever. You're kind of green, even."

She patted his big square hand, drew it to the bosom of the dark blue shirt. "What were you saying? On the stairs. Just before I had this dizzy streak. Something about Lisa Kim and her shop."

"Well, we'll forget about that."

"No, Warren. I'm shut up here at home all day. What was it?"

"Nothing you need to know. Maybe you should be taking some kind of medicine. Doc would know what kind."

"I'll go in Monday."

"Marlie, he'll be at home right now, it wouldn't take him five minutes to put down his highball, or whatever he's drinking, and come on over here."

She put his hand against her cheek and closed her eyes. "Just forget about your pal Dr. Ferrie for a minute and talk about something else. Finish telling me what you started on the stairs. Come on, darling. I want to hear your story."

"I wouldn't talk to you about that for a million bucks."

"You said someone had an accident in the bank. Got sick." This wasn't what Warren had said, and Marlie knew it. She also knew he'd be bound to straighten her out.

Her heart was beating so hard, there was such a sick taste in her mouth, it was nice just to lie there with Warren's hand against her face; and in that moment she wished that never, *never*, in her life again would she have to hear the hated name of that other man. But right now she had to. She had to find out what Warren knew.

"I said they found Tod Bonnay, murdered, in Lisa Kim's shop. The other girl—"

"Karen. I know her."

"Karen found him this morning, when she came to open the store. Of course I didn't hear about it, didn't hear anything, until a lot later. A police officer came to the side door of the bank and asked if we'd heard anything, seen anything—of course we hadn't."

"When did he die?"

"Middle of the night sometime, this officer seemed to think."

"Do they ..." Her heart was pounding so now, Warren surely must hear it. "Do they know who killed him?"

"Well, I judge they don't—" He broke off; she sensed the frown he wore. "Say, you met Tod Bonnay at Tahoe, that trip you took up there. Didn't you tell me he showed up, that somebody introduced you?"

"Yes."

"He was a bad actor, Marlie. I hope you had as little to do with him as possible."

"I didn't see him much. He was a ski fanatic."

"Yes. Always quite the sportsman."

She felt that she had to suck in an enormous breath, or she would choke, strangle; she couldn't go on talking about Tod in this quiet monotone, lying supine with Warren's hand against her cheek. She had to sit up, draw in the huge breath, and ... *scream*. The fear that beat, pounded, rattled inside her was forcing a scream into her throat.

"Warren, I've got to go right away and see my mother."

"Your mother? What can she do, when you won't even let me call Doc Ferrie—"

"I just need her. Warren, I do. I need her an awful lot. Right away."

"Well ..."

"Suzabell can help me change. And you can drive me."

Part of Warren's reluctance was based on the funny, distant way Ma had always treated him. Ma had wanted Warren to know, without any doubt, that she had no designs on his money for herself; but Warren just thought that Ma didn't want him for a son-in-law—which, come to think of it, Ma hadn't.

By pitiful cajoling, Marlie got Warren to agree to drive her across town. Suzabell came up, wary, confused, and helped her dress. Suzabell had an instinct for trouble, a nose for disaster—Marlie could see that—and what was going on here disturbed her.

In the car, Marlie tried to control her nervous hurry. Warren had lapsed into silence. Whether he was thinking about Marlie's queer behavior, or something else, Marlie couldn't tell.

He mustn't start connecting that fainting spell, and this rushing trip, with Tod Bonnay's murder. He just mustn't. The fainting spell must stay in his mind connected with her pregnancy. And this need suddenly to see her mother, the same.

Warren squinted at the street signs. "I'm not sure ..."

She directed him in a hoarse, hollow voice, clutching the purse on her lap, squeezing and relaxing her toes inside the white pointed pumps. Oh, God, let Ma be at home....

When he stopped before her mother's house, Marlie cried, "Wait for me," and jumped out without looking, and turned an ankle briefly on the uneven walk, and heard Warren protesting in the car. She ran stiff-legged up to the porch, and then saw with a vast sweep of relief that inside the patched screen, the inner door was open. Ma must be at home. They hadn't arrested her. She wasn't in jail, being given the third degree, or whatever they called it.

Marlie beat on the rim of the screen door. "Ma! Ma!"

Her mother's voice answered at once, and then dimly Marlie could make out the interior through the dusty webbing, and she saw that her mother had been stretched out on the old couch and was just now sitting up, putting her feet on the floor, "Marlie, what on earth—"

Inside, Marlie peered back at the car to make sure that Warren was still in it. "Ma, that horrible Tod Bonnay is dead, murdered! Somebody killed him last night in that pet store, the shop of Lisa Kim's, right next door to the bank. I couldn't wait to get here, to make sure that you ..." Marlie's voice ran down because her mother wasn't showing any signs of surprise, shock, or even attention. Her mother sat in a sagging heap on the couch, fumbling for her shoes with her toes, her face a mask of tiredness and disinterest.

"Don't you *understand?* Don't you see, they'll be checking on everybody—"

"Marlie, for God's sake, keep your voice down."

"But, Ma—"

"Why does Warren think you rushed over here?"

Somewhat quieter, because of her mother's attitude, Marlie told her about Warren's arrival home, what he'd said on the stairs, and her reaction.

"Why on earth didn't you let him call the doctor?"

"All I could think of … what you said, Ma, the last time I saw you. That there ought to be a way to … to …" Marlie sank into a chair; she suddenly wanted to cry. Life was too hard, too complicated to endure. There was too much to be careful about. Too much to remember. She regretted in that moment not telling Warren right away about the awful thing she'd done at Tahoe. It would have been better to be driven away, an outcast, crawling back to Ma to die … than this. This was a nightmare.

"Marlie, when are you going to get some common sense? You have no more to do with Tod Bonnay, alive and kicking or stone-cold dead, than you have with the man in the moon. He was not part of your life. You're Warren's wife, you're going to have a baby, you must take care of yourself."

"Ma—"

"When you fell on the stairs, the sensible thing would have been to be worried over your baby, just as Warren was. You should have *wanted* to see the doctor."

"Ma, I can't have Dr. Ferrie. Don't ask me why. I can't tell you, except that when I went to him, and he told me I was pregnant, there was a … a look in his eye—"

"I'll bet a damn there wasn't a word on his lips," her mother said grimly.

"Ma … Mother—you already knew Tod was dead. When I got here, I mean. You weren't a bit surprised. Did you hear it on the radio? Was it in some local news broadcast?"

"If it was I didn't hear it."

"Did you check up on him? You weren't … following him around, were you?"

"How could I follow Tod Bonnay around? Him with a big car and me on foot—"

"Isn't your car running?"

"That wreck? I'm keeping up with Tod Bonnay with a 1949 Ford?"

"But isn't it running?"

Her mother hated to admit it, Marlie saw; and this set her heart pounding again. "You *were* following him—"

"Marlie, this town is full of gossip," her mother said wearily. "And they think part-time cleaning women don't have ears, I guess. Tod Bonnay was making a play for his stepsister, for Karen Evans."

"What?" And in spite of her own fears, and apprehensions, and mixed emotions, Marlie's mind suddenly opened to the truth, to an explanation of Tod's motive in warning her to stay away from Karen. Why, he'd been afraid of *her*. He'd been afraid she might spoil things for *him!*

"There was money involved, an estate. Not his mother's," Ma was going on, "and I guess Tod wanted it. What his claim could have been, I don't know. I gather he'd tried being ugly, and that hadn't worked. Probably it isn't a lot of money compared to what some of them are sitting on, out there on Old Mill River Road—"

"That's why—" Marlie breathed, her mind fixed on the frightening interview with Tod.

"So I did sort of check, when it was handy, going and coming through town—I did kind of look over that shop to see if he was hanging around."

Marlie was looking at her mother in horror.

"And last night …"

"Ma!"

"I'd been baby-sitting until close to ten-thirty, that nice young Dr. Farmer and his wife …"

Marlie's fear was so great, her dread of what she was going to hear so terrifying, that she put out a hand as if to shut away her mother's words.

"And I thought, I'll just drive by and look, and lo and behold, there was Tod Bonnay walking toward that pet store—"

"Oh, Ma. Ma, don't tell me!"

"You're better off knowing, I see now," her mother said with weary practicality. "Must have been close to eleven, anyway, and he'd parked his car somewhere else, maybe close—I didn't see it—but there he was, as big as life, headed for the Kim girl's little shop. There was a light inside, not a bright one. A night light, maybe. And I thought, what on earth's he doing here at this hour, when the place is closed, and then he had the door open and he was sliding inside."

Marlie waited, dry-mouthed, for her mother to tell her she had stopped and had followed Tod into the store.

"And right then the damnedest thing happened. It just scared me almost senseless. You know, I'm a nervous driver. The car acts up all the time, half of the time it's sputtering, something seems to be sticking inside—well, I drive slow and I give the old wreck plenty of time. And just as Tod Bonnay disappeared inside that shop a car cut across in front of me—really, it damned near scraped my fender. Maybe it *did* scrape. I haven't looked yet—and I slammed on the brakes and almost swerved into the curb after that other car, almost hit the damned car that had cut across in front of me. The traffic was light, there wasn't more than eight or ten cars in sight on the whole street, and he didn't have to do me like that."

"What … what did you do then?"

"I drove off down the street a few blocks, and parked and tried to get my breath and to wait till my heart stopped hammering. Then I went to an all-night diner for a cup of coffee. And then I drove back past the shop. Believe me, I kept my eye peeled for any crazy idiots trying to skin off my bumpers."

"And Tod was gone?"

"I don't know. I guess not, if you say he's dead—"

Marlie wanted to scream, "Ma, you knew he was dead! You knew it when I came here!"

"But what happened next—this is just for you, Marlie, to put your mind at rest about me." Her mother seemed to be looking past Marlie into some wearying land where all bad things happened. "The Chinese girl came out. She staggered a little, and her coat flapped open, and even from across the street and with the shadowy light, I could see what was smeared all down the front of her dress."

Marlie felt again the terrifying giddiness, the numbing inertia, which had seized her on the stairs.

"You couldn't mistake it, all that blood. Marlie, are you feeling bad again?"

"Call ... call Warren, Mother," said Marlie, swimming in darkness, not afraid now, just genuinely sick and wanting her husband.

Fifteen

At around four, having waited all afternoon for Karen's call in the silent house on Edwards Street, Jim Griffin realized that if he was to eat anything that night he had to go to the store. He debated about going to a café instead, but decided that getting stuff at the store just two blocks away, cooking it at home, eating at home, would give him a better chance to catch the phone when it rang. *If* and when, he corrected. If and when it rang.

Probably Karen didn't want anything more to do with him. She had his number by now, she knew pretty well what he was. He'd been one of the sharp ones, he'd kept out of jails and prisons, but that didn't change what was underneath, the dirt.

Spread out on the kitchen table were the big sheets of tagboard and the pencils and T squares. He stacked the tagboard on the sink before he left the house.

When he came back, not more than fifteen minutes later, and pulled into the drive, he took a good long look at a car across the street that hadn't been there when he had driven away.

It was a small sedan, black, not at all shined up and not too old, either.

It was the kind of car you drove when you didn't want anybody looking at you, and this was why Jim Griffin took time to size it up.

He didn't go to the front door. He went around to the rear and stood on the step there and waited. Someone was inside; he couldn't have explained how he knew it. No odor of cop, no miasma of authority, reached him. Some other-sense, some invisible antenna of his own, searched in the house and came to him with a blank.

He opened the rear door, which was unlocked, and went in.

Sitting in the chair by the table in the kitchen, the chair Griffin himself had vacated, was a stocky square-faced man with a red bulbous nose, small dark eyes, thin red-turning-to-gray hair, and a mouth like a crack in a stone slab. On the table lay a brown hat. There wasn't a speck of dust on the hat, the man's suit was neat, he was shaved, the hand lying on the table was clean, the nails pared. His suit was blue, an inconspicuous blue, a don't-look-at-me kind of blue, like the don't-look-at-me black car across the street. Griffin said, "Who in the hell are you and what are you doing in my kitchen?"

The blunt hand lifted in a placating salute. "Your old man sent me, Griffin. Name's Chester." Seemingly he meant to offer the hand, but then let it drop to the table. "He said, come and talk."

Griffin pushed the sack of groceries onto the sink. "Talk? Talk about what?"

"Things."

"How did you get in?"

"Same way you did. Wasn't locked. I thought it best, just come in, not stand out there for the neighbors to stare at."

"How do I know my old man sent you?"

"This." Carefully, from inside the blue suit-coat, from an inner pocket, Chester drew a wallet, a black wallet, not old, now new. With a little tick of the blunt fingernails on the metal clasp he opened the wallet and withdrew a single small sheet of paper. He pushed the paper in Griffin's direction.

Jim Griffin opened the narrow sheet.

He recognized the old man's handwriting, the old-fashioned tall-lettered script, at once.

Jimmy boy, this will introduce a friend of mine, Chester. He can help us, and you can trust him. He knew The Bug real well. He knew him before, and he knew him later you'll understand what I mean.

In case you're doubting that this really came from me—and of course we've got artists in here can copy anybody's hand—I'm putting this in. Your ma had a kid sister named Victoria. Your ma had a pet name for her: Henny. I know your ma has spoken to you, years ago, about your Aunt Henny. Henny died in a car accident up close to Seattle. This is something only your old man could know, so you can rest easy. Good luck.

Aunt Henny. Yes, he remembered Aunt Henny, he remembered his mother's voice speaking of her, and knowing that his mother had loved Henny, and he thought—he couldn't be sure—that he'd seen his mother's tears when Henny had died. So far away. So long ago. Griffin took a long minute to tear the note into tiny pieces and to drop them down the sink pipe.

"So what things do we talk about?"

The man at the table sat quietly for a moment, as if listening to the world outside, and then he seemed to collect himself, and said briskly, "The bank. The bank and the money. Not the money in the bank. To hell with that. I'm no bank robber."

"You mean, the bank's money that never was found. The money that still might be in the cellar." When the other nodded, Griffin added, "What brought this on? What made my old man change his mind, drag you into it, and what's your cut?"

The dark eyes facing his were suddenly chilled, smoky with caution. "You sore, or something?"

"I just want to find out why the change was made. I just want to know why an organizer was sent—that's what you are—and why things have to be hurried up."

The careful voice said, "Keep your shirt on. No need to rush to any conclusions. Keep the peace, I always say. Make more money that way. Your old man has a chance, something he never expected, he might be paroled. And now he's impatient. Logical. And he wasn't hearing from *you*."

I should have sent word to him, Griffin thought. "He needs money?"

"Who don't?"

"I mean, lawyers for the parole, and so on."

"Yeah."

"He said it was up to me. To move. Or not to move."

"Hell, the poor old devil never expected to see outside again. You know it."

Griffin had pulled out a second chair, sat down in it. He felt tensed up inside, and warning prickles brushed from the back of his neck all the way down his spine; there was a smell in the room, the stench of deceit. "What per cent did he offer you?"

"Third."

"I don't believe it."

The other man shrugged. What Griffin was thinking, this character named Chester wouldn't come in for a twenty-thousand-plus cut. That wouldn't be worth his time. Either he expected Griffin to have everything planned, ready to roll, and the money would represent a couple of day's work, no more—or there was something here that Griffin didn't know about.

"A third of sixty-nine thousand?" Griffin persisted. "I can't believe you'd bother with it."

The tip of Chester's tongue came out and made a circle of his mouth, touching the skin where lips would have been if he'd had lips. "So what's wrong with twenty-two, twenty-three thousand? Huh?"

"For you, it smells. I know it."

"What d'you care, if *I'm* willing—"

"And what does my old man want you to do that I can't do alone?"

"He's impatient. And he's got an idea you might not do anything. He's all stirred up. He's kind of goofy right now," Chester said, as if outlining a simple lesson to a stubborn kid. "He never thought there was a ghost of a chance, parole, and now he might have—"

"He's sick. He must be dying," Griffin decided suddenly. "That's the only thing would make a parole board look at him twice."

"Well, sick or well, he wants outside. Wouldn't anybody? And he'll need something to live on."

"He starts living on money from that cellar, he'll be inside again before he can blink."

Chester gave a patient headshake. "Why don't you just relax, and we can go over what you've got so far—I see those charts of the cellar, and you've got some measurements—"

"You tell me what you're in this for," Griffin said.

Chester hesitated. "It doesn't have to be sixty-nine thousand," he said finally.

"There's more?"

"The *bank* said sixty-nine thousand."

"Why would the bank downgrade what was gone? If anything funny went on, if somebody in the bank was holding part of the loot, the figure they gave out would be bigger, not smaller. If somebody in the bank, for instance, had snagged thirty thousand—I'm just using the figure as an example—had snagged thirty thousand, then there's only thirty-nine thousand possible in the cellar. Not more. Less."

"I see you've thought about it."

"Hell, yes, I've thought about it. My guess, the way everything went haywire in the job they did, somebody in the bank took the opportunity to cover what he'd been doing. Maybe the bank's president, for all we know."

"The president got killed. Punk couldn't control his hands, let go with a blast that took the old guy right across the middle." Chester's flat brown eyes implied his hatred of all punks and his respect for careful craftsmen like himself. "But The Bug thought it was more, and he was sure it was still down there in the cellar, and the reason the bank said sixty-nine thousand, they had to give out a figure to the papers. The town was howling. The bank had to remind everybody that the money was insured, give a figure on the loss they expected to get the money back—"

"Maybe they did. Maybe somebody did."

"Nobody did. The only one who could have was the Chink. And he didn't. I'm not saying how I know, but I know. The Chink didn't, and he was the only one who knew enough to do it." Chester's barrel-shaped torso moved on the chair. "Are we going to sit here and argue all day? Why can't I see those plans on the sinkboard there, and why can't we talk about what you've seen and how we can go about this? You sure can't say your old man didn't send me," he added.

Griffin admitted to himself, while he went over and lifted the tagboard sheets, it was true; his stepfather, his tutor and guide for so long, had wanted Chester in on this thing.

He thought of the old man behind bars, wild with the hope of a parole. Someday I'll make a mistake like his, Griffin thought, and then I'll be inside and I'll know what it is to look at the empty years ahead.

He put the tagboard on the table. "This is the first sketch. It wasn't accurate. I had to wait until I could measure. But now, there's a complication."

Chester looked at the drawings and listened impassively while Griffin told him about Tod Bonnay's murder in the shop.

Chester glanced up, frowning. "This Bonnay—he have anything to do with what we're after?"

"I don't think so. He was making a play for the Evans girl, as I've explained, and for some reason he went right from Karen Evans to see Lisa Kim, in the store. My guess, Lisa Kim killed him."

"Dames," said Chester sourly, bending above the tagboard.

"What I'm getting at," Griffin continued, "is the delay. We can't move soon, there'll be too much activity—"

"That'll be over right away," Chester informed him. "You say, they got the weapon? What's left to hunt for? They're looking at people now. Not that store."

The assured way he said this gave Griffin an idea. "You went by the shop before you came here."

"Sure did. And it's locked up. Empty. I didn't know anything about a murder, of course. I just figured, Saturday afternoon, everything quiet downtown with the bank closed, the shop was closed too." He lifted his eyes to Griffin's in a slow wise look. "Closed up now till Monday morning."

Griffin knew what he meant. This was the chance, the time to move.

He hadn't been sure until just that moment that he'd had no intention of going on with the job in Lisa Kim's cellar—neither the actual breaking through into the bank, nor searching for the cash missing for these twenty years. He was through. He was not just through with this particular job, he was done for good. He'd served some kind of sentence, in a way, learning from the old man, an apprenticeship, a time of growing up and becoming what he'd been meant to be. And now he saw that he had not been meant to be what his stepfather had created, at all. He had suddenly become someone else. He had undergone a change, totally unexpected, hard to understand; he was a new self. A painfully new self.

He was going to have to tell this man, this Chester, that he didn't intend to go on with the bank job.

More: he was going to have to prevent Chester from going on with it, too. The strange new unexplored self that was James Griffin had to divert Chester from the job, not easy, since behind Chester's air of the patient expert lurked a casual violence, a ferocity, betrayed by the hungry spatulate hands and the flat brown eyes; and he would tear Lisa Kim or Karen Evans to pieces just as soon as look at them, if they got in his way. Or Griffin. Or anybody.

As soon as it was good and dark, Chester was going to want to get into the shop and look at that cellar in person.

If Griffin interfered, there might well be a second murder right where Tod Bonnay had died last night.

Mabel Winniger was sitting in Janie Ferrie's family room, knees crossed under a taut gray silk skirt, a cigarette in hand, talking in the husky voice that sounded as if she had the beginnings of bronchitis or had yelled herself hoarse competing with a steamboat whistle. Janie sat across from her, not as close, not as chummy as usual; she still wore the morning's muumuu and her face had a slack pallor.

"It's such a cute, clever idea, Janie," Mabel was saying, "that I'm kind of jealous that Mrs. Farmer thought of it, and not one of us."

"Isn't she one of us?" Janie asked, not spiritedly but as if Mabel had finally bored her.

"Oh, you know what I mean. This is going over with a bang! Everyone's going to love it! And we'll make money for Housing for Elders; she suggested we start by getting new curtains and slip covers for the women's ward lounge at County Hospital—so many senile and elderly there—and then TVs for the lobbies in that low-rent housing project, that thing they call Lodestar Homes, where everybody has to be over fifty-five, has to be over fifty-five to get in, and then—" Mabel, almost out of breath, paused for a drag on the cigarette, "—and then, when finances permit, looking into private, needy exceptional cases like old widows who can't repair their roofs—*she's actually already found three!* I'll confess to you, Janie, this little Mrs. Farmer makes the rest of us look like weed-grown wrecks!"

Janie drew a deep breath, dull-eyed. "What's the clever way of making the money?"

"Well, you've heard of golf tournaments where the husbands are matched against wives, you know—fork over the difference in scores, and stuff like that, it's not new—but Mrs. Farmer has a cute new twist. *Soul mates!*"

"Soul mates?" Janie whispered with a flinching look.

"Not your *wife*. Someone you'd like to have an affair with ..." Mabel sucked her lips and winked at her old friend.

"Won't they ... won't they run out of them awfully quick, in our circle?" Janie said. It was not a thing she would have understood a year, a month, or even two days ago. Now it was shatteringly clear.

"Oh, Janie, it'll be like drawing straws, it's just a gag, just for fun. You won't even know who your soul mate is, until it's over. That's to keep the scores from being connived over, the way husbands might do with their wives—and then there'll be a Soul Mates' Ball, and you have to come as famous soul mates, in costume, like Cleopatra and what's-his-name. Antony."

"They'll run out of *them* right away, too," Janie prophesied dully. "Quicker than the other."

"Well, it's going to be *fun*. And why on earth didn't you come to the committee meeting this afternoon? What're you doing here in that thing without even any lipstick on?"

Mabel's voice was so blithe and critical and removed from Janie's world of sick pain and horror, that Janie almost told her all about it ... all about Ronnie and Miss Barracuda, and Dr. Farmer's alarm and the stabbing thrusts inside. Almost. Not quite.

But then, of course, she really couldn't tell Mabel all of the truth, not yet, because in a way it hadn't all stopped happening, there must be more to come, maybe very unpleasant, even terrifying things, and then it would be time to cry on Mabel's shoulder the way she used to, long ago, while she'd still been hoping and praying that she and Ronnie would have a family, a lovely family of children, to bind them together forever and forever.

Sixteen

The room was growing gray. Karen glanced at the clock, then over at Lisa on the couch. "Isn't it a long time past when he said he was coming?"

"Yes."

"I'm so tired of waiting."

Lisa seemed to feel that this required no answer. She sat pinched into a corner of the couch, her shoulders narrowed, her hands folded. She had put on a green shirt and denim capris, white sandals, and she'd tied her hair back with a white scarf. With the hair pulled back her face looked leaner, bony, the slanted cheeks without color; and when she looked at Karen her gaze centered on a point just left of Karen's right shoulder.

"Did he say we *had* to wait here for him? Just ... just sitting?" Karen asked, not for the first time. She was exhausted; she wanted to lie down and shut her eyes; she wanted to forget this day and all that had happened in it.

Lisa said, "He wants us to wait. He'll come and talk to us again. There are ... new things."

Karen thought of getting another cup of coffee. How many had she drunk today? A hundred?

Then she suddenly sat up. "Listen. Somebody's coming up the stairs."

Someone heavy and big was coming up to the door from the street. Suddenly Lisa jumped off the couch as if unable to wait, rushed to the door, and jerked it open. The big detective stood outside; he had a finger pointed, centered now on Lisa's midriff. He looked ridiculously like a little boy playing that his hand was a gun. Then Karen realized that he'd been about to punch the bell.

"Come in," Lisa said, moving back. Her black eyes went all over him in a moment and then grew still. "Sit down."

"Thank you, Miss Kim." He looked at Karen. "Good afternoon."

"Good evening."

"Yes. Well, I was delayed. So much to do ..." He sat down and dropped his hat, and Karen had the dizzy impression that she was back, hours ago, in the morning; she felt kind of sick all at once. There he was, this rock of a man, hands on knees, eyes like a pair of cameras, brain—you knew—like a bear trap. "And of course, as things come in, new items, we have to go around and ask for them to be explained."

"New things, you said," Lisa said from the couch. "On the phone you said you'd found different evidence."

"We're beginning to get a pattern," he answered. "We traced the sale of the weapon, the hammer, for instance, and find that you bought it just yesterday. Along with a chisel. To remove some bricks. Would these bricks be in your cellar at the shop, Miss Kim?"

"Yes. We need more storage room down there. The ... the way the cellar is laid out is ridiculous."

"You were going to remove the brick wall yourself?"

Karen wanted to run from the room. Lisa had boxed herself into a spot where only the most obvious lie would serve as an answer. But Lisa surprised her. Almost matter-of-course she answered, "Oh, no, not Karen and I, or at least not alone. My uncle would have to do most of it."

"And when do you expect to begin this job?"

"Never."

"Never?"

Lisa touched her upper lip with her fingertips as if to brush away sudden perspiration there. "If it were possible, I would never go to the shop again. I would never go down the street outside it—"

"You'd leave town at once," he offered mildly.

"Yes. What has happened is so horrible—"

"And you knew Mr. Bonnay pretty well at one time, too, isn't that part of it? Losing an old friend, in your own shop, like this ..."

There was a change in Lisa as he spoke; it seemed that a light bloomed under her skin, paling and thinning it; you felt a sudden fragility in her, a brittle readiness to crumble. "Once we were quite ... close. Yes. That's true."

"More than three years ago."

"Quite ... quite a while past, now."

Now he used the trick Karen had noted before, the smooth and casual switch of subject, almost as if he were bored with the other tack and wanted a new one to freshen his interest. "What did you think of your stepbrother's sudden offer of friendship, Miss Evans?"

She saw the trembling relaxation that seized Lisa momentarily, as his interest left her. "I ... I was quite surprised," Karen answered lamely.

"Surely you had some suspicions about his real motive."

"I can't deny it. I did feel suspicious. And yet I was so anxious for us not to ... to be hateful ..."

She was the one who trembled now, inwardly, dreading what the next minute would bring.

"Well, it seems that it wasn't *you* who was being hateful, Miss Evans," he said, as if clearing up some small dispute.

She didn't know what to say to him.

"And then, isn't it odd when you think about it," he added, "that Mr. Bonnay died right after he approached you in this new way? Right after he reformed? Right after he came offering the olive branch, as the saying goes? Wouldn't it seem there might be a connection between Mr. Bonnay's sudden change and his getting killed? If this were an old-fashioned mystery story—excuse my little flight of fancy—we might think that somebody had hopes of inheriting from you, some *other* heir, and that they'd disposed of Mr. Bonnay in fear of losing what they'd get when you died. Meaning, naturally, they'd already planned and figured out *your* murder. But ..." He shrugged, pretending to shake off a kind of dream. "... this doesn't happen to be a story. And of course whoever inherits anything from you—"

"Lisa," Karen supplied, her wits frozen.

"You've made out a will in favor of Miss Kim?"

"It's not the way you make it sound. We both made wills. We had the business together, it's customary, and I didn't even remember at the time—"

"You didn't remember the estate left by your father? It seems incredible, Miss Evans. Here was Mr. Bonnay, constantly reminding you of it, acting nasty all over town—"

"I just ... I'm so tired, Mr.—I wish I could lie down."

"I wish I could let you lie down. Could you put up with me for a few more minutes? And the name's Block. Lieutenant Block."

Karen remembered then, he had introduced himself, given his name, that morning.

Lisa's whisper coiled at him from the couch. "Why can't you just leave us alone? Can't you see we're both exhausted?"

"As I said, I wish I could. This isn't fun for me, Miss Kim."

"Then get on with it!" Lisa's eyes were savage.

But now, the sudden change in his line of thought seemed incredible. "So. Will do. Miss Evans, do you have a blue dress, border of shiny sequins around the neck, a pale blue or white sash at the waist?"

She tried to follow the new tack, tried to comprehend. "It's the dress I wore last night on the date with Tod."

"Fine. Would you get it, please? And the wrap you wore. And the shoes." He actually gave her a smile, almost apologetic, as if showing his innate sympathy and good will. But Karen was swept by a chill, knowing somehow that this was what he had come for and that this was the point of all the meandering conversation.

Karen went to her bedroom, opened the closet, took the blue dress off its hanger, then lifted the coat from its hanger. She bent and picked up the high-heeled pumps she'd worn last night. Carrying all of these she returned to the living room.

"Just put them on the arm of the couch for now," said the detective. "Any wrinkling, any soiling, will be taken care of by the Department. Miss Kim—" Now his smile, and the near-apology, were for Lisa and Karen saw how Lisa stiffened and she could almost taste Lisa's terror in her own throat.

"Miss Kim, is there a cream-colored dress in your closet ... some kind of embroidery down the blouse? Blue or blue-gray. The skirt's pleated all around."

Karen thought, in a daze, beginning to be angry, *He's had people describe our clothes, he's been talking to people who saw us yesterday, people who noticed what we were wearing.* And under the astonishment was a feeling as if the ground were crumbling under her, as if all sureness and safety were being clawed away.

But Lisa was speaking up, quickly, her voice tight. "I don't have such a dress, no. I do have a blouse and skirt, cream-colored ... and the blouse has violet embroidery. Not blue."

Karen couldn't look at her.

Yesterday, going to work, Lisa had worn the cream-colored dress, the dress she'd bought less than a month before, the full-skirted dress with the gray lily-shaped blossoms embroidered on either side of the blouse jacket. Lisa got up swiftly and walked with an air of determined energy. She came back at once with a blouse and skirt and threw them on top of Karen's clothes and looked defiantly at the detective.

"Fine," he said. "Did you have a wrap last night, Miss Kim?"

The green coat ...

"A sweater. Do you want that, too?"

"Well ... Yes, I guess I'd better have it too." Still with the air of energy and anger, Lisa went for the sweater.

The detective stood now, and walked to where the clothes were piled, and lifted Lisa's garments from the top of the heap. "These are cream-colored, Miss Kim? I'd swear they're just white."

"They're off-white. They're what I wore yesterday, so they just must be what you want. Wouldn't you say so?"

"I'd say so." At the same moment he bent on Lisa a peculiar look. There was a warning in it. Karen thought that the look meant to let Lisa know that these clothes would be displayed to whoever had given the descriptions; that there was still time to be honest with him. But all Lisa did was to meet his gaze with one of hate and disgust.

He sighed, picked up Karen's garments, stood there with the clothes over his arm, the pumps in his hand. "Please keep yourselves available. Don't go out of town. Don't stay away from your apartment for a long while without letting us know where you are. Is all this clear?"

"Quite clear," Lisa said. She waited beside the door, to shut it behind him.

"I'm going to lie down, Lisa."

"Wait, Karen. Wait a minute."

They heard the detective's car start in the street below.

Lisa sat down on the couch again. "Do you think that I killed Tod?"

Karen thought about it. "When you brought out that blouse and skirt—yes, Lisa, I did. But now that we're alone, and I see that you're the same person I've known, I've lived with, worked with, all these months ... no. I don't know how a few minutes can make that difference, can bring a complete change—"

"Thank you, Karen."

"What happened to the cream-colored dress, Lisa?"

"It had Tod's blood all over it, and I couldn't get it clean," Lisa said with a sigh, letting her shoulders droop. "I worked like mad on it. And the coat—smeared inside. I'm so sick of lying." She shut the brilliant black eyes, and the lids looked papery, aged, withered with tiredness. "I'm sick of lying to you, Karen. Not telling you the truth *is* lying. If you'd stayed away today, avoided me, I could have kept it up, I could have hated you and believed that you had convicted me of murder in your heart. But you *didn't* stay away. You came back and you remained with me, and you've let me know, all this long afternoon, all these hours ..." All at once Lisa began to cry. She covered her face with her hands, her body shook, there was a dry sound almost like a cough in her throat.

Karen hurried to the couch and Lisa leaned against her, and Karen felt Lisa's hot breath against her shoulder, through the fabric of her dress; she felt the gusty breath that came out with Lisa's sobs.

"Don't cry. Lisa, you can't cry now. Lisa, listen to me! Where are those clothes? Where have you put them?"

Stifled, hiccupping through the sobs, Lisa got out, "They're wadded up in the bottom of the closet. Wet."

"He'll come back," Karen said, her voice stunned with dread.

"I'm too tired to care, now—"

"He'll watch to see if we try to smuggle them out," Karen said, thinking out loud. "Then, if we don't try anything, he'll come in. With a search warrant."

"I didn't kill Tod! He was dying, and I held him. Oh, Karen, I loved him so much ... and I still do. I just never stopped ..."

Karen thought, *I knew this. In spite of all that Lisa said about Tod, somehow I knew that she still loved him.*

"... even when he threw me over for somebody else. Even when he called me his ... his Chink whore ... and when I had to get rid of his baby. Not even then—"

"Hush, Lisa. Don't say any more."

The sound that Lisa was making now was like that of a hurt child, a lost child, suffering for reasons not understood, crying without hope of release. Karen ran to wet a washcloth in the bathroom, came back, tried to soothe Lisa by smoothing the wet cloth across her face. Lisa was collapsing, all control gone, her hands fluttering, her face ashy.

By main strength, Karen got her into her bedroom, into the bed, and then filled an ice bag and put it on her head. There was brandy in the cupboard, Karen remembered. She filled a liqueur glass and brought it, but Lisa turned her head at the odor and retched.

The room had grown completely dark.

Karen was curled into a chair beside the bed where Lisa lay. For a while after she had investigated the closet, had looked at Lisa's dress and coat, she had sat numbed with fright, seeing the future and what lay in it for Lisa. On her part, Lisa had gradually grown quiet; the sobs had ceased. Now for a time Karen had dozed, her head slipping sidewise to rest against the chair.

Karen awoke when Lisa's hand found hers.

"Karen?"

Karen pulled erect, feeling the aching stiffness in her body.

"Karen, will you go get my uncle, bring him here? He has to know the truth. It isn't fair, he mustn't find out when they ... when they take me away. Karen, he might even be able to help us! He might know of something to do, something better than we could think of ..."

Karen, listening to Lisa's breathless, hopeful words, found that she was thinking, not of Lisa's uncle, but of James Griffin.

James Griffin would know what to do.

It was not the time now to analyze her feeling for him, to try to figure out why the thought of turning to him brought a sense of relief and security, as well as a deep excitement, nor why she had the picture, not of conversation between them, but of creeping into his arms and of being sheltered there.

"You go, Karen. He won't stop one of us. I'll stay here. I'll be the hostage."

"All right, Lisa. I'll get ready right away."

Seventeen

Karen didn't wait for the crosstown bus, which ran sporadically after business hours. She hurried two blocks to the taxi stand, took a cab out to the house on Edwards Street. As she paid off the driver and turned to the house, she was dismayed to see it so dark. Then she noted a square of light, reflected into the yard at the rear from a kitchen window.

The cab drew away with a wide swing of its headlights. Karen went up the stairs to the porch. She pushed the button beside the door.

There was immediate movement somewhere at the back of the house, and then silence. Karen pushed the bell button again, promising herself that she would give Griffin a moment, then go to the back yard. She hadn't phoned him, she remembered, though she had promised to do so. But then, Griffin wasn't the man to be sulky over any such small thing. She half-turned to go down the stairs again; and the door opened.

She could see Griffin standing there in the shadows, behind him an open door to the lighted part of the house.

"Who is it?"

"Karen. May I come in?"

"Go away, Karen."

The tone, the sense of what he'd just said, were a shock. "What?"

But Griffin didn't answer. Another voice spoke in the dark room on the other side of the screen. "Karen Evans?"

She could see Griffin more clearly now, since her eyes were adjusting to the poor light. He had a grim look and he was shaking his head at her. She couldn't understand what was happening.

"Aren't you alone?"

"No. Please go away, Karen."

"Wait a minute," said the other voice, guttural and unctuous. "Ask Miss Evans to come in here."

"She has no part in this," Griffin said, still looking at Karen but speaking over his shoulder to the unknown man. "She doesn't belong in it. I won't involve her."

The other voice got even quieter. "Bring her in, Griffin."

There was a threat here; Jim Griffin was trying to keep her out of something, something into which she had blundered. A sense of chill swept over Karen. She tried to see past Jim, but the room was dark, the only light in it coming through the open door some distance away.

"You don't have any choice," the unknown voice continued. "Not for you and not for her. We straightened that all out. Didn't we?"

Griffin moved back into the room, away from the door. "Come in."

Karen opened the screen and stepped inside.

A short, stocky man stood where he'd been sheltered by the open door, out of sight. "Miss Evans? My name's Chester. I'm a friend of Griffin's. Sort of." His teeth gleamed in the dim light as he smiled; not at her, Karen sensed, but at some private joke. He had a hand in his right coat pocket. The pocket bulged.

Griffin was silent. Karen turned to him. Closer now, without the screen between them, she saw that the side of his face was swollen, cut and bruised, the left eye almost shut, the skin puffed and shiny, purpling. "What has happened to you?"

"Jim and I had an argument. It didn't amount to anything. Won't you come into the kitchen? We were having a last cup of coffee before we left. You can have one with us." He exuded power and ruthlessness. He was in control here. Karen turned helplessly to Griffin, not able to apprehend his manner, a mixture of regret and patience, and then walked toward the open door where the light was shining.

The short hall opened to the kitchen. A glass percolator of coffee sat on the table, along with cups, a carton of cream, an open sugar bowl. Chester motioned to a chair; Karen slid into it. Griffin didn't sit down. He stood leaning against the cabinet across the room, his arms folded. When Karen looked into his face, it seemed a mask, betraying nothing.

"I was glad to see how much you care for Jim," Chester said, setting a cup for Karen and pouring coffee. "And I'd already guessed, from things he'd said, that he's pretty fond of you. Of course you don't like to see each other hurt, feeling the way you do. That's no fun."

Karen tried to control her terror, tried to understand what sort of situation she faced here. She needed no spelling-out to know that this man, whoever he was, had no scruples and no mercy whatever. His stubby hand moved the cup so that she could touch its handle, and his heavy face was bent close, and the air of being a host, the pretense of politeness, was at once ludicrous and terrifying. Griffin said nothing. The beating had taken place long enough ago so that repairs had had time to be made—Griffin's face had been washed, the worst of the cuts dusted with what would seem to be an antiseptic powder.

Karen picked up the cup, trying to stop the shaking in her wrist by will power. "I have something private to talk over with Mr. Griffin," she said, looking up into the flat brown eyes.

"No secrets now," Chester warned. "We're three buddies, sticking together, no private talks until we get that money out of the cellar."

"She doesn't know anything about the money in the cellar," Griffin said.

"She's going to come in real useful, though," Chester corrected. "She's part owner of the place; anybody comes snooping, she can tell him to get the hell out."

"She can't tell the police to get out," Griffin warned.

"Won't be any police now. They go home, play with the kids, watch TV, go to bed and sleep eight hours just like anybody else. You ever know any twenty-four-hour police? Nunh-huh. Drink your coffee, Miss Evans. We may have a long night ahead of us. And hard work."

He was pretending a ghoulish fatherliness, bending there at the table, watching her sip the coffee. Karen thought of throwing the hot liquid into his eyes, of trying to dart back through the house. But he had a gun; his right hand never left his pocket: he would kill her or Jim Griffin before they could get away. He had pistol-whipped Jim during the argument, before she had come; and the gun was the reason for Jim's air of watchful patience. This was unexpected, this patience, this quiet waiting on Jim's part; she would have expected action and anger, and she realized at that moment that Jim Griffin had depths of control, resources of self-discipline, that she had not guessed.

"We'll take your car," he was saying now to Jim. "Miss Evans will ride in the rear seat with me. I'm sure everything will go fine, we won't exceed any speed limits or attract any attention on the way. We'll park the car around the corner, near the bank. We'll go to the front door of the shop. If anyone sees us, they'll notice Miss Evans of course. This is going to work out a lot better than the other plan, using the alley and having to break in."

Jim Griffin's eyes met Karen's for an instant; she sensed that he was trying to get a message through to her on that glance. A warning? Or was he trying to say that he'd had no part in that other plan, that he was as helpless, right now, in this situation, as she was?

Karen could think of only one thing to delay, to harass, Chester; and she stammered, "I didn't bring the keys to the shop. I don't have them with me." She tried bravely to meet the cruel eyes bending above her.

In the next instant Chester had snatched her purse off her lap, unzipped the top, dumped the contents on the table. There wasn't a lot of stuff; she hated a cluttered bag. But between the flat checkbook and the thin gilt compact lay the key ring, fat with keys.

Chester put his finger on it. "The key to the shop isn't in this bunch?"

"No."

"That's too bad." He was even closer now; she could smell the stale odor of coffee on his breath. "That's too bad, because I'll have to do something to Jim, now. The way I'm going to work it, when you don't co-operate I'll take it out on him. And when he doesn't co-operate, you pay for it. See?"

He turned from the table, the gun coming out of his pocket, locked in his fist.

"Wait."

"Huuunh?"

"It's this one."

"I still ought to rake him one."

"No. Please! How can you be ... be brutal to someone who is innocent?"

Astonishment seemed to grow slowly in his face, coming to full flower gradually, ridiculously, like a long double-take in a Bugs Bunny cartoon. "Hey. What's that you said? Innocent?" He mouthed the word as he would have a bit of bad apple. "You know what that word means, baby?"

"I'm not a baby."

"Forget it. Innocent? You think he's innocent?"

"He isn't with you because he wants to be."

"That makes him *innocent?*"

"Yes." She forced herself to meet the offensive look he gave her. "Jim Griffin is innocent and he doesn't deserve to be treated as you've treated him."

"You want to know what *really happened?*" Chester ignored her shake of the head. "Griffin was sent here to do a job. In your shop cellar. Didn't you think it was funny, the way he found an excuse to get down there? Without you? What excuse did he use? He needed time to make measurements, find out something about that brick wall." Suddenly Chester was grinning. Karen had turned to Griffin, unbelieving and yet afraid, wanting his glance to reassure her, wanting to be sure that Chester lied.

There was a quirk at the corner of Jim's mouth, almost as if he wanted to smile; his eyes seemed fixed, not on Karen, but on some diminishing landscape where he had hoped to stay. "It's true, Karen. That much is true. I came here because of what might be in the cellar."

"Lisa said that a long time ago ..." He hadn't let her finish this, in the car. "... there was a bank robbery. Afterward, some of the money must have been missing, because the shop was torn up in a search."

"Yes, it's all true," Griffin answered in the lost, careful voice.

Chester's head came up angrily. "Ahhh, we're wasting time. And time just might be what we don't have much of. So let's go. Now." He looked at Jim. "You carry the sack of tools. And be careful just *how* you carry them. The first sign you might take a swipe at me with them, you'll find out ..." He slid the gun slowly into the coat pocket, his hand going with it, his hand staying in the pocket. To Karen, then: "Get the stuff back in your purse, all but the keys. Keep them in your hand."

Karen sat as far from Chester as she could get. On his part, Chester seemed much more alert to the things outside the car, to the passing scattered traffic, to the houses and then business blocks that slid by, than he was to her or to Jim.

They parked where Chester had told Jim to park, around the corner beside the closed and darkened bank. When they got out of the car, Karen turned to Jim Griffin and said quickly, "I know you tried to keep me out of this. I'm not blaming you because I'm here."

"Karen ..." Griffin's lips drew tight against his teeth, as if he didn't really want to say anything, as if all his concentration must be directed toward Chester. "... don't waste any hopes, any sympathy, on me. I've been dreaming—"

"Shut up," said Chester. "Come along. We want to stand around like we're at a goddam garden party?"

Their steps echoed in the dark. The bank windows threw shadowy reflections on them as they passed.

Chester preceded her into the doorway area, turning swiftly to stand facing the street, the invisible gun covering Jim. Karen unlocked the door. Inside, the night light burned at the rear of the shop and everything looked neat and in place. Karen thought, Lisa's uncle had worked here to put everything right. Some of the birds stirred at the sound of footsteps; a guinea pig rustled his litter; a kitten stood up to stretch. "Don't touch the light switch," Chester warned. "That little light's going to do fine."

He motioned them ahead of him, after making sure the lock had snapped. At the top of the cellar stairs they paused, Karen and Jim waiting, Chester taking a quick look around him.

"You got lights down there." It was not a question; Chester knew there were lights.

"One light." The information about the light had to come from Jim, and Karen looked at him involuntarily. Between her and Jim there now seemed nothing but silence and an immeasurable distance. He had gone far away.

"You go first, Griffin. Switch on the light, Miss Evans."

Jim went down, carrying the tools, his black close-cropped head bent a little to clear the rim of the upper floor.

The cellar area seemed unchanged. Along the east wall the sacked fertilizers and soil conditioners stood in neat array. At the foot of the stairs everything shone in glaring brightness, while at the far end the shadows gathered. For the first time, Karen thought, I'm not really afraid of the dragon's den. I'm afraid of Chester. He's worse than any dragon I ever imagined.

"Hey, wait a minute." At the brusque anger in Chester's voice, Karen turned swiftly. Chester was looking at the brick wall. To Karen's first glance the wall seemed as it always had. Then Chester, turning and walking awkwardly so as not to take his eyes off them, slipped down the wall with his fingers on the bricks, and Karen saw where he was headed, where several of the bricks were out of line, not true with the rest of the wall.

He had the gun out. Its short black snout held fast on Jim and Karen while Chester picked with his nails. Some loose plaster spilled, cascading like a small stony avalanche, and then Chester held a brick in his left hand. "Now, ain't this something."

The stillness rang in Karen's ears.

"We've got a flashlight in that bundle," Chester told Jim. "You get it out and roll it over here. And be careful. No funny business."

Jim explored the heavy canvas sack, produced the big flashlight. But it refused to roll where Chester wanted it; there was a flange at the bulb end that kept it going in circles.

"Both of you, sit on the steps. And don't move." When they'd settled where he wanted them, Chester came forward and got the light for himself. He returned to the wall, shone in the light, seemed dissatisfied with what he saw, took out two more loose bricks. "I'll be a ..."

He stood then, as if perplexed, as if up against a problem whose solution needed heavy thinking. After a minute or so, Karen saw that his attention was centering on her. He was frowning now; the brown eyes shone with a reptilian glitter. "Who's been working down here?"

"I don't know."

"It's your shop," he warned. "Of course you know."

"I haven't been here all day. After I found ... the man who was murdered upstairs, early this morning ..." Karen's voice died because a startling and convincing idea had just occurred to her. Lisa had been down here last night, working at this wall. But Tod Bonnay had died *upstairs*. So Lisa couldn't have killed him!

Some inner common sense replied at once that Tod must have called to Lisa to come up. Lisa was the one he had come to see. And then, Lisa would have gone up carrying the hammer.

Lisa had said so little, she'd offered nothing in her own defense, just the statement that Tod had been dying and that she had held him.

Lisa must have heard Tod's murder from *down here!*

The confused ideas beat through Karen's mind, but now Chester was advancing, his jaw set, his gun out, and Jim Griffin beside her on the step was bracing himself, tightening his body for the blow.

Why didn't he jump the horrible man, defend himself?

Because of me?

But Chester came to a stop just a few feet away. "Get up, you two." He motioned with his right fist toward the rear of the cellar. "Come on back here. I want you to see something."

Eighteen

When the phone rang in the Ferrie house in the evening after eight, it was Dr. Ferrie's habit to answer, rather than Janie or Grizzie. It was almost always for the doctor, anyway.

The telephone rang that night at eight-forty, and the doctor, sitting at his desk in his study, reached to touch it and then sat still.

By his elbow was a tall drink, ice and Scotch; a hunting magazine lay open before him.

If he didn't answer the telephone in three or four rings, Grizzie would get it in the kitchen.

He lifted the receiver, put it to his ear. "Dr. Ferrie speaking."

"You ... you'd just better get downtown. You'd better get down here and see me," she said. Her voice had a hiccupy rhythm. "I'm not going to stand still for this. And you'll be s-sorry."

"Where are you now?"

"I'm in that service station phone booth, I can see your office windows. They'd better show a light inside of fifteen minutes."

"Feeling nervous?"

"You go to hell."

She sounded more nerved up, more desperate, than he'd ever heard. He knew suddenly exactly how she looked, there in the phone booth— wild and sick and shaking. And beautiful. The beautiful barracuda. The loveliness that never changed.

"All right, Betsy." He was surprised at the sound of tolerant agreeableness in his own voice. "I need a breath of air, anyway."

There was a rough gasp from her end of the wire. "A breath of air? Is that what you call it, now?"

Dr. Ferrie hung up. He took off the Paisley robe and hung it in the study closet, took out his suit coat and put it on.

Grizzie was washing out Janie's everlasting damned clutter of flower vases out in the stone-floored porch. She looked over her shoulder at him.

"Grizzie, I'm going downtown. Not for long. Will you tell Mrs. Ferrie when she comes in?"

"She's here, Doctor."

"Oh, well then—tell her I'm going." He was turning away, and then he thought, there's something the matter with Grizzie. What? She acts as if … as if something's gone horribly wrong. Out of a need to pay a little more attention to this human being who shared his home, Dr. Ferrie said, "Is she upstairs?"

"I expect. I expect she's laying down now."

The silence was charged with hidden meaning. Grizzie wanted him to say something more. But what?

"I won't be gone long."

"Yes, Doctor."

Grizzie had turned from the sink, the heap of vases. She watched him go; he sensed a narrowing of eye, disapproval, the hope that he would check himself and … and do what? What did she want of him? The thought occurred to him, through some gossip she'd got wind of Betsy. But no. It wasn't possible. And even if it were, Grizzie cared too much for her job here to betray any such knowledge.

The feeling of irritation, of puzzlement, followed him out to the garage and all the way downtown.

He went upstairs. A night light burned in the lower hall; by its reflection, shining up the stairwell, he put the key in his lock. He opened the door, clicked on the office lights. The brilliant rug, the strangely patterned wallpaper, the Indian masks, sprang into unnaturally brilliant focus. Dr. Ferrie thought, for some reason I'm tired of this place, I've gotten tired of it just today, and now it looks kind of silly. I wonder if anyone ever figured out, the place looks as if I wanted to be somewhere else…. And then, unbidden, he remembered Grizzie and what she had said, the unfinished way the little short talk had ended, and he knew that it had had something to do with Janie, Grizzie's look and her tone and her unexpressed wish for him to speak further.

Janie'd been lying down. So what was so remarkable about it?

The door opened behind him and he turned.

She was lovely and feverish. She came forward tiptoeing, her hands at her throat, at the knot there where the ribbons closed the neck of her blouse.

Dr. Ferrie watched her with remote curiosity. He felt nothing whatever about Miss Barracuda, he realized; and even the realization had no power to surprise. She was not going to be the means by which he fled this town. She was no threat. She had no power to smash his life here, the life that Janie's dad had helped him construct out of work and study and good friends and luck. She was nothing. She was a toy you built all your hopes on, strange dramatic adventurous faraway hopes, and then she just fell apart and the sawdust flew up in your eyes. That's all she was.

He even felt sorry for her at the moment, and out of this pity he spoke. "Why don't you let me help you kick it, Betsy? It doesn't have to be cold turkey. I'll help you sleep past the worst of it. Then think of what the future—"

The voice came out a whispered scream. "What're you trying to pull? Are you crazy or something?" She was yanking at the blouse; there was no brassiere under the embroidered cotton; she had dressed for this moment. Dr. Ferrie's hands twisted. His eyes were on her breasts. Then he looked away. She kicked off her pumps.

"This is going to end."

She unzipped the skirt placket, let the black tube drop, stepped out.

"You don't want it to end. *He* won't let you want it to end."

"Put your clothes on."

She came forward with the childish, knee-rubbing walk. "Just touch me."

Dr. Ferrie went over behind the desk. She peered after him, shaking her head. She was much worse off than he had expected.

"Betsy, we're all finished. Done. Through. And be glad. It isn't what I had planned for you."

"*He'll* have something to say about this."

"You know, it's a funny thing, but I haven't heard from your friend lately. He hasn't called. What's the matter with him?"

Betsy gripped the back of an upholstered chair. "He had to ... he had to go out of town. You'll be sorry if you go on treating me like this."

"How far did he go ... out of town?"

"Not far. And he knows everything you do. He knows what *everybody* does. Because I help him watch, some, but mostly because he's so smart."

Dr. Ferrie went over to the windows and adjusted the blinds there so as to keep in the light. "How old were you when Tod Bonnay got hold of you?"

"Wh-what?"

"Tod Bonnay. Killed last night. You know." Dr. Ferrie nodded toward the street. "How old were you, Betsy, when he put his claws into you?"

She stumbled around to the front of the chair and slid into it. For some minutes of silence she sat there, bent a little, looking at the rug as if studying the colors in it.

"How old?" Dr. Ferrie insisted.

"F-fifteen."

"He got you hooked on heroin?"

She nodded.

"You were in love with him."

She covered her face with her hands, rocking on the cushion. The most childish things about her were her feet, the toes overlapping and clenched together, the way a kid will do when it's frightened or hurt. The bent shoulders looked childish too, Dr. Ferrie thought. The shoulder blades stuck out. The soft hair fell across the neck like a silken veil.

"You were always so busy threatening me, and begging for drugs," the doctor said softly, "and I was always so busy …" He broke off with a twist of his mouth. "… I just never had time to see you as a seventeen-year-old kid before. A kid like other kids, I mean, the ones you see on the high-school bus or loading up on books at the library or renting a horse at Old Man Andrews' stable—"

She made half-screaming, half-weeping noises under the tent of her hair.

Why he did what he did next, Dr. Ferrie would never be able to understand. It changed everything, it changed the ending of all that had happened, wiped out his good intentions—but on this impulse which had almost no thought behind it, he opened the desk drawer and took out one of the all-day suckers that Miss Spilling kept for their infrequent child patients.

He went over and knelt in front of Betsy and pulled her hands away and tried to give her the all-day sucker, the silly blob of cherry candy crystallized on the end of a stick.

When Betsy finally got her eyes rubbed clear of tears, focused, and saw what he held, a transformation came over her. She grew cold and still. After a minute of swallowing, of headshaking, brushing her hair back, she scrambled past him and began in a rush to put her clothes on.

It only took a couple of minutes.

By the door she looked at him. "You think I'm a kid. A joke. Just because *he's* dead. But I learned a trick or two from him. The thing he always said … remember, *they're* scareder of a fuss than you are. *They* can't take a racket or a scene or a big public mess—"

"Betsy …" He stood there with the candy in his hand, feeling like a fool.

"I'm going down in the street and I'm going to start screaming," Betsy said, her tone quivering but her eyes like stones. "It's dark down there, just the street light, and maybe not many people around, but somebody'll come. You watch. You just watch."

With a secret, inward look, with almost a smile on his lips, Dr. Ferrie went to the desk, dropped the candy back into the drawer, shut the drawer noiselessly.

"Maybe they won't want to believe what I'll be yelling at them," Betsy said savagely, "but it'll start some thinking. And talking—"

"Betsy."

"And then your reputation won't be so hot, the big-shot doctor, that big r-rich bastard that—"

"Betsy."

She wiped a hand across her lips. "What is it?"

"You win."

"I win?"

"In a way. Just in a way."

She was cream-colored and slim, her hair satiny against his face, in the gloom of the examination room, stretched on the table where so many Old Hens had shyly displayed their carcasses.

"Betsy—"

"Mmmmmm ..."

"Who killed Tod Bonnay over there in that shop?"

"I don't know. I wasn't there when it happened."

"Oh, come on."

"No. Oh, it's delicious, this way, now ... when you've just—"

He put a hand on her lips. "Who killed him?"

"... don't know." She nibbled his hand dreamily, "This is the only time it's fun. Just after."

"You're kidding me. I know about the effects of narcotics."

"You know so much, try it, then."

"Who killed him?"

She was drowsing, warm inside the drug, warm inside the secret safe place where he could never follow.

"Your wife ..." she whispered suddenly, out of the dream.

"What?"

"She followed me when I left here and she sat in a booth next to us."

"When ... *when?*"

"I don't remember. A day. Let me sleep."

"You've got to get out of here." He was on his feet, he was fumbling, hurrying with his clothes. When he had dressed he yanked the dozing girl off the examination table and forced her to stand. "Put your arm in the sleeve. Wake up!" He slapped her lightly. This was what he got for giving her as big a dose as she'd craved, for making up, secretly, for those days to come when she wouldn't have any. "Who was in the booth with you?"

She goggled at the limp arm, at the sleeve he was trying to force it into. "Why, *he* was. Only, of course we didn't know she was there. Not right away."

"What were you talking about?"

She looked up at his face and crowed with a sound like a small hen's. "You. Darling. You."

He dropped what he was doing with her and stepped back. He didn't want to remember Grizzie now, he didn't want to think about that significant silence and waiting, the way she'd watched him across the room—"I expect she's laying down now"—and the bomb that had been ticking there in the house, at home, the bomb under his feet that he had sensed while he walked away and left Grizzie staring.

"Why didn't you ... why didn't you see her coming after you—"

"I did," she said, yawning, blinking. "But I was kind of dreamy. You know. We'd had some fun back here and I was going to throw my brassiere out your window—"

"Good God."

"It was only after we'd talked awhile in the booth that I remembered, this woman had driven after me in a yellow car, following me along the street, it looked silly really ..."

He went back to work getting her clothes on. When she was dressed again in the blouse and skirt, the pumps forced on her limp feet, he led her to the outer door.

With the door propped open, he switched off the lights. He closed the door, tested it to make sure the lock had caught. She was standing in the shadows, halfway between his door and the stairwell, her face soft with the desire to sleep, her eyes fixed like two jewels, unmoving.

"You stay here," he told her. "You wait until you hear my car pull away, down in the street. Then come down. Don't hang around the building... No, of course you won't do that, you'll get into bed now."

"Bed. Yes."

"Be careful." He ran down the stairs. His heart was hammering, the pulse extended all the way up into his head; he felt it in the bones of his skull. He had to go home at once, and yet even as he rushed to meet whatever waited for him, he wondered why he didn't go back, didn't clear out whatever he chose to take from the office, turn the car south, and never see the town again.

In the upper hall, Betsy clung to the railing that closed in the stairwell; the light in the hall below cast a pattern of banister rungs against the walls, making the boxlike space all angles and weird shapes, lines that led nowhere, a topsy-turvy puzzle which swam in Betsy's bemused gaze.

A car's motor whined, then roared, in the street. There was the slash of tires on paving. The sound of the motor diminished, died away.

"Must go." Betsy said the words aloud, then giggled. She put her head back, shutting her eyes for a moment. When she opened her eyes the shadowy bars tilted and quivered. She thought dreamily, I'm asleep on my feet. She felt for the first step, leaning forward upon the air, but the step wasn't where she had expected.

She fell downward with a raggedy, arm-spread, acrobatic and somehow comical grace. She lit at the landing on the nape of her neck, and there was a loud pop. Her body bounced to the second flight and flew down the stairs and rolled almost halfway across the lobby floor.

She lay like a skier who has made a final landing on his face.

It was not bright, there in the lobby, in spite of the night light. The building had long since been vacated by its workday tenants. It could be hours, it could be long past daylight, before Betsy's body would be discovered.

As it turned out, it was less than fifteen minutes. A man came by, walking a dog. He needed to start a cigarette away from the breeze, small as it was; he came close to the door, sheltering the match, and his gaze went through the pane to settle on the body, and that was it.

Nineteen

They were at the brick wall. Chester wanted them close enough to see, yet at a little distance from himself. "Look in there," Chester said, and at this moment the long howl of a police siren could first be heard in the distance.

Chester had the flashlight in his left hand, the gun in his right. He dropped both arms to stand listening. Karen was watching him, and she thought that never had she seen such evil knowingness in a face.

"Coming here?" he whispered through the lipless mouth. The question was not for them but for himself. "Coming closer, all right."

The noise of the siren rose and wavered, and funneled down into the cellar and shook itself through the bricks and on into the bank, probably; it seemed terribly loud, right above them, right over their heads.

Chester was looking at Karen and at Jim.

"Neither one of you had a chance to call the cops." He wanted to hurt, to hit, to destroy. The nose of the stubby gun was rising a little at a time.

"We wouldn't have, anyway," Jim said. "We couldn't call cop on you without involving ourselves. We're all in this together."

It didn't turn aside his desire for violence. "Somebody squealed. Somehow. I just don't see how ..."

They waited, the three of them holding their breath, but there was no sound from upstairs, no pounding at the doors, no shouts, no commands. Once the siren died outside, the night returned to its silence.

"I don't get it," Chester said worriedly, an almost human note of confusion and bafflement in his voice.

"Some traffic case," Jim said, watching the gun.

Chester grunted to show his disbelief.

Karen, in spite of her fear of Chester, of his obviously unpredictable temper, found herself looking at the place in the wall where the bricks had been removed. She had expected to peer into a black unlighted hole. What she saw was a pitted cement surface, gray in color, marked with slight ridges of white where the plaster had joined the bricks.

Chester drew a deep breath, threw a final angry glance at the ceiling, then jerked the flashlight up. "It's solid. Look." He shone the light this way and that and Karen could see that it was true, the cement wall had no smallest crack or edge where the bricks were put against it.

Jim Griffin let out his breath in a sound almost like a laugh. "The bamboo door," he said softly.

"Huh?"

"The bamboo door that wasn't there—"

"You cracking jokes or something?"

"The old man didn't know, after all. He just thought he knew."

Chester's glance grew narrow. "We're going through it. You can crack wise about your old man, but you're the baby's going to pound a hole through to what's inside."

"What's inside is the bank. Past six feet of cement. You mean to put in a week down here?"

"We don't know." He jerked his gun hand impatiently toward the bag of tools, giving Jim a sneer; but Karen knew that the question had gotten under his tough defenses, had frightened him. "Start chipping away."

Working deliberately, Jim got out a hammer and chisel and approached the cement face where the bricks were gone. He gave several preliminary taps. To Karen's ears the sound that resulted might have come out of a ten-ton boulder. She could sense no hollowness at all. Jim stuck the chisel against the cement and pounded the other end with the hammer and chips of cement flew and scattered. Jim looked over his shoulder at Chester.

Chester moistened his lipless mouth. "Take out more bricks. Do it that way. For a start."

Jim loosened bricks, pried them loose, put them in a neat stack at the base of the wall. "Somebody went to a lot of trouble," he said to Karen.

Lisa's people, Karen thought. They'd worked in secret here; constructing an impassable barrier where once had been the tunnel, the bamboo door that Jim had mentioned.... How many sacks of cement had been carried down here, mixed by hand, poured and spread until the space was filled? How many long hours of labor had gone into this work of reparation and precaution? Many, many hours, Karen sensed. And then, as if to conceal all that had been accomplished, the brick wall had been installed.

Jim worked at the brick wall, and then at the cement mass; Chester perspired, and now and then the gun hand trembled a little. Then Chester told Karen to get busy too. She was to stack bricks out of sight of the stairs, and brush up cement chips and dust.

She was kneeling beside Jim, brushing the dust into a scrap of paper, when there was a sudden burst of noise from upstairs.

A medley of sounds occurred: the door opened with a rattle of the lock, there were heavy footsteps, and then voices. Out of the confusion, Karen caught the voice of Lisa's uncle. He was saying, "I don't see what connection there could be, Lieutenant. Everything seems all right in here." And Block's voice answered, "Well, maybe no connection at all, but as it happened right across the street like that, it's kind of— Wait a minute! Look. Isn't there a light in the cellar? Is that supposed to be on?"

Karen felt thunderstruck, frozen, immobilized in the midst of fear. Chester would not be taken. He would kill Jim and her and himself first.

Then Chester moved. He motioned for Jim to give the tools to Karen. His harsh whisper emerged from the lipless mouth. "You stay here, you talk to them. And you'd better make it real good." He poked Jim with the gun. "We'll get out of sight, back there with the junk."

With Jim leading, Chester following, they forced a way past the piled stuff into the L at the end of the cellar.

Karen stood there holding the hammer and chisel. Then with a swift move she put them down and kicked a couple of empty sacks over them.

Lisa's uncle came down the stairs. "I'll take a look." He had already caught sight of Karen but nothing changed in his face. "I guess the light must have been left on by accident. Let me look around for a minute." He waited, looking upward over his shoulder, as if making sure that Block didn't intend to follow. Then he came toward Karen. She lifted a trembling hand, put a finger on her lips; and he nodded in reply.

She motioned for him to lean closer. Cupping her lips, she whispered softly into his ear. "What's back of the bricks? Please. Just trust me. Tell me."

He turned and making a funnel of his hands, answered as soundlessly as she: "Just cement. Six feet of cement."

She pointed toward the L-shaped pocket at the end of the cellar. "A man with a gun … he thinks there's a lot of money here. Money from the bank robbery, a long time ago."

Lisa's uncle stared hard at the piled stuff that made the other end of the cellar a jumble of shadow.

"He's forcing me and Jim Griffin—" She remembered that Jim had come to the shop this morning, had met Lisa's uncle, that Lisa's uncle would know whom she meant. "... forcing us to try to break through."

"A gun?"

"Yes. He'll kill Jim ..."

The Oriental face grew still, remote, with concentrated thought. Then a final whisper: "I'll pretend to leave with the detective. But I'll come back. There'll be a way—"

Upstairs, Block said loudly, "Hey, down there, Mr. Kim—"

"Coming."

He went back upstairs.

"You didn't turn off the light down there."

Lisa's uncle came back down swiftly and with an apologetic nod to Karen, clicked off the switch.

She seemed smothered and drowned in the dark. The opening of the stairs into the shop was a dim gray square; down here was blackness. There was no sound at all from the end of the cellar where Chester stood with a gun pressed to Jim's side.

And she must wait. She couldn't run to turn the light on again. It would bring Block down here and somehow she knew that Block would have as few qualms about using a gun as Chester would, though from a different motive; he would be righteous about it where Chester would simply be businesslike; and in the end Chester would probably be more efficient. Karen tried to pray, folding her hands, clenching them there in the dark, but her tongue and lips were wooden.

At last she realized that Mr. Kim and Lieutenant Block were leaving. There had been further talk from Block about something that had happened across the street. It seemed that he had sent a police cruiser to bring Lisa's uncle to unlock the shop because of some other crime in the vicinity, a thread in the nightmare that Karen couldn't comprehend.

Karen clicked on the light and turned, facing the other end of the cellar. Jim and Chester appeared, in reverse order from their going, Jim ahead with his hands raised a little, Chester in back of him showing signs of strain.

"Get the hammer and chisel," Chester growled.

Jim looked around.

"They're under the sacks there," Karen said.

Jim bent and lifted a corner of the sack. Karen wanted to scream, for she knew that this was the moment when Jim's patient waiting would end. He'd had all of Chester that he intended to take. The sacks rose in his hand in a sweeping ellipse; she felt fear beat through her, a choking pulse. The sacks seemed to rise slowly, slowly; and Chester's gun was pointed, deadly—it was going to blast Jim, blast out his life. And she loved him. There was no difficulty between them, no secret, that couldn't be dissolved if only ... if only...

The sacks whipped into Chester's face; involuntarily he put up his hand, his right hand holding the gun, to dig the burlap out of his eyes. And then Jim was on him.

Chester fell back against the stacked barrels, tried to regain his balance, flailed with his outstretched arms. There was the collapse of old wood, the cracking and crashing of the rotted barrels. Chester got his feet under him finally, but now Jim chopped at his right wrist, and the gun fell amid the debris, disappearing. Chester looked for it, then turned with his fists up, wild-eyed, the mouth pulled wide to show his crooked teeth.

"Ready to make a deal?" Jim asked, the tone wry, half-amused.

Chester pulled his mouth shut and his eyes became crafty. "Sure. Anything you want. We can both work—"

In that moment Jim brought up a blow that exploded with a crack on Chester's jaw. Karen saw the swift glaze, the sightless focus, just as Chester fell into the splintered debris. He lay there looking oddly like a plump scarecrow fallen from its crossbeam.

Jim stood there rubbing his knuckles. He spoke to Karen without looking in her direction. "My God, but I got sick of him."

"Where did he come from?"

"I guess my stepdad sent him. I was supposed to find some money down here, and rob the bank too if I felt like it and it looked easy. Nobody knew about this ton of cement. Somebody put that in when nobody was looking."

"Lisa's people."

"I guess so," he agreed. "I'm going to drag him out where I can work on him. You've got some heavy string up there, or anyway I think I saw some on your desk—"

"Yes."

"I'll need it to tie Chester up." He was pulling the inert body out upon the cleared space, away from the shattered barrels and the other stuff, old clay pots and rusted metal bird-cages and stray pieces of lumber. When Karen came back with the string, Jim had found the gun. He was emptying bullets from it. He tossed the bullets back into the clutter, exchanged the gun for the string Karen had brought. "Hide the gun somewhere safe. We may need it to make Chester think we mean business."

She watched while he trussed Chester like a chicken. "What are you going to do with him? You can't—" Then she almost bit her tongue. She'd been about to say that Jim couldn't turn him over to the police. There would be too much to explain.

"You're right, I sure can't," Jim agreed, looking up at her with a crooked smile. "And since Chester hasn't committed any crime, outside of a technical kidnaping—bringing us here unwillingly—I guess even the cops might be puzzled. Puzzled, but interested. And I suppose I'd better explain here and now that after I met you, I gave up the idea of doing anything about my old man's plans—"

"Jim!"

"So what I'd better do with Chester, is take him out of town and turn him loose. I know it's not justice. It's trouble for somebody somewhere else. But for the life of me I can't just kill him."

Jim rose to his feet, brushed at his clothes. Chester, tied hand and foot with the heavy cord, would not move until someone cut him free.

"He'll leave without any trouble. I think he kind of lost his taste for the job, anyway, when he saw that stuff behind those bricks. Come daylight, I can hand-truck him out under a load of all that fertilizer I'm supposed to be buying. And then, there'll be just me, Karen, to get rid of. If you want to." He was watching her, waiting for some sign of her feeling toward him. His eyes, that could seem masklike or mocking, couldn't conceal his hope.

Karen stepped across the distance between them.

"Karen, I'm no angel. There might be a thing or two I'd have to put right—"

"Yes."

"I want to make a new start, no worries. And I'm not even sure how I'd make our living—"

"Yes."

"But still, in spite of it all, if you want to try me—"

"I'm not going to *try* you," she told him. "This is a permanent affair."

She felt his arms go round her, strong, hard-muscled; and the smell of his clothes against her face was clean and yet intimate; and she dreaded a little that first kiss that was coming. What would it be like? He tilted her chin with his knuckle and she caught the odor of cement dust on his hand. His breath was warm against her cheek. "I love you very much, my darling," he said.

And the kiss was fine.

Twenty

Janie was lying awake when she saw the headlights reflected on her bedroom ceiling from the driveway below. The lights circled, then came to a stop in a single bright blotch near the windows. Someone was coming to the house. In surprise, Janie thought it must be very late. She lifted herself on an elbow and looked at the little clock on the nightstand. A quarter past two. Who in the world could be coming at this hour?

She slipped out of bed, got her feet into slippers, padded over to the windows. As she lifted aside the China-silk draperies, lights came on at the front of the house, illuminating the police cruiser that sat there. A man—not a uniformed officer—was getting out of the black-and-white car. A man in an ordinary suit and hat. Foreshortened, as seen from above, he seemed exceptionally stocky. Janie put her ear to the pane, trying to make out the voices below. It was not like Grizzie to answer any sound of a car before the occupant had even rung. Grizzie slept like a dead person. Ronnie must have answered the door and it must mean that Ronnie had still been up, downstairs, sitting there reading perhaps.

Or thinking about Miss Barracuda....

Janie went to the closet for a robe, wrapped it around her, tied the belt, and went out silently to the landing.

Below: "What did you say your name was?" in Ronnie's voice, and another voice answered, "Lieutenant Block, Dr. Ferrie. I know you, you've been pointed out to me, but I guess that you—"

"Oh," Ronnie said. "Well, come on in."

"Is there somewhere we can talk, Doctor?"

"In here. My study. Do you mind telling me what we're going to talk about?"

A moment of hesitation, as if the detective was looking off into Ronnie's study, preparing what he must ask. Standing above, dim in shadow, Janie felt a sort of surprise at her own calmness, her lack of fright or excitement. Of course she had known that this moment must come, and it was decent of the policeman to talk to Ronnie first and to pave the way, so to speak, for the terrible shock to follow.

"Well, I can say this much. There was a death downtown, a young person dying under some very strange circumstances ... shouldn't we talk inside your study, Doctor?"

"Why ... yes, of course."

Ronnie must have ushered the man into his study; there was the sound of the door closing, and all voices were cut off.

Janie rushed back into her room and careless now of secrecy, snapped on the lights. She hurried first into the bathroom and ransacked the medicine cabinet, but there was no help there. Downstairs, a cupboard in that little closet where she kept garden supplies, insecticides and poison dusts ... but those seemed far away-now, and the dosage problematical.

Janie sat down on the side of her bed and tried to compose herself.

Silly to gulp down something right now, anyway. She had so much explaining to do. Everything had to be cleared up so that the police would never blame anyone else. Witnesses had to be found—the person driving that car, for instance, the one she'd cut across in front of, scarring her fender....

And Ronnie had to be made to understand why she'd done it, that it was all because of him, her love and her wanting him to be happy with the girl.

It occurred to Janie, sitting down at her tiny writing desk, to wonder why the police had finally decided to come here. Well, of course there were always clues and things. And whoever had been down in the cellar during those few moments she'd been in the shop ...

She drew a piece of cream-colored paper toward her.

To Whom It May Concern:
I killed Mr. Tod Bonnay last night in the garden and pet store next to the bank.

He had been blackmailing my husband, Dr. Ronald Ferrie. I found this out by accident. I meant to kill his accomplice also, and then I realized, remembering the conversation I had overheard, that without Mr. Bonnay she would not represent any further danger to my husband.

The proof I offer, the word of another witness, is this: When I followed Mr. Bonnay into the store he was standing near the stairwell to the cellar. He had his back to me. Mr. Bonnay said rather loudly, "What are you do-ing down there?" And a woman's voice said, "Don't come down. I've been working and now I'm putting things back again."

There was a hammer on the corner of a desk there. It seemed as good a time as any so I picked up the hammer and hit Mr. Bonnay.

You must find out who the woman was, and check with her on this conversation. Only the murderer could have known what they said—isn't this right?

Yours respectfully,
Janie Linden Ferrie

Janie regarded the piece of note paper. It looked crowded and ill-written, but she had no strength to copy it again. She took an envelope and wrote *The Police* on the outside—it looked melodramatic, like a silly play on television—but she let that go, too.

Then Janie dressed, not forgetting to make up her face a little and comb her hair. Carrying the letter, she went downstairs and opened the door of Ronnie's study.

The detective's voice was saying, "... sorry, but I'll have to take you in. If it's no more than an accident, of course—"

Janie drew herself up as tall as possible and put on her best clubwoman smile.

This was the moment when she would make an offering of herself, when she would save Ronnie's world for him, when she would give him freely to that other love, the beautiful young girl...

The detective and Ronnie were both staring at her now.

She held out the letter. "Of course you won't take my husband. He had nothing to do with it. Here is *my* confession to the murder of Tod Bonnay."

The silence seemed to hum. The detective looked at the note but made no move as yet to take it.

Triumphantly, Janie looked at her husband, waiting for the gray sick expression to leave his face, waiting for the dawn of gratitude, relief, joy, and anticipation in his eyes.

For now, because of her, he would have everything ...

Warren Renick had not been to bed. He'd been at the hospital until an hour ago, until Dr. Farmer had assured him there was no more danger and that Marlie would not lose their child. When Lieutenant Block rang the bell, Warren answered the door, and unlike Dr. Ferrie, recognized him at once.

"Come in, Lieutenant. What an hour to be up and around. And what have we done?"

"It's not you, Mr. Renick. I'm just checking up some loose ends, the Bonnay killing."

"Well ..." Warren spread his big hands. "I don't know anything about it except what I've read in the papers. Marlie met the man once—"

"No, no, Mr. Renick. This is about the bank. It's just a minor detail, goes back to the robbery, all those years ago. You might not even remember—"

"Of course I remember. My father was killed that day. He died at his desk."

Block made a face as if he were disgusted at his own *faux pas*. "Well, naturally; I've just got to the point where my thinking's kind of fuzzy for lack of sleep—"

"Come into the kitchen and we'll share some coffee."

Lieutenant Block sat down where Warren indicated, in the small but beautifully arranged breakfast room. Outside, there was the first bloom of dim gray light.

"Instant coffee's all I can manage. Suzabell isn't up," Warren explained.

"Sure. Instant's fine with me." Block was studying the view, the pink iris like a motionless flock of butterflies, the pearl-like pool in its marble rim. "You've got quite a view out there, Mr. Renick."

Warren glanced into the breakfast room from across the kitchen. "Oh, yes. The morning view. My father planned it, planned just how it had to look. He must have been a frustrated artist, I guess."

"It's pretty."

When Warren had brought the coffee, had supplied Block with a bowl of lump sugar and himself with cream, Block said, "As long as I've lived here I've heard a tale about that bank robbery. And I guess, since Bonnay died at the entrance to the cellar ..."

Warren nodded. "You're talking about the money that was supposed to be lost. I know. It's a tale that never dies. And some people are sure that Lisa Kim's folks buried a ton of cash under a load of cement. Whispers and hints ... I've lived with them all these years." Warren was shaking his head. "There was a tunnel, all right. And the robbers used it, not as successfully as they should have. But the missing bundle, the cash that never was found and that the bank had to make up—that just never existed."

Block hesitated with his cup almost to his lips. "I guess I don't follow you, Mr. Renick."

"After the robbery," Warren said, "the bank's vice-president and head cashier, a man named Waterbury, went to bed with a heart attack. He had been standing next to my father when my father died. The shock almost killed Waterbury. In the next few days a lot of very excited people did some highly excitable figuring. Then the men were caught and the cash recovered, and the figures were rehashed, and whoever gave out that amount—I think it was sixty-nine thousand or so—whoever gave it out was off his rocker. It wasn't even an educated guess."

"How much was missing?" Block demanded.

"Not a cent. To the bank's embarrassment it had about fifty dollars more than it was supposed to have. And then some big news broke and filled the papers for days. If you remember those years right after the war, right after World War II, it seemed that every other day something turned up, a crisis somewhere. The bank used the big news story to cover up its mild little release, no money was gone, after all. And the thing wasn't even printed; even the local paper gave it only an inch on the back page. I finally figured it out, or I think I did. The finding of the money would have been news. But just the announcement of a mistake, no. And even now, I still run into people who've heard the story of the robbery, and who are wondering where the money is."

Block nodded.

"By the way, the bank is buying the Kim property. We're expanding. If there *is* anything in that cellar ..."

Block seemed to be laughing at himself, inwardly. At the door, saying goodbye to Warren, he turned for a last question. "Where did that extra fifty dollars come from?"

"Well, a couple of twenties and a ten were picked up off the floor of the bank after the robbery. There was an ordinary paper clip on them, which wasn't according to bank procedure." He shrugged. "My theory is that one of the robbers lost the money during the excitement, pulled it out when he went for something else."

"It could be. Goodbye, Mr. Renick."

"Goodbye for now, Lieutenant."

Opening the door of the police cruiser, nodding to the uniformed man behind the wheel, Block was thinking: Renick hadn't even asked him who Bonnay's murderer was. Didn't care, apparently. Or had other things on his mind. Maybe he hadn't even known Bonnay.

The papers had practically ignored the news of the bank's mistake over the money. But they wouldn't ignore the news of *this* night's work.

Downtown, on the way to Police Headquarters, the car passed the bank and Block found himself studying it and the adjoining shop. The day that they dig into that cellar, he promised himself, I'm going to be there. I'm going to have a look. Renick could be mistaken. He said everyone was excited and making monkeys out of themselves with the figures involved. But then, who says that there *couldn't* be ...

Then Block was grinning at himself, at the persistent thought, knowing with sudden insight why the old tale of treasure buried had never died.

THE END

Dolores Hitchens Bibliography
(1907-1973)

Novels:

As by Dolores Hitchens

Jim Sader mysteries
Sleep with Strangers (1955)
Sleep with Slander (1960)

Standalone books:
Stairway to an Empty Room
   (1951)
Nets to Catch the Wind (1952;
   reprinted as Widows Won't
   Wait, 1954)
Terror Lurks in Darkness (1953)
Beat Back the Tide (1954;
   abridged as The Fatal Flirt,
   1954)
Fool's Gold (1958)
The Watcher (1959)
Footsteps in the Night (1961)
The Abductor (1962)
The Bank with the Bamboo Door
   (1965)
The Man Who Cried All the Way
   Home (1966)
Postscript to Nightmare (1967;
   UK as Cabin of Fear, 1968)
A Collection of Strangers (1969;
   UK as Collection of Strangers,
   1970)
The Baxter Letters (1971)
In a House Unknown (1973)

As by Bert and Dolores Hitchens

F.O.B. Murder (1955)
One-Way Ticket (1956)
End of the Line (1957)

The Man Who Followed Women
   (1959)
The Grudge (1963)

As by D. B. Olsen

Rachel Murdock mysteries
Cat Saw Murder (1939)
Alarm of Black Cat (1942)
Catspaw for Murder (1943;
   reprinted as Cat's Claw, 1943)
The Cat Wears a Noose (1944)
Cats Don't Smile (1945)
Cats Don't Need Coffins (1946)
Cats Have Tall Shadows (1948)
The Cat Wears a Mask (1949)
Death Wears Cat's Eyes (1950)
Cat and Capricorn (1951)
The Cat Walk (1953)
Death Walks on Cat Feet (1956)

Prof. A. Pennyfeather mysteries
Shroud for the Bride (1945;
   reprinted as Bring the Bride a
   Shroud, 1945)
Gallows for the Groom (1947)
Devious Design (1948)
Something About Midnight
   (1950)
Love Me in Death (1951)
Enrollment Cancelled (1952;
   reprinted as Dead Babes in the
   Wood, 1954)

Lt. Stephen Mayhew mysteries
The Clue in the Clay (1938)
Death Cuts a Silhouette (1939)

As by Dolan Birkley

Blue Geranium (1944)
The Unloved (1965)

As by Noel Burke

Shivering Bough (1942)

Short Stories/Magazine Novels:

Stairway to an Empty Room
	(*Collier's*, Mar 31, Apr 7, Apr
	14, Apr 21, Apr 28 1951)
Strip for Murder (*Mercury
	Mystery Magazine*, Oct 1958)
The Watcher (*Cosmopolitan*,
	May 1959)
Footsteps in the Dark
	(*Cosmopolitan*, Feb 1961)
Abductor! Abductor! Abductor!
	(*Cosmopolitan*, July 1961)

The Unloved (*Redbook,* Oct
	1965)
If You See This Woman (*Ellery
	Queen's Mystery Magazine,* Jan
	1966)
Postscript to Nightmare
	(*Cosmopolitan*, June 1967)
A Collection of Strangers
	(*Redbook*, Sept 1969)
The Baxter Letters (*Star Weekly*,
	June 26 1971)
Blueprint for Murder (*Ellery
	Queen's Mystery Magazine*, Aug
	1973)

Plays:

A Cookie for Henry: one-act play
	for six women (1941, as Dolores
	Birk Hitchens)